The Kingdom of Rune A Child Forgotten

© Copyright 2023 Patricia Harvey

For more information, email: Patriciaharvey@phdigitallogisticsllc.com

ISBN 979-8-35097-059-3

ISBN eBook 979-8-35097-060-9

THE
KINGDOM
OF RUNE

1

A CHILD FORGOTTEN

PATRICIA HARVEY

PROLOGUE

⁓

OCTOBER 25TH, 2003

Drip, drip, drip… I found myself staring into an IV bag. The man beside me hadn't moved for hours yet; the IV just kept on dripping. The clock on the wall was ticking at the same pace the IV drips, slowing time down as I took in my surroundings. There were sounds of chaos as the tsunami neared the shore. The evacuation started hours ago. This hospital was in Bone Creek Preserve, only five miles from the shore. The hospital serves this community and three others. They had been coordinating with the other towns for months in preparation. Their hospitality would be the reason we survived this disaster. The ambulances have been driving back and forth between Bone Creek and the towns east and south of us, all day long. We knew a storm was coming, we just never knew when or how hard it would come. East of us was Rainbow Falls, East Pine Pack resides there. They were coordinating the evacuation from their high school. All evacuees are to go there to be placed in their town first. Overflow would be sent southeast to Hull Creek, where Hull Creek Pack would assist. They will then be sent to the White Mountain Pack. Sitting near Mt. St. Helens, the White Mountain Pack was the most remote.

Our towns are incredibly special; they are all werewolf communities. The rough terrain has kept humans away for centuries. We live mostly peacefully, however, we used to have wars between packs to gain more land. Wars are very few now, as most packs mind to their own business. But since the threat of this natural disaster, everyone had agreed to a treaty to work together. My mother was thankful for the treaty. Bone Creek was her original pack, but she moved when she found her mate, a Beta from White Mountain, my father. It was a huge adjustment for her. The weather here is always warm on the coast, but in the mountains a frigid winter can last up to eight months.

I gazed down at my daughter in my arms, I gave birth to her at home in the early hours of the morning. She was having trouble breathing, so I had to make the three-hour drive down to Bone Creek, regardless of the storm. I hoped I could get help for her before the evacuation started. My wolf was stirring in my head, being a werewolf had its advantages and disadvantages. Each of us gets our wolf when we turn eighteen. Once we receive our wolf, we can mentally communicate with them and our pack. I remember the first time my mind linked with my mother. It was like having a regular conversation, but our lips weren't moving.

I look down at the small package in my arms. She had been getting weaker. My wolf could feel it too, her lungs were not as they should be. She was going crazy in my head, threatening to break loose, the last thing I wanted was for her to shift right here in the middle of the hospital. My baby was sick, and I knew she couldn't be helped. I felt her chest stop moving as she let out her last breath. I felt my cheeks warm, and it took a few moments to realize it was due to my tears. A nurse came by at that time to grab the old man next to me. The nurse spoke to me; the only person to even acknowledge me since I arrived.

"Ma'am, do you need help?"

"No, you're too late, she's already gone. Please just leave me for a moment."

Werewolves were not a remorseful group, the weak died and the strong survived. It was our way. We were created by the goddess Selene, the goddess of the moon. She controls the mating. Choosing for us a soulmate we long to unite with. Selene also controls the shifting; all werewolves shift for the first time on their eighteenth birthday. After that we are free to shift back and forth between our human and wolf forms. The moon gives us energy, and we howl to it as a tribute to our goddess. My wolf was getting harder to control. She was cursing the goddess for showing us love and then taking it away.

'*It can't be helped Ria,*' I spoke to my wolf, '*she is gone, she is not coming back.*' I felt a void of emptiness at that moment. My wolf stopped talking to me. She disappeared into the back of my mind, dismissing me, shutting me out. '*Come back Ria, don't leave me too, come back.*' I felt the anger growing inside me, my desperation to have my wolf back. I couldn't handle this alone. My mate could not come with me. His wolf took over and they ran into the forest when we knew our girl was sick.

People were running everywhere as panic set in trying to move the last of the patients. All I could think about is my baby... my baby. I touched her cheek. It's still warm but getting cooler. How long had I sat here? How long had I waited? No one came.

I had been sitting there listening to the panic of others, to the fast footing across the floors, to the utter chaos around me... my mind seemed foggy like everything is in slow motion. My body ached and I just wanted to be sleeping, cuddling my baby. As a tear escaped my eye, I looked into her glossy eyes and drew my fingers down over them. She was sleeping now. Go unto the goddess my love.

A baby's cry pulled me from the fog that was my mind. I looked up to see a nurse hurriedly pushing a basinet out of the room across from me. I could see inside, the woman inside was still pushing. The doctor was telling her that she had one more, my mind wonders... one more ...one more push so... one more baby. How can the Goddess bless someone with two babies yet try to rob me of my one?

Suddenly, there was a rumbling under my feet. The hospital started shaking, and the doctor yelled for the nurse to help him stabilize the falling equipment in the room. The basinet rolled away from her, the shear panic in her eyes made me jump up and lunge forward, I grabbed the basinet.

"Do you need help? I can watch the baby. I'll stay right here."

She hesitated for just a moment before nodding and speaking "Yes, thank you."

As the nurse flew back into the room, I stared at the slumbering baby girl in the basinet. I touched her cheek, so warm. Another tear. I looked back into the room; the doctor was holding up another baby. It started crying and the nurse grabbed it, to swaddle it and place it in another bassinet. I looked down at the basinet in front of me. This was the universe telling me that this baby should be mine. This was my baby. My wolf returned to growl at me and yelled *'no, she does not belong to us,'* I reply to her, *'she does now.'* I picked up the slumbering baby and placed mine in the basinet. When the nurse returned, she started pushing both basinets towards the ambulance bay and asked if I'm waiting for transport as well. I hesitated for a moment then nodded.

She had me follow her to the ambulances and she escorted me into the first one. She yelled for a man named Robert.

"Take these two," she paused for a moment and pulled out the name card on the basinet, "Fawn babies and get them settled. I'm going back to help the doctor finish, I'll be right back, don't leave without us."

As the door closes on my ambulance, I took in the warm autumn air. The last thing I hear is the man Robert say, "this one isn't breathing." My ambulance door closes, and it takes off down the road. We headed up past Green Street and towards the Hill. My wolf was angry I had taken another, she wanted her pup, not this one in my arms. My mind didn't care what my wolf wanted, I wanted a baby and now my baby girl was in my arms.

1

A HAUNTING PAST

❧

Autum's POV

Drip, drip, drip…My blood drips from my lip to the floor, the sound echoes through my ears as I rush to grab toilet paper to clean up my mess. My mother would punish me again if she saw the floor dirty. Every time I make a mistake her wolf takes over and tries to hurt me. My mother punishes me for upsetting her wolf.

If only I hadn't broken that drinking glass while washing the dishes, she wouldn't be making me drink from it now. I've cut my tongue so many times on it I've lost feeling in it. My lips have silver lines of scars as well, my hands aren't too steady yet and it's the only glass I'm allowed to use now. I've gone three days without water just to avoid it. I tried drinking straight from the faucet last week and the bump on my head is still there from the wooden spoon she smacked me with after.

Thump, thump, thump... I can hear her coming now, but I haven't finished my chores yet. She promised me I could go to school with the other kids if I behaved. I should have started school last year, but I am six now and still have not gotten to go. My neighbor Jenny gets to go to school, I get to talk to her sometimes when mommy is going to be gone for a long time, Jenny's mom watches me. I wish she could watch me every day. Jenny tells me all about school and how much she loves it and her teacher.

So, I had to make sure to behave. Behaving meant not talking back or looking at her at all and always doing my chores, while she was out of the house all day. I still haven't cleaned the windows. I grab the window cleaner and spray it around the house, maybe she won't notice. The door squeaks as she opens it and I meet her eyes as she appears in the doorway, I look down, avoiding her gaze. She walks straight in and sets her purse down and glances around.

"Looks good in here." She sounds surprised, but I let out the breath I didn't realize I was holding in. She walks up to me and smooshes my face cheek to cheek with her hand, it makes my lips push out. She observes the many cuts and blood on my lip from the water glass and smirks.

"Good girl." She pulls a box of cheese mac from her purse and hands it to me. "Make yourself dinner," she huffs and sits in her chair and puts her feet up. "Eat quickly, I have company coming over."

She glances at me as I walk away. Company is never good, I put water on the stove and wait for it to boil. I don't want to be out here when her 'company' comes. My father died when I was too young to remember, my mother tells me. She reminds me often and says it's because he was so sad I was born that he couldn't live with it. So, he did drugs to numb the pain. I throw the noodles in early, not really caring if they are cooked, after waiting five minutes I turn off the heat and add the cheese stirring quickly, I pour it into a bowl and head straight to my room. It's not as good as my neighbor Jenny's when her mom makes it. They use milk, and we never have any.

I crawl into my closet and eat my food. My closet is my safe place. I even sleep in here most nights. I must have dozed off after a while because I'm jolted awake by a loud crash. My breath picks up and I start breathing extremely hard, very, very hard. I stand and edge closer to the closet door. I hear heavy footsteps. I reach my hand out to crack the door open to peek and the door is thrown open. My scream dies in my throat, a large hand halting my breath. I feel a sharp pain followed by a warm sensation. My vision goes black as a watch the dark shadow looming over me.

2

AWAKING FROM THE NIGHTMARE

❧

OCTOBER 2020

Autum POV

"Autum… you're ok Autum, you're at Dr. Warren's office and you are safe."

All I could hear were my harsh breaths, like I was just being suffocated. I was having a panic attack again. Did I black out? I think I did. Still, I couldn't breathe. This doctor is supposed to be helping me, not making me relive the worst moments of my life.

"Autum, remember what we practiced, take a deep breath and ground yourself where you are, what can you feel?"

Breathe damn it, I think to myself. My fingers curl to grip the soft fabric of the chair arms and I take in a harsh breath, "the chair" I reply.

"Good, good, what can you smell?"

Lady, I can't breathe, who cares what I smell. I try to take in another breath, but my throat feels restricted. "I can't breathe."

"Autum, feel the chair, and think, what can you smell?" I exhale and breathe in through my nose, "La lavender… from your …c- c- candle." That one came out a bit of a stutter.

"You're okay. Take in a deep breath in two, three, four now out two, three, four now in two, three, four and out two, three, four. How do you feel now Autum?" Getting better. Okay, maybe she does know what she's doing.

"Better." I reply, "How much longer do we have for today?" I need to get out of here.

"We are done in about twenty more minutes, but I think we need to see each other twice a week going forward. How would that make you feel?"

"Like I'm a mental case that sees a shrink, we already see each other every week."

"I understand how you feel, let's talk about why your Grandma Ellen brought you today." Well, because boys don't know how to keep their hands to themselves, and that boy got what he deserved.

"Because I punched a boy today."

She lifts an eyebrow. "Only punched him?"

Ok well no, I think I broke his nose, I mean I hope I did. Teach him a lesson for touching me, really Derek Bell thinks he's hot stuff and can get away with anything. Well not today "I may have made him bleed."

She looks up at me expectantly waiting for more of an answer, but I'm not going to give it to her. I did nothing wrong; he shouldn't have touched my ass like that. And I'm fairly sure he pet my hair first. She finally gives up and speaks.

"Autum, I'm going to recommend two visits a week, I'll speak with your grandmother. If you can't be honest with me, at least be honest with yourself. You broke that poor boy's nose for brushing up against you. Until we know what is causing these nightmares from your repressed childhood, I think more visits are a good thing. I think we have a lot to work on to get you past these moments of anger that you have so that you can manage them peacefully. Every visit ends with you in the closet and not remembering anything else. The hypnosis will help you with this trauma Autum, you just have to let it. What do you say, are you going to let me help you?"

I'm never getting out of this. My grandmother already thinks I'm crazy too, I know it. The look on her face when she saw Derek's nose. She was so disappointed in me; it almost killed me to look at her. I know I'm a disappointment. Goddess, I hate myself sometimes. Why can't I just be normal? I need to do this, I need to be better, I must be. Not only for me, but for grandma.

"Yes, ok, twice a week," I cave.

"Well then let's talk about what happened leading up to the confrontation today, something about it must have triggered your episode."

I gave a big sigh, truthfully, I didn't know what happened. I remember feeling the touch. Suddenly my mind went numb .and my senses took over, and there was a smell. The smell. Something about it made me lose it, and I didn't like feeling like how that smell was making me feel. I shook the thought and spoke.

"Dr. Warren, can smells trigger memories?" She looked at me.

"Yes, actually smells can trigger many things, including memories."

I looked down at my hands; my hands were shaking. I drew one up and touched my lips. The smell of blood often brought back the memory of the many scars on my lips, but I had always remembered the horrible way my lips became scarred. And the smell of cigarettes. I hate the smell of cigarettes. I cross my arms, my left hand sliding over the fabric that always covers my right arm. I felt myself shudder. Cigarettes always brought back memories of the burns on my arm. But I couldn't remember why I no longer liked small spaces or people touching me. My mind had blocked it from my memory but still allowed it to slowly drive me crazy with fear. I looked at Dr. Warren and spoke about my thoughts with her. She wrote some more notes on her yellow legal pad and looked up at me.

"That is why we are meeting Autum, to help unlock that memory so you can deal with it and move on from your trauma. So, you don't have to live in fear any longer, if we can figure out what the smell was. We might be able to help you move past the blockage. This is the first time you mentioned a smell. Are you sure that's what triggered it and not him touching you?"

"At school today I don't know what happened Dr. Warren. I was angry, but not because of just the touch. If I'm being honest with myself," I pause and take a deep breath. "I like Derek. But he has never shown me any attention. I remember him touching me, but I also remember wanting him to touch me, but then that smell… And then, and then after I hit him, I don't remember anything until I was in the office with Mrs. Albim. She had startled me because I didn't realize she was holding onto me, and I didn't know how I had gotten to the office."

I started panicking like I was going to black out again, and then my grandma arrived. I sighed again. "All the kids at school will think I'm a freak now. And Derek, he'll probably never talk to me again. Not that we talked much anyways." That last part I mumbled.

I looked up at the clock on the wall. My time was almost up, and Grandma should be here by now. She's probably waiting outside. Dr. Warren saw my gaze.

"Autum, I think we've made good progress today. I'm sure your friends will forgive you, but first you'll need to forgive yourself. We'll talk more about the revelations you've had here today at your next appointment."

"Thank you, Dr. Warren, if were done I'll be leaving now, I'll see you in a few days then?"

"Yes, do Tuesdays and Fridays work for you, let's say 4:30?"

"Yes, thank you Dr. Warren."

3

TAKING RESPONSIBILITY

Autum POV

I pick up my backpack and head out the door. Grandma usually waits for me outside in the front, reading her newspaper. Goddess, who reads newspapers anymore. Anyways, when I open the door, I don't see her car. I pull out my air pods and play my 'let's dance' soundtrack. I can't wait until I get my wolf and have someone to talk to, until then the positive beats keep me distracted as I wait for grandma.

As I sit on the bench outside the office the autumn air fills my lungs. I love this time of year. Maybe it's because it so closely resembles my name, but I really do love sweater weather. And damn, do I look super cute in a sweater. Plus, I don't have to wear this arm sleeve.

As I listen to the beats in my headphones, more of the day's drama comes back to me. Standing in front of my locker with Samantha. I wanted Derek to touch me. I do think he is arrogant, a bit self-centered. I guess it is to be expected from the next Alpha though. I could feel his gaze kept returning to me and I wanted to feel his touch. I was wishing for it. But then something else happened. Why… Why am I the way I am? There was darkness in me. I was doomed to never be happy, never enjoy the touch of a loved one. I just don't understand. I can hardly stand it even when my grandma embraces me. Like my skin is crawling. I just want to feel safe, for once.

As I sat there waiting, I could feel the tears start to brim in my eyes, and I looked up to the sky. Please Goddess, give me back my memories, please. I held all but one tear back. Grandma pulled up, but she didn't look to happy, oh man am I in for it now. I wipe my face and stand up off the bench and walk to the car.

"Hey Gram, where were you." I'm hesitant cause I don't know if I should walk instead, grandma looks nervous. Why is she nervous? I'm the one who completely overacted and punched Derek in the nose. His previously perfectly square nose, with his perfect arched eyebrows, and full lips. Goddess, that boy. I mean if he wasn't so damn cute, I wouldn't have been waiting there that long. I would have walked away and avoided this entire thing.

But no, not so lucky, every girl in the school ogles over him. It infuriates me to watch them so desperate for a man's attention. But none as much as Rebecca. Queen bee of the school and all surrendering to her. He's just another shallow boy at the whim of another girl who isn't me. I sigh and try to get Gram's attention again.

"Grandma, why are you so quiet? I'm sorry, I didn't mean to h-"

"Stop Autum and listen. I know why you did it, but it's your Senior Year in High School and that's the Alphas son. He is going to be taking over the pack next year, and you hit him. I just left a meeting with the Alpha and we both agree that you will need to do some type of community service for your penance. I know we've just moved here, but this is my pack Autum, and we need to be here." She sighed, "Maybe we should have come sooner, maybe I shouldn't have home schooled you for so long. Is this my fault?"

"No Gram don't say that. This is my fault; I'll be better I promise. Dr. Warren wants to see me twice a week, and today helped a lot." I kind of lied but I know I can do better.

"I love you Autum and I'll always love you, but you need to control your anger. I know about the change in your appointments, Dr. Warren called me on my drive here. I'm glad to hear you agree with her. Right now, we need to go back to the school to finish speaking with the principal. I never met up with him because Alpha Darren called for an immediate meeting. The Alpha is leaving your punishment up to your principal. I spoke to him on the phone and told him we would come as soon as my meeting with the Alpha was over. He doesn't know about your appointments but maybe he should, they know I took you to the doctor."

"Gram, I'm sorry. I'll apologize. I'll beg for forgiveness if that's what you want. I really am sorry, but please, I don't want anyone at school to know I talk to a shrink. Please Gram." Goddess, why am I such a fuck up? I drop my head back on the back rest and gaze out the window. The leaves are turning gold and red now, it's so beautiful, peaceful, silent… Grandma didn't say another word the whole rest of the trip back to the school. I need to be better for her, even if I can't do it for myself. Goddess what's wrong with me? I'm just a bad kid, I've always been a bad kid. I almost doze off when the car comes to a stop.

"We're here." Gram says. I get out of the car and walk the green mile, surely to my doom. I see a small smile creep up on Grams lips. I follow her gaze to principal Smith. "Allen?" she explores.

"Yes, Ellen is that you?"

Great my principle and my Gram know each other; this is either going to go my way or go way not my way. They embrace and start chatting, and all I can keep thinking is damn now I have another person to be disappointed in me. It's ok when you don't know the people, like why do I care what people think of me, but now, now there will be more expectations. Fuck my life.

Principle Smith leads us to his office, and we sit in the two chairs facing his desk. I haven't been here since the first day of school. It still looks the same, books cover two of the four walls with little antiquities sparsely placed throughout. Principle Smith starts talking to me but often pauses to steal a glance at my grandma.

"So, Autum, we were considering expelling you for your behavior today, but after some discussion it was decided that you would do community service, here at the school."

Yes, truly going my way.

"I had a few ideas, such as you working with the janitors after school to help clean or helping the lunch ladies." He paused after that.

I don't want to do any of those things, what will kids say when I'm working with the janitor or in the lunchroom? This is definitely not going my way.

He resumed, "but then I was thinking, you know that this year is your Senior Year, and we need more volunteers on the Prom Committee."

Ugh, I hate being around people. Not to mention preppy people with their designer clothes, and 'oh my I broke a nail' drama. Even worse, most of the people in "that" group are the Beta and Delta kids. That's just not a niche I belong in. But I'd rather that than the other.

"Volunteer to help with the committee and you'll really forgive me for what I did sir?" I asked.

"Not entirely," He replied.

Ok here we go. Lay it on thick now you old perve who just wants my grandma. I look at Gram, I need to behave, for her. She smiles at me, and I see a glint in her eyes. Her eyebrows raised for just a second, beckoning me to respond to him.

"Ok, what else would I need to do Principal Smith."

"For starters you would need to apologize to Derek, he has also agreed to apologize to you."

Interesting, really an Alpha is going to apologize to someone. I thought they never admitted when they were wrong. He continued.

"He has said that he did get too close to you and that it was his fault that he startled you and that you just reacted as such."

Probably better he says he startled me than a 5'6" brunette with beautiful blue eyes knocked him on his ass with one swing and he didn't even block it. I'll never forget the look of confusion in his eyes. He saw the punch coming; he knew he was wrong too. Then I briefly saw submission and lastly bewilderment. I mean I think it was bewilderment, that or awe. No, it was probably the former. Why would he be awe struck? I mean I know I'm impressive, but men don't like strong opinionated she wolves.

They like them petite and dainty and weak, like Becca Fawn, not my cup of tea. She practically fell over him with her big blue eyes brimming with tears and her blond hair swayed when he hit the floor. What a drama queen. Her screech could have broken glass. It definitely could have broken my ear drum. But then everything sounded like it was underwater to me, and all I could think about was that smell. Then I felt darkness around me.

I shook my head to get away from my thoughts. I'm just glad they were all focusing on Derek and not me, otherwise they would have seen the sheer panic in my eyes. I really don't know why I reacted that way, hence my visit to shrink Warren's office today.

"I'll agree that I should apologize, and I'll join the committee."

"Great! Let's head down to the auditorium now and I'll introduce you to Mrs. Albim. She leads the committees."

Ugh, Mrs. Albim is not a nice lady. I should know I have to suffer through two of her classes, first period prep class and math. She is just so boring to listen to and not motivating at all. She is in her late fifty's and has this low drawl in her voice and she speaks so damn slow, like I just want to yell, 'spit it out already.' She reminds me of Danny Glover saying he'll get us all killed someday. Great now I'll be in committee with her all the rest of the year. Goddess strike me down now. No? Well great, here we go then.

"Great Mrs. Albim, can't wait to spend more time with her."

"Glad to hear it, Autum. You'll have to wait until Friday to apologize to Derek though, Synthia pulled him from class the remainder of the week to let his nose heal."

Great a whole week of school he gets to miss, lucky. I look at Gram and see another smile on her face, ugh what now…

"Synthia, oh my, I haven't seen her in ages. How is she?" Gram gushes. Mr. Smith looks at her and smiles.

"She is well. She and Beta Elissa have their own veterinarian practice and volunteer at the animal shelter in the human city, Ilwaco."

"Oh, you must be so proud of her, to grow up to be such a well-established woman. So, the Alpha doesn't mind that she works in the city? And you work here in the school! What, retired life too boring for a past Alpha, hmm? Sorry I'm rambling now," Gram gushes.

What is happening right now, is Derek related to the principal. Oh god this could be so much worse than I thought. Gram continues.

"Oh, and you must be so proud to have your grandson here at your school, no less."

Mr. Smith grins, I like all your questions, I've been lonely since Jane passed away and the students don't care the way an old friend would." He smiled softly at her. "Alpha Darren is very happy with the Lunas ambitions. It has been so peaceful between the packs since the coordination from the Tsunami all those years ago, so she doesn't have as many duties here in the pack. And I love teaching the next generation. Even having Derek here, I mean when he isn't being inappropriate with girls and getting punched in the face."

Please Goddess, I pray, now I lay me down to sleep.

"Autum, did you hear that?" She awkwardly smiles at me. "You broke his grandson's nose."

"No, no, no. Now Ellen, don't worry about that."

He pats her hands in his. I raise my eyebrow and clear my throat, creepy old man. They both look at me and avoid eye contact. Great, the last thing I need is for this old man perve to start dating my grandma. We enter the gym and Mr. Smith approaches Mrs. Albim.

"Hello, Mrs. Albim, I'm sure you know Autum."

"Yes… Principle… Smith."

"Well, I've recruited her to join the committee this year."

"Oh… well… very… nice. We… have… a… full… plate… this… year… with… such… a… shortage… of… volunteers…"

Goddess on a crutch, come on spit it out.

"Thank… you… Principal Smith… for the… recruitment, now… follow… me… Miss Moore."

Why did they always have to use last names? Makes me feel like I'm heading onto the football field. The only thing missing is a slap on the ass, ugh, wouldn't that be a sorry sight. I'd definitely go to jail if I hit a teacher. Or I'd be banished.

4

FIRST IMPRESSIONS

Autum POV

Gram and Principal Smith started walking towards the bleachers while Mrs. Albim led me to the group sitting around the table. Great, Becca and her posse are here staring me down, of course this isn't going to go smoothly. She thinks she rules this school. I sigh to myself. She does rule this school. Rebecca starts first.

"Mrs. Albim, we can't seriously be accepting Miss Moore onto the Committee after she condoned physical violence and attacked another student. I mean how will Derek feel having his perpetrator in his presence once he returns to school."

That stupid bitch Becca. She's just rolling me over with that bus, isn't she? I don't see an end to this anytime soon.

"After all she did break his nose, I'm sure she would have hit me if Derek hadn't been blocking me."

Oh, please Becca, spare us. No one believes I was trying to hit you. I wouldn't waste my time. I mean maybe if it would keep you from using that whiney screechy voice of yours, I'd consider it.

"Miss Fawn, Principal… Smith… has decided that… Miss Moore, will… be… helping on… this… committee, any... grievance... you …have… will need… to… go… through him. As well … as… you… Miss Fawn, you… should… not... be… speaking of… such a… private … matter… so… publicly. This… is… gossip… and… disrespectful to… the parties… involved… and I… will… not… tolerate it."

I have to give credit to Mrs. Albim. I didn't like her before, but I'm starting to warm up to her now. She is fair and consistent and won't let student popularity or family position sway her. I guess I should say something now.

"Mrs. Albim, I promise to behave and be respectful to the other classmates henceforth, thank you for giving me a chance." Henceforth? Who am I? Who even uses that word? Mrs. Albim gave me a nod. That's when Amy spoke, probably trying to calm down Rebecca.

"It's not like he comes to many meetings anyways, he's usually at football practice." Rebecca just nodded still not happy I was here. Amy continued. "We were just discussing our committee's name."

"No, we were finalizing our committee's name." Rebecca sneered "And it is The Prom Com." Her arms folded and eyes scolding Amy.

Ethan spoke next "Calm down Rebecca, Amy didn't mean anything by it. The Prom Com is a great name." He sighed and then Mrs. Albim interrupted.

"Oh Autum, let… me… make… the… introductions."

Mrs. Albim went over the introductions, although none were needed. Not to mention she talks so damn slow. As she was speaking, I completely zoned out thinking of my first interactions with 'The Prom Com' group.

My first interactions with Rebecca were not the best. It started on the first day of school. Rebecca Fawn The Beta's Daughter, as lovely as ever. She was the prima donna of the school, the Queen Bee. Sadly, she really did run the school. Most girls were scared of her. She is just a cruel person and if you get in her way, she'll make you regret it.

School has only been in session for four weeks and already I'm the girl she has chosen to harass this year. She's a TA in the office for first period. She was the first student I met in the school. I walked into the reception area, and she asked me to wait for Principal Smith. She had on one of those little name badges, Rebecca. I sat on the bench when a door to my right opened, and Derek walked out of the principal's office.

Derek Bell, tall, dark, and handsome. His black hair was shaved on the sides and long on the top, he had it slicked back. He had tan skin and muscles. So many muscles, I could see them through his shirt. His hands were in his pockets, like he had just left a business meeting. His aura exuded power; he was definitely an alpha. He looked like a young Italian hit man. When we made eye contact, I felt like time was going by in slow motion. Every step he took closer to the door behind me was to the slow beat of my heart, gorgeous and his smile. If I had the chance, I'd get lost in that smile. His smile was directed at me and for the smallest of seconds I was in a fairytale.

Rebecca broke the silence; I felt my face blush and snapped my eyes to the floor. Of course, I didn't know his name until Rebecca spoke it. She did one of those loud coughs.

"Um Derek, I'm over here."

"Hey, Rebecca. TA again this year I see," he responded to back.

She gave me a smirk while flinging her hair back with her perfectly manicured nails. I remember rolling my eyes. She put her hand on his shoulder from over the counter.

"Oh, Derek you didn't comment on my outfit, you like baby?" Baby, gag, they must be dating.

"Miss Moore," Principal Smith called. "I can see you now."

As I got up to walk to the office, I heard Derek say,

"Rebecca, call me Derek!"

"It's just in fun Derek."

Hmm maybe not dating then.

After talking to the principal about my aptitude test, since I'd been home schooled, he confirmed I'd be a Senior although most my age were Juniors this year.

"Principal Smith, do you require students to shower after PE?"

"Yes Miss Moore, is that a problem?"

"Umm, well I've only ever been home schooled. It makes me a bit nervous; can you make that my last class so maybe I can wait for everyone to finish and shower last?"

"Sure Miss Moore, that should still work out with the schedule I'm preparing. Your councilor will be Mrs. Taylor. She is sick today, that's why you are seeing me, but she should be here next week if you need to change anything or need help."

My 1st was Prep: Mrs. Albim. 2nd Period: Science: Ms. Landon. 3rd Math: Mrs. Albim (again). 4th period was lunch. 5th English: Mr. Herd. 6th History: Mr. Timmer. And 7th period PE: Mrs. Timmer.

After thanking Principal Smith, I had ten minutes until 2nd period, so I headed out of the principal's office and headed out to go to class. As I was walking by Rebecca called out to me.

"Autum, is it?" Rebecca scoffed, I nodded. "I saw the way you looked at Derek. He is mine. He's been mine; you are new here. Make sure to keep your eyes off and hands to yourself."

I ignored her name badge and retorted. "What's your name again, Rebah?" I laughed to myself.

"Ewe no, Rebecca, and you'd do well to remember that." She looked pissed, but I didn't care. Rebecca continued, "I'll make your life hell if you even think of messing up what I've got going here."

"Ok got it Rebecca, I'm going to leave now." On my way to class, I found a bathroom and went in to freshen up. I can't stand girls like that. It's not like she had anything to worry about. I don't think of myself as pretty anyways, and I am new here. Ugh, first hour here and already the mean girl knows who I am.

I went into the large stall at the end of the row and when I opened the door to leave Rebecca was standing there. Goddess did she follow me in here?

"What were you doing, listening to me pee?"

"Why are you so vulgar, just came to make sure you heard me about Derek. Stay away from him."

This girl needs to move out of my way. I don't like small spaces and she is blocking my exit. "Ok I get it, now move out of my way."

"I don't think you do." She stepped closer, and stared me down with her piercing blue eyes, but something was happening to them, they were turning whiter. "Why aren't you reacting?" Rebecca almost whispered.

"Rebecca, if you don't get out of my way, you're going to regret it."

"Why, what are you going to do to her?" Goddess another one, enter, Amy. One of Rebecca's little minions.

"Good timing Amy, this bitch was making googly eyes at Derek. She needs to understand her place here, plus she's new. She was home schooled. I wonder why. And she lives with her grandmother. What, do mommy and daddy not love you enough to be with you?"

Who does this bitch think she is? "How do you even know all that? You're not allowed to look at my information."

She held up her hand to look at her manicure again, as I rolled my eyes. I could feel the sweat starting to bead on my forehead, I needed to get out of here.

"I work in the office; I have access to everything. EVERYTHING! Keep that in mind before you piss me off."

I was done I couldn't take it anymore. "Move!" I yelled. I pushed Rebecca out of my way. Amy stepped out of my way, and I ran for the exit. Other girls started entering so I slowed to a fast walk.

Rebecca was yelling behind me, "You stupid bitch, you made me break a nail! Amy why didn't you stop her?"

"Whoops," was the last thing I yelled before leaving the bathroom. I rushed to my next class, which was next to the bathroom. I saw Derek already in there. I looked down at the floor and took a seat at the front of the class. This was going to be a long year.

At the end of the day, it turned out that Rebecca was in my 2nd period class and my 7th period class. We also had lunch together. She has been tormenting me since I started school. So far, she has tripped me in front of everyone when we were leaving 2nd period that first day. She and Amy went into a fit of laughter, of course at my expense. Remembering Grams mantra, 'Just for today, I will not get angry,' I repeated this to myself several times throughout my first day. She makes it a point to mention a foul smell whenever I enter a room. When I raise my hand to answer a question, she starts answering it without being called on. She is relentless. She and her minions make it a point to call me names any chance they get. "Rank-less outsider." Is the current one. She has made it virtually impossible for me to make friends. No one will speak to me. If they do, Rebecca harasses them for the next few days. No one attempted a conversation with me after the first week of school. Lunch was the cherry on the cake though, when she pretended to talk to me in the lunch line and then blurted out.

"Lunch lady Betty is not fat! She is the kindest lunch lady we have Autum, show respect."

I'm pretty sure Betty spit in my soup that day. She glares at me every morning for breakfast so now I eat at home, and I avoid the soup and salad line at lunch. Derek was there too, he just looked at me disappointingly and met Rebecca at her table of popular kids. That was a week ago.

Now here I am four weeks in and on a freaking committee with the girl who's become my nemesis and her best friend, Amy Dord. Amy literally does anything Rebecca says. So pathetic. Her father is one of the pack trainers so naturally she is well trained. She dominates in PE and all sports. But Rebecca usually insults her for it, telling her she needs to be more feminine. Rebecca is killing Amy's confidence, and she knows it. She doesn't want just strong people by her side, she wants submissive people to do her bidding. Amy is lean, you wouldn't notice how strong she is just by looking at her. Watching her in P.E. she usually hangs with the boys, so she is challenged. Well, until Rebecca gets jealous and makes a scene. Amy pacifies her and returns to Rebecca's side. The side of non-participation. Rebecca is an observer; she doesn't like to get sweaty! Her words, not mine.

Also on the committee is Derek Bell, Alpha apparent. What's to say? Besides hanging out with Rebecca, he's almost perfect. He's never been overly nice to me, but I find him attractive. There are so many cute boys at my school. Some are nice, others try to act tough, especially in front of Rebecca. What is it with her? All these boys swooning over her, and she treats them like crap. We have several classes together, but I always sit upfront in all my classes. It's so I can exit quickly if I need to. Derek always sits in the back. I've caught him staring at me several times. I get this weird feeling, like heat is being draped over my body. When that happens, I turn and look behind me and our eyes meet every time. Have you ever felt like someone could see into your soul? That's how I feel when my eyes meet Derek's. His eyes are so dark, I could get lost in them. four weeks of secretly admiring the next Alpha. Swooning over him like every other girl here, who can't get past Rebecca.

Anyways moving on, we also have Ethan Fawn, Rebecca's brother. Nothing like Rebecca. He is cool and calculated. He seems oddly familiar like a friend you haven't seen in a long time. He is the peacekeeper. Other than having literally every class with him, we don't speak much. I didn't really notice him on the first day. Afterward, I'd notice that he always sits next to Derek in the classes they share. I came to find out that Ethan will be Derek's Beta when he takes over the pack. He also has impeccable timing. Almost any day when Rebecca is about to try and embarrass me, usually in the halls between classes, Ethan always shows up. He's always needing her help with something or has questions about their upcoming birthday party. He doesn't know it, but I secretly admire him. I'm not attracted to him but he's like my own little Rebecca whisperer. I think we could be great friends if Rebecca wasn't his sister.

Last on the committee is Samantha Rowe. She is the type that researches anything and everything before coming to a conclusion. She's reserved and quiet, the non-confrontational type, tall and slender with a natural beauty she often masks with excessive makeup. Her wardrobe leans toward long-sleeved shirts and turtlenecks. That's all I've seen her wear. She doesn't like to show off either. I can't even recall her ever wearing shorts either. In P.E she is always in stylish yoga pants and long-sleeve shirts. Her parents definitely spend the money on her wardrobe. Name brand clothes are all she wears. I met her on my first day in the lunchroom. It turns out we have all but Prep class together. She was behind me in the lunch line and knew I never said anything about Lunch Lady Betty. I remember her whispering in my ear,

"Are you going to say something back? You never said that."

"What's the point?" I whispered back. "No one will believe me, I'm new here. I'd rather not waste my breath."

And our friendship slowly began. We eat lunch together every day, it's nice to have at least one friend. Although we don't talk much, Samantha is always reading a book or on her phone researching something for a school project. Which made her very helpful when doing my homework. Usually, as she reads I would do homework, so I could pick her brain. I could finish almost all my homework during lunch and prep class.

That about sums it up. My first month going to school and how I met the group I'd now be stuck with two days a week after school. I look towards

Mrs. Albim. She literally just finished talking. I laugh to myself. She decided to excuse us, ending the meeting, since introductions took so long.

I headed over to the bleachers to meet Gram, we walked back to our car and drove home.

5

SAVED

❧

Autum POV

Gram started making tea when we got home, and we sat in the break-fast nook.

"So, Gram, you know my principal, Principal Smith?"

"Well, yes we went to school together and were good friends."

"You were good friends, so at some point you weren't?"

She hesitated, "I was always fond of him, and him me. I hoped at one point we were mated, but it turned out we weren't."

"Is that why you left Bone Creek?"

"Not entirely. I met your grandfather, and he was my mate. He was also his Alpha's beta, so I moved to his pack, White Mountain."

"Wasn't it hard leaving your family?"

Gram paused for a long time, she never really talked about her family. She tilted her head side to side. "You're old enough to know now I suppose. My mother and father died in a rogue attack when I was only sixteen."

"Oh, Gram I'm so sorry, I shouldn't have brought it up."

"No, no dear, it was a long time ago. The Alpha at the time, Allen's Father, took me in. The plan was that I'd stay at the pack house until I turned eighteen. Plans changed however, during the annual Winter banquet. The banquet had been hosted by Bone Creek for many years. It's an opportunity for all the unmated males and females to meet from all surrounding packs to give them a chance to find their mates. All males over eighteen and all females aged sixteen are encouraged to come."

"Why sixteen for the females?"

"Well, in most cases the males are always older than the females, this is the Goddess' way of ensuring the protection of the females. You can't protect your mate and your children if you are weaker than your female."

"But how would she know she's mated if she doesn't have a wolf?"

"My Autum, a clever girl indeed. Although too young to be absolutely certain, you can still feel a connection to your mate. Plus, the Alpha of the female's pack can challenge, if they feel there may be any foul play. I was seventeen when I met your grandfather. I was walking through the dance floor during the banquet, and there was a group of men. I remember one of them asking your grandfather what was wrong, he had gone completely stiff as I passed by. My arm had brushed up against him and I felt goosebumps raise across my entire arm. Out of the corner of my eye I remember seeing movement and then hearing the faint words "mate" leave his lips. He grabbed my wrist and spun me around. I recall feeling warm in his arms, and every-where he touched I felt energy. There was a distinct smell of mint and vanilla, that I was drawn to, it was his smell. All these things grew ten-fold once I had gotten my wolf. But there was something there before. I could tell he was certain, and the way he tried to please me, and treated me so gently. I could feel his words were true. I volunteered to go with him, I had no family and nothing really tied me to this place, so my Alpha didn't challenge.

"Wow Gram I never knew that, sounds like a good love story. But I do wonder what would have happened if you didn't go with him."

"I've never thought of that before. A few things could have happened I suppose. If I refused, he could have chosen to stay here, in my pack until I was of age so my wolf could name her mate. He could have challenged and threatened war. Or he could have gone home and returned the next year, although that would be difficult for him, not so much for me."

"Why is that?"

"When you're of age and you find your mate, you want to be close to them. You crave them, their touch, their smell. He already had his wolf; he would have lived in agony for a year. That's why most choose to stay with their mate's pack until they are of age unless the female chooses to leave. I didn't have my wolf, so I might have felt sad that he was gone, but I would manage just fine."

"So, you just believed him, and went. I don't know if I could do that Gram, you are very brave." I yawned.

Gram looked at her watch, "it's getting late, walk an old lady to bed, will you dear?" I helped her up off the seat and walked her to her room. She continued her story. "I did believe him and knew deep down it to be true. I guess you could say I was finally happy to know that someone could love me again. After losing my parents, I was devastated. I felt lost and abandoned. Grandpa gave me back my life." She hesitated for a moment, "I'm so sorry you never knew love Autum before you came to me. If I had known how your mother was treating you," she paused again trying to hold back tears. "My own daughter, I would have taken you away sooner. You would have never had to live through that." She touched my arm sleeve that hid my scars.

We were sitting on her bed now, holding hands. She was focused on me. She wanted me to see she really did always care for me, and that she was sorry.

"Gram you couldn't have known, and look, I turned out all right. It's getting late now, let's get some rest."

"Oh Autum, you saved me just as much as I saved you." She gave me a big kiss on the cheek and said goodnight. I headed upstairs to my room and laid on my bed. This was going to be an exhausting year; I could just feel it. Sleep took me.

6

THE APOLOGY

⌒

Autum POV

The next couple days at school were a blur. I got more stares from Becca and Amy. No surprise there. Prom Com meetings on Wednesday and Thursday discussed decorations and voting options for Prom Queen and King. It got heated fast between Rebecc and I, so Mrs. Albim sent us all home. I refused to follow her blindly. It was a committee so all could have input. She didn't allow anyone else to have input. Honestly sometimes I like her ideas but disagreed just to piss her off. Better than both of us was Samantha. Her ideas and suggestions should have been the ones everyone was listening to. I tried to agree with her the most. She was brilliant.

Now it was Friday. Sitting in 1st Period Prep class, I was trying to get ahead on assignments. I had a meeting with Dr. Warren today after school, and I didn't want to be doing homework this weekend. I wouldn't have time after school to get anything done, mostly due to the exhaustion I'd usually have after a session.

The bell rang, and I got up and headed out of class to head to the next period. When I walked into 2nd Period Derek was there. It was all over the school that he was back, everyone talking about how he is to be addressed as Alpha now. He seemed more intimidating now. Of Course, Rebecca was sitting next to him. When I saw them I just kind of stopped in the middle of the room. Derek was looking right at me, his dark eyes locked on mine. I couldn't read him at all. Goddess to know what he was thinking right now, I'd give anything. Rebecca interrupted our stare with a loud shriek,

"Autum," she yelled. "Are you just going to stand there or are you going to apologize for hitting the Alpha?"

I changed my gaze from him to her, took a slow step to the side and sat at my desk. The room was so quiet. I was not going to apologize in front of all these people, he shouldn't have touched me. My eyes were fixed to the floor. I heard rustling behind me. Preparing myself for Rebecca, I looked up ready to yell, but there in front of me stood Derek. He stared at me, almost puzzled and spoke.

"Autum, I'm sorry I grabbed you without your permission. I should have never done that. I deserved this black eye." He halfheartedly joked and looked up at everyone. "A women scorned I suppose." The class laughed with him, what was going on.

I just looked at him, now I was puzzled. Did he really just do that?

"I'm sorry too, I just reacted. I didn't actually mean to punch you, Alpha."

"Yeah, I know," he almost whispered, and rubbed the back of his neck with his hand. He started walking away back to his desk but now it was Rebecca's turn, she was fuming.

"Are you kidding me, you can't apologize to her."

"Rebecca, leave it alone, it's over with." Derek stated.

She stood up and stormed towards me. "No, I don't think so. Autum, stand up and formally apologize to your Alpha."

"Rebecca, don't you ever get tired of being such a bitch all the time?"

I stood next to her. Everyone laughed quietly to themselves, but we all heard it. Rebecca was seeing red, I could tell, her aura was all over the place. She stared out into the classroom and focused on each person and spoke. "You will all agree with me that Autum should formally apologize to Derek."

"Rebecca, you will address me as Alpha and you will stop what you're doing, just let it go."

I didn't understand what was happening, all I knew was I hated her. Her eyes had turned a brilliant white like before. She was a bully and she needed to be stopped. I saw the white slowly fade away from her eyes after Derek spoke. But then everyone turned to me and stared. I was getting anxious, I needed to remember my meetings with Dr. Warren, she told me to breathe and relax. The air in the room was stagnant, and yet it felt charged with electricity. I closed my eyes and un-fisted my hands; I rested them down at my side. I felt good, no, I felt more than good. I opened my eyes and looked out at everyone.

"I am not going to apologize again. Derek and I have already said our piece and I'm good with how it went. Derek, do you agree?"

He just stared at me, it felt odd, like he was bewildered and yet amazed, maybe because I was standing up to Rebecca. She was still trying to give death glares to everyone. Derek nodded before responding.

"Y… Yes, we are g… good." Why is he stuttering now, geez boys these days. I nodded my head back at him, took one more deep breath in and looked out at everyone, everyone was still staring at me completely ignoring Rebecca, best day ever.

"Thank you everyone." I sat down, Rebecca on the other hand started screaming just as Mrs. Landon walked in, our science teacher.

"What is wrong with all of you, you should be listening to me." Rebecca yelled. She grabbed her hair in her hands, she was definitely having a mental breakdown.

"Miss Fawn, please take your seat, it's time for class to start" Mrs. Landon said,

"No, Mrs. Landon you don't understand. Something is wrong with me; I need to go home. And you," she looked down at me. "You did something, I don't know what it was, but I'll figure it out, you little-"

"Miss Fawn that is quite enough, either sit down, or go home. This is a place of learning."

"This is just great," she yelled and stormed out of the class.

Mrs. Landon walked to the chalk board and started class, like nothing had happened. Then I remembered I called Derek by his name, eyes wide I lowered my head and looked behind me, to Derek's seat. He was staring at me, our eyes met, and he smiled softly at me. I half smiled and looked forward. What was happening? I could feel my cheeks flush. Why did Derek apologize like that? Why was he smiling at me? Why didn't he correct me like he did Rebecca? Maybe he doesn't like Rebecca like I thought he did. My mind went wild with possibilities.

7

MEETING AUTUM

ᕙᕗ

Derek POV

I don't know what just happened, but it was the most amazing thing I've ever witnessed. Autum, I thought she was just like all the other kids at this school, well until she punched me. I've always been drawn to her, but then I thought she was under Rebecca's spell. Doomed like everyone else. I don't think she even knows what she did just then. No one will, except Ethan and me. It was like she was the one persuading the class and not Rebecca. Maybe my father was right. My feelings for her have been growing since the first day of school.

I remember the first day like it was yesterday and not four weeks ago. I was speaking with my grandfather in his office, he's the principal and former Alpha.

"Grandpa, I don't want to be on the committee for Prom this year. You made me do Junior Prom last year and that was miserable. Please don't choose this. I'll do anything else." I just wanted one little favor and he wants to take advantage, cunning old man.

"Derek, consider this like an Alpha test. You are learning about the students in your school. You're having to collaborate with students you might disagree with. It's just like working with other packs, plus I find your request odd, but if you want my help than you'll do this." He smiled at me; he knew I would do it.

"Gramps this is not the same. It's the same kids every year, and you know Rebecca is just going to persuade everyone to do it her way." Grandpa looked at me puzzled.

"She's not supposed to be using that on the students."

"Right Gramps, like she can help it. She's used to getting her way; it just comes naturally for her. There's no use in even telling people she's doing it. They all just think they are wrong, and she is right. I just can't wait for school to be over with, when she'll find her mate and hopefully be more controlled."

Gramps just laughed at me. "What if she's your mate?"

"She wishes! The Goddess would never bind me to someone so self-absorbed."

Gramps didn't know it, but it was my worst fear. I know it seems so trivial, worrying about who your mate was at such a young age, but I'm to become Alpha, and my Luna needs to be strong, but also caring. And Rebecca is not caring, she is calculating and cold-hearted. Gramps looked down at his watch, and his eyes widened.

"Oh, I have a new student waiting for me in the reception area, Autum Moore. So, do we have a deal or am I changing your schedule back?"

"No, I agree." With that I hugged the old man and left the office. Autum, I repeated to myself. What a pretty name. As I walked out of the office, I saw her. Our eyes met as she sat in the office. Even from this far I could see the blue in them. Beautiful, I thought. Her brown hair was wavy and down over her shoulders. I could smell her; she smelled of morning rain and lilacs and something else faint I couldn't place. I smiled softly at her. I saw pink form on her cheeks and then the silence was snuffed out by Rebecca,

"Oh Derek, over here," she said or something I don't remember. Autum broke eye contact first and looked down at the ground. I forced myself not to roll my eyes, as a moved towards Rebecca, her voice is just so annoying. I heard my grandfather call for Autum, and then Rebecca was asking me something about her outfit and then called me baby. I focused then on Rebecca; I didn't want Autum thinking Rebecca and I were a thing. Not because I necessarily wanted Autum to know, or maybe I did. I don't know. Either way I responded, and not about her outfit.

"Derek, call me Derek, Rebecca." With that Autum disappeared into Grandpa's office.

"It's just for fun," Rebecca had tried to make light of her calling me baby. "Derek, what classes do you have this year?"

"Like you don't know Rebecca."

She giggled, not attractive.

"Well, you're right. It's funny you know we only have two classes together this year and lunch."

"You don't say." Hence the reason for my meeting with Gramps this morning. After looking at her schedule, where we had every class together, I had him change it. Now for his good deed he 'requested' I join the prom committee. It was worth every minute of it to avoid Rebecca for four hours of my day. Only four though because I still ended up with her for 2nd period, lunch, and 7th period. Plus, the committee, but it was volunteer after school, and I could join a sport and avoid most of those meetings as well.

"I thought it odd, because I distinctly remember looking at the class schedules on the last day of school last year and thought we had most of them together."

I knew she fixed it that way. "Well, it appears you were wrong." I could see her eyes start to glow white, "Rebecca calm down, you know that won't work on me."

"I wasn't going to do anything." She flicked her hair behind her shoulder and sat back down in her chair.

She sat up perfectly straight. "You know Derek, I would be the best Luna. I can't wait till we all turn eighteen and get our wolves. My white wolf and your black wolf will be gorgeous together."

"Rebecca, we don't know what our wolves look like yet, plus we don't know if we'll be mates."

"Come on Derek, I'm the oldest of my family, and have strong beta blood. I'm the strongest female here. The Goddess couldn't have planned it better herself."

She smiled up at me and deep down I knew she wasn't wrong, but I refused to believe it. It didn't feel right.

"Well, I guess only time will tell, I'm going to class now."

She smiled devilishly at me, "see you soon."

'Please Goddess not her' I prayed silently to myself as she got the last word in.

"Your birthday is in a few months, can't wait."

I am turning eighteen on December eighteenth. When I turn eighteen, I will be able to smell my mate. She won't know until she turns eighteen, but I will. And Goddess help me, if it is Rebecca, no one will know until they have to know, ugh. This is going to be the worst year ever.

At least I have Ethan. Ethan, Rebecca's brother. He will be my Beta and building a relationship with him was important. Ethan and Rebecca started school technically early. They will turn seventeen this year, but they are both very smart. It worked out so we could spend more time together to strengthen our relationship. I wonder if I have any classes with Autum. I look at my phone, and I still have fifteen minutes till my 2nd period. I decided to go drop into the library.

"Mrs. Barry, hello how are you?"

"Oh, I'm fine Derek, how are you?"

"Me? I'm good. Mrs. Berry, would you mind if I pull up my class schedule on your workbench? I just left Principal Smith's office and left my schedule in there, but now he's with another student."

"Well, it's not really allowed, just give me a minute to put these books away and I'll get it for you."

"Mrs. Barry, I only have a few minutes to get to class, I'll be quick and only look at mine, Alpha Honor."

"Ok, ok go ahead."

Yes, Alpha Honor. I'm not an alpha yet. I type in Autumn, not found… hmm maybe if I look up new student registrations, only three this year. Ah ha! Autum Moore.

Autum L Moore

Locker 249

Password: 12:9:46

1st: Prep: Mrs. Albim

2nd: Science: Mrs. Landon

3rd: Math: Mrs. Albim

4th: Lunch

5th: English: Mr. Herd

6th: History: Mr. Timmer

7th: PE: Mrs. Timmer

After I printed it, I looked it over. Five classes with Autum. Dang, she got Albim twice, well she's bound to love that. I folded the paper and stuck it in my backpack "Thank you Mrs. Barry! I'm headed to science now."

"You're welcome." With that I headed towards Mrs. Landon's class. I could hear a cat fight in the girl's room as I passed by. The bell had already rung, and more kids were filling the halls. Another day in the life of a teenager in high school, here's to another great year.

8

PROTECTION

Derek POV

I sat in a seat at the back of the class and waited for class to start. Autum and Rebecca walked in almost one right after the other. Autum chose a seat upfront while Rebecca made Eric move to another seat. He was seated by me. Eric was a friend. Who am I kidding I'm friends with everyone. But no girl will approach me for fear of Rebecca. It's real hard having good conversations with people while she is around. I can't wait until I get my wolf and I can mind link. But until then I get Rebecca the ultimate cock blocker.

I found my gaze constantly went to Autum. She was beautiful, and her scent made me feel relaxed. Her brown hair looked soft, slightly wavy, and waterfalling over her shoulders and down her back. Rebecca cleared her throat to get my attention,

"Derek, are you going to stare at her the whole time?"

"Rebecca, I'm not staring at her, I'm listening to Mrs. Landon. Maybe you should do the same and stop worrying about what I'm doing."

The class ended with Rebecca tripping Autum as the whole class exited the room, everyone saw. Amy and she had a good laugh. But Autum didn't say much, mumbled something, looked at Rebecca and kept walking. Great my paying attention to her put her on Rebecca's radar. I'm going to have to watch what I do in front of Rebecca, or she is going to make Autum's life hell. I'll need to recruit some help. 3rd period was great no Rebecca, just Autum. She again sat at the front of the class. I spent most of math class thinking about her. Really, I just felt bad for putting her in front of the firing squad. Ethan noticed I was distracted.

"Hey what's with you?"

I looked at Ethan. "The new girl Autum, have you met her?"

"No not really, just her falling skills from the last class."

When I didn't laugh, he corrected himself.

"She seems like a nice girl, but she is pretty quiet."

"Well, your sister caught me staring at her, and now I'm sure she'll be in her sight lines the rest of the year. It's why you got to admire her falling skills." I raised an eyebrow and looked at him.

Ethan scrunched his eyebrows and then smirked "Does that bother you, Alpha?" He wiggled his eyebrows at me.

I smirked, but then got more serious, "I don't know yet. Really, I'm just tired of your sister picking on any girl that even shows any interest in me or vice versa. How about for now, you just help me distract your sister whenever her and Autum are in the same room?"

Ethan nodded. Although I saw him smiling, he was a man of few words. He will make a good Beta.

"Vice Versa?" Now he looked at me with a raised eyebrow. "Since when have you ever been interested in anyone?"

I didn't answer but gave him a half smile. I was at the very least curious about her. He continued talking.

"Do you know what other classes she has?"

I looked at him contemplating for a moment then handed him her schedule out of my backpack. He was grinning ear to ear.

"Shut it."

"What? I didn't say anything." He paused for a moment looking over Autum's schedule. "Well then, I guess I'll just be her silent bodyguard."

"What do you mean."

"I have every class with her, that will make it easy."

It was settled then; Ethan wouldn't let Rebecca get out of hand and would watch over Autum for me. After class we had lunch. For the past two years, Rebecca, Ethan, Amy, and I have all sat at the same table. So, this year would not be any different. I sat with Ethan, and then the girls followed after. Rebecca always makes the excuse to sit with her twin brother Ethan, and Amy to sit with Rebecca. And that's just how it's been.

Today was like no other. I had just exited the lunch line when I heard Rebecca.

"Lunch lady Betty is not fat, she is the kindest lunch lady we have Autum, show respect."

I roll my eyes and glare towards Rebecca, who is laughing now with Amy. I meet Autum's eyes. And look away. I'm so embarrassed at how she is being treated. I feel my eyebrows scrunch together. Why can't there be one girl, one girl, Goddess, that doesn't fall prey to Rebecca? There are so many nice girls at my school, not that any of them will even consider talking to me, they stare, sure but never approach. The rest of the day went the same. Autum folding to Rebecca's persuasion time and time again. Same story different girl.

I sat in the back of all of my classes that first day, and in all my classes with Autum, she sat upfront. I wonder if she can feel me staring at her. It's how most days went. Secretly admiring her from afar. Only Ethan knew my awkward obsession with her. Why do I want her to be more than she is? I want her to be stronger. I also want to protect her. But if I try that here, it will only make it worse with Rebecca. For now, the plan with Ethan to distract Rebecca from tormenting the poor girl and others was working for the most part. Ethan has a way with his sister.

My mind kept wandering. I wonder what her laugh sounds like... Mr. Timmer pulled me from my stupor in 6th period.

"Mr. Bell, since you seem to be paying so much attention," kids laughed. Did she just laugh, I missed it. Did they all see me blanking out too? Mr. Timmer continued "Why don't you tell us how we all came together with our neighbors during the Tsunami of the year 2003."

I glanced around the room; everyone was waiting for me to respond. Most turned towards me in their seats. I glanced around the room; she was looking at me.

"Well, it actually started before that. Months before the tsunami hit, nine months to be exact." I looked to Ethan. He mouths 'show off' to me and I continue with a grin.

"There had been some abnormal weather. It had been so bad that dad, I mean, Alpha Darren, had sought advice from his Beta and other Leaders on his council. They had all agreed something much bigger was coming. And though we never really got along with the packs around us and had often been at war with some over pack lands, we knew alliances would need to be made. In case such emergencies ever arose.

As each month passed the weather became grimmer and grimmer. He started communications with the other packs and even hosted banquets. At that time, my father decided that we could build relationships with the other packs by using pack finances to help the other close packs get loans to improve their towns. It worked. Over the course of those nine months great relationships were forged. And in October of 2003 without any real notice a huge tsunami was threatening to wipe us all out, it took mere hours to evacuate the town. There were still some lives lost, but many were saved due to the forward thinking of my father and his Council. Or so it was written, The End."

Everyone clapped, except Mr. Timmer. So, I stood and bowed.

"You're a little cheeky today Mr. Bell, I think its best I inform Mrs. Timmer of your unusually high energy levels today, maybe an extra run or two will be needed in PE." He winked at me and continued the lesson.

The best part of telling that story was having all eyes on me. Usually, I didn't care who was watching, but today Autum was watching. She was intrigued, she hadn't heard this much before I could tell. I wanted to keep the story going just to keep her gaze. Her eyes were a stunning sapphire blue. I could get lost in those eyes. She was smiling as I spoke before. I rarely saw her smile, mostly because that leech Rebecca was always nearby. But I had to keep good relations with the Beta family and that meant Rebecca. She turned around and continued listening to Mr. Timmer.

I wish I knew what she was thinking. Does she like me, or even have any interest in me? I've never really wanted to know how a girl feels about me. I guess I always knew I'd wait for my mate. But hanging out with Autum would be nice. She seemed like a nice person. Anything to distract me from thinking Rebecca would be my mate. Thinking of spending time with Autum made my chest constrict. I could feel my pulse quicken, something about her just excited me.

9

THE TOUCH

❧

Derek POV

The next four weeks went by quickly. My birthday was getting close and so was Rebecca's and Ethan's. For once though she wasn't focused on her birthday at all. She always went all out on her birthday. Her family was almost richer than mine, and her parents gave her anything she ever wanted. Today however, all she talked about was how I would be eighteen soon and wanting to see my wolf.

I don't want to think of her seeing my wolf. If I could just have my family there that would be alright with me. I was nervous to shift for the first time. It was my golden birthday, and my mother was determined to make it special. I'm hoping my wolf is black like my father's, to portray strength like him.

"Derek." I looked up to see Ethan.

"Hey man, what's up?"

"Nothing really, I just wanted to ask you if you could help prep for my Beta exam later."

"Yeah, of course"

"Hey look there's Amy, come with me I want to go talk to her." Ethan was obsessed with that girl, always following her around.

"What is it with you? She is with Rebecca. I don't want to go with you, we just saw them at lunch."

"You're my wingman, I get nervous when you're not there. I don't want to cause a scene, you know. Secondly, Rebecca being there can't be helped."

What he meant was he didn't want to cause a storm in the middle of the school. His nervousness could turn into a gust of wind, then fueled by anger from not controlling himself, would result in another storm. Yes, another storm, it's happened before. His family was special, to say the least.

So, we end up standing outside Rebecca's locker, because I've got to be a good wingman. Looking around, trying to avoid Rebecca's conversation, I notice her locker number. Locker 251... Hmm that's right next to Autum's. Now I wasn't so bitter about being here. Maybe she'd swing by her locker. It's not like I didn't see her a lot, but I could never get close to her.

As Rebecca was droning on about my birthday, Autum came around the corner. I made eye contact and she looked gorgeous. Even though she was pinching her eyebrows together. She obviously didn't like that our group was standing so close to her locker. She was kind of cute when she's flustered.

"Um, excuse me, Derek."

Her voice was soft towards me. Sweet almost. I moved over to give her more room. She tucked some hair behind her ear, and I think I saw a small blush on her cheeks. Does she even know how cute she is? I may have intentionally blocked her from her locker, hoping shed brush up against me, but no luck.

Rebecca scoffed, "bit pushy there Autum, don't you think?"

Autum rolled her eyes and shut her locker, this was not going to be soft or sweet.

"Rebecca let's not start this now, okay?"

Her friend Samantha came over at that time. I nudged Ethan and looked at him like, 'distract your sister before all hell breaks loose.' He picked up what I was putting down.

"Hey Sis, you keep talking about Derek's birthday but what should we do for our birthdays? The big seventeen, its only two weeks away."

That did it Rebecca was going a million miles a minute on all her plans for their birthday.

I couldn't help it, but my gaze turned back to Autum, her back to me. I could smell the morning rain and lilac. I was drawn to it. Other girls smelt nice, but not like this. Rebecca smelt of roses, reminding me of my grandma, ewe. Amy smelled like salt taffy, the worst candy ever. And even her friend Samantha, she was like a soufflé, too rich for my blood. She always had an odd smell of antiseptic as well. Either way I didn't much like sweets.

I could still hear Rebecca talking, I'd glance at her and nod. I had no idea what she was saying. My eyes kept drifting to Autum. My eyes followed her body down, her hair still softly flowing over her shoulders and down her back. Her hair rested slightly above her ass, wow her ass was so plump. Wow, why hadn't I noticed before? I scrunch my eyebrows, why am I thinking this way? I can't get enough of her, that's why. My hand had a mind of its own as it reached out. Slowly touching her soft hair and then... My breathing hitched as I rested my hand... Touching her. I could feel tingles... Goosebumps formed on my arms, what was this? Could she feel it too? My hand was placed on her side with my thumb circling her ass cheek. No idea what came over me, it's the closest I'd ever been to her. But it only lasted a second.

Autum whipped around and her eyes found mine. She didn't look shocked more stunned. Her eyes looked sad and lost and all I could do was stare into them, trying to figure out what she was feeling. Did she feel what I felt? The electricity. The desire. The next thing I knew, I saw her right arm swing around. I could have stopped it, but I would have hurt her. And that look in her eyes... She was already hurting. It all happened in slow motion but so quickly at the same time. I drew a breath in, and I took it. I fell hard in that moment, and she has a mean right hook too.

"Fuck, I think you broke it." I winced at the pain.

I grabbed my nose and fell into the locker. Of course, Rebecca started screaming and pandering to me, asking what she should do. I wasn't hurt, not really, just stunned. The hit was harder than I expected, much harder. Curious. I snapped my nose back into place. The cracking sound almost made Rebecca pass out.

"Derek did you really have to do that?" Rebecca cried.

Yes, totally worth it to see her cringe. Time seemed to stand still for a moment, I think for Autum too. She looked phased, like someone had just smacked her. Teachers started coming towards the commotion. Mrs. Albim first, she walked straight to Autum. Samantha was behind her talking to her asking her what happened. Autum just stood there; her right hand still fisted. Her left hand on the locker. Samantha was shaking her shoulders, and nothing would phase her.

"Autum... Autum. Can you hear me? Snap out of it." Samantha tried to reach her.

She couldn't hear Samantha at all. Mrs. Albim, also unable to get a response, ushered her to the office by her shoulders. I walked behind them slowly, drowning out all the sounds, to try and hear Autum's breathing to see if she was talking yet. She was breathing calmly, but it was eerie. She looked completely lost in her thoughts. Like nothing was going on around her, completely zoned out.

I met Grandpa in the reception area outside his office, he was on the phone. He started pacing and walked back into his office again. Autum was standing there. She seemed to get her senses back as she yelled.

"D- Don't touch m me!" Autum's voice shook.

Mrs. Albim immediately moved her hands from her shoulders and stepped back.

"Autum, we have called your grandmother, Ellen. She is on her way to get you dear."

I could hear Autum's breathing pick up. But I could sense it wasn't anger, her eyes were darting around the room, and she met mine. I could see her chest rising with every harsh breath she was taking. I went to take a step towards her, but she abruptly pushed her hand out. Warning me, not to come closer. Her Grandmother walked in at that time.

"Take my hand Autum."

Her grandmother was speaking calmly, but she had a sad look in her eyes. She took Autum's hand and started walking her out of the office. She didn't even talk to my grandfather, the principal. Her phone rang just then, sounded like my dad the Alpha. When Ellen saw me, she looked apologetic.

"I'll be right there, sir, I just have to drop Autum with Dr. Warren and then I'll be right over." I heard her say to my father.

She was in and out in minutes. My grandfather came out of his office. Still talking on his phone probably to my mom since my dad was obviously on another call.

"Synthia, I don't know exactly what happened yet. I know I will expel her if that's what you want. I know I can't believe it either, who would hit the Alpha. Kids these days I understand, ok see you in a minute, bye."

I didn't give him any time to talk, "You can't expel her!"

"WHAT?!" Rebecca screamed.

How long has she been standing next to me?

"Rebecca, go home."

"But Derek you are hurt."

Hurt, what? I'm fine "I'm fine Rebecca, she barely touched me."

"She broke your nose Derek, I heard it."

"Rebecca, leave now."

She huffed, "Fine I'll go but I'm not leaving, I have Prom Com today after class," She walked away.

10

LUNA

~

Derek POV

I followed my grandfather into his office. "Derek, what happened, your mother and father are furious. They want her expelled from the school or even banished."

"What? No this was my fault; you have to call them back Gramps."

"This is out of my hands son; just be glad they aren't talking about death."

"Gramps, listen to me, this is crazy, it isn't that big a deal… She … I don't know, something was off with her, you didn't see it."

I was frustrated I didn't know how to explain what I was feeling in that moment, when my eyes met hers after she hit me.

"When my parents get here, we will talk about this."

I tried to find the words to say when my parents arrived. Gramps and I sat in silence for what seemed like forever, was only about ten minutes in actuality.

"Derek, honey, are you ok?" My mother asked as she entered the room.

"I'm fine mom."

"Derek there is blood all over you." She sighed.

"Mom, I'm fine. It wasn't Autum's fault, I provoked her."

Mom sat down as Dad walked in, "What do you mean you provoked her?"

I inhaled deeply. I hated the thought of my father being disappointed in me. And he would be.

"I... I touched her."

He seemed to think for a minute. That's my father, a man who contemplates the entire conversation before speaking. After many moments that seemed to last forever, he continued.

"That hardly seems like a reason to hit the Alpha." He mused.

I know he's not wrong, but I haven't actually allowed anyone to call me Alpha. They are all to call me Derek until I've become Alpha. I just want to be a kid like everyone else. My mother, thankfully, agreed with my decision. Otherwise, my father never would have.

"Dad, I'm not the alpha yet. Here, I'm just another kid."

He squinted his eyes at me. My mother knew this never sat well with him and looked apologetic at me.

"That's just utter stupidity, what is really going on here Derek? When I was growing up everyone called me Alpha. I didn't have the title yet; it was out of respect!" My father was angry, I had to explain this.

"I grabbed her ass."

My mom gasped, "Language!"

"Sorry mom, listen I grabbed her, and it startled her. she was just reacting. If anything, this is my fault, and I should be the one apologizing to her."

My father sat down next to my mother. All three of them just stared at me, my dad spoke next.

"What else? There is no way you didn't see it coming, you spend hours training every week."

This man could read me so well. Alphas don't take the blame for anything. Everyone is expected to listen to and respect the Alpha. Although I'm not the Alpha yet, my future title demands respect.

"There is nothing else."

Please let it go, please let it go. Don't ask me to explain how I'm feeling about her, because I don't understand it yet myself.

"Derek, you have five minutes to tell me what else is going on, because I'm going to walk out of here to go meet her grandmother and I'm going to banish that girl."

Damn, he was calling my bluff.

"Ok. Ok. I think she is battling something internally. Dad, you understand that right? She is shy and doesn't want attention most of the time. She doesn't seem to like hanging out in crowds. I'm not entirely sure but I am sure that she looked scared when she hit me, I scared her. Yes, I saw it coming, but I would have hurt her if I stopped what was about to happen. I've never had conflicts at school, you know this. I've never asked for anything, but I need you to let this go. I just heard her grandmother tell you on the phone that she was taking her to the doctor. Something is going on with her and this was not her fault, you can't banish her for this. Everyone is blowing this way out of proportion."

There was a moment of awkward silence.

"It's true, you've never had conflicts. Why now, why this girl?"

Goddess he wasn't going to let me leave without more. What more did he want, now I was just getting angry "Why... Why her, I don't know what else you want me to say."

I paused; I hated awkward silence.

"Dad, what do you want me to say?"

"Derek, I want you to say everything that is on your mind, we both know the consequences of holding in one's thoughts for too long. What is it about THIS girl?"

My father, the mind reader.

"Dad, really? What do you want to know? You want to know that she smells... Nice... Like lilacs after a morning rain. That I snuck her class schedule to see if we had more classes together on the first day I saw her leaving this very office? That I have Ethan distract Rebecca from her, so Rebecca will leave her alone? That I like to spend class sitting behind her so she doesn't see me staring? That I like the way she always wears her hair down and how it bounces when she walks? That when I stood next to her in that hall today all I could do was think of touching her? I don't know why her. Why this girl but I do know you can't banish her. Dad you can't, I- I-"

I was panting, breathing hard. I'd only known Autum for four weeks and I already knew I'd miss her if she left. But I couldn't finish that sentence, so I finally looked around. My mother's jaw was open, and my father was smiling at me, so was my grandpa.

"Ok," My father finally spoke.

"She will have community service. Allen, that's something you can arrange?"

"Yes, Darren"

"Well then, Synthia, we need to leave to meet Ellen at the Pack house. Then we will send her here to discuss her granddaughter's community service."

My father extended his hand to my mother, she stood and walked to my grandfather.

"Dad, thanks for calling, love you," she hugged my grandfather and turned to me.

"Let's go take you to the doctor as well and have them look at that nose. I think you should stay home the next few days to make sure that heals correctly." She touched my nose softly, "You did a good job setting it." She winked at me and grabbed my father's hand, "Let's go dear."

They started to the door.

"Wait." I said, were they really letting this go now? "That's it? Conversation over? Community service not banishment?"

My father's gaze met mine, a devilish gleam in his eyes, "Can't banish our future Luna now, can we?" Is all he said before he led my mother out of the office.

I looked back at my grandfather, he smiled softly at me. Grinning all the way to his eyes. I shut his door and followed my parents out to the car; it was silent as we headed home.

When we pulled up to the house, I just stared up at it through the window. Could Autum be my Luna? I never thought of that. It always seemed I'd be doomed to have Rebecca by my side. I would love to bring Autum to my home. To make this her home as well. I got out of the car. I felt happy, happy for the first time in a long time. I knew I would have to do something now, not just hide behind Ethan to help protect her from Rebecca. But I also couldn't let anyone else know she was to be my Luna. Not until she gets her wolf too and could protect herself. There was too much that could go wrong as long as Rebecca was stronger than her. I could use my Alpha voice on Rebecca to not cause harm, but then she could just persuade someone else to do it. She is obsessed with me and being Luna. I could see her trying to hurt Autum.

"Son," my father called, "You look deep in thought, what is bothering you?"

"It's Rebecca," I paused trying to choose my words carefully. "She already has it in her mind that we will be mated. And she has made that clear at school with all the other girls. I don't want anyone to know, until we are sure. And even then, I think it would be best to wait until Autum gets her wolf before we inform the council." My father and I had slowly been walking and ended up in his study.

"Why?" He asked.

"Because Rebecca can't control her persuasion. I fear she will harm Autum or have another harm her. Or have her harm herself. Autum is not strong enough to fight it yet, only when we are mated will it not affect her."

"Why have we not discussed this before, we need to speak to Beta Richard. Does he know his daughter is struggling or her mother?"

"No and there is no point. Not unless you know a way to block her gifts until she can control them. I know they don't impact us or her family but there are thousands of pack members she could influence."

My father seemed to think about this for a while. He spoke, "I will discuss with Beta Richard and your mother as well as her mother of Rebecca's gifts. We will keep your Luna a secret, for now."

"We could also talk to Dr. Warren and see if Rebecca is a threat." I suggested.

"You know she won't. Doctor patient confidentiality." He argued back.

"Then ask her as your sister-in-law." My father rolled his eyes. Dr. Warren was technically my aunt. Well, she claimed to be. My father's younger brother, Gram, left the pack to look for his mate and never returned. Dr. Warren or Emivy claimed she was his mate and that he died during a rogue attack. She sought help within our pack because Uncle Gram had told her who we were. With her being a human and my cousin, Kiel, being a wolf, she needed the help to raise him.

I nodded to him, but for the first time my father seemed like he still had something to say. "What is it?"

He smiled lightly at me. "Look who can read the room now." I grinned too. He continued, "you don't have to worry about Rebecca, I can say with certainty that she isn't your mate. Before you ask, I won't talk more about it." With that he left the study and left me completely baffled.

11

ALPHA

❧

Derek POV

I spent the next two days at home. But on Friday when I woke, I had to
see her again. I had dreamt of her the past three nights. My hands caressing
her cheek. Running my fingers along her jaw down to her collar bone, over
her shoulder and down her arms. I imagined her face, her lips parted as I
kissed her neck. Staring at me with those sapphire eyes. I woke up awkwardly
hard and sweating. It was like now that I knew my feelings my body couldn't
help but react. I got ready for school and headed downstairs. My mother
greeted me in the kitchen.

"Good morning, my sun."

"Morning mom." She always greeted me this way. She didn't mean son
but sun. She always said I was her light, and I grew up hearing the song 'You
Are My Sunshine' most mornings. I walked to her, and she kissed my cheek.

I was taller than her now, but I still remember her kissing the top of my head each morning while she'd sing.

"You are up early, you planning on school today? Do you need a ride, I can drop you on my way?"

"Yes, going to school. No, I don't need a ride. I think I'll drive today."

"Really?" She was smiling at me. "I thought you didn't want to show off and just be a normal kid, hmm? Seems you have a reason to now..."

I didn't answer her, just kissed her cheek, and walked towards the door to leave. It was time for me to grow up. No more hiding. Time to take responsibility and start earning my title. I can't be passive any longer and it would start with the school. I also needed to get Autum some more help. Ethan wouldn't be enough. First things first, I would find Samantha.

When I arrived at the school, everyone stared at me. I had never driven to school before, and my face was still bruised, both eyes black from the broken nose. My parents had bought me a nice truck, A GMC Denali, but I never really drove it. I always thought people would think I was privileged and that they would hate me for it or not respect me.

Turns out my inability to grasp my role as an Alpha was what was really hurting me. And has allowed Rebecca to dominate the school. Starting today it would be different. I had 1st period Prep with Samantha. I entered class. And my teacher Mrs. Mie turned to me.

"Derek your late, take a seat."

"Alpha"

"Excuse me" she replied.

The entire class was looking at me, so I spoke sternly.

"Everyone will address me as Alpha going forward unless I give you permission to call me otherwise. I will be turning eighteen in a couple of months and the transition will be begin, might as well start now."

I looked around and everyone was bearing their necks to me. Including Mrs. Mie, she was also smiling. A small smile appeared on my lips, but I ended it quickly. I needed to remain firm. This felt right.

"Yes Alpha," Mrs. Mie replied.

"Yes Alpha," the class replied.

I glanced around at everyone, "Samantha, move to the back of the class and switch seats with Lacy."

Both girls looked at each other, "Yes Alpha."

I walked to the back to my seat next to Samantha. "You may continue your discussion Mrs. Mie." Everyone turned to Mrs. Mie, but I turned to Samantha.

"Samantha, I need a favor."

She was hesitant, "Yes Alpha."

I had been friends with Samantha for years. Not only are we neighbors but her father was one of my father's Omegas and her family was among the brightest in our pack, they were our scholars. Well versed in all pack history and Lore. Her father and mother sat on the Council as well.

"You may call me Derek." I saw her sigh in relief. No one knew this new me yet. I liked how they were all uneasy around me right now. "You are friends with Autum?"

"You know I am, what is this about? And what is with you, I've never seen you so... confident."

"We can talk more about that later. I need you to talk to Autum and tell her about the twins." Samantha looked at me puzzled for a moment. But then nodded slowly. "Can you tell me why?"

I contemplated my words for a moment. "She needs to understand why Rebecca has so much power here, and there are other reasons that I can't share for now. I just need you to keep this conversation between the two of us and trust me."

She nodded, "I'll find a place to talk to her during lunch. And by the way, I like this new you."

I just smiled briefly at her and thought about how I would approach Autum next period. Surely, she would be uneasy after what happened Tuesday. And I'm sure Rebecca has been just making her miserable the last few days as well. After the bell rang, I walked straight to 2nd period. I sat in the back and waited for Autum to come. Several kids came in, including Rebecca. She sat next to me as per usual. I just kept staring at the door waiting for Autum to enter. Finally, she did. Our eyes met immediately, and time seemed to stand still for a moment. The silence was broken by Rebecca yelling at Autum.

Autum's eyes moved from my gaze to Rebecca's, and without uttering a single response, she took her seat and looked down at her desk. Before Rebecca could say anything else I stood up. I looked at Rebecca and she smiled at me. She was thinking I would put Autum in her place surely. I walked to the front of Autum's desk and waited for her to look up at me. When she did her eyes were dazzling.

"Autum, I'm sorry I grabbed you without your permission, I should have never done that. I deserved these black eyes." I gave a little wink to get a few laughs, it worked, "A woman scorned I suppose." The class laughed with me. She looked at me relieved and confused, she had raised one eyebrow most likely in disbelief. It's the most I've spoken to her since school started. After I brief pause, she finally responded.

"I'm sorry too, I just reacted. I didn't actually mean to punch you, Alpha."

Her voice was so sweet, but I didn't like hearing her call me Alpha. It bothered me more than I thought it would. But for now, it can't be helped. I rubbed the back of my neck and smiled at her and then nodded "Yeah, I know." I said to her. I turned and walked back to my desk. Unfortunately, it was now Rebecca's turn, and she was fuming.

"Are you kidding me, you can't apologize to her."

"Rebecca, leave it alone, it's over with." I told her.

This girl, I can't stand the sound of her voice. Also, I don't need her standing up for me. As I sat down Rebecca stood up and stormed towards the front.

"No, I don't think so. Autum! Stand up and formally apologize to your Alpha." She sneered.

I was about to speak again when Autum finally spoke up for herself, even getting out of her seat to address Rebecca.

"Rebecca, don't you ever get tired of being such a bitch all the time!" Autum retorted.

I looked at Ethan who was seated on my other side. He smirked; I think he found it amusing anytime someone tried to stand up to his sister. Usually because it ended with the other person apologizing and not even knowing why. Rebecca's eyes were starting to gleam white, and she stared out into the classroom and focused on each person and spoke.

"You will all agree with me that Autum should formally apologize to Derek." She tried to command. That was it, I was done, I stood up.

"Rebecca, you will address me as Alpha and you will stop what you're doing, just let it go."

She looked at me and then the white in her eyes slowly faded away back to their blue color. But then something else happened. Rebecca was still angry still trying to persuade the others, but now Autum. I sat back down and looked at Ethan. Was I the only one seeing this? Autum spoke again.

"I am not going to apologize again. Alpha and I have already said our piece, and I'm good with how it went. Derek, do you agree?"

Did she just address me again, I zoned out looking into her eyes. They were shining brightly, the sapphire turning almost white. I tried to speak "Y-yes, we are g-good."

"Thank you everyone." Her eyes faded back, and she took her seat. Rebecca on the other hand started screaming just as Mrs. Landon walked in. I couldn't hear what was going on, I just looked at Ethan again completely blown away with what happened. He was staring at Autum. Who was this girl and what the hell just happened? Did she just…? I don't even know what happened. It's like she took Rebecca's persuasion. Is that possible? Ethan finally looked at me, his mouth still gaping. He shook his head. He had no idea what happened either. My Luna might not be as helpless as I thought. But one thing was for sure, this was going to change everything.

12

POWERS

❦

Autum POV

Today had to be one of the strangest days I've ever had. And now I'm sitting in the hall waiting for my appointment with Dr. Warren, Friday at 4:30 on the dot. I can't be late, but I have to come early to sit around and wait. I felt like I was bursting at the seams, I needed to talk to someone about today and all the information I had learned about the Fawn twins. My doctor can't tell anyone cause of patient/doctor confidentiality, so I was going to spill everything.

"Miss Moore, are you ready?"

"Yes." Finally. I needed to get this all off my chest and then I seriously needed a nap. I almost fell asleep in 3rd period math with Mrs. Albim after my little confrontation with Rebecca. I felt so energized whilst we had our little yelling match, then felt completely drained. It must be all the emotional turmoil of the day. Not to mention Mrs. Albim's slow drawl, it was enough to put anyone to sleep.

I walked in and took a seat on the sofa. Dr. Warren asked if I wanted anything to drink. I did not. I was hoping she would let me skip EMDR today. EMDR or eye movement desensitization and reprocessing, is a type of mental health therapy. Some would say it's like hypnosis. This method involves moving your eyes in a specific way while you process traumatic memories. Dr. Warren uses a light bar to accomplish this.

"Dr. Warren, before you start asking me questions and we do the thing that we do I really just need to talk and get some things off my chest."

"That's what I'm here for Autum. If you just want to talk, we can talk. We can continue EMDR next session."

"Thank you." I started by telling her of 2nd period and my encounter with Rebecca. I felt in control and confident for probably the first time ever since I can remember. But the more interesting story was what happened at lunch. My friend Samantha and I had one of the realest conversations that we have ever had. Usually Samantha just reads during lunch, and I work on homework or people watch. We talk sometimes, but we've never really talked, talked. We both kind of do our own thing, and it's nice not to be sitting alone. Today however, Samantha dropped the biggest bomb on me, and I just can't believe it. It started when she noticed me falling asleep at our lunch table.

"Autum, girl, how can you fall asleep here with all this noise?"

"Samantha, just wake me up when lunch is over. I just need a quick nap. I'm emotionally drained from my altercation with Rebecca and then sitting through an hour of class with Mrs. Albim in Math."

"Ooh, you had an altercation with Rebecca, do tell. Did it end the usual way with you just walking away?"

"You're not going to let me sleep, are you?" She laughed and shook her head. "Ugh, fine, I'll tell." After describing the whole ordeal and how Rebecca left school sick, she laughed. Then she looked around the cafeteria.

"That explains why it's so noisy today. Look at everyone. They are talking and laughing with each other. Usually everyone is on edge waiting for Rebecca to have an outburst."

"You're right, I hadn't noticed until you said so. Anyways it was the best class of the year. And listening to her whine 'you're supposed to be listening to me' cherry on the cake. It was the first time I've seen so many people defy her at the same time." We both laughed at that.

Samantha replied, "Can't really blame her, after so many years of people literally being persuaded by her every minute of the day. It became second nature to her. I'm sure she really did feel like she was going crazy."

"Right, but why would she go crazy? it's not like they have to listen to her."

"Well, actually Autum, most kind of do."

My puzzled look must have invited the next explanation she gave me.

"The Fawn twins have abilities." she had said. I just looked at her dumb founded. I have never heard of this, wolves with abilities.

"What do you mean?" I asked, mouth open.

"Rebecca has an actual gift of Persuasion. She's like a siren, and she uses the Siren Gaze to get all the males to do what she wants. It even works on women, it's not as strong but still effective. The only ones it doesn't work on are her family, mated wolves, and Alphas.

"Omg, I have never heard of this, so many things make more sense now. And her brother Ethan, what can he do?"

"He can manipulate the weather. That's why he is always so calm, if he gets angry then he can cause a storm. Because of this though, Ethan was forced to control his gift."

This girl is blowing my mind right now, I can't even believe the words she is saying.

"So has he ever gotten angry?"

"Well, there was this time in first grade that was really bad. We had been watching some documentary on Penguins and Ethan saw the snow. When the teacher told him we didn't get snow on the coast he had a tantrum. That night it snowed nine inches!"

"That doesn't sound so bad."

"Think about it, a community that never gets snow has no plan to deal with snow. School was closed all week. Cars couldn't drive up our steep hills and valleys, most were stuck in their homes. Not to mention we lost a ton of crops. It only melted after Ethan got tired of the cold after five days and made it hot again. For the kids, we all had a blast. But when my parents talk about it, it was the second worst disaster they've had here."

"Oh, I guess that would be bad. So, two bad disasters and nothing else?"

"All I can say for certain is that we have had a lot of storms, most that came out of nowhere. Usually right over the Fawn Residence through the years. Ethan has gotten better and better controlling his emotions as he grows older."

"You said the adults only counted the snowstorm as the second worst event, what was the first?"

She got really quiet. "Have you ever heard about the tsunami that almost wiped this pack out?"

"Yeah, who hasn't?"

"Really, you know of it, how?"

I didn't want to go down this rabbit whole yet, I'm way too interested in Ethan now.

"You tell me first," I replied. "My story is longer than yours."

She hesitated then continued

"Now, none of this has been confirmed, but there was no scientific reason for that tsunami. It just appeared out of nowhere. And it just so happens that Ethan's mother, Elissa, was giving birth at the time. Their birthday is the same day as the tsunami!" She just stared at me after that, probably waiting for a response, but I just was trying to fathom everything she had said.

"Samantha, I feel like you're pulling one on me, are you for real?"

"Totally, it's like an urban legend now and no one talks about it. The Tsunami that is."

"Why wouldn't people talk about it?"

"Well lives were lost, even after attempting to prepare for a disaster they felt was coming. They just never fathomed it would be something so colossal. The pack lands remained underwater for months afterwards. All the houses were washed away and the whole town had to be rebuilt." She obviously knew a lot about the town. She began again.

"So, your turn, how did you hear of the tsunami?"

"My grandma is from this pack. She met her mate at a banquet here and moved to White Mountain Pack to be with him. She told me she actually took in some of her old pack during the Tsunami. My Grandma taught me a lot about the packs. I didn't even know I was a werewolf until Gram explained to me. She home schooled me until this year, obviously. She decided I needed some social skills and to do that it was time for me to join my peers and go to school." Samantha kept quiet, waiting, probably wanting to know more about me, not knowing I was a werewolf.

"How old where you, when your grandma told you you're a wolf?"

"I think I was six, I knew my mother had a wolf. I just didn't fully understand that I had one, but-"

The bell rang, abruptly ending our conversation.

"So that was my day." I looked to Dr. Warren. Hoping to catch a surprised look on her face. But she had no expression at all. She was still writing notes on her legal pad.

"Dr. Warren, did you hear me? Isn't it crazy that there are wolves with like superpowers?

"Actually Autum, I already knew about that. The Fawn family is a family of white wolves. White wolves are known to have powers. The part that is unknown is how many white wolves there are. It is extremely rare."

I felt completely deflated, so much for my exciting news.

"Dr. Warren, how is it you know and the kids at the school don't know?"

"Well, it's no secret that I'm a psychiatrist, I know a lot of secrets. But don't worry. I'll keep you knowing our little secret."

"I didn't get anyone in trouble, right?"

"No, Autum its fine, you would've known eventually. After all they will be turning eighteen next year. But let's talk about some of the other revelations you had today."

"What do you mean?" what did I say that made her think I had made other revelations today...

"Going back to the story you just told me you used the words confident and energized. Not only that, but you also walked into my office and knew exactly what you wanted. So, who is this new Autum before me today? This Autum is not the same girl I just saw on Tuesday, so what changed?"

I had to think about that for a minute. What had changed since Tuesday? I was a mess on Tuesday. I felt like a mess all week actually. Today was different. The only thing different today was, maybe Derek apologizing to me. And not just to me but in front of the whole class.

I told Dr. Warren my thoughts. She followed with "Why do you think the Alpha apologizing to you made you more confident and energized?"

She called him Alpha, am I supposed to do that here too? Everything changed so quickly. I forgot.

"I think the… Alpha apologizing to me, confirmed that I wasn't in the wrong and that what I did was justified. It also helped me stick up for myself against Rebecca. Once I knew I had his support."

"This is very good progress Autum."

"Thanks Dr. Warren, it was like a weight was lifted and I was done allowing her to be cruel to me any longer."

"Autum I would like to review a few things from last session also, if you remember, we ran out of time. I believe you had some revelations during that session that will help us break through your blockage."

I nodded to her; I couldn't remember everything I had said on Tuesday. She has a way of picking through my stories though and pulling out the pieces that pique her interest the most.

"So last week you discussed smells bringing back memories and you also talked about the Alpha touching you. The part I'm curious about is not that he touched you, but how you said you wanted him to touch you. I know how you feel about physical contact, so that statement I want to revisit."

"I don't know where to begin on that. I remember wanting him to touch me, I almost remember feeling goosebumps when he did, but when the smell hit me, it washed away everything that I was feeling and brought me to darkness."

"Do you know what the smell was?"

"No, something musky maybe."

"Could it have been his cologne?"

I looked at Dr. Warren and she must have seen the light bulb go off with my facial expression.

"Autum if you can confirm that it was his cologne, and we can get it. We might be able to use it in session to break through your memories?"

Listening to her say that and thinking it might be possible. Suddenly I didn't know if I wanted to. It was true everything she said. Today I was different. Today I was confident and a little fearless. Today I was happy. Did I really want to know? Did I want to relive what happened in my childhood and drudge it back up again? As if she was reading my memory, Dr. Warren spoke.

"Autum, we don't have to do it right away. When you're ready, we can try. I just want you to be the same girl that walked in today and decided what we would be doing."

I nodded to her again, still working everything out in my head.

"Well Autum, session is over for today. I think this has been the best session yet."

"That was definitely the quickest one, time went by so quickly. Thank you, Dr. Warren, I'll think about what you said. See you next week."

On my way home I just kept thinking of everything that I was feeling. And the conversation with Dr. Warren about Derek touching me. I did feel something, didn't I? As I ponder the question, Gram pulls into the driveway. We settled in the house, and I tell her all about today. I go to bed early feeling exceptionally exhausted and let sleep take me away.

13

FLIRTING

❧

Autum POV

The weekend flew by. I really couldn't wait to go to school today. I just had a feeling it was going to be a good day. Gram dropped me off, and I met up with Samantha before we parted for 1st period. She told me that Rebecca was going to miss school all week. Her parents were punishing her for using her powers on the students. I knew today was going to be a good day, turns out the whole week might be the best week ever. Classes went by quickly before lunch. Derek smiled at me as I entered each time, he always seemed to beat me to class.

My stomach was growling almost the whole 4th period. I was so excited to come to school I forgot to eat breakfast before I left. Lunch Lady Betty was the only server for breakfast. She was still giving me the stink eye, so I didn't eat breakfast at school either. As soon as the bell rung, I headed straight to the cafeteria. After getting my tray I looked for Samantha. She was exiting the salad line and made eye contact with me and smiled. We met in the middle and started walking towards our table. That's when Derek called her.

"Samantha, come sit with us, I need your help with something."

Samantha looked at me and smiled, I was not smiling back.

"Come on," she said. "It won't be that bad."

I rolled my eyes and reluctantly followed. When she got to the table, she cleared her throat.

"I'm a party of two." She winked at me.

Derek smiled. "Autum is welcome to sit with us, if she'd like to." He turned to face me waiting for my response.

"Yes, thank you Alpha." I said softly.

I took my seat next to Samantha and next to Amy. Ugh, Amy. Ethan sat next to Amy and Derek next to him. The table was round, so Samantha separated Derek and I. Derek looked disgruntled for a moment as I sat down, but it quickly faded. He got his senses back and addressed Samantha.

"Samantha, what have you read on white wolves?"

"Well, not much, my family only has one book that I'm aware of. It's pretty old."

Derek looked disappointed, but continued, "Do you remember it saying anything about how to block their abilities?"

"No." Slightly hesitated, glancing at Ethan and then at Amy.

I'm sure we were thinking the same thing. First that is Rebecca's brother and her best friend. If he's asking to stop Rebecca's powers. Won't they tell her?

"Samantha, it's just a question for now. This conversation doesn't leave this table."

As if to confirm Derek's statement. Ethan and Amy both nod.

After thinking for a moment, Samantha responded, "There might be something in that book about the types of powers or abilities white wolves have been known to have. I'm unsure of all of its contents. It didn't seem practical to finish reading it when the only white wolves in current existence are in my pack, and I know more about them than anything in that book."

"Can I borrow it?"

"Good luck with that, like I said it's an old book. There is no way my father will let it leave the house."

Derek contemplated for a moment, "Then can we come over and look at it?"

Samantha smiled, "My parents are out of town. Sleepover!" She burst out.

Derek looked amused, "And who will be invited to this sleep over?"

"All of you," she looked at me, "That means you too."

"Me? I will only get in the way. You don't want me there, plus there will be people there that don't like me." I glanced at Amy.

"Autum, you have to come. You've never been to my house, come on, it will be fun. Amy, tell her." Samantha spoke.

Amy glanced at me and spoke, "Autum, I don't ever recall not liking you. All those times I laughed or made fun of you are because Rebecca told me too. And as I'm sure you are aware, now, it couldn't be helped."

How awful it is to live like that, not having control of your own actions. I felt bad for Amy. I felt bad for anyone that she persuaded like that. I finally nodded and replied. "Ok I'll come."

"Then I'm in too," Derek affirmed quickly after me.

I felt my face warm; Goddess I hope they don't see me blushing. I've never been to a sleepover before. I've never really had friends before. Right after Ethan and Amy both said they'd come too. Samantha went on to make the plans.

"So, we will do it this Thursday, and we can meet after school and ride together."

"Why Thursday?" I asked.

"Didn't you hear school is canceled on Friday."

I shook my head no.

"There is a storm coming, it's just a precaution. But it's supposed to get bad Friday. So, no school. But don't worry, we'll be fine. If it gets bad, all our houses have storm cellars as well."

"All your houses?" What did she mean all their houses?

"Yes, all of us. We're all neighbors."

My face was on fire now. I hummed in response. I was going to be next to Derek's house. I hadn't seen any of their houses. Oh, but Rebecca will be close too then. "Will we have to worry about Rebecca coming over?"

Samantha looked at Ethan and raised an eyebrow. He actually rolled his eyes before replying.

"No, she is grounded to the house. She's not allowed to leave. Plus, my parents have helped this week with her. You really freaked her out Autum, Friday when you stood up to her. She's been a mental case all weekend."

Everyone was looking at me. "Ok, guys, stop staring at me. I didn't do anything. She was just being a bully. Seriously stop looking, I don't think my face can take it."

I put my hands on my cheeks. How embarrassing. I'm definitely flushed. The bell finally rang, and I was glad to be able to walk away. We all got up to walk to class. Ethan and Derek following me. I looked at them suspiciously. Derek spoke.

"We aren't following you on purpose, we have the same class next."

"I know that." No, I didn't, completely forgot. His presence made me flustered. I needed to find a bathroom to splash my face with cold water. They sped up a little, so we were side by side.

Derek and Ethan were on either side of me. My mind was racing, and I could feel my heartbeat getting louder. I took a chance and looked at Derek.

He was already looking at me. He smiled. His eyes were so soft towards me, and he had a genuine smile. He moved his hand over the top of his head to pull some of the loose hairs back into place.

"It's weird, right?" He asked.

Was he talking to me? Looking at him he was still staring at me. Yes, he was talking to me. Say something Autum. The guy you've been drooling over is talking to you.

"Weird?" I asked back.

"Yea, to not be worried about Rebecca interrupting us?" He smiled at me.

I slowed my pace just slightly, still looking at him. Was he flirting with me? I smiled back at him. "It's not weird."

He raised an eyebrow, "It's not?"

"No." I paused, "It's nice."

With that, I took a step back and to the side. Going behind Derek. Ducking my head down, face flush with heat. I stepped into the girl's restroom. Avoiding all eye contact but not able to prevent the smile that crept to my face.

14

THE STORM
APPROACHES

Autum POV

The next two days came and went. Derek and I stealing glances throughout the day. He even walked me to a few classes we shared. The walk was usually silent, but it was a comfortable silence. Derek even opened a few doors for me as we entered class. This usually got everyone's attention. The boys looked indifferent, but the girls all glared at me.

During lunch break, Derek and Ethan got to the table after us. Derek sat next to me. It surprised me to say the least. His arm brushed mine several times and his leg bumped me under the table twice. We talked a little bit about school and how I was getting along with the teachers and students. I felt like he really was an Alpha checking in on a pack member. I just wished it was more than that. I wished he'd grab my hand and hold it or place his hand on my leg. It would definitely help the nervous energy that had been building up since he sat next to me. No, that was never going to happen, wake up from your fairytale Autum. Dr. Warren canceled both my meetings this week and Mrs. Albim canceled the Prom Committee meeting. Most of the adults were preparing the town for the storm that was approaching.

It had been cloudy most of the week, the dark clouds foreboding the storm that would come soon. Though the weather was not the best, it was still quite warm outside. Definitely a little breezy but not horrible. This was good for my current predicament. Because today I was walking home after school. The wind was strong enough to push my hair around, so I decided to do a side braid as I strolled down the road. Typically, I would have had Prom Com and Gram would get me at 5:30. Today however, school was out at 3:30 and No Prom Com, so I was without a ride.

Gram and I spoke of it Monday night after we were notified of all the cancellations for the week. She had made prior plans, though she wouldn't tell me what they were. After pressing for a short time, she seemed to be anxious, so I dropped it. I remember giving her a hug and telling her not to worry about it, that I could have Samantha give me a ride. I never asked Samantha and had already resigned myself to the fact that I would walk. We only lived five miles from the school, I figured it would take me about an hour and half to get home. Plenty of time before Gram got back. She would never know.

I had only walked a few blocks from the school. The town really was beautiful. Lush greenery and the coast only a mile south. The clouds looked rolled together where the shore met the sand. I couldn't see the ocean, but I knew that was where the coastline was. The cool air from the sea meets the warm air from the land. I hadn't even noticed the truck pull up next to me.

"Autum? I thought that was you, what are you doing?"

Looking over I saw Derek. This was going to be awkward.

"Alpha, hi." I was hesitant, "I'm walking home, it's no big deal."

He got out of his truck, the wind tossing his hair, gorgeous! The sight of him took my breath away. What was wrong with me?

"Don't be silly Autum, let me give you a ride." He wasn't really asking.

"Um, no that's quite all right, I don't want to be a bother. It's not that far, I'll be fine."

Derek walked around his truck to the passenger side and opened the door.

"Autum, I insist. I can't let you walk home in this wind. What kind of Alpha would I be, hmm?" He persisted.

"Fine, thank you." I gripped the inner door to hoist myself up.

Once in, he shut the door for me. Watching him walk back around the truck, the wind was picking up a bit. It probably would have taken longer fighting the wind while I walked. Derek got in the truck, and it was awkwardly silent for quite a few moments. Then he spoke.

"So," he paused, "Are you going to tell me where we are going?"

I could feel my cheeks flush.

"Right sorry," I cleared my throat, "I live on Burbank Road, it's the last house at the end of the road."

I'm an idiot. If I was a meme, I'd be face-palming myself. I wrinkled my nose slightly; his cologne was strong in this small space. I didn't like his cologne. But our proximity was also making me feel flustered. This was going to be the longest ride ever.

Derek's POV

"Well then, I'm glad I found you. It would have taken you two hours to walk there in this wind." Her scent was perfuming my truck. It made me happy. Her side braid was long, draped over her right shoulder. She's never done that to her hair before. I liked it. Some hair had fallen out and framed her face. With the light pink glow of her cheeks, she was the perfect beauty. She slightly coughed to get my attention.

"Alpha, do you need me to tell you how to get there?" She asked shyly.

She had caught me staring, but I couldn't care less. I put the truck in drive and pulled back onto the road. She was quiet, and her breathing was shallow. I caught her breathing from her mouth a few times. Her hand would move to her head and massage it for a second. Did she have a headache?

She kept glancing around out the window, like she was enjoying the scenery. Every time her gaze landed on me; I could feel it. Like a heat gun had been directed at me. Her gaze captivated me. Why did it feel that way? When I would look at her, she would look past me and turn her head away.

"Why were you walking?" I attempted to break the silence.

"Oh, um my Gram had something going on, so she couldn't pick me up today." She answered, again placing her hand on her head to massage her temple.

"Hmm," I paused. "Your hair is different," I paused again. "It looks nice like that; in the braid I mean." Complementing her was hard. I was nervous. I had never been nervous in my life. I was afraid she wouldn't like what I said. I found myself curious to know how she felt, I wanted to know everything about her.

She smiled softly, "Thanks. The wind was having its way with it."

She moved her hand from her temple to her braid. Smoothing her hair all the way down to the end. I focused back on the road. I really was captivated by her every movement. I couldn't focus.

"Derek, stop! You passed my road." Her face became beat red, "Alpha, I meant Alpha, sorry." She quickly apologized.

I got angry. I didn't like her calling me Alpha.

"Sorry, I didn't mean to disrespect you." She dropped her head.

Damn it, I had scared her. She thinks I'm mad because she called me by my name. I saw her cross her arms. Rubbing her elbow through her arm sleeve that she always wore. I saw her do this before when she was nervous.

I wondered what she was hiding under there. Had she hurt herself? Had someone else hurt her? Before I became angry again, I let the thought go.

"What? No, I'm not mad at you, its fine." I tried to assure her.

Goddess, we really need to figure this out. Binding Rebecca's powers, it was driving me mad. Her calling me Alpha, she was to be my equal. I pulled up outside her home. It was a rather large house. The front yard manicured with shrubs and bushes and a large weeping willow. The backyard is blocked by a large wood fence. Flowering vines covered the fence, appearing to come from the backyard. Her Grandmother must be well off and employee some gardeners to keep up with its appearance. I saw her reach for her door handle.

"Wait!" I spoke hurriedly. She looked confused for a moment. I jumped out and walked around the truck and opened her door. I held my hand out, so she'd take it to step down.

"Alpha, it's not necessary. I can get down on my own."

"I saw you holding your head, like you had a headache. Just let me help you, please."

She looked shocked that I had noticed this about her. She nodded and took my hand. Immediately, I felt tingles in my fingers and goosebumps rose up my entire arm. I could feel the small hairs on the back of my neck stand. She stepped down and let go of my hand. I observed her. She stared at her hand for a moment rubbing her thumb and fingers together. What was that, was that real or did I imagine that? Whatever it was, she felt it too! I could still see the goosebumps on her arms.

"Are you alright, do you feel ok?" I asked sincerely. I hoped her headache had vanished.

"Yeah, fine" She took a deep breath in. Like she hadn't smelt fresh air before.

"Come on," I spoke, "I'll walk you to your door."

As we walked, I couldn't help but think maybe I smelt bad to her. She was breathing through her mouth most of the ride here. She smelt absolutely divine to me. Was it not the same for her? I wanted to ask but then stopped myself.

"Do you have something you'd like to say Alpha?" She asked.

Had she noticed my internal struggle?

"Do I smell bad to you?" I found the courage to ask.

I didn't really want the answer, what would it me for us. I thought mates smelt good to each other. If she was unable to be near me... I couldn't go down this rabbit hole because Rebecca was waiting on the other side. I was dragged back from my inner monologue when I heard her choke and start laughing.

"Is it really that funny?" I asked, almost offended. Almost.

Her laugh was magical. I wanted to hear more of it. I pulled my shirt up to sniff it.

"No, I'm sorry. How did you know? I mean, it's not you, it's me." She laughed some more.

I grinned, "Famous last words of a doomed relationship, and this one hasn't even begun yet?" I winked at her.

That stifled her laughter quickly. Her cheeks flushed again. Her body giving her away at every turn. She liked me, I know she did.

She cleared her throat, "What I meant was, it's me. It's the smell of your cologne."

I was puzzled for a moment, "My cologne smells bad and was giving you a headache?"

She nodded, "It doesn't smell... bad." She hesitated, "I'm sure you smell much better without it though."

She was biting her bottom lip, probably to stifle another laugh. Her cheeks were on fire. Her body really did react to me. Was this the mate bond? We reached the porch and walked up the stairs. I reached for the front door to open it for her, but she stopped me.

"I'm going to sit out here for a minute, the fresh air will help my head-ache." She spoke softly.

"Is it really that bad?"

We both laughed and I followed her to the porch swing. I didn't want to leave yet. I like being in her company, something about it just felt right. We sat on the swing, each of us at one end. Leaving a huge gap in the middle. I wanted to bridge that gap, but I didn't want to startle her. Not again.

"You don't have to stay Alpha, I'll be fine."

"Derek."

"What?" She asked, confused.

"Call me Derek, Autum."

This moment was perfect, she looked absolutely stunning, pink was permanent on her skin now. Her sapphire eyes almost blazed as our eyes met. Lilacs and morning rain run through my senses.

"Alright, Derek" It came out a little louder than a whisper.

The way my name rolled off her tongue made me want her more. I needed to distract myself before I did something and got another black eye.

15

THE GARDEN

Autum POV

"So, Autum," he started as he rubbed the back of his neck with his hand. "Why'd your grandma decide to move back here?"

I told him about my grandma being mated to the Beta of another Pack and how she moved away. How this was her first pack and her home. I asked about his parents and growing up as the Alpha's son. It was so easy to talk to him. Time went by quickly before I knew it an hour had gone by.

"How are you feeling?" He asked me.

"Better, thank you for sitting with me. My grandma should be home soon, you don't need to stay and babysit me." I smiled.

"Right, I should be heading off now anyways., I need to go get my mother some flowers. It's my parent's anniversary today."

"That's sweet of you, how long have they been married?" I asked.

"I think like thirty years or something."

"Wow, your parents look so young. Werewolf aging is definitely good for the skin." We both laughed, "I have a garden. You can pick some flowers for your mother here, if you'd like, that is."

"Yes, I'd like that." He answered almost too quickly.

I felt like he wanted to spend more time with me. We got up off the porch swing and walked to my front door. He picked up his pace and opened the door for me. I glanced at him and smiled as I entered the house.

"So, this is my house," I spoke softly.

The interior of our home mirrored the shades of blue seen on the outside, with one notable exception: a warm yellow focal wall. Adorned with an assortment of trinkets, a long table graced the yellow wall. Amidst the array of decorations, attention inevitably gravitated towards a large pink salt statue and smoldering plate of dried sage. The aroma of the sage wafted through the air. There were pictures of flowers and plants hung on the walls and several flower arrangements placed around the room. Derek followed me through the living room as I toured him around. We ventured next into the kitchen to pass through to the backyard, to my garden. I stopped by the backdoor and removed my shoes before stepping outside.

"Why did you take off your shoes to go outside?" He laughed softly, obviously amused.

"I love to feel the grass on my feet, it relaxes me."

"Am I making you nervous?" He grinned.

"I've never had anyone over to my house before or into my garden." Yes, I was quite nervous. I went to almost never speaking to Derek, to sitting with him at lunch, walking with him to class, and now he's giving me rides home in less than a weeks' time. It was all so fast. But I wanted it. Dreamt about it, often. It was a bag of mixed emotions for me, some so foreign yet so familiar. "But I'm glad you're here." I don't know where this bravery came from, but I liked it.

Derek was silent for another moment as he looked around, the silence was making me more nervous. Did he like my house? Did he want to be here too? It was agonizing waiting for him to respond. He finally spoke.

"I'm glad to be your first." He winked at me.

Was he trying to get a rise out of me? He was successful, if so. I don't think a minute had gone by when I wasn't flustered. I knew the pink had found its way to my cheeks again. I knew because as soon as I felt the heat, Derek smiled shamelessly.

"Your garden is beautiful. You have such a variety of plants and flowers. Can you help pick some out for my mother?" Although embarrassed by his previous comment, I couldn't wait to help him. I loved my garden and showing it to him might be the highlight of my year so far. I walked back into the house to grab some scissors and then proceeded to show him around the yard.

"Well, we have quite a lot, what is your mothers favorite color?"

"Yellow," he said.

"Oh, that's perfect. Over here we have sunflowers and marigolds, oh and black-eyed Susans." I said, pointing to each flower as I went.

He raised an eyebrow at that one, "really?"

I laughed, "Yes that's really its name. We can put it with some white flowers. I have white hyacinth, jasmine, and lilacs, these will all make your house smell fantastic. Oh, and we should put some rue in there. It will add some green and it also has a yellow flower."

Derek's POV

As I followed Autum around her garden, I couldn't help but notice how happy she was. This place really did relax her. As we were walking, she would point out areas with certain plants. One particular section stood out, the herb garden. Autum always smelled like morning rain, lilac, and a subtle hint of something else I couldn't place till today.

"Autum," I called to get her attention. "What is this herb, this one with the soft purple flowers?"

Autum approached.

She smiled softly, "This is thyme. Gram likes to cook with it, but I like it as an essential oil. It also smells nice to put into the flower arrangements in the house."

"What benefit does it give as an essential oil?" I was intrigued, this was the other smell I could always slightly make out on her.

"Well beside the immune support, and don't laugh at me, it helps relax me when I go to bed. I usually place a few drops behind my ears." She paused for a moment before continuing, "It's also said that thyme can ward off nightmares and keep bad vibes away. It's believed to bring courage to the bearer."

I liked how she was opening up to me. She was becoming more comfortable. I tried not to look at her critically as she spoke about the plants in her garden. I didn't know anything about plants and their healing abilities. Heck, some of it I found hard to believe. But she believed it, and I would not make her feel like a fool.

"Is there something about it that made you want to know?" She asked.

"If I were to answer honestly, it's one of the things you smell like. And I wanted to know the name of it." Her eyes briefly widened as I continued, "I certainly know more about it now than I thought I would. Do you know this much about all the plants in your garden?" I smiled at her.

"Y- Yes," she answered meekly. Her surprise was not hidden from my confession.

"Can you tell me more about the lilacs then?" I paused, "They also smell like you."

She tried to hide the shock on her face. Failing miserably, she straightened her posture before answering.

"The lilacs, umm, lilac oil can be used to treat fever and can also reduce stress and anxiety. Purple lilacs symbolize spirituality, while white lilacs represent purity… and innocence." She answered confidently as I took a step closer to her.

I couldn't look away from her as she spoke. I was a goner; I knew it now. She was the most innocent, sincere, and enchanting female I had ever met. I felt her voice was getting softer and softer as she spoke.

"Anything else about the flowers you picked for my mother? What about this closed flower?" I just wanted her to keep talking. Her voice was like a siren, and I found myself longing for it.

"That's jasmine, it blooms at night. It will fill your home with its sweet fragrance, it symbolizes love, beauty, and sensuality. And the rue," she was breathing heavier now. I kept stepping closer to her as her voice grew fainter. "The rue is like a repellent; it repels insects and also bad energy."

Did she realize how soft she was speaking, almost inviting me to come closer? I took another step forward. "What about me Autum, is there anything in your garden that smells like me?" She looked almost embarrassed to say. Her eyes glanced down at the bouquet in her hands, and she smiled as she prepared to answer. She turned her eyes back to me.

"The sunflowers," she smiled softly. "Sunflower seeds are considered a superfood. The oil can protect skin, hydrate, and minimize signs of aging. The sunflower symbolizes loyalty and adoration and because of their association with the sun are well-known to brighten someone's mood."

The atmosphere was getting charged, our bodies so close together. I didn't speak, so she continued.

"You also smell like sage." She cleared her throat a little. "When burning white sage, it is believed that it provides a barrier that prevents negative energy from entering. Sage oil can ease muscle and joint pain as well as eliminate toxins. Sage means domestic virtue. It is said that a sage plant will be healthy when all is well but wilt when things go badly. It also symbolizes wisdom, believed to improve memory, and grant wisdom to the bearer."

We were both breathing heavily now. I could see the rise and fall of her chest. I felt like I wanted to kiss her, and I was sure she could feel it too. But I felt that she wasn't ready for that yet. I watched as her sapphire eyes turned lighter; they were absolutely stunning. Goddess I just wanted to caress her. To feel her soft lips on mine. I wanted to run my fingers down her cheek, to her chin, to pull her lips to mine. I felt no panic from her. She was just as captivated as I was. When my resolve was just about to break. The silence was broken.

"What are you two doing out here and in this weather?"

"Gram, oh hi, when did you get here?" She stepped away from me.

The spell had been broken, as if an invisible bucket of cold water had been poured from above. Her grandmother breaking our trance. The wind had picked up quite a bit, but I hadn't noticed at all.

"Gram, can I use one of your old newspapers to wrap these flowers?" She asked her. Her grandmother nodded in agreement.

"Autum, if it's not too much trouble can you make me a second bouquet?" I asked her.

"Sure." Autum smiled.

"Alpha, do mind giving an old lady a hand to the swing, just there."

"Of course, ma'am." I stepped over to lend her my arm and help her to the swing.

"Don't be silly call me Ellen, Alpha."

"Yes ma'am, I mean Ellen." I smiled down at the old lady, "Then I also must insist you call me Derek." She smiled back at me. Autum was walking back around the garden making a second bouquet.

"As you wish. So, what brings you to my home Derek?" Ellen questioned.

"I gave Autum a ride home ma'am, sorry, old habits die hard." She laughed quietly.

"That was over two hours ago. You've been here the whole time, just walking around the garden?" Her eyebrow was raised.

"Well, she was telling me all about the plants here and I guess we lost track of time." This lady was reading me like a book.

"Yes, the garden is quite lovely, isn't it? I could spend all day out here and get lost in it. Nature holds a special energy, and it calms an old women like me." She smiled happily.

Autum walked back over to us, two bouquets in hand. "Here you are Derek."

"Thank you." I held my hand out to her grandmother to offer her assistance back into the house now that we were done outside. She took it. Autum spoke again.

"Why do you need two, are you giving your father one too?"

I laughed out loud, "My father, no, he wouldn't know what to do with them. It's a funny story actually. You see my mother thinks their anniversary is today October seventeenth, but my father believes it is tomorrow, the eighteenth. They were married so long ago. When the tsunami hit, it washed away the whole town, and most records were lost. So, neither of them can prove which day it is. Not to mention, neither will admit they are wrong. So, I give my mother a bouquet on both days."

"That is funny and sweet of you," Autum replied.

"They actually don't mind it; I think they prefer it honestly. My mother makes my father dinner on the seventeenth and my father cooks for my mother on the eighteenth. They do the same thing with gifts. It's quite the family tradition." We walked into the house, and I helped Ellen to the kitchen table.

"Autum, would you make me some tea, dear?" Ellen requested.

"Yes, grandma, what are you wanting today? You are looking a little tired, are you feeling okay?"

"Yes dear, make me some manipura, please."

Ellen sat quietly at the table while Autum prepared the water. I joined her at the stove. All kinds of herbs were shelved above the stove. Autum pulled ingredients out from the cupboard while I watched.

"What is manipura?" I finally asked.

She laughed quietly, "It's a type of tea. It helps with vitality. It's made with turmeric, ginger, black peppercorn, cloves, cinnamon, chamomile, and lemon balm." She explained.

"Autum, put some sage leaves in it as well, will you?" Her grandmother asked.

"Yes Gram. Umm... Derek do you mind going outside and grabbing a few leaves off the sage plant I showed you when we were outside just now?" She asked hesitantly.

I could see she was embarrassed, thinking of our intimate moment out there. It had to be what was keeping the permanent pink on her cheeks and neck. I liked knowing I did this to her. I was craving her too. I nodded and stepped outside. After grabbing the sage, I stopped before entering back into the house. I could hear them talking about me and didn't want to interrupt the conversation.

"Nice boy that one is," her grandmother spoke.

"Yes, I think so too." Autum replied.

A smile plastered my face. Verbal confirmation. I felt good, Autum was a high I hadn't experienced before. I wanted more. Opening the door, I headed back inside.

"Gram are you really feeling okay?" She was asking her grandmother as I entered.

"Just for today my dear, do not worry, hmm." She responded.

Autum gave a half smile to her grandmother. I handed her the leaves and Autum placed them in a mortar and used the pestle to grind them down. I watched, fascinated. We didn't make tea like this. She put the ingredients into a round mesh ball and dropped it into the hot water she had already poured into the cup.

I could feel the tension in the air. Autum was worried about her grandmother. Ellen on the other had remained indifferent. She truly wasn't going to speak to Autum about it.

"I should be heading home now. Autum, will you see me out?" I asked her.

Autum nodded, and I took one last look around her house before we walked out. Sunflowers decorated many of the vases and the lingering smell of the burnt sage was still perfuming the air. I decided to be bold and after stepping outside and shutting the door I grabbed her hand to hold it. We stood there on the porch for a moment, her looking down at our hands.

"I feel it too... you know... the sparks" I whispered to her.

She looked up at me, her soft eyes blazing again, the pink on her cheeks was now showing on her neck as well. She went to open her mouth to speak but then closed it again. I made her speechless. I smiled inwardly.

"Thank you for the flowers. I'm sure my mother will think they're beautiful, I know I do." I didn't look at the flowers when I said that, just kept my gaze on her. I saw her wrinkle her nose and I smirked and laughed to myself silently. I was never wearing this cologne again. I pulled her hand to my lips and kissed the back of it. She gasped quietly but didn't pull away. I lowered her hand and released it and took a step back. She finally spoke.

"I'll see you tomorrow then, at school?" she asked softly.

"Yes, and then Samantha's house for her slumber party." I winked at her then turned around to walk to my truck.

Best day ever. I turned around one last time to look at her. Her gaze was still on me, and she had one hand on her check, probably trying to cool it. I got in my truck and started backing down the driveway. Her gaze on me until I was out of sight.

16

THE PACK HOUSE

❧

Autum POV

The next morning, I woke excited for the day to be over all ready, thinking of the sleep over at Samantha's. I had never been to a sleepover before. I packed some pajamas and a change of clothes in my backpack.

First period dragged on with Mrs. Albim but knowing I would see Derek during second period left me watching the clock. The bell finally rang, and I headed to second period. Derek was already there; he always beat me there. He looked amused as I rushed in, stopping abruptly when I noticed him sitting directly in the seat behind mine. I raised an eyebrow at him and sat down. Ethan came in after me glancing at us, he looked at me and smirked.

"Hey speed racer, I guess I see why you took off so fast." Ethan looked at Derek and laughed while I lowered my head and fumbled with my backpack.

Ethan made the kid next to Derek move and took his seat beside him. Derek leaned forward and I felt a tug on my hair. My hair was in a bun this morning; I got ready so fast this morning I didn't have time to do anything with it. My hair suddenly fell from the bun. I turned around to see Derek holding my ponytail, he then put it on his wrist.

"Derek, what are you doing," I asked.

A gasp was heard from several students. Was I not supposed to call him Derek in front of people?

Derek was smirking. "I like it down, the way it curls," he pulled a curl and let it bounce back. "It's quite beautiful."

I didn't know how to respond. I liked the compliment, but everyone was now staring at me. I didn't like the attention. I mustered a quiet okay before I paused. "I will need my ponytail back though."

"Why," he asked.

I cleared my throat a little. "I will need it for PE."

He leaned forward, whispering back, "Well, then I will give it back to you at PE."

He paused looking at my ponytail on his wrist. He put it to his nose and inhaled the sent, "Lilac and thyme, I think I will enjoy having it until then."

He leaned back in his desk. I looked forward, trying not to smile. I was glad my hair was down now so no one could see me blushing. I could heat this whole damn school with the number of times I heat up throughout the day.

The rest of the day went quickly. The last period was almost over, and we were picking up the equipment. Amy put us all to shame during three-on-three basketball practice, and I really needed a shower. That girl was like a one woman show. Amy had it out with Mrs. Timmer because she split girls from boys and had each of us on different sides to only play against our gender. I mean, I was happy to just play against the girls, but Amy needed a challenge. This was just boring for her; she didn't even break a sweat.

Most people headed to the showers, but Amy walked over to Derek and Ethan to get some real game play on for a minute while Samantha and I cleaned up the equipment. We walked the ball bags over to the sports closet. We threw them in, and the boys and Amy walked over.

Amy threw her ball to me and said, "put it in the bag for me, will ya?"

I looked into the closet, the bag deep inside and threw the ball back to her and responded, "I don't do closets."

I walked away headed for the showers. I could hear them all talking about me, but it wasn't something I knew how to explain. Samantha and Amy caught up and we headed into the showers as everyone else was headed out. Amy shouted back to the guys that we'd meet out front in ten. I could tell the girls wanted to ask me questions, but I quickly grabbed my change of clothes from my locker and headed for the large shower at the end of the room. It was the only private shower; all others were open. And being naked wasn't really a big deal to werewolves, since once you shift back you are naked for all to see.

A light in the equipment closet has been burnt out for weeks, no way I was going in there. I don't even like taking showers in this stall, but the lighting is good, so it doesn't bother me as much. I'm really just trying to hide all my scars. I never take off my arm sleeve and my hips, my poor hips. I was in an apartment fire as a child and had burned most of my body. A lot of it healed but the deep burns on my sides from the beam that nearly killed me were really the only memories I have of that day. I know my mother died that day, but I don't remember it. I mostly remember Gram picking me up from the hospital two days later. I hadn't been able to speak when I was taken to the hospital and the building was burned down. Police didn't know who to contact, with my mother burned inside and me not talking. Luckily, Jenny's mom saw me, and they were able to get ahold of Gram. I only remember her holding me in her embrace from the hospital bed. I was there for months in recovery. Gram was there every day after that praying to the Goddess, she'd say, "Just for today my dear, we will not worry." I showered quickly before getting dressed and meeting the girls so we could walk together.

I asked Samantha, "Can I ride with you?"

"I didn't drive today," she replied.

"Oh, so who are you riding with then?" I was surprised she didn't drive; she always drives.

"Derek said he was giving us all a ride," She smiled devilishly.

Derek pulled up in his truck and Ethan opened the back door and hollered, "Amy, Samantha, sit back here with me."

I whipped my head to stare at the girls, who both smirked and climbed into the back seat. I guessed that meant I was sitting up front with Derek. What a ride this will be. Derek pushed the door open from the inside. I'd be lying if I said I wasn't a little disappointed he didn't walk around and open it from the outside. Mostly, I just want him to offer his hand to me again to feel his touch. But also, Derek's truck was lifted and didn't have any steps. Climbing in this thing was a real bitch. I threw my bag in and reached for the door handle to help pull myself in.

"Need a hand?" Derek asked as he reached across the seat and extended his hand.

"Thanks" I replied. Silently thanking the Moon Goddess. Grabbing the door with my right and Derek's hand with my left, he heaved me up. Pulling me so hard I flew into his lap. Snickering from the backseat could be heard, so I quickly sat up and moved to my seat. I shut the door, silently cursing to myself.

"Sorry," he muttered. "Don't know my own strength sometimes." He rubbed the back of his neck.

"Its fine, really." I answered quickly.

I could feel the heat coming off my face and chest. I literally just had my ass in Derek's lap, and I couldn't stop thinking about it. I buckled myself and glanced up towards the rearview mirror. I raised an eyebrow when I noticed dried thyme and lilacs hanging from it. It was only a small amount, but the inside of his truck smelt so fresh. Ethan and the girls were still having fits of laughter every so often as we drove. Derek seemed amused at some point and asked.

"What's so funny back there?" He peered at them through the rear-view mirror.

Ethan replied first. "Derek, why do you have flowers hanging from your mirror, and when did you get this truck detailed, its spotless. I was just in here a few days ago; it wasn't this clean. You have some kind of special occasion going on man?"

Derek slanted his eyes at Ethan. Ethan put his hands up but didn't continue talking.

I peered up at the rearview mirror again. A small smile creeping on my lips the small bundle of thyme and a single lilac hanging from it. I could see Derek stealing glances at me through my peripheral vision, so I quickly turned to peer out the window to avoid him. Knowing he intentionally wanted his truck to smell like me made me feel something, Something I hadn't felt before... wanted. But I couldn't let myself get comfortable with the feeling. Rebecca would be back at school on Monday and if she saw Derek and I getting close, there was no telling what she'd do. I felt a small sigh leave my lips, resting my forehead on the window I peered out to take in the beautiful view.

We emerged from the tree line and five houses came into view. They were all huge and surrounded by trees and lush bushes. The houses were situated with one very large, dare I say, mansion in the back. That must be the Pack house. There were three houses to the left and one house on the right side with a good amount of distance between each of them. As we started driving by the houses, Samantha piped up, "Derek, you passed my house, what are we doing now?"

"I need to go to my house first. I have some more books I need to grab; my father didn't want me taking them to school."

Derek parked and everyone started getting out of his truck. I turned to the back seat and asked, "Are we all going in?" Ethan smiled at me and said, "Well we are. You're welcome to also, the pack house is open to all."

As I turned in my seat, about to open my door, Derek appeared in my doorway with his hand outstretched. I grabbed his hand and jumped down, but to my surprise, he didn't let go.

"Come on," he said. "Let's show you the pack house."

I turned to look at the girls behind me, both smirking. I faced forward and let Derek guide me to the front door. My mind started going wild. Will his parents be in there or other pack members? What would they say if they saw us holding hands, what did this mean?

I got close to Derek and whispered, "What are you doing?"

He leaned in and whispered back, "Relax, it will be fine."

He had to feel my anxiety. The only thing keeping me from ripping my hand away was the subtle tingles spreading across my palm from the contact. Derek started making circles on the top of my hand with his thumb. I took a deep breath as he pushed the door open and walked in. I started repeating my grandmother's mantra in my head, 'just for today, I will not be scared, just for today, just for today.' My anxiety was through the roof, but I had no idea why. This is the pack house everyone is welcome, I told myself to calm down.

I felt a warm hand on my cheek. "Breathe Autum, you're ok."

I opened my eyes; I hadn't realized I had closed them. Derek was looking into my eyes. I let out the breath I was holding, and he stepped back.

"Thank you, I'm sorry. I don't know why I'm so anxious." I spoke softly.

"There's nothing to apologize for." Guiding me into the very large great room. The pack house was beautiful. Huge stones for walls were covered by large tapestries. Every wall had one. One was the Pack code of Arms. Another a huge map of the surrounding lands. The map was something I'd never seen before. It was beautiful, showing the mountains and rivers. It had all the cities and known locations for other packs. It had an image of a castle perched atop a mountain. I hadn't heard of a castle before. I looked at Derek.

"What is this castle there," I pointed to the large tapestry.

Derek guided me closer to it. "That is the Kingdom of Rune."

He must have noticed my confused look, so he continued, "The Kingdom of Rune was buried deep in the mountains. An old kingdom that once ruled here with Lycan Kings and Queens. There hasn't been a King in four centuries and a Queen in two centuries. The castle is said to be all but rubble now. Lycans were the first Werewolves. Only shifting during a full moon. Then the Mood Goddess mated us to humans, and we were created. Lycans held the power of the light and the dark. An ancient power that gave and took life. In the center of the castle was said to be a tree of life. When the last Lycan Queen defeated the Heiress of Darkness it was said the tree was struck down by lightning. The tapestry depicts this tree here."

He pointed to the tree growing out of the castle, and resumed the story, "It grew out from the center of the castle. One half green and living, the other half bare and dying. No one has seen the castle in centuries since the Queens death. It's said to be lost in the mountains, overtaken by the forest. No one has possessed the same power as the Lycans. The only ones who have come close are the white wolves. Direct descendants of the Lycans, their powers are muted in comparison."

He glanced at Ethan who was beaming with pride. Amy shoved him. "Stop grinning! we get it the almighty white wolf," she gave him a little bow, and they all walked towards the kitchen.

I could smell chocolate chip cookies, I looked towards Derek, "That's a crazy story, I've never heard it before."

"Glad you liked it, come on let's go get a cookie. And you can meet my mom." He winked at me.

He half had to pull me into the kitchen. As we walked in, his mother was pulling out fresh cookies from the oven. She looked over to see us walk in. Us, hand in hand. She smiled at us, "Hello, you must be Autum." She asked. She put the tray down and extended her hand. Derek finally let go of my hand and I reached to shake hers. But she didn't shake my hand instead pulling me in for a hug "I'm so glad to meet you, Autum."

"Nice to meet you as well, Luna Synthia." I replied.

"Oh, just Synthia dear." She responded, "Here have a seat, you look flushed dear. Derek get the poor girl a glass of water." She ushered me into a chair with a smile.

I looked to the others in the room, Amy, Samantha, and Ethan all broke out in smiles as they all took cookies and sat down on the bench. Derek got me a glass of water and sat next to me. His mother placed the whole tray of cookies in front of us.

"So, what are you kids up to today?"

Derek replied, "We are just grabbing the books from Dad's office for our research project." He winked at his mother, "He said I could take them to Samantha's tonight."

She must have known what we were trying to do, and she seemed ok with it.

"Oh right," she said, "I also have a book for you. It's about the King-dom of Rune and the power of the Queen of Light. But you should hurry along before-"

She was cut off by a 'ding' sound and that's when I noticed the elevator. It was on the back wall of the great room next to the winding staircase. Makes sense to have an elevator when you live in a five-story mansion. It looked to only have three floors, but each level was- My thoughts were cut off when the elevator door opened, and Rebecca stepped out with Dr. Warren. I averted my eyes right away. This is the last person I wanted to see. Now I knew why I was so anxious.

"What is she doing here?" Rebecca's voice was shrill.

"This is the pack house. Everyone is welcome here Rebecca," Synthia responded. "Derek take your friends to the office and get your things and go." Synthia walked towards Rebecca and Dr. Warren.

Everyone stood from the bench, and I followed behind the others. They obviously knew where the office was.

Rebecca wasn't through with us though, "So I'm gone for a few days, and you all replace me. Is that what is happening here?"

"No one has replaced you Rebecca, calm down." Ethan replied.

"Rebecca, perhaps we should go back up to the roof top garden and relax some more." Dr. Warren suggested.

"I don't need to relax; I need that little bitch to go back to where she came from. She is going to ruin everything!"

Rebecca went to lunge forward but Dr. Warren grabbed her arm. Derek grabbed me and pushed me behind him. Samantha was behind me now and Ethan had moved Amy behind him.

"Rebecca that is enough," Derek boomed. "You will not come in here and throw insults." He and Rebecca were locked in a stare down.

"Fine I'll go back to the roof with Dr. Warren, but I want Amy to accompany me." She smirked.

"That is up to Amy," Derek replied.

"I'll go and I'll meet you guys later." Amy was quick to respond and walked towards Rebecca and Dr. Warren.

"I'll go to." Ethan spoke and met them at the elevator.

Synthia waited with us until the elevator door closed and then we all went to the office. No one said anything for a moment.

Synthia broke the silence. "I'm sorry son, I forgot she was up there. But I see now why you've been concerned."

He shot his mother a warning look and I scrunched my eyebrows and looked at him. Was she talking about me? Was Derek concerned for me?

"Derek, maybe you should just take me home, I don't want to cause problems." I sighed.

"Absolutely not, I'm not going to let Rebecca intimidate you or anyone else, any longer." He said matter of fact.

"I second that," Samantha chimed in. "Plus, you are a guest in my house tonight. Let's just carry on and figure out how we can fix this."

I let out a breath and sat in one of the chairs. Derek and his mother grabbed several books off the shelf and placed them in a bag. She then swung open a large full length body mirror that was on the wall that was hiding a large safe. Inside the safe she pulled up a fake bottom and pulled out two more very old-looking books.

"These are from the Kingdom of Rune. They are very old and talk about the Queen of Light and how she defeated the Heiress of Darkness. These belong to Ethan's mother, Beta Elissa. She gave them to us for safe keeping. I've read them several times, and I'm sure there is something in there we can use to help bind Rebecca's powers. I'm just unsure of what that is. Samantha, dear you are very clever I'm hoping you can crack this. The only other option we have is to have your father command her, but it would be very painful for her." She gave a long sigh and handed Samantha the books.

Derek walked to the door, opening it for us to exit and we left the office. He told us to go wait for him by the door so he could talk to his mother.

"Autum, stop worrying," Samantha said to me while we waited by the door. "She is all bark and no bite." She laughed awkwardly.

"We both know that is just not true." I retorted, "She can literally command someone to hurt me, or worse." Rebecca had it out for me and there was nothing anyone could do. "What am I going to do at school on Monday?" The question had been plaguing me all week and now even more. Derek approached and he reached for my hand, I was biting my nails.

"Don't do that to yourself, I won't let her hurt you." he said calmly, grabbing ahold of my hand.

"Why?" I asked.

Derek regarded my question, "Because you're my pack."

He left it at that, and we walked out to his truck still holding hands. I could feel someone staring at me. Derek opened my door and helped me up. After he closed the door, I looked up to the roof top to see Rebecca peering down. She had Amy beside her. She looked as if she was staring straight through me. It sent a shiver down my spine. Derek got in the truck and followed my gaze; he grabbed my hand. "Don't worry about her, okay?" I nodded. He reversed out the driveway and drove and pulled into Samantha's house. The first house on the block.

17

SLUMBER PARTY

Autum POV

Walking into Samantha's house was like walking into a library. Book-shelves and maps of our land and the continents covered her walls. From what you could see of the walls, they were deep colors of maroons and browns. Everything in this house was pristine. There was not one thing out of place. Even the books on the shelves were perfectly placed. Looking around, I saw not one speck of dust. I couldn't even start to think how long it would take to clean this house to such perfection. Samantha led us upstairs to her room.

Her room was large and much lighter in color than downstairs, but she also had a large bookshelf full of books. Maps and exotic landscapes covered her walls. Just like downstairs, everything was clean and organized. She had three giant bean bags and a king size bed. Large accordion glass doors led to her private balcony. Walking out onto the balcony the view was beautiful.

It overlooked her backyard and the forest. The clouds above us were dark and ominous. You could hear the thunder in the distance and the wind was starting to pick up.

I leaned against the balcony, arms on the railing, taking in a deep breath. I could feel the energy in the air, this was going to be a big thunderstorm. I didn't even hear Derek come up behind me until he spoke.

"What are you thinking about?" He asked.

"Nothing really, so, um who owns the house next door?" I asked.

"The houses on this block belong to the Pack. The tenant, if you will, is whomever the Alpha gives that title to during their rule. So, this house is the Omega house. Currently occupied by Omega Julian and his wife Amber, Samantha's Parents. The next House is the Gamma house. Occupied by Gamma Richard, he goes by Rick. He has no children, and his mate has passed. The house next to mine is the Beta House, occupied by the Fawns. And the house across the street is the Delta House, Occupied by Amy's parents, Delta Anthony, and his wife Lyla. That house has the training grounds on the property, that's why it sits alone on that side. We need a lot of room for training." He explained.

"So, what happens if you name someone else during your rule, what happens to the current occupant?" I asked.

"The pack gifts them a house. The pack owns many houses in town and on the out skirts. Some own their own homes outside the Pack homes already and would just move back into those," He answered. "Come on, Samantha headed down to the kitchen. Let's go meet her and get something to eat while we wait for Amy and Ethan."

After making many snack trays we headed back up to Samantha's room. We had a meat and cheese tray, a fruit tray, a tray of PB&J sandwiches, two bowls of popcorn and a box of capri suns. I think we were set for the night.

"Where are your parents at tonight, Samantha?" I asked her.

"My parents went out of town." She replied.

"Oh, you didn't go with them?" I asked.

"Samantha actually travels a lot with her parents." Derek interrupted.

Samantha looked uncomfortable for a moment but covered it up quickly. I wonder what that is about.

"So, are we gonna get started to figure out what to do about the psycho?" Samantha changed the subject.

"Hey, don't call my sister a psycho." Ethan popped off entering the room.

"It's about time you two got here." Samantha replied, "Sorry but I don't have another word to describe her currently. Only speaking truth here."

Ethan frowned, "It's not entirely her fault, she shouldn't even have this kind of power yet. Neither of us should. My mom thinks our wolves are very powerful and the energy can't be contained. Once we get our wolves, they will help us control our powers." He sighed and grabbed Amy by the hips and flopped into a big bean bag, pulling her on top of him. She screamed, and we all laughed.

"Ok, Samantha where do we start?" Derek asked.

She got excited, "I have already started reading books about white wolves, I've made it through these three here. I have two more on white wolves and one on the Kingdom of Rune, but I'd bet the ones your mother gave us will have more information than this one." She responded. "Ethan and Amy can read these two on white wolves, I'll take the one I have about the Kingdom of Rune. You and Autum can split up the two your mom gave me."

Derek nodded and Samantha handed out the books. She was so excited right now. It was nice to see her with so much emotion when she usually had none. Ever the recluse. I had a few questions too, so I asked, "Samantha, do you have any books on energy crystals? I brought some books from my house about chakras and reiki. We may be able to temporarily block her energy source. We have more books, but we haven't finished unpacking everything yet and I couldn't find them before tonight."

"I'm not sure, come with me downstairs and we'll see if we can find something." She replied.

We returned not finding anything on crystals, we'll just have to go on my memory until I find our books. We all settled in. I took one of the bean bags between Derek and Ethan. Amy still sat on Ethan's lap. Samantha sat on her bed, books organized, and she was taking notes as she read. Her notes were in tight little stacks. Derek handed me the book from his mother on the Kingdom of Rune. It was one of the oldest books I had ever seen. The notes inside were handwritten, faded calligraphy, hardly readable. The pages felt thicker than a book you would see today, the edges frayed, and the paper yellowed from time. The leather, soft from years of handling, was a dark brown. The language was hard to understand. "Hey, Samantha, do you have an Old English or Angelo Saxon alphabet book?" I asked her.

"Yes, I do have that," She jumped off the bed and ran downstairs.

Derek looked at me and laughed. "Here," he said handing me his mother's other book. "I thought it was in another language, you obviously know more about this than I do."

I laughed too and blushed a little, "You can read my books on chakras and reiki, I pretty much have them memorized already."

He nodded and we traded. He asked, "You want a snack while I'm up?" I nodded.

He walked over to the table Samantha had set up and grabbed one of the bowls of popcorn and threw some sandwiches on top and some of the meat from the tray. He moved his bean bag closer to mine and put the bowl between us. Then he handed me a napkin. Probably a good idea not to get any grease on these books, they were so old.

Samantha returned a big grin on her face, "Found it!" she exclaimed and handed me the book. She walked to her desk and pulled out a pencil, a notebook and a pair of white gloves and brought them to me as well. "You'll want these to take notes. The gloves are for the old books, so you don't get popcorn grease on them." She said.

"Yes, thank you" I replied.

We all continued reading. The thunder was getting closer, and we could hear the wind banging against the house outside. A couple hours had passed, and I was now sprawled out on the floor, multiple papers spread out with my notes and passages I had pulled from the books. Samantha's bed was still organized with all her notes. Derek was still reading my books and Ethan and Amy had fallen asleep. Party poopers. I stood to stretch and turned to Samantha. "Where is the bathroom. I need to change; these jeans are not comfortable being hunched over like this."

"It's right there, the door on the right. The left door is my closet." She pointed with her pencil as she kept reading.

I grabbed my bag and walked in. The bathroom was huge with a giant walk-in shower. Oh, to be rich, I thought. I washed my face and changed into my pjs, a pair of shorts and a tank top that read 'coffee, because adulting is hard.' I exited the bathroom and walked to Samantha's bed.

"Should we discuss what we've found?" I asked her.

She nodded and Derek stood up also, he stretched and looked at me and smirked. I put my hand on my hip and questioned, "What?"

He put his hands up, "Nothing, I just thought your shirt was funny." He walked into the bathroom.

Samantha looked up at my shirt and laughed. "Truth," she said.

"Damn straight" I replied.

I grabbed my papers off the floor and Samantha made room for us on her bed. Derek came out of the bathroom in a pair of sweatpants and no shirt. He needed to put a shirt on. I could not tear my eyes away. Sweatpants on that boy should be illegal. His muscles were carved, and you could see his v line disappear beneath them, I visibly shivered. He could mark me any day. It's what all wolves hoped for. To find their mate and be marked by them. Marking your mate involved biting them on the neck to claim them. They say when you mark your mate it's like your souls join together. You become inseparable, bound to each other. You can mind link with each other and will have an uncanny sense of where they are. My mind started conjuring images of Derek marking me. Derek cleared his throat, "Eyes are up here, Autum."

Breaking from my gaze that had landed in his nether regions. I responded, "Then put a shirt on, you can't blame a girl can you." I could feel the fifty shades of red creeping up my face and down my chest.

Derek walked over and whispered in my ear, "I'm not putting on a shirt, I like you looking."

He then walked around the bed and sat on the other side. I looked at Samantha and she burst into laughter, "Shut it." I yelled and threw some popcorn at her.

"Okay, okay, I didn't say anything" she laughed again.

"Anyways, what did you find out Samantha?" I asked her.

She was grinning still, but she answered, "I found a lot on powers held by white wolves, those that have been found anyways. Common gifts listed are super strength, super speed, fire starter, mind reading, the ability to talk to animals, and lots of nature gifts like growing plants and moving the ground. Then there were some very rare ones listed like Ethan's weather manipulation, Rebecca's Power of Persuasion and even their grandmother's power of Healing is rare."

"Wait did you say their grandmother can heal people." I asked, astonished.

"I did." She replied and then continued. "The rarest power recorded was the gift of power absorption. No one has held this power since the last Lycan Kingdom of Rune. But this gift is able to absorb the power of others and harness it. The Lycan Queen used this power to harness the light and defeat the Heiress of darkness. That's all the books say. Nothing about how it was done." She finished.

I was still processing that Ethan's grandmother could heal people. That sounded like something out of a fairytale, yet here I am a werewolf so to say.

I look at my notes next. "I only got through part of the book on the Kingdom of Rune. I was betting the white wolf one had similar writings as your other books, so we can still explore that on another day," I yawned. "Sorry, anyways this book also talks about the Queen of Light. It doesn't talk about the power absorption being how she harnesses it, but then again, my old English isn't that good. It mentions harnessing the power and has a picture of a circle with a triangle inside the circle and a tree inside the triangle. I realize that's a bit off subject I just found it interesting that its similar to what you found." I continued.

"There were also a lot of symbols in this passage. I haven't made complete sense of the passage but the symbols I was able to match up mean 'gift', 'hail disruption', 'destruction', 'creative focus', 'self-defense and protection' and multiple symbols for 'god' its repeated in three's multiple times. If I keep looking for this symbol for 'self-defense and Protection' maybe, we can find a way to do a protection spell on the whole pack against her powers, so they won't work on the pack."

"I also found a super creepy nursery rhyme; it has been translated multiple times and it appears it was turned into a nursery rhyme so that it will be remembered. A lot of good that did. It doesn't have anything to do with our current goal but nonetheless," I paused.

Derek shrugged and jested for me to read it.

"It seems to be additional verses to the song *You Are My Sunshine*."

I am the Heiress of all the darkness,

I get my powers when darkness reigns,

And when the time comes, death will follow,

All will bow or feel all that pains,

And in the darkness, most will parish,

Greed of man will be his despair,

And the dark Queen will have risen,

To take her claim on all that is fare,

When the light seeks out the purest,

Touched by darkness but not consumed,

Saving those lost to the Heiress,

The queen of light will once again Rule.

There was a long silence after I finished reading. Derek and Samantha looked creeped out now.

"So, Derek, did you read anything good," I broke the awkward silence.

He cleared his throat, "First off my mother sings me that song and now I'm never going to think of it the same way again." He really did look disturbed. He continued though, "I'm sure you know everything I read, but I must say it's not anything I've been familiar with before. It almost seems like we could find a way to block her Third Eye Chakra and Crown Chakra. It says all energy moves through the Third Eye Chakra. So maybe there is a way to block her energy this way. I really am not sure, and I'm still confused about all of it. But after reading this, I can see that this is the way you live, Autum. Your garden and all the crystals and sage burning in your home. Maybe you can do something to remove negative energy from their home or something." Derek rubbed the back of his neck.

I noticed he did this when he was nervous, and it was cute. "I'll talk to my Gram and see if I can find some crystals. We can definitely do things now to help remove negative energy from their house. It will improve her mood and there are teas she can drink that will also help."

Samantha jumped off her bed and went to her closet and pulled out some blankets and threw one over Ethan and Amy and then handed one to me and one to Derek.

"Enough talking," she yawned. "Time for sleep. You can sleep on my bed with me if you want Autum, or you can sleep on that bean bag."

"I'll take the bean bag" I answered.

It was right next to Derek's. This was a chance to sleep close to him. His presence brought me comfort. I laid down and so did Derek. Samantha turned off the light and crawled into her bed. The wind was howling outside, and her accordion doors were shaking slightly. But none of that mattered. I was in my little bubble and Derek was in it with me. The thing about being werewolves was although we didn't have our wolves yet, we could see in the dark. And there were two eyes peering at me and I peered right back. I exhaled, content with how the evening had gone. Derek reached across the small gap between our beanbags and placed his hand on top of mine. I left it there and smiled at him. I closed my eyes and let darkness take me.

I was awoken to a loud thud. I opened my eyes and looked around. Everyone was still sleeping. Samantha's alarm clock read two a.m. Why was I awake? I looked at Derek. He looked peaceful sleeping. The wind was really going now. I sat up and took another glance around. Movement out the balcony door caught my eye. There was a large bird lying on its side outside the door. It must have hit the door and that's what woke me. I got up and walked to the door. The bird was still breathing. I looked around the room again. Everyone was still sleeping. I cracked the accordion door open and stepped outside. The poor bird was barely breathing. I looked out over the balcony to see that there were fallen trees and broken branches scattered everywhere across all three lawns I could view from up here.

There was a beautiful flash of lightning that splintered across the sky. I kneeled next to the bird and put my flat palm above its body, feeling for its energy like Gram had shown me, thinking about channeling my energy into the bird to help heal it. I had only been practicing Reiki for a short time, Gram was the expert, but I was starting to believe in all this Buddhist stuff. I swear I saw smoke swirling below my palm. It looked like gold smoke, then suddenly the bird jumped up and I jumped back further onto the balcony. It worked to my surprise, or the bird wasn't as injured as I thought. I went to step back inside but Amy stopped me. She pushed through the door and joined me on the balcony. "Hope I didn't wake you," I said to her.

"You need to leave Autum." She talked so monotoned.

"What are you talking about Amy, are you sleepwalking or something?" She was staring at me vacantly not blinking, and I know it can be dangerous to wake a person that is sleepwalking. I put my hand on her shoulder to gently guide her back inside. But she pushed my arm away with one hand and then grabbed my throat with the other. I had no time to react.

"Amy stop! What are you doing? I don't want to hurt you," I pleaded with her, my voice barely leaving my lips.

"You need to leave Autum," she repeated she pushed me to the railing still holding my throat. Her grip got tighter. She was so strong. Who was I kidding, there was no way I could beat her in a fight. I've never trained and that's all she does. I could feel her hand getting tighter. I was clawing at her hand with my nails now, pleading with her.

"Amy let go." I could feel the fear inside me growing and I was starting to panic. Suddenly there was a huge crack of lightning it felt like it hit right behind us. Then another and another. The warm air was swirling around us. Before I knew it the sky was bright like daylight as I stared up into it. You could feel the heat coming off the sky and time slowed for a minute. Was I going to pass out? I felt… light. I could see the light coming towards me. My vision half blurred and fading around the edges. My life was slipping away, "Help… me," I whispered with my last breath. I felt my hands fall to my side and my hair was floating around me from the static. I could taste something, something like copper. A single tear fell from my eye, and I felt the calm wash over me.

Suddenly I was jolted, arms wrapped around me, and we were flying. A loud thunderous boom resounded followed by the brightest light I had ever seen. Debris was flying everywhere. The ringing in my ears was so loud it drowned out the sound around me. Derek and Ethan were yelling to each other; I could see lips moving but no sound. Derek was looking at me talking. But I couldn't hear him. What happened? The air around me started to move in waves and the ringing slowly started to fade. I could see Derek yelling to Ethan, but it came out like a whisper to me.

"Ethan, control the goddamn lighting" Derek was yelling.

"I can't, I don't know what's happening!" He yells back.

My chest was rising and falling rapidly. The wind was blowing so strong. I tried to get my bearings, Derek was shielding me, we were back in the bedroom. I looked to the side out the back door. The balcony was gone… Just gone. Samantha was trying to shut the doors; the wind pushing in was making everything fly around us. The glass on her doors completely shattered but still in place. And to my other side Amy was pinned under Ethan. Derek looked down at me and brushed my cheek with his hand. I had been crying, why was I crying?

"Are you okay?" He asked.

I turned to face him. And my breath stilled, I was completely mesmerized by his eyes. They were like blue fire.

"Your eyes," I whispered, "Beautiful fire" I could hear the exhaustion in my voice.

He leaned in close and shooshed me. "Those aren't my eyes Autum… They're yours. And beautiful doesn't begin to describe them."

My eyes, I could see my eyes reflecting in his? I heard Samantha finally shut the doors and Derek picked me up bridal style. I felt so tired, I could barely keep my eyes open.

"Derek, why do I feel like this?" I barely managed to say, "What happened?"

"Shh, its ok Autum you can close your eyes if you're tired. I'll explain in a moment, or you can sleep we can talk about it tomorrow." I closed my eyes and heard him move towards the door and open it.

Samantha asked, "Where are you going?"

"I'm taking her to the spare room, I'm not letting her sleep in here with Amy. We can all talk about this tomorrow."

Derek walked across the hall into another room. He placed me on the bed and pulled the blankets over me. He went to walk away, but I opened my eyes and grabbed his arm.

"Where are you going?" It came out almost panicked.

"I'm going to go grab another blanket and sleep on the floor, I'm not going to leave you Autum." he said, "I'll be right back."

"No, don't… go." I felt tears brimming in my eyes. "I almost died," I whispered, I remembered now, Amy tried to kill me. A tear slipped from my eye. Derek wiped it away. He nodded and climbed in the bed with me. He held me close, and I buried my face into his chest. His warm skin comforted me.

"I'm sorry," I said.

He pulled away a little bit and looked at me, "Why are you sorry?"

"For crying, I know its weak."

"What? Don't be ridiculous." He pulled my chin up to look at him, "You don't have to hide yourself from me Autum, if you need to cry, cry." I nodded and he pulled me closer. I felt the flood gates open, and they poured from my eyes. I made no sound, and we laid there in silence. I closed my eyes and let Derek's scent comfort me.

"Sleep Autum, I won't let anything happen to you," he brushed my hair back with his hand from my wet face. Then kept gently stroking my hair next to my temple. Sleep took me.

18

AFTERMATH

❦

Autum POV

I woke up to the sun peeking through my curtains. I let out a long yawn
and stretched my body. Wait, my curtains? I sat up quickly, I was in my room.
How did I get here, how long was I sleeping to wake up here? I felt good, I
stretched again climbing out of bed and got dressed. On my nightstand was
a vase of fresh flowers, sunflowers and sage, my new favorites. There was also
some rue and thyme in the vase. The burning plate with white sage on it, that
is usually in the living room was on my dresser, peculiar. Gram must have
been worried to have all this up in my room. Heading downstairs I noticed
Gram laying on the couch, a book in her hand. She dropped her book and
smiled, "Good, you're awake, you should go drink some water and eat something dear," she said as she sat up.

My throat was really dry now that she mentioned it. I walked to the couch and followed Gram into the kitchen. I grabbed a glass of water, while Gram made me a sandwich. After drinking four glasses. I finally asked, "How long was I sleeping?"

"Today is Sunday love," she said.

I bit back the bile I felt rising in my throat, and I walked to the kitchen table and sat down. I slept for three days. "How is that possible? I slept for almost two days Gram!"

"From what I heard, you were struck by lightning, or close to it. That kind of event is sure to warrant a good rest." Gram sat across from me, setting my plate down in front of me.

After taking a few bites of my sandwich I asked, "Is that all you heard?"

She raised an eyebrow at me, "Yes, that's all I heard. Why is there more?" "No, um… I was just wondering what else has happened since I've been sleeping." Glad I could come up with something so quickly. "Oh, how did I get here by the way, who brought me home?"

Gram smiled at me, "Derek brought you home."

"He did?"

"He's been coming every day to check on you. I'm actually surprised he's not here yet." She looked up at the clock, "This is about the time he makes me my tea."

I knitted my eyebrows together, "He comes and makes you tea?" I asked, biting back a laugh.

"Yes, he's quite a lovely young man. He comes and makes me tea, and then he goes out and cleans up more of the garden. After the storm it was a mess out there. You definitely still have a lot of work left to do; the wind damage was significant dear."

I felt myself grimace at the thought of what my garden might look like. Gram continued speaking. "He even wanted to know what plants would help you. After pointing out a few that helped with removing negative energy and help relax the mind. He filled the vases in the living room and your bedroom, throwing a few of the scents you like in as well dear."

I sat there in awkward silence for a moment, then I realized my mouth was open. And I felt myself slowly start nodding. I got up and put some water on the stove for tea.

"Are you all right dear?" Gram asked.

"I'm just… processing Gram. It all feels so surreal. I just am having a hard time thinking about everything that happened and-"

I was cut off by the doorbell ringing; I turned my head sharply towards the front door. Suddenly I felt like my heart was going to jump out of my chest. Was that Derek? Were things going to be weird now? I cried in front of him. No, I bawled and then passed out. I touched my hand to my head. I had a sudden sharp pain there now, but my mind was still trying to process everything Gram said. He brought me here. He carried me to my bed and has been back every day for the last three days to check on me. He put flowers in my room, helped Gram with the garden. He's been making her tea.

"Are you going to get the door dear?" Gram questioned.

I just looked at her. Nope. I'm not ready to face him I think to myself. As I absentmindedly shake my head no, I turn on my heal and step out the backdoor.

Oh, my goddess, my poor garden. My breath hitches when I see every-thing that has been damaged. The tree had lost several branches, but they were nowhere in sight. There were divots all over the grass, most likely from the branches crashing down. Most of the sunflowers were toppled over. We would need a lot of stakes for those and some twine. Most of the arborvitaes were split in half, some missing whole sides. The flowers lower to the ground looked fine. But some were oddly flattened. I walked to a flattened section of jasmine and the wood fence slats were missing behind it. The fence must have blown over. I looked around to find there were multiple fence slats missing around the whole yard. All the debris has been cleaned away, but you can still see what the damage was. The bird bath was missing, so that must have been crushed by a tree branch too. This could all be fixed, yes, I could fix all this. The hard part had already been done, clearing the debris. I walked over towards the swing and noticed one of the chains looked brand new. I ran my hand down it. I feel my eyebrows scrunch together, did Derek fix this?

"It's safe to sit on, I promise you." Derek walks out of the back door.

I nod my head and sit down slowly. I kind of bounce a little just to see if it moves. I look up to see Derek smirking and shaking his head at me. He has a throw blanket in his hand and a mug.

"May I sit with you?" He asks. I nodded and he handed me a small pill and the mug of tea. He then drapes the blanket over the back of the seat between us and takes a seat.

"What's this pill?" I ask.

He clears his throat, "That's an aspirin. I saw you walking around out here through the window, and you were holding your head. The cup is chamomile and rosemary tea." He usually avoids eye contact, but that is not the case today. Today I am the one avoiding eye contact.

He made me tea- tea known to reduce stress. I had this tight feeling in my chest. It was like Derek cared for me. Besides my Gram, no one has ever made me feel like that. I look at the cup in my hands and avoid his gaze.

"A penny for your thoughts?" he asks.

I chuckled nervously, "You'd need a hundred pennies to hear all the thoughts I'm thinking right now. And even then, I'm really not sure that would be enough." I start thinking of the questions he will ask, I'm not ready to talk about this yet. Not ready to face what happened. I felt so uncomfortable thinking of school tomorrow. I could not go to school tomorrow; Rebecca would be there and Amy…

He cautiously laughs too. "So, Autum," he rubs the back of his neck with his hand, "Do you want to talk about what happened at Samantha's and what's been going on the last few days? Are you ready for that, or do you just want to sit here and enjoy the view?"

I look up at him and our eyes meet, and as if he is reading my mind he speaks again, "I don't mind just sitting here and enjoying the view. It's quite beautiful" he smiles at me, and I'm lost in his dark brown eyes. Derek's eyes were almost black, it was like looking into a mirror. It was as if my soul was staring back at me.

I hear the back door open, and Gram sticks her head out. "Autum, I'm going to drive over to Ilwaco with Mary today. We are going to get supplies from the local apothecary shop there. Do you need anything, it will be late when I get home?"

"Gram, do you want me to come? That's a two-hour drive one way." Not to mention the human town can be unsafe for our kind.

"Oh, no dear. You need your rest. Mary and I will be fine." She replies.

I really did want to go though, to get out of this situation with Derek for a few more hours, to just pretend that what happened didn't happen.

"Gram, really, it could be unsafe for you two to go alone. I don't mind riding along," I half pleaded.

Gram looked at me and smirked. "Dear you've been couped up in your room for three days. Stay and enjoy the fresh air," she paused dramatically, "and the view." She winked at me and closed the door. That cunning old lady, was she eaves dropping? I slowly shook my head and noticed Derek was now frowning too.

"What's wrong?" I asked him.

"Your grandma knows Mary?" He questions.

"Well, if it's the same Mary, yeah, I guess so. She grew up here. Mary visited us in White Mountain Pack too. Why what's wrong with that?"

"Nothing I guess, did you know Mary is Rebecca and Ethan's grandma?" he says, glancing up at me again to gage my reaction.

I shake my head, "I did not know that. Mary is the one who can heal then, right?"

He nods. That's definitely a good piece of info to know. I had known Mary since I was a child. She was the one who taught Gram about herbs and chakras, who then taught me. She would visit often, and we'd spend hours meditating. I always thought her healing was just from using the energy from the earth and living things. I never thought it was an ability that she was born with in this way.

"So," he begins, pulling me from my thoughts. "You were struck by lightning, and you've been asleep for several days, how do you feel?"

"I feel good, actually. But for real though, I wasn't actually struck by lightning. I would have burn marks or something."

Derek slowly shakes his head, "No we were definitely hit by the lightning."

"We?" I ask.

"Yes, you and me and Amy." I hear him say, but I don't believe it.

"We should be dead, or seriously injured, come on don't joke about this. That was already a horrible night." I slowly reached up my fingers grazing my neck where Amy held me. I remembered everything, the choking, the words she spoke, the bright light, Derek saving me, the balcony disappearing, Derek taking me away and the crying, ugh why did I have to cry in front of him. I looked down at the ground, upset, embarrassed, so many emotions were plaguing me. I couldn't decide exactly how I felt about this whole thing. I knew I was scared of Rebecca's powers and whatever she did to Amy to make her attack me. And I know that I definitely didn't want to see her at school tomorrow. But the strongest emotion I was having right now was for the boy in front of me. He comforted me and made me feel safe. He took care of me. Right now, all I could think about was him.

"Autum, did you hear me?"

Was I just spacing completely out? "Um no, sorry."

"I said the lightning moved around you."

"I don't understand."

He cleared his throat and started rubbing the back of his neck again, "You and I were…protected. It was like we were in a cocoon of energy, the lightning it- it went around us. I pulled Amy from you and then she was thrown into the room. I jumped from the balcony into the room a second later, I could feel the balcony giving way below my feet."

I felt my eyebrows pinch together, "That makes no sense. You're not making sense, lightning doesn't move around people, it follows a path. What you're saying is not possible. You must be delirious. You were with me, maybe it fried your brain."

"Samantha and Ethan saw it too Autum. I have sworn them to secrecy."

"What do you mean, why does it need to be a secret?" I shivered thinking about what he was telling me.

He let out a long sigh and moved closer to me. Placing the throw on me. "Autum, you were… floating on the balcony, your toes barely touching. Your arms were raised to your sides and your head was tilted back looking up to the sky, it was like you were calling on the lightning… to save you."

I was gripping the blanket tightly with one hand, the teacup gripped in the other, I was speechless. I remembered feeling light, and looking up to the sky, I thought I was dying… "That's not right. I- I can't control lightning. Ethan- it had to be E-"

"Autum," He placed his hands on mine and took the cup placing it on the ground. "Ethan tried to stop it, but…he couldn't. He didn't have any of his power. Autum, do you remember your eyes?"

"My eyes… they looked like a blue flame, they were glowing."

"Yes, they were. And that's what Ethan and Rebecca's eyes do when they are using their powers."

He paused for a long time.

"Autum, do you remember that day in class when Rebecca stormed out, the day I came back to school?"

I just nodded, I couldn't speak any words, what had I done? None of this could be possible, I don't have powers. I can't be a white wolf; they are so rare. Gram isn't a white wolf, and neither was my mom.

"In class, that day, when you were telling Rebecca off, your eyes did the same thing, Ethan and I saw it. We were completely dumbfounded. We didn't know what it was that we saw. That day, Rebecca stormed out, not able to persuade the rest of the class, but you did. They were all listening to you."

"What are you trying to say Derek?" I was shaking my head, "that I somehow took their powers. That's even crazier sounding than the lightning bent around me."

I put my hand to my head again. My headache was worse than before.

Derek stood up, "That's enough talk for now. You are still unwell. Maybe you should go rest for a bit before we continue."

"Continue?"

"A lot has happened in the last few days. Things you should know. But I don't want to overwhelm you."

Derek picked up the teacup from the ground and held out his hand. "Come, I'll get you some more tea and we can go sit inside, it's getting chilly out here."

I took his hand, but he didn't let it go, we walked into the house hand in hand. Derek sat me on the couch and went to the kitchen to make more tea. I sat there trying to process everything. Had I always had these 'powers'? Am I a white wolf? If it's not from my mother or grandmother maybe my dad was a white wolf. I never knew my father. I know his family still lives in White Mountain. Maybe Gram and I could take a trip over there. I don't know anyone on that side of my family. Gram reached out to them when my mother died, to see about my father. It's then that she learned he was dead too. She was hoping my story of his death was exaggerated, after all who would believe the word of a 6-year-old. They didn't want anything to do with me.

They blamed me for his death. Neither my grandmother nor I understood it. Enough time has passed, maybe they would see me now.

Derek returned to the living room. I told him about what I'd been thinking about with my father's family.

"Do you think they'd talk to you now that so much time has passed?" He asked.

"I don't know, but it's worth a shot. I don't know anything about him or them. I was too young I only know what Gram told me, that they didn't want anything to do with me."

He nodded, "How's your headache?"

"Getting better, thanks for the tea."

He smiled at me. "Are you ready to hear more about what happened the last few days?"

"Yes, like why Amy tried to kill me, what did she have to say about that?" I questioned.

"Autum, Amy hasn't been able to be questioned yet, she's… in the hospital."

My eyes went wide while he continued.

"She seemed fine after the lightning strike but the next morning she had awoke screaming and writhing in pain, she was covered in blisters. The lightning burned most of her body, she is in a medically induced coma. Her body is healing fast, and they plan on waking her on Tuesday."

"She wasn't protected like we were?"

"No, I told you. I think you were calling the lightning to help you. She was- She was strangling you."

"Are you saying I hurt Amy." I felt ashamed, I'd never hurt someone so severally. How could I do that and not know I was doing that. I felt my chest getting tight and my breathing become harsher. I controlled lightning, but I protected myself and Derek. How is any of this possible? I started grabbing at my chest, I couldn't get enough air. I stood up, I was hyperventilating and couldn't stop myself. What had I done? What if I had hurt Samantha or Ethan? I could have hurt Derek or killed myself. My vision started blurring around the edges. A sharp pain searing through my head engulfed my vision in light.

"Autum?"

That was the last thing I heard Derek say…

Drip, Drip, Drip… I sink tap was dripping again. I was back in my mother's apartment, how'd I get here? I was standing in the hall I looked behind me to my bedroom., There was a man on the floor in my room. I was breathing hard. My body felt hot. I looked at my hands and they were glowing. I was shaking. I was scared. Why was I scared, what had just happened? I ran to my mother. She was laying motion less on the floor in the living room.

"Mommy, wake up."

She wasn't moving, her skin was blistered where I just touched her. What did I do? I could smell something funny. Smoke. I looked back towards my room, there was smoke coming from my room. The man, the man was standing in the doorway. I felt my breathing get faster.

"No, stay away from me."

I put my hands out in front of me and started backing up towards the door. The man lunged for me.

"Come little Kitty" he roared.

"No!"

A bright light shot out of my hands. I was thrown against the wall. There was a loud explosion and then I heard nothing but the ringing in my ears. My eyes slowly fluttered open. Everything was on fire; the smoke was thick…

"Mommy, where are you? Mommy, help me." I was coughing and I couldn't breathe. Flames, all I could see were flames. And then I saw it. "Mommy, no!" I screamed; she was on fire! "No!" I tried to run to her, but I couldn't move. I was stuck. There was a flaming beam lying over me. I was going to die. "Mommy, help me. Mommy!" Suddenly there was a loud bang, and the door was kicked in. The smoke was getting thick, I could hardly make out the person who just barged in.

"Autum!" It was Jenny's mom. "Come on baby let's get you out of here." With a heavy sigh she lifted the beam and pulled me free.

"Let me go, let me go, get my mom, save my mom!" I was screaming. What had I done? I killed her. I killed my mother.

Jenny's mom carried me outside while I was kicking and screaming. "Go back, go back, go get my mom, please GO back." I was sobbing, my words coming out more and more like nonsense.

"Honey I'm sorry, she is gone."

"NO, she can't be gone!" I was trying to fight against her, but I was losing my energy. I suddenly felt tired, and my body ached all over. "No, she can't be..."

19

THE FIRST OF MANY

❧

Autum POV

"Autum!"

"Autum, wake up!"

"Autum! You're heating up! Wake up! AUTUM!"

I opened my eyes. We were sitting on the floor up against the couch. My back to Derek's chest. His legs were over mine holding them down and my hands were together gripped between one of Derek's hands. His other arm was holding my head to his chest. I was breathing hard, my chest moving rapidly up and down. My hands. My hands were glowing.

"Derek?"

"Autum, I'm going to let go of your hands. Keep them out in front of you, ok?"

"Derek, I-"

"Autum, please concentrate, I need to let go."

I didn't know what was happening. Derek let go of my hands and I kept them extended out in front of me. My hands were glowing, just like in my memory of my mother's house. Oh god, my mother. I killed my mother.

"Autum, you're going to be ok," Derek was trying to calm me down.

"I'm not Derek, I'm not okay."

"You are, I'm going to help you stand up, and then we are going to go outside to the backyard. Okay?"

I nodded. Derek put his arms under my armpits and lifted me using his forearms. I looked down at his hands, they were blistered.

"Did I do that to you?" I'm a god damn monster, what have I done?

"Autum, I'm fine. Let's just focus on one thing at a time, okay? Come on let's go outside."

"Ok." I blubbered.

Derek carefully opened the back door for me, and we stepped outside. My body felt like it was on fire. My hands were still glowing.

"Derek, what did I do, what happened?"

"You blacked out and I caught you. You started screaming and then all of the power in the house went out and you started to glow." I didn't know how to stop myself from glowing. I was still breathing hard. "I don't know how to make it stop!"

"How do you usually relax yourself?"

"I meditate."

"Let's try that then" he said. I sat down on the grass and crossed my legs. My face was wet from the tears. I was still crying I couldn't stop. I put my palms face up and connected pointer finger and my thumb on each hand.

"I can't quiet my mind" I cried.

"Just listen to my voice Autum, breathe in, breathe out. Everything will be ok. Just breathe in and breathe out." Derek sat in front of me and reached for my face.

"Don't touch me, I don't want to hurt you!"

"I'm not scared of you Autum, and your face, your face isn't glowing." He reached for my face and with the back of his fingers he wiped away my tears. "Your eyes are absolutely stunning" he whispered. "Just focus on me Autum."

I got lost in Derek's eyes, the reflection of mine in his. He placed one of his hands gingerly on my chest. And we breathed together. I remembered one of the mantras Gram and I spoke as I sat there.

"I call back all the energy that belongs to me and release all energy that does not. I call back all the energy that belongs to me and release all energy that does not. I call back all the energy that belongs to me and release all energy that does not." I whispered with shaky breath.

I felt the energy leave my body and flow down into the earth. I opened my eyes and looked down at my hands, they felt cool again and were no longer glowing. I let out another sob.

Derek pulled me onto his lap, and I cried. "I killed my mother," a sobbed into his shoulder. "I killed her." Derek tried to stand up still holding me.

"No, wait your hands, I burned you!" I frantically pulled his hands towards me to look.

"I'm fine Autum, look they're already healing."

"How? I saw them, they were bad. I- I hurt you. Why did you stay, why didn't you run away, aren't you scared of me?"

"Autum," he brushed my hair from my wet face. "I'm fine, I'm not leaving you, I'm not-"

"Derek, why are you doing this? Why are you here? Why are you so nice to me?" I cut him off. I couldn't help it anymore, I had to ask him. I felt so vulnerable in front of him. I could have really hurt him. I didn't know what I was doing or how to control it. I could have killed him.

Derek braced me and stood up before he started carrying me back towards the house. "I'm doing this because you're a good person Autum. I'm here because you needed me, and why am I nice to you? I'm nice to you because... because I like you. And you deserve to have people around you that care about you."

"Derek, I'm dangerous."

"No, you're not, you just need to learn to control it. It's connected to your emotions. I will help you."

Derek carried me to the couch. And leaned over to put me down. But I didn't let go of his neck. He half smirked and stood back up. He sat on the couch, me on his lap instead.

"So, you wanna talk about what it was that made you go all werewolf zombie, again?"

I lifted an eyebrow and looked at him, "Werewolf zombie and again?"

"Yeah, the same thing happened when you broke my nose. You were completely zoned out. Only this time you were talking."

"What did I say?"

"At first you weren't making sense, something about water dripping. Then you said mommy wake up. You said you could smell smoke. After that you were yelling at someone to stay away from you. Your hands started glowing and that's when you fell. I caught you, but your hands burned me. You were screaming about a fire, I had to pin you down and hold your head from all the thrashing. You were screaming... screaming about your mother."

I gulped, "I. Killed. Her. I used my powers and caught the apartment on fire. She burned to death."

"I don't believe that Autum. You were yelling at her to wake up before you talked about the fire. What else do you remember?"

"I um, burned her with my hands, when I was trying to wake her."

"Autum… it sounds like she was already gone. If you burned her, it would have hurt. She would have woken up."

Derek rubbed his thumbs under my eyes. Goddess I was crying again. How could she have already been dead? "The man, the man could have done it."

"Do you know who the man was?" He asked.

"No, I don't remember. He was in my room. I think I saw him before. In one of my sessions with Dr Warren. When I um, broke your nose. I was hiding in my closet, and he found me. But the flashback ended there. I don't remember what happened after that. Well except for this part where I lit the entire complex ablaze. I don't even know if that man is still alive."

"Did your fear of small places start after that?"

Did I want to answer that? Did I even know? Thinking back on it. I used to hide in my closet a lot, even slept in there instead of my bed most nights. It did change after that.

"I guess it did, I never really thought about it till now. I would sleep in my closet when my mother brought men over. When I moved in with Gram I slept in my bed. I never used my closet after that." I was playing with Derek's hair line at the back of his neck. He was rubbing his hands in small circles on my lower back.

"Are you starting to feel better?" he asked.

I shook my head no, not wanting to get off his lap yet. The small tingles where he was touching me were relaxing. My fingers were buzzing where I was touching him too. Derek got goosebumps on the back of his neck. I smiled at him when I felt them.

"It tickles a little" he responded without me asking a question. I laughed.

"That's better, I love the sound of your laugh." I avoided his gaze and looked down; I could feel my face heating. I glanced at my hands to make sure they weren't starting to glow again. The last thing I wanted to do was hurt him again. Derek tilted my chin up until our eyes met.

"Why do you look away?" He held my chin firmly but still soft. I could not look away. I could not avoid the question. I didn't want to either; I didn't want to lie.

"I… I get embarrassed when you compliment me."

"Why?" His piercing eyes had me mesmerized.

"I think because I haven't heard them before. Compliments. And it scares me." He tucked some of my loose hair behind my ears. And he scrunched his eyebrows slightly. Contemplating my reply.

"My compliments scare you?" He asked confused. I felt my eyes well up, but I didn't let the tears fall. They did scare me. No one had ever been this kind to me. I'd never had someone like Derek. He took care of me, checked on me, took care of my garden because it was important to me. He helped calm the storm inside me. He wasn't afraid of the things I had done. He didn't judge me.

"Say something, please." He looked sad, like he thought his words had somehow hurt me.

"Yes, they scare me." I looked away again as his hands fell to his side. "They scare me because I don't want them to stop. I'm scared that I'm imagining all of this. That I'm imagining you. I fear that I'll wake up tomorrow and everything will go back to the way it was. That you'll ignore me. I… I… Couldn't handle that, not now that I know how it feels."

Derek raised both hands to my face. "Autum, don't punch me again, ok?" He whispered. His hands caressed my cheeks so softly.

"Why would I pun-"

Wide-eyed, I watched as our lips met, feeling our souls unite. The tears fell as sparks flew between us. I was floating on a cloud. Sensations I had never felt before were thrumming through my body. My hands were on his chest, fisting his t-shirt as if he would disappear at any moment. Pulling him closer to me. I felt his tongue lick my lower lip and my mouth opened. It felt so natural, so right. His tongue explored my mouth. Heat spread through my body, the energy swirling as if it had brought new life to me. My body moved on its own as it tried to get even closer to him.

He reached one arm behind my back and pulled me in. His hand slipping under my shirt, my body welcomed his warm embrace. Sparks danced across my skin as each finger pressed into me, leaving a trail of goosebumps along my back. In that moment, it was only the two of us. No one else existed. Everything that had happened fell away; it led me to this moment. It led me to Derek.

We broke the kiss, both taking air in greedily. Our chests matched rhythm as they rose and fell. Derek leaned his forehead to mine. His hand still on my back was rubbing in circles. I knew he could smell my arousal. I felt heat pool between my legs, I had never felt this way before. I didn't know how to act. I would have been more embarrassed if I couldn't feel the bulge in his pants.

"I will never stop complimenting you. You're brave, beautiful, and intelligent. You're not imagining this. You're not imagining me. No matter what happens today, tomorrow, or in the future, I will stand by you. I'm also scared. Scared you'll realize I'm not good enough for you."

He gently wiped the tears from my eyes. I didn't know how to respond to any of that. How could he say he wasn't good enough for me? I'm the nobody, he's the future Alpha. But I believed every word he spoke.

"I've wanted you since I first saw you, but I wouldn't allow myself to dream that big." I whispered back. He pulled me in and hugged me. His embrace warmed my heart.

"This isn't a dream, babe. This is real, and I'm here to stay." I finally relaxed. I would believe his words. I stayed in his embrace, allowing the beating of his heart to soothe me.

20

JOINING BONE CREEK PACK

കൗ

Autum POV

I woke up sweating. Derek was sleeping, still holding me. But we had a throw over us. It was still light outside, I found the clock on the wall, it said two p.m. We'd only been sleeping a few hours. I went to get off his lap, his hands tightened on my thighs as soon as I moved.

"What's wrong?" He asked.

"Um nothing, we fell asleep. I need to use the bathroom."

"Wait," he said before I could get up. He leaned in and gave me a kiss. Nothing like before, but it was soft and sensual. I kissed him back. We pulled away and I couldn't hide my smile. He let me up and stood as well and stretched.

"Can I make something to eat? Are you hungry too?" he asked.

"Yes, I'll help you, be right back," I responded.

Derek was rummaging through the fridge when I got to the kitchen. "There's left over chicken noodle soup, its pretty good. I can make tuna melts with it," I said.

Derek threw a weird face and scrunched up his nose. "No tuna for me," he said.

I laughed. "So grilled cheese it is and chicken noodle soup?" I asked. He nodded. We made lunch and sat at the table.

"How do you feel after your little cat nap?" He asked.

I smiled, "Pretty good. Sorry I fell asleep on you like that."

"You seem to get pretty exhausted after using your powers, like you don't have any energy left. You are also emotionally exhausted. I'm glad you were able to relax enough to fall asleep on me. So, um… My parents plan on visiting you and your grandma tonight. They want to talk about Rebecca with all of us here."

I frowned, "Why?"

"My parents know everything, well except what happened here today. I don't think we should tell anybody else. My father will help protect you until we can learn more about your lineage."

I slowly nodded, taking in what he was saying. "I don't want my gram to know. I will have to tell Dr. Warren about some of this, but I don't want her to know about my powers either. I don't want them to be scared of me."

"I don't think they would be scared of you; your grandma loves you, Autum. But I do agree that less people should know about your powers. Until we know more."

"So, when are they coming here?" I asked.

"I'll call them and let them know your grandma headed to Ilwaco. We can call them when she gets back, it's only a ten-minute drive here from the

Pack House." I nodded in agreement. "Also, there are a few more things you should know before they come."

"Okay, like what?"

"Well for starters the ground below where the balcony was had a marking burned into it. It looked like the 'Tree of Knowledge' symbol we saw in my mother's old books. The tree inside the triangle inside the circle. It looked funny though. The right side of the tree looked like a pine tree, but the left side had two branches off the trunk like a 'V' shape. It was odd."

"'The Tree of Knowledge' has also been referred to as the 'Tree of Good and Evil' and the 'Tree of Life and Death.' That could be why each side looks different. But why would the 'Tree of Knowledge' appear, when I made lighting strike, that doesn't make sense." I replied.

"I know, I'm not sure either." He said, "Also Rebecca will not be at school the next few days. She admitted that she told Amy to scare you, but not hurt you. I think that is part of the reason why my parents are coming here. To discuss what we should do about it. Dr. Warren has practically been living at the Fawn Residents the last two weeks." I didn't know how to respond to Derek, so I just nodded. "Are you okay, Autum?"

"It's just that, Amy was going to kill me. She was overpowering me. It was no fight at all. I'm weak."

"Hey, don't say that about yourself. You can start training; you will learn to protect yourself. I'll make sure of it, okay?"

"Sure."

I was not confident in my ability to learn how to fight, but I would try. We finished our lunch. I called my grandma and told her about the meeting with the Alpha and Luna. She said she could be home by seven p.m. I relayed this to Derek who in turn called his parents to inform them. Derek also mentioned he planned on working in my garden today. So, we went to his truck where he had brought twine and dowels for the sunflowers to reinforce them. He had also brought fence slats to replace the missing ones.

Gram and he had gotten close the last couple of days and had discussed what would be needed for the garden. I was glad to have the help and the distraction. I could tell Derek was trying hard to keep my mind and my hands busy. The upcoming meeting with Alpha Darren and Luna Synthia was making me nervous. I heard a cawing sound from a bird and looked up. There was a black raven in the tree. His cawing was more like a croaking sound. I watched him for a minute.

"That bird has been here every day. Probably missing the bird bath." Derek laughed.

"He looks like the bird from the balcony."

"The one you said you saved?" He questioned.

"Yes" The bird flew down from the tree and landed right in front of me. I sat in the grass and crossed my legs.

"Hey, my pretty bird, you look much better." I spoke to him.

"How do you know its him?"

"His eyes, they are blue. I've never seen a raven with blue eyes before. It's unheard of," I explain.

He jumped closer to me and tilted his head side to side. I extended my hand and he waited. I know he's not a dog, it's not like he was going to sniff my hand, but I didn't know what else to do. He jumped again and put his head under my hand. I started to pet him, like a damn dog. I laughed out loud.

"That has got to be the craziest thing I have seen," Derek exclaimed.

"Really?" I raised my eyes to look at him and raised my hands to him.

"Ok, maybe not the craziest thing I have seen, but it's in my top five." He laughed.

"You have a top five?"

"Well after meeting you I do!" He exclaims.

We both laughed.

"Wait, what's your number one?"

We looked at each other. "The lightning strike," we say at the same time. Laughing again. I can't help but feel happy, even with all the horrible things that have happened. Derek brings out the joy in me. I feed my pretty bird some bird seed. And we finish in the garden.

Derek and I made something to eat around five and then I went to take a shower and clean up. When I came back downstairs Derek was sitting on the couch. We still had a little less than an hour before his parents would arrive.

"Derek, do you mind if I go and meditate while we wait. I haven't been able to do my full routine in a few days?"

"Can I come with you?" he asked.

I felt it would be awkward to have Derek watching me, but I didn't want him sitting in the living room bored while he waited. "Sure," I said. Derek followed me to the meditation room.

"You have a whole room just for meditating?" he asked.

I laughed, "Yes, we do it almost every day. It's good to have a space dedicated to it."

I pulled out a yoga mat and Derek grabbed one as well. I looked at him one eyebrow raised, "Are you planning on joining?"

"Well, I don't know how to do it, will you teach me?"

I shook my head, this should be interesting, "Sure."

We set down the mats and I showed him the first position. "This is the root chakra pose," we stretched into a warrior pose, arms extended. "The mantra for this pose is 'I am.'" After a few minutes we moved into the second pose. Sitting on the floor with our legs stretched to the sides. Elbows on the floor in front of us and leaning forward. "This is the Sacral Chakra, its mantra is 'I Feel.'" I started laughing as Derek tried to lean forward.

"Hey, don't laugh at me, I'm trying" he retorted.

"I'm sorry, I'm sorry. Just wait until the next one," I snickered. Derek was not as flexible as I thought he should be. He could barely place his elbows on the floor to lean forward.

"Don't you train every day, Alpha?" I raised my eyebrows questionably at him as I laughed.

"This is different, you are much more flexible it seems." He replied. I needed to keep my head out of the gutter, I could feel my face heat up just a little. So, I looked away from him quickly. Not before I saw a smile smirk cross his lips.

"Let's move onto the next one. The third one is the Solar Plexus Chakra." I showed Derek how to sit and cross his leg over the other. Knee up, left elbow to right knee. "The Mantra for this pose is 'I Do.'"

Derek laughed, "I do …not think I can do this one." We both laughed after that one.

"Ok well move onto the fourth one. This one is the Heart Chakra. Lay on your belly, place your palms down and then lift yourself up keeping your hips to the floor. This mantra is 'I love.'"

Now Derek's face was turning pink. "This pose seems a little precarious." He smirked.

I cleared my throat, "Let's move on. The fifth is the Throat Chakra. Now we lay on our back's feet firmly on the ground, knees up. Place your arms at your sides, palms down and lift your pelvis until you are flat as a board from your knees to your chest. The mantra for this is 'I Speak.'"

"I doubt that you can't really speak while in this pose." He laughed.

I fell to the floor, laughing. "You are making this very difficult you know." I looked over at him, both of us laying on the floor laughing now.

"I'm sorry" he said still laughing.

"Okay, okay the next two are easy and less, precarious, as you so put it." I winked at him. "The sixth pose is the Third eye Chakra. You sit and cross your legs and place your hands on your legs, index finger and thumbs touching. The mantra for this is 'I See.'" And the last one is very similar except your feet are crossed on top of your legs and the Mantra for this is 'I understand.' This last one is the Crown Chakra."

"So, you do this every day?" He asked.

"If I can, I do it most days."

Derek got up and walked around the little room. "This is the poster of the exercises we just did, but what is this poster? It has the same chakras but different poses?" He asked.

I cleared my throat, "Yes those poses on that poster are for unlocking your chakra's energy. I have a hard time with them."

"Really, why, you are obviously flexible enough." He smirked.

"I, um, have a hard time with the mantras." Before Derek could respond the doorbell rang. I was relieved by the distraction. To unlock your chakras, you have to believe you are worthy, believe you have purpose, that you have strength and unconditional love for yourself. I am weak, I don't view myself as worthy.

Derek sat with his parents on the couch while I got tea for everyone. Gram arrived while I was preparing the tea and I entered into the living room in awkward silence.

"Anyone want tea?" I asked. Both Luna Synthia and Gram took tea along with me. Sipping slowly, I stared up to Alpha Darren and we made eye contact. He smiled at me warmly before he began.

"Ellen, Autum, I asked to meet you tonight so we could discuss the events that took place at Omega Julian's place. It seems that you all were having a sleepover with their daughter Samantha. To my understanding Amy and Ethan were there as well."

I nodded my head and he continued.

"I know from Derek's account of things what happened after the lightning struck but can you tell me what you remember from before, like why you were out on the balcony to begin with?"

I looked to my grandma, and she smiled at me sweetly. She had no idea what truths I was about to speak. She will be furious that I didn't tell her how Amy attacked me. With a deep breath I began, I told Alpha Darren about that night. First about the bird. I took time to look at each person in the room to gauge their reactions. Derek seemed awe struck, his parents skeptical, and Gram looked proud. I told them about Amy meeting me on the balcony and about the words she spoke, telling me to leave. I described the feeling of lightness and told them I thought I was dead before Derek hurled us through the doors. Again, I looked around the room. Derek was blushing his parents seemed mortified at my ordeal and Gram... Gram was fuming, not that any of them could tell. But I could read her like a book. She was disappointed in me for not confiding in her.

"Now you know everything I know Alpha Darren." I spoke.

He paused for a moment deep in thought. "Autum, thank you for filling me in." I nodded at him, and he continued. "I did something today that I thought I would never have to do," he paused. "Today I used my Alpha command to prevent Rebecca from using her powers on Pack Members."

"Forgive me for asking sir, but why didn't you do that sooner?" I asked. Gram gasped at my forward question, but Alpha Darren waved it away.

"No, she's right. Using my Alpha power in this way is not looked upon in a positive way. Some might have said I was abusing my power as Alpha. But when Rebecca chose to try and injure a pack member the council and I had no other choice." I didn't know what to think about this. I was happy to think she couldn't hurt me through others by persuasion but that wouldn't stop her from just out right hurting or killing me. Alpha Darren continued.

"This is also not permanent. Rebecca could leave the pack and reject me as her Alpha, this would break my command. It's also possible that once she gets her wolf, that her wolf could break my command." I was puzzled after that and so was Gram. I even saw some bewilderment on Derek's face. Derek was the one to ask the next question - all our minds.

"Father, how would her wolf break the command?"

After a long pause, Synthia placed her hands on Darren's. She spoke next.

"Rebecca's mother, Elissa, is not just a white wolf. She has the ability to speak and command animals."

We looked at her questionably, that still doesn't answer how her wolf could break an Alpha Command, after a brief pause, she continued.

"To be able to command animals, all animals, one cannot just simply be a Beta or even an Alpha wolf. Elissa's wolf is a Sigma." I looked at Gram bewildered. She looked the same but was still looking at Synthia, I looked to Derek. He was frowning.

"What is a sigma?" I asked no one unparticular.

Alpha Darren responded, "A sigma is equal to an alpha. But instead of sitting at the top of the hierarchy, like the alpha, the sigma sits outside the hierarchy. Sigmas don't follow the structure of the social ranks. They don't conform, they don't care if they are liked or hated, they have high self-esteem and confidence but are neither a leader nor a follower."

"If that's the case, how is she mated to a Beta?" I asked. This time Gram was on board with my questioning showing it with a nod.

"Rebecca's father, Richard, is a beta and his wolf was mated to Elissa's wolf. But because Elissa is a sigma, she was able to choose. Her wolf had to choose Richard. She could have walked away, and the mate bond would not have impacted her the same way it would have hurt Richard. When it comes to love a Sigma can go for anyone they see fit. Sigmas care deeply for those they choose to extend their love to. But again, it is their choice."

I had another question, my mind was going a million miles a minute, "Why hasn't Elissa commanded Rebecca then. She obviously has the power to command right, being an equal to an Alpha?"

Darren let out a sigh. "Her wolf does not conform. She refused to bind her own pup and doesn't see the problem in her pup controlling others. Elissa on the other hand does see the problem in it and that is why she allowed me to command her."

I slowly nodded as the understanding washed over me. He continued.

"I apologize again Autum, for everything that has happened to you, and I would like to ask both you and your grandmother something."

I looked at Gram and we both nodded, Gram spoke next. "You have already given us so much to think over, what would you like to ask?"

"You are both still a part of the White Mountain Pack. I would ask you at this time to reject White Mountain as your pack and officially join Bone Creek Pack. I have commanded Rebecca to not hurt any pack members but you two are not pack members yet." He turned to Gram, "You asked to come back here, now I ask that you make it official."

I was startled, I hadn't even realized we weren't a part of the pack. Gram looked forlorn. This would be the last part of Grandpa she would lose. To leave his pack. She looked to me. I could see the tears welling in her eyes. But she stood and nodded. She walked to the kitchen and returned with a knife.

She stood in front of Alpha Darren and spoke, "I Ellen Moore reject White Mountain as my pack." She let out a yell and Synthia stood to steady her. Alpha Darren cut his palm and dripped blood into Gram's mouth. "I, Ellen Moore, accept Bone Creek as my pack and Alpha Darren Bell as my Alpha." She again let out a cry and nearly fell to the floor. I jumped up to help catch her. Staring into her eyes. She placed her hand on my cheek. "I'm fine dear, now you." She paused for a moment and looked me in the eye, something sad was there. She leaned over to whisper in my ear, "Autum, everything will be all right, remember that I love you."

I stood nervously; I remember doing this when I was six. I just remember it hurting and falling asleep after. Derek stood and stepped next to me. I nodded to him as he held my arm with one hand and wrapped the other around my waist. I looked to Alpha Darren.

"I, Autum Moore, reject White Mountain Pack," I clenched my teeth and felt my knees give. The pain in my head was like a needle being pushed in and then a heard a snap like a lifeline breaking. I felt a tear run down my face. Alpha Darren cut his hand again and dripped blood into my mouth, I resumed, "I, Autum Moore, accept Bone Creek Pack and Alpha Darren Bell as my Alpha."

Alpha Darren replied to this with a loud resounding "I accept Ellen Moore and Autum Moore into Bone Creek Pack." Again, my head felt like it was in a vise, and I heard another crack, a new line snapping into place. A lifeline that would connect me to the Bone Creek Pack Alpha, Alpha Darren. Now if I die, he will feel it. Like he would with any pack member. There was something else now too, something else I was not ready for. My head started throbbing. I saw Luna Synthia and Alpha Darren escorting my grandma out the back door.

"I need… to sit down." I stammered. My head was throbbing to the beating of my heart. The sound vibrating my very being. I reached up to cover my ears. I felt Derek set me on the floor.

"Autum, are you alright?" Derek was asking but I could hardly make out his words.

"Make it stop!" I raised my voice. "This is not right. Something is not right." I could hear a loud whooshing almost like helicopter blades before other sounds faded around me.

21

THE PAST

⁓

Autum POV

The whooshing sound turned into the sound of flames, and I was standing in my old apartment. What was happening? I had been having headaches for weeks, and now my head was clearing like a mental block had been lifted. I stood as a spectator in my own dream. The room was on fire and now everything froze as if time stopped.

I looked around, the beam was on me, and there I was, lying there, fear evident on my tiny 6-year-old face. Time started moving backwards and the beam lifted. Tiny me stood up. I was stark naked. The flash of light retracted towards her, and I could see the flames disappear. The man was standing in the living room now walking backwards to the room. I followed. He lay on the floor and tiny me came in after. Tiny me had another blast come in towards her. So, I used it twice that night.

The scene kept on reversing the man redressing and tiny me redressing. What was he doing? I reversed time faster and faster until I was sitting in my closet eating my Mac and Cheese. I stopped time again and now moved it forward. Tiny me was sleeping I walked through the wall and saw the man. He was with my mother. They were arguing in the living room.

"I want to see her." he yelled.

"She is not who you think she is." she screamed back.

"No, she isn't but she will do."

He picked her up and threw her at the coffee table. Blood spilled from her head. She was dead. I felt nothing seeing her lying there. I could feel no emotions.

The man, he had evil in his eyes. He looked possessed. He walked to my room and pushed open the closet.

"Come little kitten, it's time to play." he said in his sickly voice.

He grabbed her by her throat and threw her on the bed.

"I don't want to play with you, you are scaring me."

"Oh, little kitten, it will be like before." He purred.

"I don't know you" she cried.

"No, well you look just like her kitten."

"Please let me go, I want my mommy."

The man started to undress, "If you take off your clothes and be a good girl, I'll let you see your mother."

She took off her clothes. The man's face contorted.

"What has she done to you!" He yelled.

I looked and saw the many scars on my body, the burns on my arm, the scars on my lips.

"I was b- b- bad" She cried. The man put his hands on her, and I felt my emotions come back tenfold.

"I'll make you feel better, now be a good girl." He purred.

I could not watch this. "NO! Get off of her!" I tried to yell.

She was crying, and I could do nothing but watch. I could feel the pain of his actions. I watched as she started to burn bright. Her face looked void as she shot her arms out and she shot light from her hands. The man flew from her, and the room caught fire. She ran from the room to our mother.

Time stopped again.

I drew in a deep breath. How could I have forgotten all of that? He stole my innocence from me, and I never knew. I am damaged, I am worthless. Anger consumed me. Why did I forget? Why did Gram tell me to remember she loved me, what did she do? She knew this would cause my mind to break, rejecting and accepting a new pack. I fast forward time till I was in the hospital. There she was 6-year-old me. Sleeping with Gram by my side. The doctor entered.

"We have the results back Mrs. Moore, I'm afraid the damage is more extensive than we may have thought."

"What does that mean doctor?"

"I'm afraid at this time her chances of ever having children will be slim. The burns are starting to heal but will leave significant scarring, but not as much damage as the emotional scarring of her experiences."

"Yes, I see. Today will be a day she may never forget."

"It's more than that ma'am." The Dr. cleared his throat, "the burns on her arm are old, some I'd say a few years old and some as recent as a couple weeks ago. The scars on her lips are the same, but some as recent as I'd say today. It also appears that she has had multiple broken arms and broken ribs, she's lucky they healed properly."

Gram looked up at the doctor teary eyed, "and the sexual assault, is there old scarring for that as well?"

"No ma'am. That was recent, today ma'am."

The doctor left and Gram burst into tears. "Oh, my darling, I'm so sorry." She cried. "You are so brave and so strong, and no one will ever hurt you again, I promise." She leaned down and kissed my forehead. She started fidgeting with her phone. She placed it to her ear.

"Hello, Mary? …Yes, it's Ellen… It has been a long time and I'm sorry for calling like this out of the blue… I'd love to catch up but first I need your help… Can you come to White Mountain Pack?"

I fast forward again to when Mary arrives, what was she planning.

"Ellen?"

"Mary, thank the Goddess, thank you for coming."

Mary entered the room and was taken aback when she saw me lying in the bed. "She is so young; you didn't tell me she was this young."

"Does it matter?"

"No, but," Mary looked at me with a gleam in her eye. "This is your daughter's child, Kimberly's child?"

"Yes, Kimberly's child, my granddaughter. Can you help her?"

The old women had a strange look in her eye. Then I saw it, her eyes started to glow, and she placed her hand on my stomach. She started praying to the Moon Goddess. Then she did something else. This was something from the Reiki, she placed one hand on my chest over my heart chakra and the other on my head over my third eye chakra. She was mumbling something about awareness, intuition, and thought. Then she mumbled 'love, healing, and acceptance.'

"What are you doing now?" Gram asked.

"Looking into her memories."

"Which ones?"

"All of them!"

Light started to flow out of the girl into the old women. She leaned in and whispered into the child's ear. I could not hear what she said, but when the old women stepped away, she had been crying. Her eyes slowly faded back to normal.

"Is it done?" Gram asked.

"It is. She won't remember most of it. The really bad stuff I put up a very large wall."

"A wall, can't you just remove it completely?" Gram asked.

"No!" She brushed the hair away from my face, "These experiences will make her who she is. It is her destiny to step through these challenges and come out on the other side stronger. But she is young, and because of that I have put up walls. They will fall one by one until she is ready to see. Until then I will visit often, and I will train her in the way of Reiki. She must learn to control her emotions and meditate. Reiki is an energy healing technique that promotes relaxation, reduces stress and anxiety through gentle touch. It will improve the flow and balance of her energy to support healing. Her destiny is a great one. She has been touched by darkness, but only through darkness may we find the light."

Then the old women looked at me. Not the little me, the actual me. The me watching this entire thing unfold. The me lost as to how this old woman was looking into the deepest part of me. Could she see me? She walked to me.

"Can you see me?" I whispered.

The old women nodded. Gram was looking at little me in the bed. Mary came to stand right in front of me. Invisible me. How could she see me? She reached up and touched my chest and head again. A light came from the places she touched. Gram seemed to be unaware of what was happening. Mary whispered to me. "You have been touched by darkness where others have been consumed. You are being called upon to fulfill your destiny child. I will give you back that which I took from you. I call back all energy that belongs to me and release all energy that does not." She whispered.

Then as if I had known what to say I spoke, "I call back my energy from all sources and release all negative energy bestowed upon me. I reclaim my power and take my place in the light."

Light illuminated us and a wave of warm light flew up from Mary and spun around above us. Light then poured in from all around me, coming from every wall before flowing into me. I was filled with warmth. I felt strong. I looked at the old women before me. She looked sickly and weak. Her hand still on my head started to burn, then she yelled, "Its time, WAKE UP!"

The air around me started to bend and wave. I blinked and when I opened my eyes I was on the floor in Derek's arms. "There you are you had me worried for a minute." He smiled down at me sweetly.

"How long was I out?" I asked.

"Only a few minutes" He replied.

"What? Really? It felt like hours went by." I tried to sit up, but I immediately started to fall again.

"Woah, slow down. Just give yourself a minute." Derek paused, "You've had a lot of activity today, you need rest."

"Where is everyone else?" I asked.

"Your Grandmother needed some air; my parents took her to the garden." I remembered now, watching them lead her outside. She told them she needed air.

Derek didn't help me stand, instead he picked me up and sat on the couch. "Passing out happens a lot when we accept new members, it's normal. What do you need?" He asked. He was so gentle, but I didn't deserve him. I was no longer pure, I'm damaged. I turned from his gaze holding back the tears that threatened to fall.

"I need... time." I pulled my hand from his and placed my hands in my lap.

"I don't understand... what's changed?" He asked.

"I can't explain it right now. I just, I need to speak to my grandmother." Derek stood, hands laced behind his head and started pacing. We gazed at each other, having a silent conversation. I could see the hurt in his eyes, and he could see the regret in mine.

Gram, Alpha Darren, and Luna Synthia walked in at that time. Feeling the tension in the room Alpha Darren asked, "Is everything alright?"

"We need to leave." Derek answered.

Gram stepped forward hesitantly but made her way to me. "Autum?" I stood, holding myself. The Alpha and Luna looked lost as to what had happened. Grams eyes met mine and tears instantly fell from my eyes. She rushed to me, embracing me. We fell to the floor in a heap. The sounds that escaped me were heart breaking. Luna Synthia stood speechless, one hand covering her mouth.

"I remember everything." I sobbed. "EVERYTHING." I yelled. "Let me go, let go of me." I tried to push her away.

"I won't," Gram cried back. "I will never let go. Scream. Kick. Yell. I won't let go, I'm sorry my love, so sorry."

I let my body go limp, I was too exhausted to fight her. "I'm broken." I cried.

"You are the strongest person I know Autum."

"No, I'm not. I loved you; how could you hide this from me and for so long? All the counseling and you knew." Did Dr. Warren know too? Was this all some big waste of time to hide the truth from me? To keep everything from me, my past, my abilities, who am I? She loosened her grip.

I looked up to her. "Who else knows, does Dr. Warren?"

"No, No," She whispered, "Just Mary and I."

I nodded to her, and we stood up.

"I need space," I said lowly, "I need space from you, I can't stay here." I stepped away from my grandmother. She had sorrow in her eyes but also acceptance.

Synthia stepped forward, "You can stay with us."

"Synthia?" Alpha Darren questioned.

"She stays with us!" She stated with finality.

"Thank you, I just need a few days… to process everything." I swallowed hard.

I went to my room to pack a few things. When I returned to the living room it was quiet. We all walked towards the door to exit.

"I love you, Autum" Gram said.

"I love you, too."

We walked out of the house into the brisk night air. I was taken aback when Derek opened my door for me. Same as Alpha Darren for Luna Synthia. I looked at him and he tilted his head to the side to tell me to get in. I needed to sleep. I felt drained. The trees and houses blurred together as we drove to the pack house.

My mind was somewhere else. How could I have been so stupid as a child? My mother was so cruel to me, and yet I loved her. My body riddle with scars, broken bones and still… I loved her. My chest hurt with the pain of betrayal. How could a mother do these things to her child and how could I still love her? Tears fell silent from my eyes. Derek moved to sit next to me. And I know what he saw in my eyes. I was lost, completely and utterly lost.

When we arrived at the pack house Derek showed me to the room I'd be sleeping in.

"My room is next door, if you need anything." He placed my backpack on the bed. Then moved to another door in the room. "This is your bathroom. And that door is your closet." He spoke softly.

I nodded to him. I sat on the bed and opened my backpack. Seeing I hadn't packed anything to sleep in I lay on the bed fully dressed, shoes and all.

"Autum?" Derek spoke soothingly. He walked to the bed and kneeled by me.

"I'm just tired, I'll be better tomorrow." I said flatly.

"What do you need, are going to sleep like that? In your clothes?" he asked gently.

"I didn't bring anything else, its fine."

Derek left the room and returned a few minutes later. He had changed his clothes and had more in his hands.

"Here's a shirt and some shorts, they will probably be a bit big on you, but they will do."

I sat up and nodded. As Derek approached, I raised my arms. He visibly gulped when he realized I wanted him to help me. He needed to see. See that I was damaged. He needed to know why we could never be together. To see it. To see me.

"Autum, I can't."

I just looked at him, our eyes not straying from each other. At some point, understanding crossed his eyes and he dropped his head and sighed. He reached down and grabbed the bottom of my shirt. He pulled my shirt up over my head and he went stiff. My chest and stomach were riddled with scars. Some small, some large. I turned my head to the side, not wanting to look him in the eyes. I slid my arm sleeve off my burnt arm then I stood and unbuttoned my jeans. Derek lowered to one knee and slowly pulled them down over my hips and to the floor. His breath hitched as he saw the burns around my hips. He looked up and saw my arm. Round burns covered my arm.

I sat on the bed while Derek removed my shoes and then pulled off my jeans. Still afraid to look at him, I stared at the wall. He grabbed the shorts and held them open for me to step into. After, I turned around and looked over my shoulder. I cleared my throat to pull his attention from the scars on my back.

"My bra." Derek reached up and unclasped it. Keeping my back to him I grabbed the shirt from the bed and put it on. It was his shirt. I turned around and lifted the shirt to my nose and inhaled deeply.

"Thank you," I said.

"I have questions."

"Tomorrow." Was all I said before I laid down in the bed.

"Can I lay with you?" He asked.

I gave a heavy sigh, "I think that's… a bad idea."

"Why?"

I felt my eyebrows pinch together, "Why… Why… Derek, you saw me. I'm- I'm not good enough for you. You need someone stronger, someone worthy of you. I'm not any of those things. I'm- I'm broken, I'm damaged." I closed my eyes and rolled onto my side. My heart was racing, my chest rising and falling with each heavy breath I took. I heard Derek's steps getting farther away and my heart ached. I was angry at myself for pushing him away, but I knew it needed to be done. Derek was to be the next Alpha; he needed a strong Luna.

Derek shut off the light and then there was an awkward silence in the room. Instead of leaving he walked back towards the bed. He started to climb in.

"Derek, you c-"

"Autum, enough."

He sounded gruff, like he was holding back.

"Derek, I'm sorry. I didn't mean to hurt your feelings, but I'm-"

"Don't you dare." He cut me off.

"Excuse me?"

"Don't say another hateful thing about yourself. I won't listen to it."

I was dumb founded. Derek scooted closer. I rolled over to face him, and he patted his chest. I gave a sigh and hesitated, our eyes met in the dark and his eyes were fierce. I'd never seen him like this. Almost protective but for me.

"Derek?"

"Autum, just surrender for tonight. I need to be close to you. I know you need me too."

I did, I surrendered. I laid my head on his chest, and he put his arms around me. His touch instantly calmed me.

"You are the most beautiful person I have ever met; beauty comes from the inside Autum." First, he pointed to my head and then to my heart. I opened my mouth to speak.

"Don't." Those were his only words. I closed my mouth. I rested my hand over his heart and let sleep take me.

22

DEATH WAITS
FOR NO ONE

❧

Autum POV

I woke the next morning to a knock on my door. I sat up and remembered I was not at home. Looking around I found that the bed was empty beside me. I looked at the time next. It was ten a.m. I'd never slept in so late. The knock came again. I jumped out of the bed and went to the door. Opening it Luna Synthia appeared.

"Good morning" she said.

"Good morning, Luna"

"Call me Synthia dear. How are you feeling this morning, may I come in?"

"Oh, yes come in. I'm feeling better. I don't really know what I should be doing though. With the time I have." We walked into the bedroom and sat at the end of the bed.

"Well first I recommend taking a shower. Getting a meal in you should be second." I nodded; a shower did sound nice. "Also, a trip to Beta Richards house next door is in order," she said.

"Rebecca's house? Why?"

"Because Mary is asking for you dear." She smiled at me softly.

I nodded. Synthia left the room, and I grabbed some clothes from my bag and my hairbrush. I headed to the shower. The bathroom was large. Colors of greys and whites decorated the walls and floors. A large shower was in the back with multiple shower heads and a rain shower head above. The bathtub was separate and looked like it had jets in it. I would definitely need to take advantage of that while I was here.

I brushed my hair while the water warmed up in the shower. As I stepped into the shower, I noticed shampoo and conditioner bottles already inside. I popped the top of the shampoo to smell it. Mango, yum. I washed my hair and then grabbed the loofah to wash my body. Every ridge I washed over of scars, every burn I felt below the loofah. I closed my eyes and raised my head up, washing my neck then my chest. I didn't realize how hard I was scrubbing or that I had turned up the hot water. I just needed to be clean. To wash away the memories. Over and over again I cleaned myself. Until I felt nothing, I stood there in the shower letting the water pour over me, down my body to the drain, where it washed all my pain away.

I finally decided to leave the shower when my stomach growled in protest. Getting dressed was difficult, my red and irritated skin did not agree with the confines of my jeans, nor my bra or shirt. Looking in the mirror I gave a heavy sigh. What did I do to myself? I shook my head, disappointed that I did so much more damage. I couldn't go downstairs like this. I sat on the edge of my bed contemplating what to do next when there was a knock on my door. Might as well face the music.

"Come in." I sighed. The door slowly opened, and Synthia peeked her head inside.

"Are you ready for br-" She stopped abruptly. And walked hurriedly towards me. "Oh, Autum! What did you do?"

I was not looking at her, I couldn't. "I just wanted to wash it all away. I didn't mean to do... this" I outstretched my arms.

She knelt on one knee to be at my level. "Autum?" The way she was looking at me, the pity in her eyes.

"Please don't look at me like that, I can't handle anyone else looking at me like that, with pity."

"It's not pity Autum, its... understanding."

I looked at her, startled, "You know?" I almost panicked. Who told her? How did she know?

"No. No, I don't know Autum, but I do *know*." Sudden clarity hit me. Startled by her omission, I reached out and hugged her. I didn't want to let go. She knew what I had been through. We shared that experience. She hugged me back tight.

"Come, let's go see Mary first. Then we'll eat. She'll fix you up right as rain."

"Are you sure it works like that?" I asked pulling away from our embrace.

"Oh, yes dear. She's done it for me before." She gave me a soft smile. And tucked my hair behind my ear.

"Can I braid your hair?" She asked. I nodded. My mother used to brush and braid my hair. It might be the only good memory I have of her.

"Where is Derek?"

"I made him go to school today."

"Oh, right."

"You have earned yourself a pass. Derek, on the other hand, has not. It also gives him the opportunity to monitor Rebecca back at school today. Ethan will be bringing your class assignments since you have the same classes." We walked to Beta Richards House and knocked on the door. I was surprised when he opened the door. I think I surprised him as well.

"Hello Beta Richard" Synthia spoke.

"Luna" He bowed slightly to her. "And who is this?"

"This is Autum." Synthia replied. His eyes, still slightly wide, took me in.

Synthia cleared her throat. "Are you going to invite us in?"

"Sorry, yes, come in. Forgive me for staring. But your-"

Synthia cut him off, "Yes, yes, her skin. She's had an… allergic reaction, but she'll be fine. We are here to see Mary; she is expecting us."

Beta Richard led us through the house. The house was very warm and inviting. The cool colors of the house brought life to the rooms. Most of the walls were painted in teal, blue, and white. The decorations were more modern and sleeker. No tapestries were in this home. But more modern works of art hung on the walls. When we entered Mary's room, I felt like I was home. Herbs, flowers, and Himalayan salt sculptures decorated her room. She was burning white sage near her bed. She had crystals hanging off of everything. The lamps, the pictures, around the vases and in the windows. I walked to her bedside, and she opened her eyes as I reached her.

"Autum, how are you?"

"I'm fine, I'm fine. You look ill Mary. What happened to you?" I asked.

"She was doing good until last night. All of a sudden, she fainted, and we had to carry her up to bed?" Beta Richard replied.

Mary was shooting daggers at the man. "The question was for me; I can talk all by myself you know." He went to open his mouth but then shut it again. "I need to speak to Autum alone." Mary said. Everyone eyed each other then finally nodded. Synthia patted me on the shoulder and left the room as well. Mary looked at me with curious eyes. She reached for my hand and turned my arm over to look at it.

"Child, what did you do to yourself hmmm?" I just shook my head and looked down at the ground. She reached for my chin next and pulled my head up to look at me. "You are more, Autum, so much more."

"What do you mean?"

"That will come in time dear, for now, let's get you fixed up." I pulled my hand from hers

"No, you're too weak. It could kill you."

"Yes, your right, that's why you are going to do it."

"Me?" I said in a very high-pitched voice.

She laughed. "Yes, you. Now listen closely dear. You have a very unique set of gifts."

"Gifts, like more than one?" I said incredulously.

She laughed again and nodded this time. "You dear have the ability to," she paused and bobbed her head back and forth, "let's say the word is 'borrow' another's gifts."

"Borrow?" I said skeptically.

"Mmhmm, I've sensed you'd borrowed Rebecca's gift before and Ethan's, that lightning struck a little too close to home at Samantha's, if you know what I mean."

I did know what she meant, but I don't know how I did it. "I don't know how it happened, it just happened."

"Yes, I suspect you were under duress, but you will learn to control it and today just happens to be one of those occasions."

I took a deep breath, "What do I need to do?"

Before she could answer she started coughing and wheezing. "Water," she choked. I handed her the glass on her nightstand and helped her take a sip. Slowly she continued.

"You need to reach out and feel for it. To me it feels like a string tugging at my ribs. Then I feel either energy leaving or entering my body, depending on what I'm doing." I calmed myself and tried to reach out for the feeling as she said. Nothing happened.

"I don't think I can do this" I said.

"Remember the bird dear?"

"The bird from Samantha's balcony?"

"That would be the one, how did you do that?"

"That was different, I was pulling natural energy from around me, from the earth."

"Yes, that's it, I felt you pulling that night. I was only a couple houses away. Autum, you are so strong, you just need to concentrate and let the energy flow."

I thought about her words, the bird came so naturally to me. I was just trying to do something good, to save a life. I looked into Mary's eyes then I closed mine. I put both her hands in mine, placing one on her chest and one on mine. I thought about what my intentions were that night with the bird. To transfer energy into the bird. Tonight, I wanted to transfer energy into me. I started to feel a tug, it was gentle but then I felt the flow of energy into me. Tingles spread across my body and after a few minutes I released it and opened my eyes.

Mary had a large grin across her face. I peered down at my arms and the rash was gone. I stumbled back in disbelief and sat on her bed. "I did it?"

"Yes dear, that was all you. Now you just need to release it back to me."

"I still have your abilities? How do you know?"

Mary reached for the mirror on her nightstand. And handed it to me. I turned it over and gasped. My eyes were such a brilliant blue. A blue flame of sapphire. I closed my eyes and thought about sending it back. And I mumbled the Mantra about releasing energy that does not belong to me. I opened my eyes and watched as they faded back to normal.

I laughed, "How'd you know I still had your abilities and not my own?"

"Well, I didn't see any light shooting from your hands so." We both laughed.

"Now Autum, I asked you here for a reason. This old lady's light is about to burn out and there are some things you need to know."

"Mary, don't talk like that."

"It's just a fact of life dear, nothing to fret over. I'm old."

She started coughing and wheezing again and I helped her with more water. Her breaths were becoming more labored.

She took my hands in hers. "Listen to me child and hear my words. There is a darkness here. It grows day by day. At first it was but a whisper. The smallest of doubts that has started to fester. I fear she is here. At first, I believed that what I had felt was nothing, that the whisper was the imagination of an old lady."

She leaned in closer to me, pulling my hands tighter. "Last night that whisper broke through the silence, it was but for a mere second, but I saw her. Saw her through the ripple of time as you called back the energy that belonged to you. She had been shielding herself from me, using your energy as her shield. She disguised herself and infiltrated us. She must be close to you child, to have used your energy. You must go back. You must see what I saw. You must find her." She started coughing again.

"Calm down, don't overdo it. I don't understand, who is she?"

"The Heiress my child." She lowered her voice to that of a whisper, "The Heiress of Darkness."

I tried to pull my hand from her grip. She pulled me closer. "She does not know who you are. She's been using energy, wherever she can find it. Steeling the essence from whomever she can. Be cautious who you trust. Find her before she discovers who and what you are."

"Who and what I am? You're not making sense. And how will I know who I can trust?" I asked.

She pointed to my heart. "You will be able to feel it here, the heart cannot lie."

She was talking in riddles. "Who am I?"

"In time my dear." She pointed to my head. "The wall will fall when you need to know, knowing now will only put you in more danger."

"I need to know now; how can I protect myself if there are more secrets?"

"To find the who, you'll need to go back to the beginning. To find the what, you need only look inside yourself." Her hands loosened and she repositioned herself in her bed, "I believed for a time that the prophecy would not come true. That it had been broken when there were only two, but then I found you." She released my hands and placed her hands on my face. "You were there in the hospital, and I couldn't believe my eyes, and then when I saw it, I knew. You were where you needed to be. Hidden from the darkness."

"I was not hidden from darkness; I was living in it. You saw what I went through. How could you say I was where I needed to be?" I stood from the bed.

"Wait," she gasped. I turned to look at her, I didn't understand what she wanted me to do. I didn't understand what I was meant to do. I didn't speak. I stared at her lost. She continued.

"When I'm gone, you can watch it again. You can go into the ripple and watch it again." Then she spoke in another language. "Eerht fo eno era uoy."

She repeated it over and over again until her breath gave out. She started to wheeze. "Mary!" I ran back to her bed and kneeled beside it. Beta Richard and Luna Synthia came running in after hearing me yell.

"Mary?" Richard Spoke

"Tell my daughter I love her," She spoke softly.

Richard nodded. Synthia came up behind me, beckoning for me to stand, to leave Mary with Beta Richard. But I couldn't. I couldn't leave her. Synthia reached for me.

"No" Mary choked; it came out like a whisper. She pulled me in closer. "When I'm gone, you'll see what's left of me. You need to take it."

"What? Mary, no, what do you mean? Your life?" I whispered back.

"No, it will be the last essence of my gift. If you don't take it, it will be lost to the energy of time. You will need it. Don't use it until the end. She is looking for you. She is here." Mary lifted her hand and placed it on the mirror on her nightstand.

"I don't understand."

"It's going to be ok. Take it now child, before it's too late." Her breath was fading.

I knelt my head down to kiss her forehead, and I pulled what was left of her gift from her, like I had done before. Our eyes met. "Very good my child."

I heard her take her last breath and saw a single tear leave her eye. Our hands were still locked together. I sagged to the floor. I felt my cheeks wet from tears. The room was quiet. I kept my eyes closed. Not wanting anyone to see them glowing. I tried to relax myself to store the energy I didn't need to use. I needed the mirror. I slowly stood up keeping my eyes down cast. I slowly pulled my hands from Mary's and rested her hands on her chest. I turned to her nightstand and peered down into the mirror. My eyes were slowly fading.

I picked up the mirror. I hadn't noticed it before, but the mirror was quite beautiful. It was old and intricate and looked to be made of obsidian. The design twisted all the way up the handle and framed in the mirror. I held it to my chest and turned to see Beta Richard and Luna Synthia looking at me. At that moment, the door burst open and a beautiful women ran in.

"I'm too late" She cried, looking to Richard and then back down to Mary. "I came as soon as you mind linked me, but then I felt her leave just now." Her tears flowed freely as she walked to her mother. I could only gather that this was Elissa, Rebecca, and Ethan's mother. I backed up to Synthia, and she rubbed my arms up and down. I was tense and still crying as well. It was then that Elissa looked up and saw me for the first time.

She seemed startled at first, staring at me, "Who are you?" She asked.

"I'm... Autum." I said softly. I was still gripping the mirror as if my life depended on it.

"Autum." She looked at Richard and they seemed to be having a conversation amongst themselves. Mind linking. "Okay, Autum. My mother spoke of you often. When she would travel to White Mountain Pack to visit Ellen and you. It's nice to put a face to the name, but I do wish it was under better circumstances."

She looked back down at her mother and leaned down to kiss her. "We need to get Dr. Warren and make the arrangements." She wiped her eyes and walked past me. "You can keep the mirror. You must have been important to her, if she asked for you to be here in her last moments." We all walked out of the room and to the living area. We sat in silence for a while. Elissa broke the silence.

"We will be having a gathering to celebrate her life. Let's plan it for Wednesday."

"That soon?" Richard asked.

"The twins' birthdays are this weekend; we can't do it then." She sighed and placed her head in her hands, "I just can't believe she's really gone."

Richard leaned in comforting his wife.

"You will be invited too Autum, I know that you and Rebecca aren't friends, and I mean she tried to kill you." Wow, this woman is blunt.

"She used to be such a sweet girl, but she's gotten it into her head that she can do whatever she wants. It will be safer now that Alpha Darren has commanded her. But the only real way to deal with her is head on. You can't hide from her."

"I'll think about that," I said. I stood up "It was a pleasure to meet you both, my condolences to your family." Luna Synthia stood up and offered condolences as well. We left the house and headed back across the street. When we got inside, I let out a huge breath. She did the same.

"I'm so sorry Autum, I hadn't realized she was so sick. Or I would have never taken you over there."

"I needed to see her, I'm glad I was there for her. I need to call my grandmother. Mary was her best friend."

"Of course, of course."

Synthia led me to the study, and I called Gram. This week had been full of trauma and tears, and I was ready for it to be over already. After I got off the phone, I told Synthia I wanted to lay down. I went back to my room to think over everything Mary had told me. I pulled out my notebook and wrote it all down. Then I wrote down some of the events of last night. I needed to talk to Samantha and Derek. We were going to need to start documenting everything if I was going to solve this Heiress of Darkness thing. A light bulb went on in my head at that moment. The Nursery Rhyme. I needed that book!

23

SECRETS

❧

Autum POV

A knock on my door broke me from my intense focus on the book I had borrowed from Synthia.

"Come in."

Derek peaked his head in. "Hey, how are you doing?" He rubbed the back of his neck as he walked in.

"I mean, why do you ask? It's not like all my memories came pouring in last night and had me reliving the worst moments of my childhood and then today I got to watch one of the most influential people in my life die."

"Right, that was a stupid question."

I sighed, "No, I'm sorry. Thank you for asking. I'm keeping my mind busy reading this book. Samantha's dad let me borrow their Old English dictionary and your mother let me borrow those books we had that night at Samantha's."

"Fun," he raised his eyebrows garnering a laugh from me. He flopped on the bed. "So," he sat up and moved until he was sitting across from me. He crossed his legs like mine and scooted closer until our knees touched. I ignored him and kept reading. He rolled his eyes and started grabbing all my papers and putting them into a nice pile.

"Hey." I protested.

"It's tomorrow, you said I could ask questions tomorrow, and that is today," he said. He looked desperate for answers. And I didn't want to give them.

"I'm not ready." I said shakily. It was too soon to re-live what happened. I wasn't done processing for myself.

"Maybe talking about it will help?" He questioned.

I drew in a big breath. "I just feel like-" I couldn't even finish the sentence. I blew the air out. Tears already welling in my eyes. I was fisting the blanket in my lap. Thinking. Thinking how he could not be disgusted by what my body looks like. How could he even want me still?

"Autum," he put his hands over mine to stop me from fidgeting. "You feel like what?" he asked.

"Weren't you disgusted... when you saw me?" I turned my head to look at the wall again. I felt so unworthy. I wanted to tear my skin away, to start over. I didn't want to see the disgust in his eyes. Derek reached up and placed his hand on my cheek. He was so gentle. His touch sent a warm sensation through me, and I leaned into it. He slowly pulled me to face him.

"Look at me." he breathed softly.

I slowly raised my eyes to meet his. Derek unfolded his legs and then put one on either side of me. He motioned for me to do the same. I did, laying mine on top of his, my knees bent. He pulled us closer together. Our noses practically touching, he whispered softly.

"You. Are. Beautiful." He let out a small, forced breath and pushed a strand of hair behind my ear. Leaning into my ear. He whispered again. "Anyone who says different will have to answer to me."

I looked to him again. His eyes were full of sincerity. I was speechless. How could he see me this way when I couldn't see myself this way? I went to speak but he put his finger to my lips.

"I have questions, answer them if you can, okay?" I hesitated but then nodded in submission.

Derek reached to my left arm and pulled my fabric sleeve off. He ran his fingers gingerly over my scars. I felt myself shutter at the feeling. He asked, "What is this from?"

With a deep breath I spoke, "I will answer…What I can. But you have to agree not to get angry when I answer. No matter what."

"Why?" he asked as he already was tensing.

"Because I won't know if you are mad at me or someone else. And the thought of you being mad at me…" he was shaking his head no in response, but I finished, "I know it sounds irrational. Please, I just-"

"Okay," he cut me off reluctantly.

I let out a huge breath and could feel my chest slightly heaving. I was scared. He nodded his head to me, telling me to go ahead with my answer.

"Cigarettes." My one-word answer was clearly not enough as he slightly raised an eyebrow to tell me to keep going. "They are scars from a cigarette."

"How many do y-" he started to ask.

I cut him off, "forty-seven." I sighed. I tried to pull my arm away, but he held it firm. His strong fingers were gently wrapped around me. He lifted my arm and kissed it softly before putting it back down. I felt a tear slip from my face. He wiped it away.

"The scars… On your body… What are they from?"

"A belt."

"A belt did all of that?"

"Well, when you use it like a whip with the clasp side out." Derek stiffened, I could feel his hands getting clammy and he was starting to sweat. I turned my head to stare at the wall again. He was getting angry.

"Don't do that," he finally spoke.

"Do what?"

"Bare your neck to me like that, like you're submitting. I don't like it."

"I didn't mean to. That's not what I was meaning to do." I said softly.

"Just don't do it to anyone… ever again." His voice was firm. His eyes refocused. He leaned down and kissed the scars on my chest. Then lower, he lifted my shirt to kiss above my belly. He straightened back up. He ran his thumb over my lips. The sparks ignited and I felt them run down my spine to the tips of my toes. He cleared his throat before speaking, obviously having just as much trouble as me.

"What happened to your lips?"

"When I was little, I broke a glass washing the dishes." I paused for a moment. "For my punishment, I was only allowed to drink from the broken glass cup." He leaned forward and kissed my lips gently. He made all my hurt disappear, like it never existed. Pulling away he took in a deep breath.

"Autum, how did you survive, all this?" He gestured to my body. "And really, for breaking the cup?" He grabbed my hands holding them tight.

"Yes, you'd think I would have learned better after the first time, you know, to be careful with the dishes."

"What happened the first time?" he asked.

"I broke the ash tray."

His hands tightened around mine. There was an eerie silence that followed. Neither of us wanted to move from each other, but we were both still uncomfortable with the entire situation. I decided to try to get up, I didn't like seeing him angry. It was making me more uncomfortable than I already was.

"Wait!" he said, "Just a few more questions. I'm calm now. I just- I need another minute."

I let out a breath but gave him the time he asked for. His hands loosened, but he didn't let go.

"The scars on your hips and legs, they look like burns." Not really a question, more of a statement, but I answered.

"They are burns. From when the apartment caught fire." I paused and corrected myself, "When I caught the apartment on fire. The ceiling partially collapsed on me."

"How'd you escape?"

"A neighbor pulled me from the fire."

Derek took a few minutes to think of everything I'd told him. "So, you said before that your father was dead, so your mother?" He didn't quite finish the question. I knew what he was going to insinuate.

"Yes, my mother did all this to me."

"And you are just now remembering all of this for the first time? Where is your grandmother in all of this? Why are you angry with her?" I was slowly shaking my head in response to his questions.

"No. I, um, remembered most of what I told you. Though it's much clearer now. My grandmother didn't know about how I was being treated until that day." My voice grew quieter, and I could hear the tremble in it. I squeezed my eyes shut, trying to push the awful memories away. I felt my body shaking thinking of that man touching me.

"Autum? What is it, what's happening?"

"There's more, so much more." I cried.

Derek pulled me into his chest. Rubbing circles on my back while I cried, "Answer if you can," he said softly.

"I can't say it... not those words..."

"Think of different ones then, hmm." he hummed, the sound vibrating his chest where my head laid. Helping me calm down.

"I'm not-" I pushed my head into the crook of his neck, inhaling deeply, his scent comforting me. I fisted his shirt as I came to terms with what I was about to say. I felt the warm tears spill from my face as I pulled away to look at him. He looked distraught seeing me like this. I readied myself for the rejection. "I lost my innocence that day, the day of the fire. I'm no longer pure."

His eyes grew large, then quickly softened. I was tense, I was waiting to see how he'd react. The suspense making my mind go wild with rejection. He quickly pulled me into his embrace.

"Breathe." he said smoothly into my ear.

It was then that I realized I was holding my breath. I took in the most air I ever had. My body shook as I exhaled, the sobs escaping me as I let my soul bleed out. Derek rocked us back and forth as he tried to sooth me. I didn't understand him. How he could be so caring after everything I told him? So gentle? I tried not to think about it. Instead focusing on the feeling of his hands on me. I'd never let anyone hold me like this, ever. And never had I felt the need to be so close to another being. We stayed this way for a while. Until long after I stopped crying. The sound of Derek's heart beating in my ear as I leaned on him soothed me.

"Are you hungry?" he asked softly. I shook my head no. "Have you spoke to your grandmother today?" I shook my head yes, but I had only called and told her about Mary. We didn't talk about us. He pulled away slightly to look at me, but I couldn't look at him. I kept my eyes down. I felt disgusted with myself. Dirty.

"Autum." I still didn't look up. Derek reached with both hands to each side of my face, forcing my head up. I closed my eyes. "Autum, why won't you look at me?"

"I'm scared."

"Don't be scarred of me Autum, I won't hurt you."

"I know, not physically."

"Autum." His voice deeper, "Open your eyes."

I did, reluctantly. Knowing I would see his pity, he would be looking at me as damaged. My breath caught when I looked into his eyes. I saw none of that. I inhaled sharply and let out a shaky breath.

"You are still the same Autum that I met on that first day of school. The same Autum that stood up to Rebecca at school. The same Autum that walked with me in her garden. And you are so much more... To me."

I didn't say anything, but I could still feel the tears running down my cheeks. They wouldn't stop. I hated how emotional I was. I wanted to be strong. Derek made me want to be strong, want to be confident. I wanted to believe him, that he wanted more from me. I wanted more from him.

So, I took what I wanted, I kissed him. He tensed at first, surprised I had initiated the kiss. He kissed me back. I moved my hands to his neck and pulled him closer. His hands on my back did the same. This feeling was like a fairytale. I was a lost princess who just found her prince.

I pulled away first. Derek looked at me and wiped away the remaining tears. I moved to look around him and saw that it was 7:30 at night.

"What is it?" he asked.

"Is it too early to go to bed?"

He smiled at me, "No, not if you're tired. You are emotionally drained hmm?"

I nodded. "Will you lay with me?" I asked softly.

"Yes." he spoke just as softly, pushing some hair behind my ear. "I wouldn't leave, even if you asked me to." Derek got up and turned off the light. I changed into his shorts I used the night before and his shirt. He stripped to his boxers, laid in the bed, and spooned me.

"Thank you." I spoke.

"For what?"

"Being here."

"I won't leave. Ever, Autum."

"You don't know that." I said to him, finding it easier to talk now that the lights were off, and we weren't staring at each other.

Derek's hand reached under my shirt and rubbed across my stomach. "Do you feel that? The tingling? I pray every day to the Moon Goddess, Autum, that you will be my mate. But I know even without the prayers that you are."

"Yes, I feel it." Grabbing hold of some more courage from Goddess knows where I continued, "I crave it, miss it when you're not here." I moved my hand on top of his on my stomach.

He kissed my shoulder. "Sorry I didn't come see you sooner today after school. Mondays I do pack business with my dad."

As the tingles subsided from his kiss, I rolled my shoulder. "It's fine. I didn't mean for it to sound like that. Like I'm needy." Goddess, I did sound needy.

"I want you to need me." He lifted his hand and, starting at my shoulder, lightly dragged his fingers down my arm and up again. "I crave you too. And I longed to taste your lips on mine again and… More." He moved his fingers to my jaw and slightly turned my head towards him.

I wanted more too; I just was scared of my thoughts that were plagued in darkness…

"Talk to me Autum. Nothing you say will make me feel differently about you."

I inhaled a sharp breath. "I want you; I've never felt safer than I do right now. It's hard for me to believe that I could be so lucky. To hope that I could be your mate, but-"

"But what?" He asked.

"When I close my eyes… Now I see things in the darkness. Things that bring up bad memories." I exhaled, "And I don't know if I'll ever believe that the sight of my body doesn't repulse you. I don't know if or when I'll feel comfortable taking the next step."

"I will make it my life's goal to shower you in compliments, praise every inch of your skin. I am patient. I will wait for you to be comfortable. We won't do more than kissing until you ask, until you're ready. I will hold you every night if I have to, to chase away the darkness, if that's what you need. I'll keep you safe, protect you from the nightmares."

I grabbed his hand that was now resting on my stomach again. I lifted it to my lips and kissed his palm. Lacing our fingers, I placed it back around me. Derek tightened his grip and pulled me in tighter. His lips on the back of my head were the last things I felt as I drifted to sleep, protected against the nightmares.

24

MEETING LANA

❧

Autum POV

I woke alone to the lights dimmed low. It was ten a.m. I slept in late, but I still felt tired. I got up and went to the bathroom. Taking a shower, I thought about my conversation with Derek. After my shower I put Derek's clothes back on. I had planned on going to go downstairs but instead I took a deep breath and then let myself fall back onto the pillow. Looking up at the ceiling, I scrunched my nose. I could smell sunflowers and sage, but Derek wasn't in the room. Lifting my body up, I turned to look at the pillow.

A soft giggle left my lips when I saw the pillow tucked into Derek's shirt like a pillowcase. I fell face first into it, breathing deeply. Wrapping my hands around it, I gave it a big squeeze and let some of my anxiety go. I couldn't help but think of the possibility of being with Derek. Really being with him. I fell back to sleep, letting his scent calm me and dreaming of the possibilities.

I woke several hours later. I could hear a bit of laughter coming from outside the room. I sat up and looked towards the alarm clock, it was four p.m. A note sat on the nightstand.

"Good evening sleepy head, I'm downstairs babysitting. Come down when you're ready." – Derek

Walking to the bathroom I startled myself when I looked in the mirror. I looked like death. Sleep really did not help, I touched the bags under my swollen eyes, probably from crying and oversleeping. Sighing, I washed my face and put on a bit of concealer. I threw my hair up into a messy bun. I went to the closet and pulled out the second pair of clothes I had brought with me. I would need to do some laundry. Looking in the mirror, I still looked unwell but better. It could not be helped. So, I left the room and headed downstairs.

I could hear three voices now. Two men and a girl. As I neared the stairs Derek and Ethan came into view. They stopped talking as I walked down the stairs. Glancing around the room a small set of eyes peered at me from over the coach. She slowly raised her head higher. She was young, looked to be around ten. Her hair was the same dark color as Derek's, though much curlier. Derek, catching my gaze, made the introduction.

"This is my little sister Lana. Lana this is Autum."

I put on a soft smile. "Nice to meet you, Lana." The girl looked like she was about to burst. The excitement in her eyes. She had a bowl of popcorn that was flying everywhere as she softly bounced on the couch.

"I heard we had another girl staying here. I can't wait to play with you or watch movies with you." I sat down near her, and she bounced a little closer. I let out a small laugh. She continued, "I'm watching Mulan right now, it's a great movie. About a girl who everyone thinks is weak, but she gets strong and learns how to fight." Lana jumped off the couch. She flung the bowl of popcorn to me. She landed on the floor in a crouch then jumped up and did some crazy punching kicking combo that looked like it came right out of the movie. She smiled triumphally.

"Wow, that was pretty good." I said to her.

"I know," She responded. She did a little flip of her hair with her hand and sat back down on the couch. Taking back the bowl of popcorn. I looked at her in awe. Holding back a laugh, I looked up to Derek who was standing behind the couch with Ethan. Both watching in amusement.

"And that is my little sister!" Derek exclaimed. I let my laugh out then.

Derek came around the couch and put his hand out for me to take. "Come on, you must be hungry?"

I was. I took his hand and we walked to the kitchen. Ethan following. Derek didn't let go of my hand. I felt shy. Shyer than earlier. Maybe now because I knew how he felt about me. He wanted to be with me, mated to me, and me to him.

After we entered the kitchen and out of ear shot of his sister Derek asked, "How are you feeling?"

"I feel good actually."

I felt myself blush a little and Derek looked at me with an eyebrow raised. Turning towards him I laced our fingers together and leaned into his ear. "Thank you by the way."

"What for?" He asked.

"The shirt pillow," I softly smiled at him and put a light peck on his lips.

His eyes widened in surprise at my forwardness, most likely because Ethan was in the room. I smiled softly and Derek's eyes softened. I took a step back and turned to sit at the kitchen Island. Ethan's and I's eyes met and the look of surprise on his face confirmed my earlier thought. I quickly looked at the ground clearing my throat.

"So, what do you guys have to eat in this house?" I asked.

Derek, realizing he had completely gone immobile, started walking around the island to the stove. He was rubbing the back of his neck with his hand again. "I can make you some Spaghetti."

"That sounds good." I replied.

"If your making spaghetti, then I'm staying too!" Ethan exclaimed almost too excitedly and took the seat next to me. I looked at him amused. While Derek let out a small laugh.

"What?" Ethan asked.

"Are you really that excited over a box of noodles and a can of sauce?" I inquired. Ethan laughed this time and Derek let out a loud huff.

"Did I miss something?" I asked.

"A can of sauce," Derek said dramatically. "I'll let you know that I make the best spaghetti. I have a secret ingredient." He bragged.

"Well then, my apologies to the chef."

His sister walked into the kitchen at that time. On a mission from the looks of it. She was humming one of the songs from Mulan. She opened the kitchen closet and pulled out the broom. Derek rolled his eyes and helped her loosen and remove the broom end. She walked out of the kitchen with just the handle.

"Every day, I swear." I heard Derek mumble.

Curious, I got up as Lana walked back into the living room. Peering around the wall I watched her. She un-paused the movie and it was right at the beginning of 'Let's get down to business, to defeat the Huns.' Lana was twirling the broom stick like the characters in the movie and singing along. I couldn't help but smile.

I walked back and took my seat. "Your sister-" I started to say.

"Is a handful," Ethan cut me off.

"Is annoying and predictable," Derek cut him off.

It was my turn, "She's amazing and I already love her!"

Derek smirked and shook his head. "Just wait. You won't think that after listening to Mulan and Shrek every single day. And when I say every single day, I mean. Every. Single. Day."

"Anyways," I began. "What brings you over Ethan?" I turned to look at him.

"I actually came by to bring you your schoolwork." He walked out to the living room and returned with some folders. He was humming to one of the songs of Mulan.

I raised an eyebrow at him. He slowly let a smile creep to his face. "What?" He asked, "It's catchy." Derek took that opportunity to throw a dish towel at him.

"For real though, I hear it every day, do not bring that into my kitchen." Derek warned.

"Thanks for bringing my schoolwork, Ethan." I spoke. He slid the folders to me.

"So?" Ethan asked me, "How are you doing?"

Derek seemed to be busy at the stove. Close enough to be listening, but too busy to interact. He was pulling all sorts of seasonings out of the cupboard to season the meat. Turning slightly to talk to Ethan, but still watching Derek. I wanted to see his 'special' ingredients.

"I'm doing better. I definitely needed the sleep." I answered him.

He nodded for a few seconds, contemplating. "When's the last time you meditated?" Ethan asked.

Surprised by his question, "It's been a few days. But the last time doesn't really count, someone was distracting me." I shot a look towards Derek, who looked over his shoulder and smirked.

"What, really?" Ethan asked astonished. "Derek, you have never meditated with me. I've asked so many times."

"Well, what can I say, I've never really wanted to watch you bend over Ethan." Derek replied. Caught off by his amused vulgarity, my face warmed and I knew I was blushing.

"Anyways. Moving on," I said. "So, where are your parents, Derek?"

"Right, my parents. I meant to tell you that when you got up. They went to the hospital. They went to see Amy; they woke her up today."

"My parents are there too." Ethan spoke, "They wouldn't let me go." He looked angry. I know he cared for her. But I was still having trouble forgiving her. I started thinking about that night.

"Nope!" Derek clapped his hands. He walked around the island and hugged me from behind. "What do you need?" He asked me. Then turning to Ethan, "And you, you both are getting into your heads, let's not do that right now. There is nothing you can do about what happened or what is happening right now! So, what do we need?"

I looked at Ethan. We spoke together, "I need to meditate."

Derek looked at each of us. "Creepy but ok. I'll let you guys know when dinner is done. You have about thirty minutes." Derek kissed the top of my head and walked back to the stove. I watched him for a moment, cooking, then turned and led Ethan to my room.

25

A NEW FRIEND

❧

Autum POV

Ethan and I walked into my room. Leaving the door open so we could hear Derek when he called us down for dinner. We both walked to the largest open spot in my room and immediately took up the warrior pose.

"I'm impressed." I spoke.

"Really? You know," He paused. "Knew my grandmother. She made us do this."

"I'm sorry for your loss Ethan."

We stayed quiet for a moment. "You know I used to fuss so much when I was little, and grandma would make me stretch with her. Then at the end she would sit for hours. I used to think I was sneaky, getting away while her eyes were closed."

I nodded in understanding. "It was the only thing that kept me grounded growing up. Your grandmother meant a lot to me. Thank you for sharing her."

He looked at me briefly before nodding. "She kept me grounded too. When my powers started so young my parents were really lost. They sent me to Dr. Warren first. They thought maybe she could help me learn to self sooth and calm myself down. When that didn't work gram started making me meditate with her. She would go through these stretches. I thought I was so smart, learning them so quickly." He laughed to himself. "And grandma always made me feel like it too. She would praise me. I would sit with her for what felt like to 6-year-old me, forever. Then I would sneak off. And she would let me. Now I would give anything to be sitting next to her again." he finished.

We transitioned into the Sacral Chakra from the Root Chakra. Sitting on the floor and pushing both legs out as far as they would go, I leaned forward onto my arms. I could almost do the splits I'd done this so many times. I was feeling good about myself in that sliver of a moment. "Your grandma gave me back my life. I know it sounds dramatic, but she really did. Knowing what I know now," I shook my head softly. "I really don't think I would have chosen to live."

I could feel Ethan looking at me. But I didn't meet his gaze. I couldn't. "I'm sorry you couldn't be there. In her last moments," I said.

"I'm glad that someone was." He responded. "Besides, it's like she knew it was coming. She called us all to her bedside the night before. My mother thought she was being overly dramatic. Turns out she wasn't. I'm sure she is angry at herself for not spending that time with her. My grandmother literally told my mother 'Death waits for no one' the night before she died."

We moved into the next pose. The Solar Plexus Chakra. This was a sitting position. One leg bent on the floor, one up over the other. Body twisted looking to the side. With one arm pushing against your knee. Ethan transposed his legs, so we were looking at each other.

He continued, "Not that it matters much, she was mostly talking in riddles."

"How do you mean?" I asked.

"At first, she was telling us her time had come. My mother wasn't having it so she told her she would call the doctor and have her checked out. Grandma waved her away, said there was no point. I remember my mother rolling her eyes. She kissed grandma on the head and told her goodnight before she and Dad left for bed. Rebecca and I were both there with her, on either side of her. She held our hands in each of hers. She asked us to sit next to her, so we did. She told us that she loves us and to keep each other safe." Ethan paused.

"That doesn't sound like riddles to me," I spoke.

Ethan dropped his eyes for a second. "She started staring at Rebecca for a long time. It was uncomfortable how long she stared. Rebecca glanced at me several times and I shrugged my shoulders at her. We didn't know how to react to the awkward silence. Rebecca tried to get up to leave but grandma held her firm. Her words were eerie, but I'll never forget them."

"'Child you have an evil in you.' Gram let go of my hand and she reached for Rebecca's cheek. 'Oh child, the light will find you and when it does let it in' Rebecca stood and walked out of the room. I thought I saw her crying, but I didn't understand what grandma was saying. She turned to me next and clasped both of my hands. She leaned in closer to me."

"'There's a prophecy coming undone, and you will have to be as one. The evil is here, it exists, we can no longer live in this bliss. When the time comes you will join, through brush you will travel to the poin. Through the darkness you must seek, to the one who's heart is not feeble nor weak.' I tried telling her she wasn't making sense. She just patted my hand and said she couldn't say more."

"'She is always listening when you call her name' grandma whispered. Who grandma, I had asked her. 'The Heiress my boy, the Heiress of darkness.' She was looking past me at that moment. Like someone else was in the room. I felt a shiver as she pulled my hands until I was leaning close enough, she could whisper in my ear. she cannot see all, she does not know that she has arrived' she had said. I asked who. She spoke but two words 'our queen.' That was the last thing she said to me." He finished.

I was speechless, looking at each other we moved into the heart chakra. It was like a downward dog pose. I exhaled deeply.

"Your grandmother was the same way when I visited." I took another deep breath. "She was telling me that the evil had been but a whisper but now it was here. She said that a prophecy she thought was gone was actually happening. She told me to be careful who I trust." At those words we glanced in each other's direction.

He asked, "So is this you trusting me?"

"Well, you did see my eyes glow when I borrowed Rebecca's powers at school and I'm sure you realized the lightning at Samantha's was not your doing?" He nodded, so I continued, "Well I didn't have anyone banging down my doors demanding answers. You also opening up to me now proves you have nothing you're trying to hide. Also, I just have a genuinely good feeling about you, so yes, I'm choosing to trust you."

He didn't offer any other words, so I continued, "Your grandmother said that you know who, is here and that she has been blocking herself with the energy she collects around her."

"You know who?" he questioned.

"Your gram said that she could hear her name being called, I'm not chancing it. I felt a shiver that morning with her, I believed her."

"Who you guys talking about?" Lana walked into my room asking.

Ethan and I moved into the Throat Chakra pose. Remembering Derek trying this pose made me smile to myself. We lay flat on our backs, feet on the floor, knees up, then lift our hips. Bracing your body with your hands still on the floor. It was difficult to talk like this. I took a deep breath and then exhaled.

"Nothing you should concern yourself with little one," I answered Lana.

She moved to stand over me, "Who are you calling little?" Hands on her hips and a very serious face. I fell to the floor trying to hold in my laugh.

"Hey now, I didn't mean anything by it. You're a warrior, your just little still." I responded to her.

She nodded in approval and started mimicking Ethan and me. "So, what are you two doing anyways, Derek wanted me to tell you dinner would be ready in ten minutes." I repositioned myself into the correct posture and watched as Lana copied.

"We are moving through the Chakra poses and at the end we meditate to calm our minds and find peace within ourselves," I answered with a smile. I couldn't see Lana's face now as we were all lying on the floor. But I could imagine her face looked like disbelief. Most People didn't believe in this stuff.

"Sounds good. Why doesn't everyone do this?" She surprised me when she answered.

I let out a small laugh and decided to move into the Third eye and Crown Chakra pose. They were in similar positions; sitting with legs crossed. Ethan followed me and so did Lana.

"So, who is 'you know who'?" she did little air quotes with her hands.

I sighed she must have heard us walking into the room. I responded, "She is an evil woman, we can't speak her name, or she could hear us." Thinking this bit of information shouldn't be too much and knowing she'd keep asking if I didn't give her something.

She jumped up from the floor, "Oh, I know! We need a code name!" she said excitedly.

Thinking on it she was right, "That's actually a good idea. You know any evil women names we could use Lana?"

She put her hands together, tapping her fingers together sinisterly and smiled, "I have a name." wide eyed she continued, "Lilith."

"Why Lilith?" Ethan asked before I could.

"Well," she began, "Lilith is the mean girl at my school, and she is just rotten." She huffed.

I shook my head at her amusingly. "Lilith sounds like the perfect code word, thanks little one." I winked at her, and she smiled like she'd won a prize.

"Thanks, I'm going to go finish my movie." She looked down at her watch, "Dinner in five minutes." She said before walking out.

We both sat there in silence focusing within ourselves. I felt the air move around me, and a lightness took over. I opened my eyes, and I was floating above my body. I was made of light, like before when I remembered everything. I looked around the room and saw Ethan. Still sitting with perfect posture and completely relaxed. My eyes widened as I took in the figure sitting in front of him.

"Mary?"

"Hello child."

"How are you here?"

"The easy answer is that I'm not." She smiled playfully at me. Seeing that I wasn't amused she continued, "This is the last of my soul. Once I've decided to move on, I'll be reborn. But for now, there is too much unfinished business."

She stood up and held out her hand. "Come we need to go see Amy."

"What do you mean?"

"You just need to think of Amy, and we will go there" she replied.

I did as she said, closing my eyes, when I opened them, we were outside her house. I looked at her in amazement. "But I'm not really here, right?" I asked her.

"Your body is not here, but your energy is," she said.

"How?" is all I managed to say.

"It is one of your gifts, your white wolf gifts."

"How do I have these gifts when I don't have my wolf yet?" I asked.

She looked thoughtful for a moment. "We all have our wolves when we are born, their souls attached to our souls. They just don't materialize until we are eighteen, when your mind and body are strong enough to cope with the change of having two souls in one body and one mind. You though," she paused and placed her hand on my cheek. "You had a very traumatic event as a child, and you were given your moon gifts early to help protect you. They are not at their full strength; however, they will get stronger the closer you get to your birthday." She gave me a knowing smile but didn't continue.

"So how do we do this, we just walk through the wall?" I ask somewhat sarcastically.

She nodded, "Yes, but I would like you to rewind it back to the time they arrive so we can watch the whole interaction." She asked.

"Why don't you do it?"

She laughed. "Child, I don't have that gift. I'm just here because I haven't moved on yet, but I will eventually. For now, I'm here for you. There are so many things you don't know, and I'll be here to answer the questions that I can." She answered.

"One more question before I do this," I paused. "How did you see me at the hospital?"

She shrugged, "I don't know exactly, maybe it had something to do with the way I'm able to heal. I use energy from the earth and myself to heal others. Your gift seems to be 'power absorption' of some kind. You can use all types of energy. That's why you were able to help the bird. I don't know how strong your healing will be, but you should be able to do that and so much more when you get your wolf. I can see energy moving around us when I'm using my gift. You were using your energy like you are now and I was healing you in the hospital, then I saw it, your energy. I saw you."

I didn't know what to say when she finished. So, I lifted my hand and made a swirling motion with my hand counterclockwise. Time started reversing and I stopped it when I saw cars approaching. I looked down at my hands, disbelief apparent on my face.

"You are more Autum, so much more." I didn't respond.

Alpha Darren and Luna Synthia parked at the pack house and walked over while everyone else parked in front of Amy's residence. Amy's parents, Delta Anthony, and Lyla, were on either side of her as she held herself and walked in the house. Dr. Warren walking close behind. Beta Richard and Elissa were also there. We followed them inside. I sped up time slightly, I couldn't be late for dinner, and I had already far surpassed the five minutes Lana warned about.

Amy sat on the couch between her parents. Her mother placed her hand around her shoulders and Amy leaned on her.

"Alpha, thank you for moving the meeting to my house. We needed to get Amy out of the hospital, she'll feel more comfortable being at home for this discussion." Delta Anthony said, he looked to his wife and daughter.

Lyla nodded and looked down at Amy, "Ok, honey tell the Alpha what you told us at the hospital."

Amy looked up to Alpha Darren who was still standing. Tears instantly streamed down her face. "It's like you've already heard... that I was... choking Autum." Then she addressed Beta Richard and Synthia, "But, I don't think it was Rebecca." Everyone looked confused. Amy continued, "When Rebecca persuades me, I don't know she's doing it. I think it is my idea. I have to be told that she was persuading me."

"And you do remember?" Alpha Darren asked.

She nodded frantically. She was holding herself so tight her knuckles were turning white. "I wasn't in control of my body. I could see and feel everything I was doing and saying but I couldn't stop myself. I was screaming in my head, screaming so loud." She paused again, her voice shaking, "I was telling myself to stop, to let her go. No one could hear me, hear my plea to stop. I can still hear the screaming." She grabbed her head covering her ears like she was reliving the event again in her head. She was trying to rock herself to calm down. Her mother, Lyla, held her tighter rocking with her.

Dr. Warren stepped in, taking Amy's hand in hers, "Breathe Amy, in two, three, four. Out two, three, four. Again...very good." She nodded to Alpha Darren to continue.

"When did you get your functions back?" He asked.

"I- I don't know... that next morning maybe or while I was sleeping. When the lightning hit me, I was mute, I still couldn't talk or move. I just laid there, my body in pain and no one could hear me writhing. The pain," she paused. "It was like nothing I'd felt before. I blacked out from it. The next morning when I woke up screaming and Ethan could hear me, I thought the whole thing had been a nightmare. Until I realized my skin still felt like it was on fire. I blacked out a second time from the pain."

Alpha Darren seemed to ponder for a moment. "How do you feel now?"

"Scared." One word is all she managed to say. Her eyes seemed to glaze over as she lay there on her mother. She was lost in her thoughts, probably trapped there.

"I came here tonight ready to hand out punishment for your actions." He looked at Amy and knelt down beside her, "but I see now that you are also a victim in this. I am going to call a council meeting and we will all discuss everything you said happened and look into how it happened." Alpha Darren looked stressed; he was worried about something but wasn't saying it.

Everything slowed down to real time, and I looked at Mary confused. "What happened?" I asked her.

"Looks like you can't see into the future, only watch what has already happened and what is presently happening."

Dr. Warren stood from her position next to Amy. "Alpha, I would formally like to request a seat on the council. Given the events that are taking place, you could use all the help you can get."

"I'm sorry Doctor, but you are not a ranked member of the pack. That's not a request you can make. We've discussed this before." Alpha Darren responded.

For a split second you could see Dr. Warren was angry. She quickly recovered, "Then sir, let me sit in as a special consultant. I have information that I think would be helpful with this." She glanced down at Amy.

"I'll consider it with the council. I'll get back to you tomorrow." He spoke.

I looked to Mary who had her eyebrows scrunched up. I wanted to ask her about this ranked member of the pack thing, but she looked worried.

"What is it?" I asked her.

"I feel…" she paused, "Darkness."

I paused to take in my surroundings, I could feel something too. It made my stomach knot up. "I feel it too. What is it?"

"I think SHE is here, maybe watching too."

"You mean the Heir-"

She cut me off, "Watch your tongue child."

"Right, sorry. We actually have a code name now, curtesy of Lana. We call her Lilith."

"Lilith?"

"Yes." I explained how we came to the name.

"Ok, so Lilith, I can work with that," Mary replied. "I can feel her negative energy. She must be close or watching like we are watching."

"Will she be able to see us?" I asked, almost panicked.

"No, no, no. Don't worry. But she can probably feel our presence like we can feel hers." She glanced around, "They are finishing up anyways we should head back."

I took us back to the pack house, to my room. "So, how do I get back into my body?"

As I asked the question, Ethan stood and walked over to me. He put his hand on my shoulder and called my name. It was an odd sensation. I could feel his hand on my shoulder, although I wasn't in my body. His voice echoed when he spoke. Like talking in a long tunnel, the sound muffled but you can still make out the words.

"Just think it, and you will open your eyes in your own body." She replied. So, I did just that, I closed my eyes and when I opened them Ethan was in my face staring at me. "Can I help you?" I asked him.

He started laughing, "You didn't hear me?" He questioned.

I backed up from him, "Come on, we are late for dinner."

He smirked, "Late, I'm never late for anything. It's been exactly five minutes."

I looked at him, one eyebrow lifted. "It's been at least an hour or two."

"Stop messing around, and let's go eat." He spoke.

I stopped him at the door. "No, wait. Seriously though, how long has it been since Lana walked out."

"Autum, it's only been five minutes." I must have looked completely dumfounded.

"Are you ok?" He asked.

"I'm fine, just forget it. Let's go eat." It was slowly making sense. Time didn't move at the same speed when I was in that energy state. The same thing happened when I joined Bone Creek Pack. Derek said it had only been minutes that day as well. It felt like at least an hour.

26

SECRET INGREDIENT

࿐

Autum POV

When we opened the door the smell of spices filled the air. I could smell the sausage and the Italian seasoning, the basil and so much more. Derek was dishing up the plates when we arrived in the kitchen. Lana was standing next to him with a dirty plate and spaghetti sauce all over her face. She was holding her plate up for more.

A small laugh left my lips, "Is it really that good?"

"No, its awful tasting, you should give your plate to me." Lana said in complete seriousness.

Derek laughed at her and gave her another heaping helping. "That's it though Lana, mom and dad will want some too. They are on their way back from Delta Anthonys." Derek handed Ethan and I each a plate. We all walked to the table. A timer started going off as we sat down, "Oh yeah, forgot the biscuits." Derek jumped up.

"You made biscuits too?" I asked incredulously.

"My famous drop biscuits, you're going to love them." Derek gave us each a biscuit and we dug in.

Oh, my Goddess! This is the best spaghetti I have ever tasted! I swallowed the first bite, "What did you put in this, this is amazing." I took another bite.

Derek was smirking, but before he could answer his parents walked into the kitchen. His father answered, "He made it with love, that's the special ingredient!"

"Ok, but really what did you put in it?" I asked.

Derek laughed, "No, he's right, you could try and duplicate it, but you won't be able to!" Alpha Darren and Luna Synthia dished themselves up a plate and joined us for dinner. Lana had already finished her second plate and was told to go wash up and get ready for bed.

"So," Alpha Darren started, "We have spoken to Amy, and I believe the events that took place where not her fault." He looked at me. I nodded. Seeing what I saw when Amy told her story, I believed her. Ethan visibly relaxed a little. I knew he liked Amy. Alpha Darren interrupted my thoughts.

"You seem ok with that decision Autum, though you look like you have questions?"

"No sir, I believed her. I mean you, I believe you." I gulped, that was a slip up I didn't expect to make. Derek and Ethan didn't look like they suspected anything, but Alpha Darren and now Synthia were both looking at me. I looked down at my plate and kept eating. Avoiding eye contact.

Alpha Darren continued, "I also believe that Rebecca was being honest when she said she didn't tell Amy to try and kill you." I only nodded this time, not wanting to overshare again. Ethan actually let out a long breath. Poor guy, stuck between his sister and Amy and the things that they did must have been hard for him. Luna Synthia patted his hand. We all felt a bit relieved for him.

Lana walked back in and gave her parents a kiss good night. She walked over to Derek, and he kissed her cheek and gave her a hug. Such a good big brother. Lana came to me and hugged me. I was surprised and wide eyed I hugged her back. Then she paused in front of me and pointed to her cheek. Did she want me to kiss her too? I looked at Derek. He laughed, "She won't go to bed without a kiss good night," he said.

I couldn't help but think this child was special. I kissed her cheek. She was making me feel like part of the family. Lana left for bed. Ethan stood at that time and went and washed his plate and put it in the dish washer.

"It's time for me to head home. Thank you, Alpha, Luna." He bowed slightly. Then he turned to Derek and Me, "See you two at school tomorrow." I nodded and Derek got up to hug him. They embraced a little longer than usual. They always seemed close. Ethan relaxed more, needing the reassurance everything was going to work out from Derek.

After, we sat there in silence while we finished eating for a moment. Luna Synthia broke the silence, "So you plan on going to school tomorrow, Autum?"

"Yes, I think I need to. Knowing that Amy and Rebecca weren't being malicious has helped me relax enough to know that I will be ok seeing them."

"You mean 'hearing' that Amy and Rebecca weren't being malicious." Alpha Darren corrected me, lifting his eyebrow at me in question.

"Right, hearing you say that they weren't," I said softly.

"How long are you going to lie to me Autum?" Alpha Darren questioned.

Derek intervened, "What would she be lying about, she-" I stopped him by placing my hand on his. I didn't look at him but to Alpha Darren.

"I didn't intentionally lie Alpha," I started. I looked down at the table for a second and took a breath. "I didn't know I could... see things."

"Explain it to me." Alpha Darren asked in a lighter tone this time. I looked at Derek, he squeezed my hand in reassurance and nodded. Telling me I could trust his father and mother.

"When I meditate now, I can go to places, and I can watch what is happening." I replied.

"And you couldn't do this before?" He questioned.

"No sir."

"When did it start?"

"After you accepted me into the pack sir, but I've only done it twice."

"What have you witnessed happening during these two meditations?"

I must have started crying because Derek lifted his hand to my face to wipe the tear that escaped. His mother moved and took the other seat next to me, she placed one hand on my knee and one on my shoulder.

"You don't have to say that." She gave me a pointed look then turned a sharp eye to her husband. He looked baffled. It wasn't his fault, he didn't know. "Just tell us what you saw the second time?" She clarified.

I nodded, "Tonight I was meditating in my room with Ethan." I paused for a long time. Should I tell them about Mary? Would they think I'm crazy? I let out a loud sigh. Here goes nothing, "I saw my physical self, sitting on the floor, but I was floating above; made from energy, I looked like translucent gold light. And." I took another deep breath, "I saw Mary too." Everyone looked shocked. I almost felt embarrassed. I felt like, I sounded like a crazy person.

"Why Mary?" Luna Synthia asked.

"I don't know all the whys. I only know she told me it's because she hasn't moved on yet, that there is still too much unfinished business and too much that I do not know."

"She said that, that there was too much you didn't know?" Alpha Darren asked.

I nodded. "I don't know all that she meant, only that a darkness is coming. We have named her Lilith as to not speak her title."

"I've heard that as well, that if you speak her name, you are inviting her into your conversation." Luna Synthia responded.

Alpha Darren nodded. "What else happened?"

"I was able to transport myself to Amy's house. Mary and I watched the conversation with all of you."

"And this has no physical strain on you?" Alpha Darren asked.

"It does make me tired, but I've learned to replenish myself with the energy from the earth. My ability, from what Mary and I can tell is 'power absorption.' I can absorb energy from almost anywhere. I can even absorb others energy."

"To what end?" Alpha Darren asked.

"I don't know yet sir. So far, I've been able to absorb Rebecca and Ethan's gifts, leaving them unable to use them temporarily. I've also been able to focus energy and… project it from my hands." I say hesitantly.

Alpha Darren and Luna Synthia glanced to each other. "I am having a council meeting tomorrow while you two are at school. Although Autum, you already knew that didn't you?" He smiled at me.

That one gesture helped me. The dread I was having after telling him about my abilities was making me feel uneasy. I was worried they'd reject me, want nothing to do with me. He continued, "Nothing you have said tonight leaves this room. Nothing. Don't tell your friends and don't tell anyone on the council." He expressed with concern.

I looked at Derek and we both nodded, Derek spoke, "Ethan already knows some of it, not all of it but he knows she can take other's abilities."

"You need to call him, before you go to bed," His father replied. "And Autum, we need to find your fathers family." He paused in thought, "You have to be a white wolf with the abilities you have. And your grandmother didn't know. White wolves are highly coveted, you could have been in danger.

Although I don't understand why you got your moon gifts before your wolf presented itself, none the less we need to know if you have siblings or if you were the first born." Alpha Darren said.

"Three things," I interjected, "One, Mary told me she believes I got my gift early because of the traumatic events that happened when I was a child." I briefly looked to Luna Synthia, "Second, why would I have been in danger? You have white wolves here. And thirdly, siblings and being born first, why does any of that matter?"

Luna Synthia answered my first question, "No one outside the pack knows that we have a white wolf family here. We have gone to great lengths to protect them. Beta Richard goes with Elissa anytime she goes on a run as well as extra pack warriors, to monitor the borders. It will be more difficult after the twins get their wolves, but we are already prepared."

"Why are you prepared so early?" I questioned. Luna Synthia looked to Alpha Darren. Something seemed off, what were they hiding? I looked at Derek, he seemed just as concerned as I was.

"Dad?" Derek questioned.

"We were going to wait until after the council meeting to talk to the two of you. We are concerned that Rebecca and Ethan will phase early."

Wide eyed I asked, "Really? Why? Has it happened before?"

"It has before in white wolves. With them getting their abilities early as well, it is highly likely."

"Do they know?" Derek asked.

"No, not yet."

"Then why tell us?" I asked.

"Because you can absorb their abilities. We will need you there in case their bodies and minds are overwhelmed with the change. Not to mention I'm unsure about Rebecca. She seems better but I don't know if it's an act. She may be subdued for now, but we don't know about her wolf and how she will take my command on her." Alpha Darren responded. This was such a big bomb to drop on me. And how would I absorb their abilities without anyone seeing? Derek instantly started rubbing my back, he must have seen the panic on my face.

"You can't ask her to do that. Everyone will be able to see she has gifts too." Derek protested.

Synthia asked, "How would others know, just don't use them."

"My eyes glow. How do you know I'm strong enough to take on both of them at the same time?" I asked as I stood up and started pacing.

Synthia stood and walked over to me. Stepping in front of me, she started rubbing my arms. "Look at me Autum." I did. She spoke again. "You are strong. You can feel it." She put one of her hands on my chest. "Your abilities are growing too." She nodded at me. She was right. I could feel that I was getting stronger. Able to control the energy flowing through me.

"I have school for the first time tomorrow with Rebecca," I paused. "I will let you know after school, how I feel about it." Alpha Darren, satisfied with my answer, nodded.

"And no one can know what I can do. I know Ethan knows, and there is a possibility that their parents know, because of Mary. Mary knew." I spoke.

"Did you ever tell Dr. Warren during any of your sessions?" Alpha Darren asked.

"No, she has been canceling our appointments since I found out. She's been needing to be with Rebecca. I'm not even sure I still need to see her. The whole purpose was to unlock my memories. I did that without her." Derek stood from the chair and came and stood next to me. He placed his hand on my lower back. His touch relaxed me. His presence calmed me. I met his eyes.

Derek asked, "Do you know if you have any siblings or if you were the first born?"

I shook my head, "No, but why does being first born matter?" I questioned.

Alpha Darren responded, "The first born gets certain privileges. Like for Derek, he will become Alpha, and he will be the strongest of his siblings. For you…" He hesitated. "If you were the first born it could be why you have such a unique gift."

"I'm not following" I said.

Synthia replied, "We have two facts that have held true. One, that all first born are the strongest of any sibling. Two, that all white wolves get a moon gift. So, following with that logic, most have speculated that if a wolf is white and first born, there is chance for them to be granted the gift from the original family."

"So, you think my gift of power absorption is a gift from the original family?"

"Yes and no," Synthia responded. "It's getting late, why don't we finish this conversation tomorrow after you two get home from school."

"We also have the funeral to go to tomorrow evening," Alpha Darren added.

I had so many questions, I didn't want to go to bed. "Come on," Derek pushed, "I'll walk you to your room."

"But-" I started to say but Synthia interrupted.

"I promise, we'll answer more of your questions tomorrow." I nodded and let Derek lead me upstairs to bed.

27

MIDNIGHT RENDEZVOUS

❧

Autum POV

Derek walked me to my room, opening my door for me. I didn't want him to go. His parents walked by us; I swear I saw his mother smirk at me. Ignoring that I saw anything, I walked into my room and turned around to face Derek. He was leaning in the doorway. He had been watching me walk in and his eyes were still low. Probably looking at my ass. The feelings between us had been growing. With each day, each kiss, I craved him more. I wanted to feel his touch on my body. He was taking me all in. I cleared my throat to get his attention.

"Sorry," he mumbled as he met my eyes.

"Mmhmm."

He turned his head and pointed at his cheek.

"What, do you want a kiss good night too?" I asked.

"Well, you gave Lana one, it's only fair." He smirked.

I took a few steps back to him and leaned to kiss his cheek. Then I kissed the other one. Finally, I placed a soft kiss on his lips, while I gazed into his eyes. He reached out and grabbed my hips. Startling me, I gasped at his touch as my shirt rode up and his hands were on my bare skin. We stood there in silence for a moment. Our eyes didn't leave each other's, and I could hardly make out my own breathing, my breaths were that shallow. Derek lifted his hand to my cheek, and I leaned into it. His eyes were on my lips again, but he looked hungry. I licked my lips feeling the heat from his gaze. Remembering his words from the night before. He wanted more when I was ready... How much more could I give him tonight? I felt my face heat up.

"Kiss me again." His breath warm on my face.

I didn't say anything, he wasn't asking for permission. It was a command. It surprised me how much I wanted to obey. I wanted to make him happy too, like he has done for me. I closed my eyes and leaned in. I felt myself shiver.

"Open your eyes Autum," he whispered. He gently moved his hand to the nape of my neck and my eyes opened. Derek's lips connected with mine and I could see into his soul in that moment.

His lips on mine tingled and another shiver went down my body. This kiss was not gentle. He was dominating my mouth. He kissed me like he needed me. I kissed him back, adding pressure to the kiss. His hand on my lower back pulled me in closer. My arm moved up around his neck, and my hands fisted his hair. I wanted more... So much more. The kiss deepened before we pulled apart, both taking in a deep breath. I could feel my chest heaving and see him doing the same. He took a step forward, forcing me into the room farther. He shut the door and turned me around. My back now against the door. My body wanting more of him, I leaned in and kissed him. He answered my kiss with more force than the first one.

His hands started roaming down my back. One under my ass pulled me in as he squeezed it. My body wanted him, my hips rolled against him as a soft moan left my lips. He licked my bottom lip, and I parted them, inviting him in. His tongue was silky and tasted every inch of my mouth. My hands were on his chest now as I felt every ripple of his muscles through his shirt. My hands moved lower as he kissed me. I felt the bottom of his shirt hem and pushed my hands up inside his shirt. His skin was so warm, and I knew he could feel the sparks wherever my hands touched him.

His hands squeezed my ass and lifted me up. I wrapped my legs around him. One hand had moved to my front and brushed against my nipples. They were so hard it was almost painful. I didn't stop him as he started massaging my breast. My mind wanted his lips on them too. I started to think what it would feel like to have his hot breath caressing my most sensitive parts.

We parted to take another breath and he started kissing my neck. He kissed and sucked on my marking spot where my neck meets my collar bone. Another moan left me, and I felt the wetness between my legs. I felt my face redden as I heated up. I would never get used to feeling like this. I had started to crave it and I knew my arousal would perfume the room. Derek stiffened as the scent hit him and I felt him instantly harden under me. I suddenly became hyper aware of what we were headed towards. I wasn't ready for sex and just like that my mind took over and I felt my body tense. Derek felt it too. He leaned his head onto my shoulder with a soft sigh.

"Sorry," He spoke softly.

"No," is all I said. He pulled his head up to look at me. "I wanted you to," I said shyly, "I'm just not ready for-"

He gave me quick peck cutting me off, "I know." He put me down. "I should sleep in my room tonight." He rubbed the back of his neck and adjusted his pants. I nodded. It was a good idea. I don't think I could stop myself if he slept in my bed. I knew I wasn't ready, but I also knew I wanted him. I felt my face blush and bit my bottom lip. I looked at the ground.

"It drives me crazy when you do that, you know."

"Do what?" I asked.

He stepped forward rubbing his thumb across my bottom lip. "When you bite your lip like that." He pulled my lip from my teeth and kissed me softly. I let out a shaky breath. "And when you get flushed." His thumb caressed my cheek, and he kissed me again.

"I'm going to go now, Good Night Autum." His hand fell from my cheek, and he stepped back towards the door, still watching me.

I smiled and said good night. Derek slipped out of my door leaving me heated and my core throbbing. I didn't know what to do with myself.

I paced in my room for a few minutes. I couldn't stop thinking of Derek and his hands on me and his lips. I touched my lips at the thought of his lips on mine. Frustrated, mostly at myself, I walked to my bathroom and got the shower ready. I undressed and let the hot water run over me. Thoughts of his hands caressing my ass and remembering the heat and wetness I felt, filled my head.

I turned the shower to cold. Yes, a cold shower. I finished washing and got out of the shower. I put on some underwear and Derek's shirt I had worn the night before. It still smelt like him, though faint, it would have to do. I tried to lay down, but I couldn't take my mind off Derek. I looked at the clock. It had only been thirty minutes since he left, but it seemed like hours already. What was wrong with me? I felt like screaming into my pillow. These emotions were so strong, I was longing for him to just touch me again. I grabbed my pillow, holding it over my face. This was crazy right? I was acting crazy. I inhaled his scent from his shirt pillow. It just made me want him more.

I got out of bed and walked to my door. I needed tea or something to calm down. I was not going to sleep like this. I cracked the door open and looked both ways down the hall. No one was awake. I slipped downstairs to the kitchen and started rummaging through the cupboards. I found a small box of chamomile tea. Not like what we have at our house, but it would have to do. I grabbed two from the box, convincing myself this would help me sleep. I found a tea pot in one of the cupboards and put some water on the stove.

Waiting for the water to boil was excruciating. How could Derek be asleep right now? Was he not feeling what I felt? I was facing the counter and leaned down. Elbows on the counter I put my face in my hands. Crossing my legs to help with the throbbing. I'd almost consider touching myself at this point. Never had I tried but this was becoming painful.

I felt my eyes start to brim with tears. How could I go from punching him to craving him, this was madness. I was angry at myself for feeling this way. My body was aching, it started to hurt all over as my muscles contracted and released over and over again. Trying to hold myself together. I felt the tears escape my eyes. Suddenly I felt warm sparks on my sides and knew Derek was behind me. I took a sharp breath. And sat up. My back to his chest.

"Your upset, what's wrong?" He asked.

"Um, nothing I'm fine." I wiped my eyes.

Derek turned me around. He laid his hand on my cheek, "You were crying." He pinched his eyebrows together, then softened his expression, "I'm sorry, I went too far earlier."

"No, I- I-" I didn't finish. I was embarrassed. How could I tell him I needed this, needed him to hold me. Needed his hands on me. The comfort and security I felt with him. I wanted him. I started shaking my head.

"Tell me what's wrong, you can tell me. I won't be mad." He pleaded.

I didn't know what to say. I couldn't say what I wanted to say. I reached up and grabbed his face in both hands. Pulling him into a kiss. He kissed me back gently; he was being cautious. He pulled away.

"Are you kissing me because that's what I want?" He asked.

Shaking my head, no, his hands slowly traveled down my sides to the bottom of the shirt. When he realized I wasn't wearing shorts his eyebrows shot up in surprise. I bit my bottom lip and felt my body heat again. My core already throbbing from earlier needed almost no motivation to start pulsing again. My heart was pounding in my chest and all I could do was stare into his eyes. I was mesmerized. My arms around his neck now played with his hair line.

"I told you that when you bite your lip like that it drives me crazy." He smiled playfully.

He leaned in for another kiss, grabbing my nape with one hand and his other still playing with my silky underwear, grabbing my ass cheek. I felt the heat and throb at my core, dampening my underwear. My arousal started making itself known. He pulled his lips from mine. "So, you weren't upset with me?" he asked softly.

"No," I answered. "With myself."

"Why?" he probed, now peppering kisses down my neck. I tilted my neck to the side giving him more access. He kissed my marking spot, and I stifled a moan. "Autum?"

"I was feeling… I… wanted… you." I let out in small pants as he sucked on my neck.

He stopped kissing me, and looked at me, smiling to his eyes. "Why didn't you just, you know, take care of yourself if you were that distressed."

I buried my head in his chest, not wanting to meet his eyes, shaking my head no, "I've never." Is all I said.

I don't know what his face looked like after learning that bit of information. But his hands started sliding up my sides. His thumbs grazing the sides of my breasts. My nipples instantly hardened, and I could feel the fabric of the shirt rubbing on them from the movement of his hands. I parted my lips, letting a small breath escape. Derek captured my lips with his, moving his tongue in quickly. I was lost in his touch.

Derek started kissing my jaw and moved one hand to cover my breast completely. His other hand started moving south. As his lips descended my neck to my marking spot his hand was gliding across my stomach leaving goosebumps everywhere he touched. Reaching the top of my panties, he slowed, hesitating, waiting for me.

"Don't stop." I breathed out.

Slowly, he continued. His hand on the outside of my panties moved south. The small amount of pressure from his touch building the pressure inside me. Reaching my clit, he pressed firmer but continued down, till he felt they were damp. I could feel him smile through our kiss as he moved his hand cupping my throbbing core. Rubbing his fingers softly back and forth until my underwear became much wetter. I covered my mouth with the back of my hand, unable to hold back the moans. He slid his finger under the side of my underwear. When I didn't protest, he slid them to the side and when his warm hands touched me, my head fell back. My core instantly clenched.

The pressure was building, my body hot and wanting. I moved one hand to the counter for support as my legs started shaking. He kept circling my clit with his whole hand, touching every sensitive spot I had. My thoughts kept moving from one action to the next. Derek's hot breath on my neck as he left love bites all over my neck and his fingers still circling my clit had me wanting to scream. In one swift motion Derek moved his hand under my ass and lifted me to the counter. He used his body to spread my legs wider and inserted one finger. My moan was silenced when he captured my lips with his. My breathing became harsh as he slowly pumped his finger in and out. My juices coating his hand, his thumb still circling my clit. He curled his finger and started moving faster. My body moved to his rhythm as he strummed me and kissed me and touched every inch of my body.

Derek released my lips, "Your so wet." His husky voice in my ear driving me nearer to my orgasm. Derek added a second finger and pushed them in. Holding for a moment to let me stretch around them. Then he went deeper and faster, still curling his two fingers. His hands were large and rough, the ridges massaging my core and making me wetter. "Are you going to come for me, Autum?"

"Yes." I managed between breaths.

He started breathing harder into my ear, "Come for me Autum." His voice was deep and menacing as he moved faster inside me until my core clenched.

I felt my orgasm roll over me in waves of heat. I dropped my head back and felt my toes curl. My knees were shaking and clenching to Derek's side. My moans lost behind the sound of the tea kettle finally going off. Derek slowed his movements and then slowly pulled his fingers from me as my orgasm subsided. Still breathing heavily, he met my eyes. He leaned his forehead against mine. His smile so sincere he pecked me on the lips and moved to take the tea kettle off the stove. He washed his hands and returned to me, still sitting on the counter.

"Do you still want the tea?" He asked.

"Um... No."

I smiled at him as he lifted me off the counter. Pulling my shirt back down he laced his fingers with mine and we walked back to our rooms. Reaching the top of the stairs he opened my door. He stopped outside the door, but I pulled him in with me. He shut the door and turned off the light.

"I'm going to go clean up in the bathroom." I spoke softly.

He nodded to me. I went to my closet and grabbed some clean underwear. I looked at Derek, "Do you think I could get another one of your shirts, to sleep in." Derek grinned and took the shirt off his back and held it out for me. Laughing I grabbed it and headed into the bathroom.

I changed slowly, every time I touched my body, I sent chills down my spine reliving our moment downstairs. I finally finished changing and took one last look in the mirror. Noticing the hickies all over my neck I gasped. It was going to take a miracle to cover all of this. The hickey on my marking spot was the most prominent. Did he realize he basically just claimed me? I bit my lip thinking about what we had just done.

I heard a knock on the bathroom door, "Autum, are you okay in there?"

I opened the door and smiled up at him through my eyelashes. "You left a lot of hickies."

"Yeah, I got a little carried away, sorry." He rubbed the back of his head.

"And this one," I pointed to my marking spot.

"That one is for everyone else," he moved closer to me, "to tell them you are taken."

"Is that so?" I asked, "And what about you? Are you…taken?" I probed.

He laughed and pulled me into an embrace and started walking backwards towards the bed, "Oh, yes definitely taken." He sat on the bed pushing his legs between mine and pulled me to sit on his lap facing him. As I straddled him, he grinned and turned his head to the side. "Give me one, give me a love bite," he said.

I hesitated, "How?" I asked embarrassingly.

"Just kiss me until you feel the pull on where you would mark me. Instead of biting me just suck on that spot. It will make a hickey."

I started kissing his neck slowly and softly going lower. Derek had his hands on my hips, his grip getting tighter the more I kissed him. I kissed the spot where his neck met his collar bone. I pulled away and looked at it.

"That's the spot, love," he said.

I leaned in and started sucking on his neck. My lips felt a little bruised from all the kissing we had already done. Now, sucking on his neck was putting an odd pressure on them. My mouth felt watery, and my teeth were tingling. This must be how it feels before your canines come in. Odd, I thought to myself. I pulled away, looking at my handy work. After a few more times of deepening it. I was satisfied. I pulled away and looked at Derek. He put his hand on my cheek and smiled. Then he grabbed me and threw me into the bed over his shoulder. We laughed as we got under the blankets. Derek patted his chest for me to lay on him. I fell asleep immediately.

28

DREAM STATE

Autum POV

I was sitting near a lake, surrounded by huge stone walls. The sound of falling water to my left as I gazed at my surroundings. The waterfall's melody soothed me. I felt any and all anxiety leave me. Flowers, bushes, shrubs, trees of all sizes and flowering vines covered the ground and walls. I was in a garden. Looking down at my hands I saw they were translucent, made of golden light. I walked to the edge of the lake and peered at myself. It was what I had looked like in my meditation state but now I was sure I had been dreaming.

"You made it." A voice sounded behind me.

"Mary?"

"Hello child."

"Where am I and why am I here, how are you here?" I asked.

"I told you before, too much unfinished business." She stated matter-of-factly. "Now, for where you are and why, well that will all come with time."

"Not more riddles Mary." I groaned.

She laughed, "We are in a garden, it is safe here. I have been calling you here for months." She stated.

"Mary, you've only been gone a few days."

"Time moves differently here. Days out there are months in here." She sighed. "It doesn't matter, it's not like I have anything else to do."

I looked at her, my eyebrows pinched. "I'm sorry, what? You've just been sitting here, waiting for me?" I understood what she meant about the time difference, having gone through it twice already.

"Yes dear, we need to work on your mental strength. We should also work on some combat training."

Before I could respond, a flicker of light caught my eye. Turning my gaze, I was mesmerized by a sea of glimmering…wind, dust, smoke? I was unsure what I was seeing. It seemed to move as if dancing in the air. It came closer swirling around me. My eyes wide in shock as it moved around me, their little bodies becoming visible.

"Those are fairies dear." Mary answered my question without me speaking.

"They are so beautiful; how can they see me?"

"They recognize your energy dear; they are why you are protected here. Don't let their appearance fool you, fairies are a vicious bunch." She laughed.

"I'm so confused." I looked at her skeptically.

"Let me explain. This place is a special place, it is a safe place for you to meditate. The fairies protect this place, it is their home. I need to help you work on your mental strength and after what you've experienced this week, we should look at some combat training."

"You can help me do all that?" I was talking to her but still watching the fairies. I reached out my hand and they swirled around it. Not touching me but still dancing around me. They moved on and I watched as they took their flight further from me.

"Yes child, it will take some time. But fortunately for us, being here we have plenty of that."

"How does it work, being here, how did I get here?" I asked, intrigued.

"You had to clear your mind. You've finally been able to drop most of the walls I put up when you were a child. Then the mental blocks from the emotions you've had this week. Something must have happened tonight that allowed you to let go. It allowed you to come here." She finished.

If I weren't made of gold light right now, I would have been as red as a cherry. Something had happened all right, I let my guard down with Derek. He took me to new heights, so to speak, freed me from myself!

"I was so wrapped up in how others would see me, see how damaged I am. I wasn't being myself. I was hiding myself away, only showing those around me what I thought they wanted to see."

"And that has changed now?" She questioned.

"I think I have made small steps in realizing that I am who I am, I don't need to hide myself. I'm not completely there yet, but Derek is helping me."

"That's excellent my child! I think the Root Chakra will be the easiest for you. You already know how to ground yourself. The others will take longer and lots of training! It's going to be a long week here, but we can do it!" she said excitedly.

"A week!?" My voice raised, "I'm not staying here for a-" Mary cut me off, her startled voice when the fairies surrounded her. Their shimmering light turning from golden to a redden glow.

"Oh my," Mary gasped.

"What's going on?" I asked surprised by the turn of event. "You said this was a safe place!"

"Yes, a safe place for you. They think I have hurt you."

"Me? She hasn't hurt me. I was just surprised. Please leave her alone." The fairies light changed again, and they moved on.

"Explain this to me, what is going on?"

Mary sighed, "I can only say so much. Giving you too much information could change events and it's not allowed. Everything needs to happen in the order it needs to happen."

Holding my head in frustration, I looked to her. This time, in a calm voice, I continued our conversation. "A week is a long time to be here. It's too long."

"Oh dear, it will only be eight hours in real time, just while your body sleeps. We can accomplish so much while you are sleeping."

"You think we can do all that in a week." I asked hesitantly.

"Oh no child! We will get through the Root Chakra this week and start training. Each night your body is sleeping we'll work through another Chakra. The others will take more time though."

"This will take months." I said still not believing this was really happening.

"All good things come with time dear."

"How do we begin?"

"First, we identify situations in your life that don't make you feel rooted, safe, grounded, or secure. We figure out how to change those situations for future circumstances. This will give you the tools you need to feel centered when things get...hectic."

"Hectic." I repeated.

She smiled and nodded at me. "Let's start with this statement, repeat after me dear. 'I am exactly where I am supposed to be,' She smiled at me waiting for me to repeat.

29

NEW CONFIDENCE

Autum POV

Derek was spooning me as I woke the next morning. I felt the most relaxed I'd ever felt. His arm draped across my stomach. His fingers softly rubbing right above the lace of my panties.

He leaned in behind my ear, "Good morning." I smiled to myself and turned around to face him. It had been a week to me since I'd seen him. I missed him. I leaned in and kissed him longingly, both hands on either side of his face. I felt him smile through our kiss.

The sound of someone clearing their throat had both of us jolting straight up. "Did you two sleep well?" Luna Synthia asked. She had one eyebrow raised as she stared us down. "I hope you two are using protection." She asked.

"What! Mom no, we haven't done that."

"None the less, better to be prepared." She tossed a box of condoms to Derek. His eyes just about bulged out of his head. I felt my face heat in embarrassment as I covered my face with my hands.

"Mom, we don't need-"

She cut him off. "Stop, I used to be a teenager, stuff can happen. Stop making such a fuss." With that she turned and walked out of the room, closing the door behind her.

Derek turned to me, "I am… so sorry." I caught him off guard when I burst out laughing.

"You're not upset?" he asked.

"No, I think I love your mother now too." I laughed.

He raised an eyebrow. "Too?"

I smiled at him and gave him a grin, "Yes, as in also." I leaned in and gave him another kiss. Goddess a week was so long and yet not long at all. I could feel his presence the entire time, small tingles were felt in my dream state as he held by body. I played with the hair on the back of his neck for a moment while we gazed at each other.

"You seem different, are you okay?" He asked.

"I am more than okay." I rolled out of the bed and headed for the bathroom, not elaborating.

Derek jumped out of the bed and followed me; I stopped him at the bathroom door. "Can I help you?" I asked.

He grabbed me by the hips and pulled me in close and kissed me. My hands landed on his chest as I gently pushed him away. "I need to get ready." I tried to walk away. Derek grabbed my hand and pulled me back to him.

"Wait… who else do you love?" He asked.

I laughed, "Your sister of course, she's amazing. Fell in love with her right from the get-go." I pushed him away, "Now go get ready for school." He stumbled backwards, holding his chest like I had just wounded him. I laughed again and closed the bathroom door. I leaned against it, waiting to hear Derek leaving the bedroom. When I heard the click of the door closing, I released a breath I hadn't realized I was holding.

I walked to the sink and washed my face. Looking at my reflection in the mirror, it felt so weird to be back here, to be solid again. Seeing all the hickies on my neck and remembering what had actually happened last night and not a week ago. I had a startling realization. Thinking of Derek all week, in my dream state, had been my driving motivation. He was what got me through it. I gazed at myself, my eyes becoming brighter as my emotions grew. I loved Derek Bell. Biting my bottom lip, flashes of Derek's hands on me last night sent goosebumps everywhere. I touched my neck, leaning in closer to the mirror to look at Derek's love bite. And I spoke out loud to myself, "And Derek Bell loves me."

I quickly put on some light makeup. I covered most of the love bites Derek left on my neck, leaving the one on my marking spot for everyone to see. Leaving the bathroom, I stopped when I saw Luna Synthia laying out some clothes on my bed.

"I noticed you didn't bring much with you, these should all fit you. There's also a black dress for later."

"I couldn't possibly accept these, Luna Synthia."

"Call me Synthia, Autum. And of course, you can. I haven't worn them in a long time."

"They are too nice." My voice felt small.

"Autum," She approached me. "I've witnessed you go from completely devastated to a confident woman in mere days." I blushed at her comment and looked down at the ground. If she only knew it had been much longer for me. She was speaking to me like a mother would. She reached out and lifted my chin so our eyes would meet.

"Whatever you decide, whoever it is you want to be. I will support you. The girl I saw last night, the one demanding her Alpha we keep her gifts a secret."

Oh my Goddess I did do that; my eyes went wide. I should have never talked to Alpha Darren that way.

Synthia laughed, "Its fine Autum. We weren't angry. More proud than anything."

"Why… why are you so nice to me?"

"Well," she stepped away and walked to the clothes on the bed. "It's becoming more and more likely that you will be mated to my son, Autum. And more than that, even if you're not. You are a white wolf. We told you they are highly coveted. We will protect you either way. You are a part of our pack now." She lifted up a mint green dress. It was beautiful.

"It's not too much, too flashy for school?" I asked her. I know Rebecca is always dressed nicely at school, but it was more than I had ever dressed for school.

She was shaking her head no, "I think it's time they all see what we all see here."

I approached her, taking the dress, "And what's that?" I asked.

"Someone who is starting to accept all that they are. An intelligent, brave, and forgiving women. You will have power beyond your imagination Autum. Its time others start to take notice, you will not be pushed around!"

I nodded to her. She was right, she was talking about Rebecca. I could be that confident woman she was talking about. The one I knew was buried deep down inside me. I sighed to myself. I could do this. Be brave. Be confident. Refuse to be treated poorly and still keep that part of myself that wouldn't allow myself to hate anyone. I mean look at what my mother did, and I still loved her. And I forgave Amy and Rebecca already in my mind. Synthia was right I forgive easily; it was my empathy for others.

I looked down at the dress in my arms and walked to the full-length mirror in the closet. Slipping into the dress, its long sleeves covered my scars, while the length extended past my knees. It was a beautiful casual dress. The top hugged my curves and then flared out at the bottom. I walked out of the closet to show Synthia.

"Just beautiful," she said before she walked out of my room.

I looked at my reflection for a few more minutes. I grabbed my white flats and put them on. They went well with the dress. Taking a deep breath, I left my room and descended the stairs. Derek was in the kitchen with his parents. His back was to me as he leaned over the counter. Synthia cleared her throat when I entered.

Alpha Darren speaking first, "You look nice today, Autum."

"Thank you, Alpha."

"Darren," he corrected me.

I smiled and nodded to him. Derek turned around then, "Are you re-" he paused mid-sentence as he turned and made eye contact. I smiled at him as he looked me up and down. "You are beautiful," he said softly as he approached me.

"Thank you. It's not too much?" I asked.

He smiled, "No, you are just as beautiful on the inside, now everyone else will see what was already there too."

I felt the blush on my cheeks. Derek took my backpack in one hand and my hand in his other. Walking to the front door he yelled out to his parents that we would see them later. When he opened the door Ethan was getting ready to knock. Ethan took a step back and smiled at me. Nodding in approval he turned to Derek.

"Can Rebecca and I ride with you guys to school?" Ethan asked.

Derek looked at me. He wanted my permission. Well, I guess it was now or never. Might as well get it over with. I nodded. Derek gave my hand a squeeze. Letting me know he was here for me. I smiled at him, and we walked to his truck where Rebecca was waiting. I instantly straightened my posture and made eye contact with her. Her eyes went immediately to my neck. Her eyes went wide. Then she looked at Derek's neck. We stopped in front of her. Anger was radiating off of her.

"Are you sleeping with this slut?" She addressed Derek.

SLAP!

My hand burned as my gaze met Rebecca's. She was not going to speak about me like that anymore. Derek stood there with his mouth open. Ethan did the same.

"Now Rebecca, that is none of your business." I spoke, she had her hand on her cheek. "You will not speak to me like that ever again, nor will you treat me like you have been," I said.

"And if I do?" she asked snarky.

"Rebecca," Ethan started.

In one motion I pushed Rebecca into the truck.

"Autum?" Derek questioned.

"I'm in control." I took a deep breath looking into Rebecca's eyes. I could see my eyes starting to glow in the reflection and I smiled. I stepped back from her. I left one hand on her sternum. I let my energy flow through my hand, just enough for her to start to feel the heat. Her eyes went wide when she looked down.

"If you make the wrong decision, I will make the right one for you." I stated. I let her go. "You won't tell a single soul about my gifts either." She nodded. I released her from my gaze, and I looked at Derek. He had the biggest smile I'd ever seen on him. He took my hand and lifted it to his lips, kissing it.

"Oh, one last thing Rebecca, to quote your words, I saw the way you looked at Derek. He is mine. He's been mine. Make sure to keep your eyes off and hands to yourself. Now get in the truck or walk. I don't care either way." She stomped her foot and huffed. Ethan opened her door, and she got in the truck.

Derek opened my door and lifted his hand to help me in. When I took it, he pulled me into him instead and spoke into my ear. "That was hot!" I laughed and he helped me into the truck.

When we got to school Samantha was waiting for us. Derek parked the truck and Rebecca got out instantly slamming the door as she stormed into the school.

Derek was shaking his head at her behavior, "Let me get your door." He got out and came around to help me out. As soon as my feet hit the ground I was mauled by Samantha. I embraced her even though she was squeezing all the air from my lungs.

"I missed you too," I said.

She pulled away and took me in. "You look good, better than good. Are you alright?" She asked.

I laughed, "Yes I'm good, actually I'm exactly where I was meant to be." I looked at Derek, he reached for my hand pulling me to his side. Samantha's eyes found my neck and she smiled.

"Well, it seems that you really are." With that we headed into the school.

30

COUNCIL MEETING

⁓

Luna Synthia POV

The council meeting was scheduled to start in thirty more minutes. I grabbed some pitchers of water. Cutting up some cucumbers and oranges to add to the pitchers. I brought the pitchers in and took my seat next to Darren. I could see the worry on his face. Reaching for his hand, he looked at me.

"It will be okay love," I spoke to him.

He nodded. Picking my hand up and kissing it. He rested it on my thigh after. I looped my arm under his to get comfortable and laid my head on his shoulder. He looked stoic now. Not letting his emotions show on his face. Ever the Alpha, the protector.

We were in for a tough year. The Heiress was back, that much was apparent. We knew as soon as we heard Amy's story. Blood magic is the only way to control a person like Amy was controlled. But who the Heiress was and where she was hiding was yet to be known. How long had she been lingering? She could be anyone. There are no known books with her picture. How had she survived and why was she back?

Beta Richard and Elissa showed up early. Walking in, they took their seats next to Darren. I straightened up.

"Elissa, have you spoken to the twins about their birthday?"

"No Luna, I plan on discussing it with them tomorrow. I wanted to get past the funeral first." Elissa hung her head slightly.

"Before everyone else arrives," Darren started, "How familiar are you with Autum Moore?" he asked them.

Beta Richard spoke first after glancing at his wife, "Mary told us about Autum. We had put some of it together after Rebecca had come home from school the day of one of their encounters."

"Does Rebecca know?" Darren asked.

"She doesn't know what she knows, honestly." Elissa responded.

"Elissa, you are most familiar with the prophecy," He paused in thought. "Do you think she could have been brought here to complete the power of three?

He asked even though he didn't want to. The four of us were the only four that knew that Elissa gave birth to triplets that day at the hospital now that Mary was gone. She still struggled with it every day. Being the Luna, it was my job to care for the women and children of the pack. I could feel her heart ache through the bond we all shared.

She visited the grave almost every day. Her children only knew she had miscarried in a later pregnancy, not that it was, in fact, their triplet sister. She always swore she could feel the link to her baby. She refused to believe she had died until we convinced her after several months. Even then, she struggled for years. When a loved one dies, you feel it. Like something breaking inside you, a tether snapping. The Alpha feels every death in his pack as well. There had been many that day of the Tsunami.

Elissa had a complicated pregnancy. Growing three pups was unheard of. When the weather changes started happening, we knew her babies were in duress. She spent most of her pregnancy on bed rest. When the first child died, we hypothesized that Baby Ethan was in duress from the loss of his sibling. He and Rebecca were restless. They had to sleep together for months.

We thought we were clear of the prophecy, since one of the children had died. That it would happen in another time, not our time. We were wrong. The Heiress was back, and we were not prepared.

"I think it could be a possibility. I felt something when she was in my home on Sunday. There is a connection there. She is definitely a white wolf. Do we know anything about her father, and is she first born?" Elissa responded.

"We don't know that information yet. Autum is unsure. If she is first born, we will have to watch her closely. We are all familiar with the prophecy, that the Queen reincarnate will be first born of a white wolf." Darren Stated.

"Has she shown any other powers other than to absorb other's abilities?" Elissa asked.

"Not that we are aware of." Darren lied. It wasn't safe to share Autum's gifts with anyone until we knew for sure she could protect herself.

'What if Autum's the Queen?' I mind-linked Darren.

He looked at me, his eyes had turned black, just as mine had. It's what happened when we used the mind link, our wolves came forward. It would be obvious to everyone we were having a private conversation.

'I had the same thought last night when she told us of her gifts. But we shouldn't jump to conclusions, either way she is special.' He mind-linked back.

"What are you two discussing, care to share?" Beta Richard asked.

"Not at this time. Once we have more information, we'll share." Darren said.

Gamma Richard, or Rick, walked in at that time followed by Delta Anthony and Lyla, Amy's parents and Omega Julian and Amber, Samantha's parents. Rick walked straight to the bar and poured a vodka and cranberry. Poor man was always drinking. It helped numb the pain of losing his mate. She died from cancer last year and they had no children. Wolves could live to be hundreds of years old. After mating, even the looks of aging slowed. But if your mate died you were lucky to survive. The tear of the bond was devastating to our wolves and could drive them mad, most committing suicide after a mate dies. Rick drank to numb the pain. Mary numbed the pain with her healing abilities. Even Ellen, Autum's grandmother, had survived. She survived for Autum, raising her was the only thing keeping her wolf sane. But you could see she was getting sicker with each passing day.

The only other hope wolves had was a second chance mate. It was more common when we still had wars. Many wolves would die from pack wars and then hundreds more after losing their mates. Moon Goddess Selene gave us second chance mates. A way to mate those who had lost their mates, giving them a second chance to live.

"Did you start the meeting without us?" Asked Gamma Rick

"No of course not, you are right on time." Darren replied.

Darren started the meeting, "Thank you all for meeting on such short notice. We have new information after speaking with Amy last night," he paused. "Omega Anthony, would you like to tell the council what your daughter said?"

Anthony cleared his throat, "Amy claims that her body was being controlled by an outside force. That she could see and hear everything she was doing, unable to stop herself."

Everyone looked at each other briefly before resting their eyes to Beta Richard and Elissa. Elissa turned towards Darren to speak. "It has to be blood magic," she stated.

Elissa had some knowledge on witchcraft, since Mary was fascinated with it, and it was carried down in their blood line. Neither of them could harness it. It is said that is how the White Queen defeated the Heiress in her past lifetime. The Queens gifts where stronger due to her blood line, she had a blood line descended from all three original Lycan families and one from a witch. The Queens blood line was named Leoht. With such the gift was also named 'The Gift of Leoht.' The gift could manifest in the first born but didn't mean it would. It is said that the child also had to be pure of heart.

Darren nodded, "Yes, we thought the same thing."

Omega Julian spoke next, "We will return home immediately and start researching."

Julian was very dedicated to the pack. He helped write many reports, he was very thorough. He and Amber took many trips to further their studies, even taking Samantha at times. We would always allow her to miss school for those trips, since it was furthering her education abroad.

"Wait," Darren interrupted. "Dr. Warren has requested a special seat on the council just to help navigate through this threat. She said she has insight that will be valuable."

"Unless she knows a witch, how could she help? I am pretty well versed on witchcraft," Elissa stated.

I spoke up next. "We don't know how she would be helpful; she should be here shortly. Why don't we listen to what she has to say first? Then we can vote on allowing her to sit with us as a temporary condition of this situation."

Everyone nodded in agreement. While we waited for Dr. Warren we moved onto the next topic.

"Beta Richard, please address your concerns with the council about the twin's birthday." Darren asked.

"We believe they will phase early." Richard said.

"What?! Why would you think that? They are only turning seventeen, that's a whole year early," Amber interrupted. Julian looked at Amber sternly. She became quiet and dropped her head. She had a point though. That's what the meetings were for, for them to voice their concerns.

"We all know they received their moon gifts early, too. None of us were expecting to have snow when Ethan used his powers the first time, or to have to command Rebecca to stop persuading the other kids at school." Beta Richard replied, scrubbing a hand down his face.

Elissa continued. "Both of them are experiencing night sweats, their teeth and gums are sore and Rebecca's mood swings have been unpredictable."

Gamma Rick swirled his drink, "Well Rebecca has been commanded not to use her gift on pack members, but what about Ethan? Are we expecting another Tsunami?"

Everyone's eyes shot towards Darren. I was definitely not thinking about that, and neither was he by the look on his face. Maybe it was something we should be prepared for though. The party was planned for the beach of all places. But we had a backup plan. Autum. Autum was our backup plan.

"Richard, Elissa, is that something we should be concerned with?" He asked them.

Richard seemed to ponder the question, but Elissa answered confidently, "No. Ethan has had control of his power for a long time. Even with the added symptoms of his phase coming, we have not had any weather anomalies."

"You call my daughters balcony being blown to smithereens not a weather anomaly." Omega Julian asked skeptically. His brows were pinched together. His wife, Amy, nodding in agreement.

Delta Anthony and Lyla seconded that, "And our daughter ended up in the hospital." They had valid concerns, but they didn't know what I and Darren knew or Richard and Elissa. That Autum had done that when her life was in danger.

"Can't you command him too Alpha?" Gamma Rick asked.

"I mean I can try, it's not the same. Rebecca's command prevents her from using her power on our pack, but she can still use it. How that would work for Ethan, I'm not sure. I don't think he'd target the pack intentionally, and I can't command him to not use it at all. That could be dangerous to him as he shifts, not being able to pull from all his strength." Darren responded.

"I don't think Ethan will be a danger," Elissa interjected, "If he is, no one will be around by that time. I have planned their birthday party for Saturday from 5pm-10pm. Their birthdays are not until Sunday, if they phase, it will be at midnight on Saturday. The party will have ended. We will stay on the beach to ensure the rest of the pack is out of harm's way in case something happens."

"Does the council agree that these terms are reasonable?" Darren asked.

"If you will also be there, Alpha, we will agree." Delta Anthony and Lyla responded.

"Same," Omega Julian and Amber stated. Gamma Rick raised his glass, saying he agreed.

"It is settled then, I agree. Synthia and I will both stay during the phasing." He finished. I nodded in agreement.

Hearing a car pull up, we all stood and waited for Dr. Warren to enter the house. I waited for her at the Door. Dr. Warren came to us from the human city of Ilwaco. She had gone there to go to school to be a doctor. Her full name is Emivy Warren, and she was a human, but her child was a wolf. She approached our pack ten years ago. Her husband, she claimed, was Gram Bell, Darren's younger brother. She claimed they were rogues on the account that she was human. It was unheard of to be mated to a human in this day and age. Most packs looked down on it thinking it was a weakness. They were shunned because she brought no strength to the pack. She was a liability. Darren has always had a problem believing her story. He said he would have known if his brother was a rogue. She said Gram died by the hands of another Rogue. Emivy decided to go to medical school so she could be an asset to a community like ours. Elissa and I were only veterinarians. We needed a doctor, and she needed help raising her son. Her son, Kiel, was following in her footsteps. After graduating he left for college in Ilwaco. It was a four-year program. She has gone to visit him multiple times, but he would be coming home soon.

"Emivy," I greeted her. We gave each other a small embrace.

"Luna," she greeted back, slightly bowing after our hug. She joined us at the table, and Darren didn't hold back.

"Alright Dr. Warren now is your time to tell us how you can help. The council has agreed to hear you out. If they feel you provide a valuable service, we will grant you a temporary seat as a Special Consultant." Darren finished.

"Before I say what I came to say, I'd like to apologize." She held her hand up since Darren was about to interject. She finished, "I apologize for not telling you this before, but I was worried you would deny my request for the packs help in raising my son. But with what is currently happening around us, I feel I have no choice but to offer my assistance. I hope you will accept it and I hope my ten years here will help in knowing you can trust me." She paused for a moment, "I am a witch."

I think Elissa looked the most startled. Darren didn't even bat an eye. He was very good at hiding his emotions. Gamma Rick was pretty laid back, and why wouldn't he be? He had already thrown back four drinks in the last hour. Delta Anthony and Omega Julian and their wives were silent. Everyone's eyes were black. All having conversations with their mates on how they wanted to proceed.

'What do you think?' Darren mind-linked me.

'Well, she has been here for ten years. She performed multiple operations on members of the pack. Not to mention she has been a therapist to most of our children. If we trusted her to do those things before not knowing she was a witch. Why wouldn't we trust her now?' I mind-linked back.

"How would you help with this current situation?" Darren asked Dr. Warren.

"First, I would request permission to do a thorough walk through of the school."

"Why the school?" I asked.

"Well, because Amy was cursed. Someone would have had to be close to cast a spell to use Blood Magic on her. And beside her home, where I was last night and I felt no residual magic, the only other logical place for contact would be the school." She answered.

"What would the witch have needed to cast the spell." Elissa asked. I knew she was fully aware; this was a test.

"Something that belonged to her, a picture of her, or a piece of her, like hair or blood. This spell was strong though, blood would have been needed." Dr. Warren answered.

Darren mind-linked me, *'I just mind linked Elissa, that is accurate. What do you think?'*

'Ask her If she thinks it could be the Heiress of Darkness?' I mind linked back.

"Doctor, do you think the blood magic witch is the Heiress?" Darren asked.

A gasp left Julian's lips, "You aren't supposed to speak her name Alpha."

"My apology Julian, but the question needed asking."

Dr. Warren responded, "Julian do not worry, she can only hear you if you speak her true name."

Delta Anthony and Julian looked skeptical; they were after all the scholars of the pack. They were about to ask their question when Dr. Warren continued.

"It is said in legends that the Heiress can be summoned when called by her name. Her nickname, the Heiress of Darkness, was given to her by the towns people so they could talk without her listening. It is also said the Heiress had a sister. She was very jealous of this sister. They were twins, the sister having been born first had the chance to receive the gift of Leoht."

Julian and Amber kept mind-linking, but only Julain spoke.

"Wait," Julian cute her off, "are you saying the Heiress was a white wolf?"

"Yes and no"

"But I have never read anything on this." Julia continued.

"If I'm not mistaken several thousand of your books were lost during the Tsunami. The literature you choose to save was heavily weighted towards Lycan Lore."

"That may be true, but then how do you know." Julian questioned.

"Because I didn't grow up here. I was raised in a human city among other witches. We studied our history."

Darren interjected, "Please continue doctor, your answer was yes and no to the white wolf question."

"As I was saying, the sister had the chance to receive the gift of Leoht. The sister, also being of pure heart, did in fact get the gift of Leoht. On her seventeenth birthday she phased, and her gift became known. A huge beacon of light surrounded her body as she transitioned into her white wolf. It was a glorious day for the young Queen."

"So, the sister became our Queen?" Darren asked.

Everyone was engrossed in her story as she continued.

"Yes, she became Queen Patrina. Her sister, however, had a much different day. She never phased on her seventieth birthday or on any birthday after that. She was wolf-less. The only power she wielded was that from her witch blood line. Filled with sorrow she begged Patrina to use her gift to bless her, to change her fate, to bless her with a moon gift and give her a wolf. Patrina said she couldn't, that she didn't have the power to do that. Sorrow turned to jealousy and rage; she cursed her sister. Vowed to take back that which should have belonged to her. What should have been her birth right. She started working with dark magic. Learned to wield it and as the years passed became stronger. Focused on becoming more powerful than Patrina, she fueled herself with peoples' darkest fears, their nightmares, and their sinful desires. Taking their negative energy, she grew stronger. She raised a Rogue army and had them attacking packs, killing thousands. Spreading rumors that Patrina could save them but refused. This fueled their rage, thinking their Queen was selfish. Their rage only making the sister stronger. Her dark ways became known giving her the nick name, Heiress of Darkness. She hid herself until the time was right."

Dr. Warren reached for her glass of water and took a sip. "You were taught in your books that the White Queen won. That both sisters died in a fiery death and peace followed. We were told differently. We were told the White Queen did indeed parish, sacrificing her life for that of her people. Binding her evil sisters' powers to herself and to a tree. You know it as the Tree of Knowledge, but it also has another name. The Tree of Good and Evil. The Heiress did not die but was stripped of the last remaining power she wielded. Cursed to live the remainder of her life as an ordinary human. The Moon Goddess taking pity on the Heiress, created mates. Although wolf-less, her blood still pure with its heritage, would eventually match her to another. This was a chance for the Heiress to find love and to finally live without hate in her heart."

After a long pause, Julian asked, "So what happened, did she find love?"

"No one knows, it is not written anywhere. But to answer the Alphas question from before I went on with my rambling. Yes, it could be the Heiress, or it could be an heir of hers. No one knows what happened to her, she disappeared."

There was a moment of silence in the room, Dr. Warren was definitely earning her keep with that story. But we still needed to know how she could help us find out what exactly we are dealing with here. I mind linked Darren and he agreed. He asked her the next question.

"Dr. Warren, what would you look for at the school that would help us?" He asked her.

"First, I would tour every classroom then bathrooms, janitor closets, offices. I'd check the cafeteria, the kitchens, the gym, and the library. I would be looking for residual magic. If the ritual was performed at the school, there would be traces of it. While doing that I'd be checking for physical signs, such as markings on the walls or alters of any sorts."

"What could you do if you did find any of those things?" He asked.

"I would use the residual magic to track the witch to their lair. I would also ensure to remove any markings that are inviting the darkness in. Lastly, I would take measure to protect Rebecca."

That caught most of us off guard. "Why Rebecca?" Elissa asked.

"She is the first born of a white wolf," She nodded to Elissa, "The witch might be trying to establish a relationship with her. We all know that the first born of white wolves have a chance of receiving the gift of Leoht. Maybe this witch is planning on using her."

Elissa was shaking her head before speaking, "Then why go after Autum? Why use Amy to try and kill her?"

"From what I've discussed with Rebecca during her sessions, she believes Autum is ruining her life. She has taken her boyfriend, her position within the pack, her friends, and now her powers. This has made Rebecca unstable. We don't know what kind of powers Rebecca will have, but maybe this witch was trying to get Autum out of the way in the hopes of stabilizing Rebecca. If she really believes Rebecca is her chance to get all her powers back. She'll probably stop at nothing until that happens."

"What do you mean get her powers back?" Darren asked.

"If Rebecca gets the gift of Leoht, she would be able to unbind the Heiresses powers from the Tree of Good and Evil."

"So, she doesn't have her powers now? Then how did Amy get possessed?"

"That I'm not entirely sure, it could be she found a way to get some of her craft back or she stole another witch's craft by having her killed and performing the ritual of Yfel. Alpha, you have many wolves in your pack, and some are also descendants of witches. You'd be a fool if you didn't believe some of them are practicing their craft. There is also a large coven in Ilwaco. But I will know more after searching the school."

"Yfel?" Julian interrupted. Hesitating, He spoke again, "That word translates to Evil. What exactly is the ritual of Yfel?" He directed his question to Dr. Warren.

"It is complicated, but basically, she could take another witch's power after she dies. The ritual would allow her to transfer the power to herself as long as the witch didn't die by her hands."

Darren took a deep breath. This was going to be difficult to figure out. The Heiress may or may not have her powers. She could be using another witch, or she could be somehow killing witches and taking their powers.

"I will give you permission to search the school, but Elissa will go with you to help. She may not have had it manifest in her, but she still holds the blood line and is knowledgeable." Darren spoke.

"And what of my request to join as a consultant?" Dr. Warren asked him.

"We will vote on it after you leave. I will call you tomorrow and let you know. Regardless, you will still help us find this Heiress or other witch who is threatening our pack." He says with finality.

She stands and nods. Looking at the clock on the wall. She speaks, "I should probably head over to your house Beta Richard, today was the first day with Rebecca at school with Autum. I would like to be there when she gets home." Beta Richard nods in agreement. I stand with her to walk her out.

"I have one more question." Darren says, "What is the Heiresses real name?" He askes

She paused before answering, "It was lost to time, Alpha, forgotten."

I walk her out. When I return to the room, we vote to allow Dr. Warren sit on the council as a special consultant. We discussed what Dr. Warren said about the two sisters. It is decided that Elissa will go to the school tomorrow with Dr. Warren. We also discussed sending out scouts to locate the lost Kingdom of Rune. If there is a possibility that the Heiress can get her powers back, we need to know if the tree really exists. Everyone stands to leave, but Elissa asks us for help with some last-minute funeral arrangements. Darren stays seated while I walk everyone else out.

31

DISTRACTION

❧

Synthia POV

I return to the conference room in the middle of a heated debate.

"So, we are going to just allow my daughter to be used as bate!" Elissa yells

Darren and Elissa are both standing now. His Alpha aura is strong in the room, but her wolf is a sigma and doesn't have to head to his command. She chooses to be a part of the pack, but currently her wolf is refusing to listen. Elissa's eyes keep flickering black and her wolf is trying to take over. Her hands gripping the table, knuckles white, trying to keep control.

"Elissa, we will put extra guards on the school and at your home. We can't chance them finding out about Autum." Darren tries to reason.

"My wolf, Emeka, she won't allow it, we've already lost one daughter." Elissa strains to talk, still fighting her wolf for control.

"Can you let her forward without giving up control, let me talk to her?" Darren asks.

Elissa's eyes turn to a brighter blue, as she lets Emeka forward. Still in her human form and still straining to keep it that way. Richard has his hands around her waist trying to comfort her and hold her back. Darren could subdue her if she shifts, but it would take everything he has, this room would be destroyed.

"Emeka, listen to me. I won't let anything happen to Rebecca. We will protect her too. We can't save her by putting another at risk. Rebecca will turn seventeen on Sunday, then everyone will know she doesn't have the gift of Leoht, and none will be the wiser as to why. Please see reason. It's only four days. Just wait four days." Darren tries to reason with her.

"Four days." Is all Emeka says, and Elissa's body goes limp in Beta Richards arms. She is panting as he moves her back to the chair. Completely exhausted from using so much energy, she pants, "I'm sorry Alpha, but thank you."

Darren walks over to her putting a hand on her shoulder. "I will protect Rebecca. We will figure this out." He steps away still speaking, "What's the plan again for the twin's birthday?" He asks.

Beta Richard speaks, "With their birthday being on Sunday, the party will be Saturday at the beach. We will have everyone clear out early and keep the kids down at the beach. If the phase happens it will be just past midnight. We will have wide open space in case anything happens. Autum can absorb their ability if necessary. Although what you said about them possibly needing all the energy, they have to phase easier also has me worried. It might be a bad idea to have her take it from them. The phase could be more painful than it needs to be."

"We'll cross that bridge if it comes to that." Darren replied.

Looking at the time the kids should be back from school, and we should all be getting ready for the Funeral. Beta Richard and Elissa stood to leave. While Darren and I prepared for the conversation we promised Autum after school.

Autum POV

Derek and I walked into the pack house. The conference room door was still closed, and we could hear people talking in there.

"Come on let's get a snack." Derek said as he pulled me to the kitchen.

"I don't think I can eat. My nerves are on end, knowing I'm going to see my grandma for the first time since..." I didn't finish my sentence, holding my stomach with one hand. Derek directed me to the bench, and I sat down.

Derek eyed me, "How about some toast or saltine crackers to settle your stomach."

I nodded, "Crackers sound ok." You'd think that with how much time had passed for me, that I would be okay with seeing my grandmother. I knew I was, but my body was so shaky that I must be subconsciously dreading it. I didn't give much thought to it being Mary's funeral either, since for me, she was still very much alive.

Derek made toast for himself and came and sat next to me. We snacked for a minute, Derek's hand resting on my thigh while he ate with his other hand, his thumb slowly drawing circles on my leg. It was comforting. I glanced at him and smiled.

"What?" he asked.

"Nothing," I just smiled back at him.

"Hmm," he leaned in towards me. "You were pretty hot at school today."

"Is that so?"

"Oh yes, the way you held yourself all day, confident. Not sure where this all came from," He looked me up and down, admiring my dress again, "but I like it." He gave me quick peck on the lips, "Come on let's go get dressed for the funeral."

With Mary's help I would grow quickly. I could already see a difference in myself. I liked it. I would take everyone by surprise at how rapidly I made self-progress. The only thing was the lapse in time. It was difficult remembering what had happened last here. Remembering what was important a week ago. And just like that the memories came back to me.

"Your parents said I could ask more questions today." I replied.

"Let's get dressed and come back down, we'll talk to them before the funeral... or after," he stated.

I reluctantly agreed and we went upstairs. Luna Synthia had given me a black dress. First, I brushed my hair and brushed my teeth. I slipped the black dress on but couldn't quite get the zipper all the way up. Giving up, I returned to the bathroom to touch up my makeup. There was a knock on my door. "Come in," I yelled from the bathroom. Derek entered; I knew it was him from his smell. I noticed a small smile on my face. Goddess, I'm so captivated by him, his mere presence makes me happy. I look over my shoulder as he enters the bathroom. I put on some black earrings and a black necklace.

"Do you need help with this?" Derek reaches for my zipper. I pull my hair to the side. I can see him smiling through the reflection in the mirror as he pulls it up. The dress has long sleeves and is a few inches below my knees. The neckline is a wide scoop and lays right above my breasts. Keeping my hair to the side, I start to braid it as Derek pulls my hips towards him. He rests his chin on my exposed shoulder. "You look beautiful." He turns towards my neck and inhales, "And you smell nice."

"Thank you," I laugh.

"You feel a little warm though," He reaches for my chin turning me to face him and puts his lips to my forehead. "Are you feeling okay?"

"I feel jittery, but otherwise okay. I guess my mind feels restless, like something is going to happen."

"I can make something happen, maybe give your mind a reason to rest, hmm." He started kissing my neck slowly. His hands roaming, one to the fabric covering my breast the other moving lower. As he palmed my breast, sparks ignited where his lips met my skin. Derek spun me around, my back now to the counter and pushed against me. His lips met mine and I kissed him back. Reaching my arms up around his neck, I pulled him in for a deeper kiss. He lifted me, sitting me on the counter. My mouth parted inviting him in as he tasted every inch of my mouth. His hands roamed up my thighs as he spread them to move closer to me. I wrapped my legs around him, pulling him in. He moved to my jaw, kissing it, and working down to my neck. I dropped my head back giving him more access as he licked and sucked on my neck. He moved his mouth to my ear as his hands moved closer to my core.

"I've been thinking of this all day,"

I hear his raspy voice in my ear as his thumb brushes the outside of my panties against my slit. A shiver runs through me as my arousal perfumes the air. I had been thinking of this all week, he had no idea! Derek hooked a finger through the side of my panties and his warm fingers grazed my opening.

"You're wet." He growls deep and low. A soft moan left my lips as he captured them, stealing my breath away.

His fingers moved between my slit, down and back up. Coating his fingers in my juices as he slowly started circling my clit. The tingles from his contact on my skin had me moving my hips against him, wanting more.

"Derek," I let out a breathy moan.

"Do you want me to stop?" he panted as he moved his hand to the back of my dress, unzipping it.

I pulled it down, giving him access to my breasts. "Don't stop" it came out like a shallow whisper. Derek's mouth went to one breast while his hand went to the other. His fingers pinched and rolled my nipple. His tongue was circling and sucking on the other.

I reached for his pants, unbuttoning them, and pushing them down. His manhood sprung free. I couldn't see it, but I could feel it. He was massive. I wrapped my hand around him and started stroking him. He groaned and it ignited my arousal.

My core was throbbing as his other hand still circled my clit. He moved lower inserting two fingers and as I rolled my hips into him, letting out another moan. I could feel my wetness spill out. It coated his hand as he pushed and pulled his fingers from me. His thumb adding pressure to my clit as it makes circles. He speeds up and the noises that left my lips didn't sound like me. They were loud and resonated off the walls as I came closer to my climax. It's true what they say, 'absence makes the heart grow fonder.' I wanted him, missed him, craved him.

I pulled Derek's lips to mine to capture the sounds leaving me. He sped up, pumping his fingers faster and moving his hips fast as my hand stroked him. As my climax burst through me, my head flew back, and Derek kissed my neck, each wave hitting me in succession as he pushed his fingers deeper and harder. My breathing was harsh as I tried not to hyperventilate.

The heat left me, and Derek pulled his fingers from me. He put them in his mouth, tasting me. His eyes focused on mine as he did it. I felt heat prick at my core as I watched him suck his fingers clean. My hand wrapped around his throbbing shaft. I jumped off the counter and kneeled in front of him.

"Autum, you don't have to," he tried to pull me up.

"I want to," I had no idea what I was doing. I wet my lips and put them around him. Tasting him as precum coated my cheeks. Keeping one hand at the base, I started moving my mouth on him. His groan fueled me, I moved faster. He put his hand on the back of my head but then moved it. I pulled his hand back. He wrapped my braid around it and added pressure to the back of my head, pushing me deeper.

I moaned, my throat vibrating, and he thrust his hips into me. I ran my free hand up his leg till I reached his ass. Grabbing it I pulled him in, taking him in even deeper. I saw his head tilt back as his pace increased. My head moved faster as his hand pushed me. His movements were starting to become more erratic. I looked up at him and our eyes met. He watched as my mouth took him in and out. Feeling him grow larger, I know he was close. My hand squeezes his ass as he moves faster. The vibration from my throat pushed him over the edge, and I felt his hot seed hit the back of my throat. My hand stayed on his member, squeezing as his final thrusts slow.

Derek pulls me up. "Did you just...?" He looked at my lips, my tongue sweeping across them, cleaning them. He smashed into me, our lips locking. Tasting each other, he slowed down, pulling me against him. Parting my lips, his tongue felt like silk against mine. He took his time as he reached down pulling my dress up and reaching around, he zipped it back up. Pulling away from our kiss, he reached the bottom hem of my dress and pulled it up. Pulling on the elastic of my panties and letting it snap against my skin.

"You might want to change those." He rasped next to my ear.

I laughed as he spun me around and slapped my ass, pushing me out of the bathroom. I changed and Derek walked out of the bathroom dressed and ready. While I had to fix my hair and my makeup. I also brushed my teeth, again. Trying to finish quickly was difficult, I could feel his eyes on me. Derek leaned in the doorway watching me reapply my makeup. I finished up with some light lip gloss. Smacking my lips at the end and peering at him through the mirror. He smirked. I saw him reach down and readjust himself. I raised an eyebrow at him.

"What? That was hot, and I was just reliving it and thinking of those lips on me all over again."

I felt my face heat at the thought. Derek walked in and grabbed my hand. Pulling me from the bathroom, "Can we go out in the yard and walk around for a minute?" I asked him as we walked out of the room. He nodded.

I took my shoes off and we headed out the backdoor. "I was hoping I was enough of a distraction for you," Derek said wiggling his eyebrows at me.

I laughed, "That was the best distraction, the most amazing distraction I've ever had."

"Then why this?" he asked as he spun me towards him. He looked down at my bare feet. He held both my hands and leaned in touching our foreheads together.

"This is different, this helps me relax by grounding myself."

"How?" he asked.

He made me do a little spin with his hand then pulled me in from behind, and we just kind of swayed for a moment like we were dancing. I leaned my head back on him and stared up at the clear night sky.

"It's hard to explain. I can feel it. The earth's energy. It grounds me. Roots me in this place. I can let it flow in and out of me." I speak. I pulled his hand, leading him to a tree in the yard.

"This tree, it has energy." I tried to explain. I placed my hand on it and then my forehead. "I can feel it. It is alive. It takes the negative energy from me and it kind of like recycles it and puts it back out into the universe clean. I can also feed it energy if that makes sense?"

"What does it feel like?" Derek asked.

I turn from the tree and smile up at him, "That one's easier to answer."

I spun him around pushing him into the tree. I pushed up on my tip toes to reach his neck and breathed hot air all down his neck and slowly ran my nails up his arms. Goosebumps covered him wherever I touched. "Those goosebumps, that's what it feels like." I whispered into his ear.

He leaned in to kiss me, but I put my fingers to his lips. "Don't you dare make me fix this again." I turned on my heel and ran for the backdoor, laughing as he sprinted to catch me. He lifted me off my feet as he spun me around.

"Got ya!" He laughed as he brought me down to the ground and turned me to look at him.

He pushed some fallen hair behind my ear, "You do seem better now." He smiled down at me. Lacing our fingers together he led the way back into the house. His parents were in the kitchen.

"How was school today?" Synthia asked.

"School was good," Derek replied. I put my shoes back on and followed him to the kitchen table.

"We have an hour until the funeral. Do you two want to talk now or after?" Darren asked.

"Now!" I rushed to reply. Derek shook his head at me but smiled. He bent his elbow out for me to lace my arm through. Pulling me closer to him on the bench seat. He rested his hand on my thigh. His mother smiled at our closeness, and I blushed.

"Would you like a cup of tea Autum?" His mother asked.

"Yes, thank you." She poured two cups of tea, not bothering to ask the boys if they wanted any.

"So" she began, "We learned quite a lot at the council meeting today. I think I should start with that."

32

THE CALLING

❧

Autum POV

She began by telling us about the Queen and the Heiress being sisters. And their relationship and how the war ended. Next, she talked about how Dr. Warren thinks Rebecca is involved in all of this. That led to why they believed I was targeted. I kept mental notes as she talked so I could ask questions when she was done. She finished by telling us the plan for the twin's birthday on Saturday.

"Last night you spoke about the original families, what are their names?" I asked Synthia.

"It's important to note that they aren't just names, they were characteristics as well. Each family had something the other two needed. Together they were whole.

"First, there were the Boerns. This family name means warrior. The Boern pack were protectors, they had strength and honesty. They were the caregivers. They were huge. Their black wolves were second to none, not even a dire wolf could match their strength."

"Second, there were the Gewitts. Gewitt means intellectuals. The Gewitt pack had good problem solving, verbal comprehension, and reasoning skills. They had great war strategies but lacked emotion and feelings, they were extremely rational. Their wolves were sandy brown."

"Third, were the Haelan, meaning naturals. They were empaths, forgivers, and even tempered. These were the white wolves gifted with abilities to help cultivate the earth. They could heal animals and even speak to them. Their abilities were far and wide. Seers, elementals, energy bending. Anything and everything having to do with life itself." Synthia finished.

"So, what was the witch blood line called?" I asked.

"The witch line was Poer. Their name meant power. Like the others there are types of witches. I'm not familiar with the types. We can get more info from Elissa on witches." Synthia spoke.

"Okay, if my understanding is correct. At some point all the bloodlines merged after a few centuries of mating. But that didn't mean you would necessarily get all the characteristics of each bloodline. Some things manifested and some didn't?"

"Correct." Synthia clapped her hands together.

"So, the Leoht bloodline was named specifically for the Queen. Because all the characteristics manifested in her. A girl, first born of white wolves, who was also pure of heart?"

"Yes" Synthia smiled at me. I rubbed my head; this was so much information to take in.

"And what is the thing about the power of three?" I asked her. She moved her head side to side for a moment, choosing her words carefully.

"There is a prophecy. It says that the Heiress will return in the presence of the power of three. In many of our books, like the ones I lent you, it speaks of a God of light, and it is surrounded by symbols of three. We had to translate it from Old English so it might not be completely accurate. We are not sure exactly what it means though. We believe that it means that it will take three Gods or three beings of some kind to defeat the Heiress for good," Synthia stated.

"Last night when I asked if my gift of power absorption was a gift from the original family you said yes and no. What did you mean?" I asked Synthia. Synthia sighed loudly and her and Darren's eyes went black. I looked at Derek. He glanced down at the table. My eyebrows scrunched and I tilted my head, looking at Derek. He was hiding something from me. I felt his hand on my thigh tense. And I squeezed my arm that was laced through his.

"You tell me." I said to him. He looked up at his parents.

"Derek! What are you not telling me?" I tried to pull my arm from his.

"Stop, nothing that I can prove yet." He held my arm tighter.

"What does that even mean?" I was getting angry, and I could feel my face heating up. I felt hot and my breathing was becoming harsher.

"Hey, hey," He reached up with his free hand and putting it on my cheek, pulled me to look at him. "Autum, I'm not keeping anything from you, it's just a feeling..." he trailed off.

"Someone tell me. Please!" I begged.

"Okay, okay." Synthia put her hands palm down on the table.

"Yes, your power absorption is a gift from the Haelan Family. You will be a white wolf. Only white wolves get moon gifts." She answered.

"Ok, so I'm a Haelan, a natural," I said. Derek squeezed my leg, making me turn to look at him.

"You're more, so much more." He lifted my hand lacing our fingers. Bringing the back of my hand to his lips, he kissed it softly. Placing our hands on top of the table. He finished his thought, "The light Autum, the light you harness is more." I was shaking my head, not understanding what he was talking about. Derek unlaced our hands and turned my palm up.

"Wait," I breathed out loudly. "You're not saying-" I didn't finish the sentence. My mind was going a million miles a minute. I stood from the bench. Holding my hands, rubbing my thumb into my palm. "I can't be." I said looking up to all of them. They were all staring at me.

Derek got up from his seat, approaching me. I just started shaking my head. He pulled me in, embracing me. My hands covering my face as he spoke into my ear, "Why not you?"

I peered up at him, laying my hands flat on his chest. "You know why, know what I've lived through. I'm not pure Derek," I answered.

"Pure of heart, Autum. Pure of heart. And as for what you've lived through. It's like the nursery rhyme said." I gave him a puzzled look.

He finished, "Touched by darkness but not consumed." As he spoke the words. I had a moment of clarity, was it possible? My legs felt weak, as Derek held me firm against him. His mother came up behind us.

"We can finish this later; we need to go." Synthia said.

I looked at Derek. "We'll know more after your birthday." He said, giving me a quick peck. "Are you ok to walk?" I looked down realizing Derek was holding most of my body weight, his arms wrapped around my waist.

"I need a minute." Nodding, he sat me down on the bench and told his parents we would catch up in a minute. Mary knows. That's why she is training me. It all made sense now, why she was pushing me. How long had she known? I would find out tonight.

"Autum." I looked up to Derek, focusing on him.

"Hey where'd you go just then, huh? You didn't hear anything I said, did you?" He kneeled down on one knee to be level with me. Placing one hand on my leg and another on my cheek. I leaned into his hand and closed my eyes for a second.

"Sorry."

"Don't be sorry, just tell me what you're thinking. I want to help."

"I saw Mary again." I paused to gauge his reaction. He didn't have one, so I continued. "She came to me in my sleep, or I guess I went to her."

He nodded but remained silent, prompting me to finish my thoughts.

"It's somewhat complicated, but the short story is that Mary started training me last night. She wouldn't say why, but now it makes sense. She knew what I might be."

"What you are." He corrected.

I just shook my head at him. "Time is different there... its longer."

"How much longer?"

"Days there are equal to hours here." I answered, he looked surprised.

"So last night, was more than a night to you. When you woke up?"

"Yes, an entire week had passed for me."

"No wonder you missed me!" he smirked.

I smacked his arm but smiled warmly at him. "You don't think I'm crazy?" I asked.

"No, I knew you were special." With that he stood and extended his hand to me. I took it. Bending his elbow out, I laced my arm through, and we made our way over to Beta Richards house.

"Where is Lana?" I asked as we walked across the street.

"Amy is watching her."

"Oh," I said.

"Why?" he asked.

"Um, nothing. I missed her too. I actually want to watch Mulan with her." Derek laughed and shook his head. Walking into the Beta house, I couldn't help but notice that it was packed. There were hundreds of pack members here. I felt a bit overwhelmed with the information I had just learned and being around so many people. I gripped Derek's arm a little tighter.

"Do you want to go to the backyard? It will be quieter out there." He asked me. I nodded.

Derek took a throw blanket from the back of the couch. We went through the kitchen to the patio. There were still people outside, but it was quieter. Laying the blanket down next to a tree, we sat down. Derek had his back to the tree and then pulled me between his legs.

"Are you going to take off your shoes." He asked.

I laughed nervously, "I was thinking about it." I leaned forward and pulled my flats off. Then laughing I pulled Derek's off too and his socks.

"Hey," he laughed back.

Derek pulled the blanket closer to us and we put our feet in the grass. I laid back on him. Trying to relax. He took my hands in his and embraced me, making me hug myself. I let myself relax.

"What are you thinking about?" He asked. I turned my head to look at him.

"I have so many questions. Who am I? Where did I come from? Who was my father?" I let out a long breath. "What if I'm not what you and Mary think I am? What if I'm just a regular white wolf? Not the Que- I can't even say it, it feels wrong, like I'm an imposter. You could be wrong about." My voice was cut off as Derek silenced me with a kiss.

"Could you two go a day without being all over each other. Goddess." Rebecca said walking over to us. I rolled my eyes. I went to get up, but Derek held me firm. I smiled, turned, facing Rebecca.

It was her turn to roll her eyes. "We are starting inside; I was told to come get you two." She stormed off back inside. We put our shoes back on and walked inside. They were passing out champaign glasses to everyone. Elissa stood at the front of the grand room. On a small table by her side was a silver urn with a wolf engraved on it. Around the urn was a pink heart necklace with a gem in the center of it.

I felt a light touch on my arm and looked to my left. Gram was standing next to me. We silently stared at each other for a moment. I made the first move, embracing her. She started silently crying as soon as we touched. Relief flooding her that I was no longer mad at her. We pulled away from each other as Elissa began her speech.

"My mother was proceeded in death by her granddaughter Elizabeth." She paused and ran her fingers over the pink heart necklace around the urn, "and is survived by me, Rebecca, and Ethan. Today we honor the life of a women who was truly amazing. Who was kind, loving, and forgiving. I can honestly say she was my best friend. She dedicated her life to family and friends. Nothing was more important to her."

"No one ever felt anything other than love from her. She sacrificed more than I'll ever know. We were all fortunate enough to know her and I for one am in awe of all that she achieved. The warmth and happiness she brought to us cannot be overstated."

"She gave herself to others, healing their outside wounds as well as the ones within. Leaving a part of her with them always. I loved her more than words could ever possibly say, and she will live on within my heart forever more." She lifted her champaign glass, "To Mary."

"To Mary." The room echoed. Everyone walked around for a minute. A line formed to offer condolences to the family, who still stood at the front of the room. Derek walked us towards the kitchen, and Gram and I sat down.

"I'm going to go talk to Ethan, make sure he's doing okay. You and your grandma should catch up." He kissed the back of my hand and walked away. Gram and I were sitting next to each other at the table. Awkward silence filled the air.

"So, how have you been dear? Looks like your relationship is blossoming." She smiled at me.

I grabbed both her hands in mine. "It is!" I said excitedly. We continued to talk, and I filled Gram in on everything except the queen thing. Talking as softly as possible to not attract any attention.

"You have grown so much in the last few days. Just look at you, you look radiant dear." Gram said as she placed a hand on my cheek.

"Thank you, Gram." I responded.

"But you feel a little warm. How are you feeling?" Gram leaned forward putting her lips to my forehead. I laughed, déjà vu, I thought.

"What's funny?" She asked.

"Derek did the same early today, the exact thing."

"Oh," she laughed too.

"But I feel fine. I just think it's the nerves of today. Seeing Rebecca for the first time since the incident, going back to school, seeing you."

"That's understandable." She paused for a moment. "Will you be coming home now? Now that we have settled things?" She asked.

My eyes drifted to the Grand Room where I could see Derek standing with Ethan. As if he could feel me staring, Derek's eyes met mine. He smirked at me and winked. Making me blush my eyes look down for a moment but return. The heat from his stare stirred all kinds of emotions in me. My lips parted.

"Oh my," Gram said, startling me out of my stupor. I was flushed and definitely heated. Gram gaped at me.

"What," I said as innocently as possible. Pulling my gaze from him to look at her.

"Honey, the way you two are reacting to each other. I'm surprised you're still sitting here." She laughed.

"What are you talking about, Gram? It was just a glance."

"Dear, you two have a very strong connection. Did you see the way he felt your gaze? Like you called to him."

I nodded, "It was just a coincidence, good timing."

"No, that was a calling, dear."

"I thought you had to have your wolf to do that." I asked her. A 'calling' was one of our more animalistic tendencies. A wolf would use the calling to seduce their mate. Putting them into a sexual frenzy that must be sated.

"Yes, that is usually the case. Your birthday is only a couple of weeks away. If they are expecting the twin's wolves early, then it is possible you will also get yours soon too. Could also explain why you're so warm." Gram says while she pats my arm.

"So, you think my wolf will want Derek? That's why I already feel a pull to him?" I asked curiously.

She smiled sheepishly. "I'm going to miss not living with you," she said.

"Gram, I never said I wasn't moving back."

"I love you Autum but look at you two. He hasn't taken his eyes off you," she said. I looked at Derek again. He was still stealing glances at me. Still engrossed in conversation with Ethan, but still watching me. I bit my lip.

"Autum did you hear me?" Gram asked.

"Sorry, did you say something?" I spoke.

"You wouldn't last the night apart and you're not even mated yet." She shook her head at me.

"What do you mean?" I asked her.

"The feelings will get stronger until your wolf comes," she said.

"And then what will happen, will it subside?" I asked her. But I wasn't looking at her. My skin itched to be touched by him.

"Not exactly," I could feel her uneasiness, but it felt more like embarrassment.

"Why are you embarrassed?" I asked her.

"Autum! You can feel that?" Her startled voice made me look at her. Although every inch of me wanted him, wanted Derek. "I'm embarrassed because you're calling to him Autum, stop staring at him or this funeral is going to get very interesting."

"Everything is heightened in me. I could always sense your feelings; it's just getting stronger right now." I answered her.

"Listen to me, these are symptoms for days before a phase, not weeks before. Your wolf is strong, you need to be careful. Your emotions are going to be all over the place. You don't want him to go into a frenzy here Autum. Pull your gaze away." Gram warned.

I stood up distracted, not hearing a word she said. Things started moving in slow motion to me. Maybe it was the burning fury in me as I watched Rebecca try and grab Derek's arm. He was headed past her towards me, trying to ignore her. She spun him around and kissed him. She KISSED him.

My legs started moving on their own as I ran towards them. Derek slapped her, but then she tackled him to the ground. Ethan saw me coming, squared off his shoulders and stopped me, like running into a brick wall. Grabbing me he spun us around, forcing me back into the kitchen.

"Calm down, she didn't mean it. Her emotions are all over the place. She's not herself." He begged.

33

IT WILL NEVER BE YOU

Ethan POV

I didn't know what was going on with Derek tonight. He came over to talk but hasn't said more than a few words to me. I can see him looking past me. I shift, looking behind myself. I see Autum and him in a heated gaze.

"Derek, are you going to be alright?" I asked him.

"You need to look at me bro. Or you might just fuck her right here." I spoke again. My man was not himself. I stepped in front of him to block his view. He shook his head.

"Sorry, thanks." He rubbed the back of his neck. "I can't stop thinking about her. Everything I want to do to those plump pink lips of hers."

"Yeah, I can see that. Why don't you take her home, before my house becomes the next episode of 'Wild and Dangerous Animals,'" I joked.

Derek nodded and stepped around me. It was crazy watching him react to her like that. Derek, who had never shown interest in a girl before, was now ass over tea kettles for Autum Moore. I know they haven't had sex yet, but I'm surprised Derek didn't give Autum the tea my mother made for me and Rebecca. It helps calm the need of the calling. They should both be drinking it; they won't be able to fight the calling if they don't. I wish Amy was here. I could think of a few things I wanted her plump lips to be doing too. She wouldn't come tonight. Understandably just getting home from the hospital last night. She needed to rest.

The next few seconds happened so quickly I could hardly grasp what was happening. I turned to see Rebecca grab Derek's arm. He flung it off like it burned him. The rage in his eyes was unmistakable. He was furious. Made even worse when she threw herself at him. His eyes went wide when their lips met. He pulled back slapping her off of him.

The sound of the slap shocking me back to reality to see Autum coming straight at us. Her eyes were a murderous glow. She would kill my sister for touching him. The last thing I needed was for her to cause a storm or do something crazy if she absorbed my abilities. I took a few steps forward. I saw Rebecca jump from the floor and tackle Derek a second time. I knew he could take care of himself. I blocked Autum as she came barreling into me knocking the air from my lungs, but I had no time to waste. I spun us around. Asking her to calm down. Explaining to her how Rebecca had been out of control, that she didn't mean it. We were both startled when we heard Derek's Alpha voice. It stunned us into submission as we turned to watch.

Rebecca's POV

I couldn't stand being here anymore. Standing up here with the family while everyone apologized to us for my grandma dying. My mother put Elizabeth's pink heart pendant around my grandma's urn to pay homage to both of them, it was just depressing. We never met Elizabeth, my mother said she miscarried shortly after having us, so we don't remember it. I thought my night would get better when I saw Derek approaching us, but what a waste of time that thought was. He was talking to Ethan the whole time. Mom and Dad on the other side of the table were talking amongst themselves. I stepped back leaning against the wall. Derek and Ethan's conversation was boring. Not that Derek was even paying attention. Ethan was losing his best friend, and he didn't even know it. I could see Autum in the kitchen sitting next to her grandmother.

She kept eyeing Derek the entire time. Derek kept gazing at her. It made me sick to my stomach. I liked him first. They don't even have their wolves yet. They don't even know if they are mated. But that hasn't stopped them from acting like it. Derek won't even look at me anymore. The way they were cozied up outside earlier was pathetic, she is making him weak.

Derek needed a strong female. I know now that Autum must be a white wolf too. She has some kind of heat ability or something. The way she touched me the today, I will never forget. Like she was holding a hotplate to my chest.

If only Derek would consider me. My ability will be useful. What is she going to do? Heat up his soup? My birthday is in four days, the party three. Why couldn't he just wait to see, see if it's me. I felt something for him. I know it, there is something there. I just need him to feel it too. I watch as he ends the conversation with Ethan and goes to step around him.

He needed to see me. He needed to see what we could be. I grab his arm just wanting to talk. But he flings my arm off like I am diseased. The way he is looking at me with disgust turns something deep in me and it hurts. He is going to hear me out one way or another. I pull him again and throw myself at him, landing a kiss on his lips. I was expecting sparks or something. Like what all the mated wolves say it feels like. But there is nothing. Sorrow fills me, but it is short lived as Derek's hand comes down on my face. He fucking slapped me. Just like that slut did today before school.

Rage replaced my sorrow as I fell to the floor. I was seeing red, I jumped from the floor flying at him. His eyes match mine with the same rage. We tussled for a second before Derek flipped me to my back, pinning me down.

"Yes, just like that." I purred into his ear.

"It's never going to be you." He grunted back. He sat up, my dad helping him up and my mother helping me. Fucking asshole, lucky for him I like it rough.

"You were supposed to want me!" I cried out. My anger was trying to take over again.

"Don't ever touch me again!" Derek gritted through his teeth.

"Derek, wait." I tried to stop him from walking away.

"YOU WILL CALL ME ALPHA. IF YOU EVER TOUCH ME AGAIN, I'LL KILL YOU!" He boomed.

Autum POV

Beta Richard reached for Derek's arm, but he pulled it away. Derek looked at me, still being held back by Ethan. Not that I still needed to be. We were both stunned by what we had just watched. Well, I was more flustered, hearing him be so dominant hit me in all the right places.

"Let her go." He directed Ethan. Ethan released me immediately. Holding his hands up and bowing in submission. I walked to Derek, everyone moving out of my way as I approached. He reached for my hand, and I gave it to him. The skin contact, noticeably relaxing us both. Derek looked at Beta Richard and Elissa, now standing next to each other and both holding Rebecca.

"You need to explain to them what is happening to their bodies. I won't be having this conversation a second time!" He said sternly. Derek was still fuming. The scent coming off of him was pure rage and everyone could smell it. He was the same height as Beta Richard and just as broad, even for only being seventeen. His Alpha aura radiating off him like hot steam after getting out of the shower. Mmm a shower sounded nice. Goddess my dirty thoughts were getting the best of me. Derek squeezed my hand, getting my attention. I looked at him. He had one eyebrow raised, staring down at me.

I leaned in and whispered, "Can we... leave?" He nodded and everyone moved out of our way as we headed to the door. His parents met us there.

"You two should stay, make sure they tell the twins why Rebecca just mauled me." Derek said to his parents.

"We had the same thought." His father replied.

Synthia reached for me and pulled me in for an awkward hug. Made awkward because Derek wouldn't release my hand. A small laugh left her lips, "You're the only thing keeping him calm right now." She said into my ear.

"We'll take care of things here; we'll see you two at home later." Synthia waved us away.

Home, what a word. I needed to talk to my grandma. Because home to me was wherever Derek was. I could just feel it. It felt... right.

We ran into Amy outside. Lana holding her hand as they crossed the street over to us. Lana came barreling towards us, I thought to jump on her brother. Nope, she ran to me. I smiled down at her.

"Hey little one, why are you out here?" I asked.

Amy answered. "Sorry," she was acting very timid. Not the Amy we all knew. "I just felt funny, like I needed to see Ethan." Her face flushed. I immediately thought of the calling. He must have been thinking of her. She was acting on instincts and didn't know it.

"We can take Lana. Can you ask my grandmother to come outside for me please?" I asked her. She nodded and took a very large path around us. I felt bad for her. I hadn't spoken to her since the incident. But I knew now after seeing her, I had no ill will towards her.

"Are you ok?" Derek asked.

"Yeah, that was strange talking to her for the first time. But I'm good. She seemed scared though," I answered.

"She did," He agreed. "Did you and your grandma need more time to talk? She can come over." He spoke softly.

"No, we had a good conversation. She asked me when I was coming home." I spoke. Derek stiffened and so did Lana as she still clung to my waist.

"You can't leave," Lana whined. Gram walked out of the house then.

"Looks like someone likes you." Gram said as she approached, looking down at Lana.

"Yes, it appears so. I was just telling them that you asked when I was moving home." I spoke.

"Oh yes, about that. I was just speaking to Alpha Darren and Luna Synthia to that regard."

"You were?" Derek asked.

"Yes," Gram said, "If that scuffle in there was any indication of anything, then we should do it soon. So, when should we get your things?" She said, directing the question at me.

"Tomorrow, works for me." I responded.

"Wait, Autum. You don't have to leave. Ellen, I will protect her. What happened in there wasn't anyone's fault." He tried to reason with her. I started laughing and so did Gram. Lana and Derek now giving me death glares.

"I will see you tomorrow then." I said to Gram. Giving her a one-handed hug. Because Derek was still refusing to let go of my hand. Silly boy. Gram kissed my forehead.

"Get some rest dear. You are still a bit warm." She said to me. Rolling my eyes, I nodded to her. Derek was looking at me totally lost.

"What's going on?" He asked as my grandmother went back inside the house.

"Apparently, I'm moving in with you and your parents have already approved." I smiled at him.

"You little brat," he laughed, "letting me think you were leaving." He finished.

"Would you have let me leave?" I asked, smiling up at him.

"Not in a million years, but your gonna pay for that." He picked me up throwing me over his shoulders.

"Put me down." I laughed, "Lana, help me." I cried out.

"Nope, you deserve a spanking for that one Autum." Lana teased.

"You think so little sister. Should we spank her?" Derek asked her. I flailed in his grasp, as he walked towards the pack house, every bounce sending vibrations to my core. My face was hot at the thought of being spanked by Derek. It shouldn't have aroused me, but it did. Goddess how it did.

Lana bounced up and down excitedly as we walked back to the pack house. "You're getting a spanking." She sang.

"Lana, stop making it sound like fun." I laughed at her.

"It is fun, when you're not the one being spanked." She taunted back. We entered the house, but Derek didn't put me down.

"Lana, I'm going to take Autum upstairs and give her a good spanking. But I need you to stay down here." He started to say.

"But why," Lana pouted.

"Because Autum is going to want some time alone after we are done. But she has been talking all day about watching Mulan with you. So, you get the movie and popcorn ready, and we'll be back down in a bit, okay?"

Lana started jumping up and down. "Yes! You are gonna watch too?"

"Sure am," Derek answered her as he trudged up the stairs.

I saw Lana bounce off to the kitchen as Derek took me up the stairs. Moving one of his hands up my leg under my dress. His warm hands sent goosebumps wherever he touched. He reached my ass and squeezed hard. "I'm going to spank this little ass of yours until its red." He groaned out.

"No," I meant it to come out stern, but it was airy and sensual.

"If I didn't know any better, I'd think you like being spanked. I thought you were a good girl, Autum." Derek teased.

"I am, I am. I'm good, I'll be good." I pleaded although, not asking him not to spank me, the thought had my arousal flooding the hall as we entered Derek's room. He closed the door behind us.

SMACK!

"Ow!" I yelled. It stung where he smacked me, but then his hand massaged my cheek. The sparks distracting me, the tingle making my core throb.

Derek inhaled loudly through his nose, "but you liked it." I couldn't see his devilish grin, but I could hear it in his voice.

SMACK!

The second one elicited a moan. The vibration sending shockwaves to my bud below. It stung more, but again Derek kept his hand there, massaging the sting away.

"Are you going to deceive me like that again?" Derek asked in a low, deep voice.

"No," I breathed out. But I was thinking yes, the way he was man handling me, was thrilling me.

"Did you just lie to me?" he asked. His voice was so deep, even the sound was making me wet. I felt his hand lift.

SMACK!

"Lying only gets you more." He rang out as I bit my lip stifling another moan. "You want more don't you?" He lifted me off his shoulder tossing me on the bed. I bounced as Derek pushed my legs apart, climbing onto the bed.

He loomed over me and brought his head to my ear, "Answer me, you want more? You like it?" he asked.

"No," I lied, biting my lip. I could see the mischief in his eyes. He pushed off the bed. Grabbing my legs, he twisted quickly. Flipping me to my stomach. He pulled me till my feet were planted on the floor. My ass in the air. He pushed my dress up over it. I tried to cover my ass with my hands. Derek grabbed them with one of his hands, holding them on my back.

SMACK!

I buried my face in the blanket, moaning. He cupped my pussy with one hand.

"So wet, this will be the second time you've had to change these panties today."

Goddess, I wanted him, all of him. To be consumed by him.

34

PILLOW FIGHT

❦

Autum POV

With my arms still pinned behind my back, Derek pulled them towards himself, forcing me to stand. He released them, so they fell to my sides before unzipping the back of my dress. Leaning into me, breathing on my neck. "Come take a shower with me?" he asked. He caressed down my arms until he reached my hands. He laced our fingers together. "Please?" He asked again.

"You'll see me." I answered.

"I've already seen you."

"That was different." I spoke.

"I won't look." He replied.

Turning my head to look at him. My back still pressed against his chest. "You won't look?"

"I'll keep my eyes right above here." He lifted my hands in his and moved them over my covered breasts. I would have never thought touching myself would elicit the response he got, but I couldn't have been more wrong. My nipples instantly harden. The stiff peaks showing through my dress. Derek groaned in my ear. Sending a chill down by entire body and finding its resting place deep in my core. My body felt like it was on fire. Already flushed from the spanking and now dawning a tinge of pink and red that seemed to take a permanent residence as his hands on me fueled my arousal.

"Ok." I answered.

Derek quickly dropped one of my hands and pulled me with the other towards his bathroom. He turned on the lights but dimmed them low. I smiled to myself at his thoughtfulness. He turned the shower on first so it could get warmed up. Then grabbed two towels from the cabinet. He went to the sink and started brushing his teeth.

I laughed, "What are you doing?"

"Getting her off of me." He scrunched his eyebrows as he looked in the mirror. The disgust of what had happened earlier now on his mind. I was glad he was angry. It helped me not to be. I walked up behind him and hugged him. Resting my head on his back. I felt the tension leave his body as he relaxed into my touch.

He finished brushing and turned around. Looking into my eyes he helped me pull my arms out of the sleeves and the dress fell to the floor. I wore no bra with this dress, so one less thing to remove. I found the bottom hem of his shirt and lifted it off of him. Biting my lip, I reached for my panties and pushed them down. Stepping out of them I walked to the shower. Looking over my shoulder I expected Derek to have peaked at my ass, but his eyes met mine. A small smile on my lips. "Are you coming?" I asked him as I opened the shower door and stepped in.

"Oh, I plan to be." He answered, getting a giggle from me.

The shower was perfect and steamy, just how I imagined it earlier. Derek came in behind me. My breath stilled as I felt his chest touch my back. His manhood was already ready and pushing up against me.

His hand reached for the loofa, and after putting soap on it, he started washing me with it. His bare hand mimicking the same movement rubbing and massaging every inch of my body. The shower spray rinsing it away as he moved slowly, getting every part of me. His lips grazed my neck as he pulled my still braided hair to one side. Sucking on my marking spot deepening the hickey. The rising steam carrying the scent with it. Derek ran the loofa over my arms, and I took it from him as he reached my hands.

Turning, I started cleaning him, duplicating his actions. I ran my fingers over every ridge of his chest. Reaching my arms around him, I pressed my breasts into his chest. My nipples hardened with the contact of his skin. I started to wash his back, but Derek leaned in and kissed me. It was a deep kiss. Full of want. Moaning into his mouth, I dropped the loofa. Derek slowly pushed me to the wall. One hand around me, stopping my back from hitting the cold tile. The other rolling my nipple between his fingers.

"I want your scent all over me. I want to taste every part of you." Derek said as he kissed down my neck. Moving farther down he took my nipple in his mouth.

"Yes," I cried out. I wanted him all over me. I wanted his lips to taste all of me as he rolled my nipple with his tongue.

Derek reached for the tap, shutting the shower off. He lifted me up and I wrapped my legs around him. He carried me out of the shower, kissing me harder, needily. He ripped the towel from the holder and wrapped it around my back while still carrying me. He walked to his dresser and pushed everything on it to the floor. He sat me there. Pressing me against the wall, he moved his lips back to my breast, massaging the other with his hand. I leaned my head back, letting the euphoric feeling wash over me as he moved his lips to my exposed neck.

One of his hands stayed on my breast while the other traveled lower until he brushed my slit with his fingers. He parted them, causing my sweet scent to grow stronger. Derek started kissing lower. My legs fell from around his waist. He reached around and pulled me to the edge of the dresser. Then used both hands to push my knees wider.

"Derek?" I questioned.

"Tonight, when your sleeping, will it feel like a week for you again?" he asked. Finding it hard to concentrate with his fingers teasing my clit, I only nodded. He smiled up at me, his mischievous grin. "Then let's give you something to remember me by while you're gone."

My eyes went wide as his silky tongue made contact with my pussy. My head flew back. My moan was airy and long. I grabbed his head with one hand, getting a fist full of hair. The other gripped the edge of the dresser as I leaned my shoulders back touching the wall. His tongue circled my clit as his mouth sucked. Then it dived inside of me. He pushed his tongue in and out of me. Then moved back to my clit. Covering my whole pussy with his mouth. My stomach was clenching, my core throbbing, coming closer to my climax as his tongue touched every inch of me, tasting me.

"Grab your knees," He rasped out. I did, pulling them further back for him, exposing my wet pussy for him. He inserted two fingers coating his hand in my juices. Pumping them in and out, wetting my thighs. He pulled his fingers from me, reaching down and started stroking himself.

My body was on fire, watching him touch himself. I was going to come. Come for him. He increased his speed. And I watched him with bated breath. His hot mouth went down on me again. His tongue going flat and moving back and forth on my sensitive bud. Groaning, he lifted his head. And using his free hand dove deep into my pussy with three fingers, his thumb on my clit and his pinky rubbing on my ass. I cried out at the new feeling. Unexpectedly, it sent a chill through me. My hips were pulsing, liking the new pressure. He stroked himself faster and faster. He captured my lips with his, making me taste myself. He pulled away and moved to my ear, biting it.

"More pressure" I moaned out.

"Where?" Guessing, he added pressure to his thumb on my clit.

"Yes, Goddess yes."

His eyes went wide with excitement. I rocked my hips, enjoying the pressure as heat enveloped my entire body. I would never, could never, get enough of him.

"I'm going to come, Autum." His voice deep

"Oh goddess," I cried out.

He pushed his fingers faster and deeper, my pussy throbbing, my juices spilling out coating my ass as his fingers pushed in further.

"Come for me Autum."

And I did. His lips moved, capturing my cry as I was pushed over the edge. The air was electric as my muffled moans filled it. The sound of our wet flesh making me come undone wave after wave. I rode out my orgasm as he found his own release. He slowed his pumping. He hardened our kiss, spilling his seed onto my stomach.

We stayed there, our breathing heavy. I let my legs fall. And put my arms around Derek's neck. Derek leaned his head onto my shoulder with his hands on either side of me on the wall.

He leaned down and kissed both of my breasts, then lifted his head to look at me. I smiled at him. I could feel that my face was still flushed, and my chest was still heaving with each breath I took. I leaned forward to kiss him. He kissed me back. Grabbing the nape of my neck, he pulled me in to deepen the kiss.

"You wanna go jump in the shower, to clean that up?" He pointed to my stomach, and I laughed. Nodding, he helped me down off the dresser and I used the towel to clean most of it up. He gave me another kiss.

"I'll go grab some of your clothes while you're in there. I'll meet you downstairs. I'm going to go check on Lana."

When I got out of the shower, I glanced at myself in the mirror. Swiping the fog away I opened my mouth to look at my teeth. They were throbbing. I was nervous to shift for the first time, my birthday was two weeks away. If I got my wolf before Derek, I would know if he's my mate first. The thought thrilled me, that I would know so soon. I stepped out of the bathroom, walking to the bed where my clothes were laid out to get dressed. I looked at Derek's perfectly made bed and smirked. I jumped into it, rolling around wrapping myself in his blanket. I felt his scent engulfing me. I breathed it in and let all the anxiety leave me.

"What are you doing?" A small voice asked.

Peering through the blankets, I saw Lana. I rolled myself out of the blankets and laughed.

"Just making your brothers perfect bed a mess, as payback." I grinned at her.

She looked at me with her big doe eyes. "Can we jump on it?" Lana asked.

"Let's do it." I stood on the bed, grabbing her hands to pull her up.

Her laugh was infectious as we jumped on the bed. She was jumping doing her karate moves. The blankets on the floor and the sheets coming up over their corners, I laughed at what Derek would do when he saw.

"What are you two doing?" Derek asked sternly as if I had summoned him by mere thought. Lana and I fell to our butts.

"It was her idea." Lana said pointing at me.

"Traitor," I laughed as Derek approached his bed. I panicked grabbing his pillow.

"Pillow fight!" I yelled.

"Don't you dare," Derek warned. I picked up one of the pillows, and Lana followed suit. I threw the pillow at him, and he caught it.

"Oh no." Lana cried, jumping off the bed. Derek went for her first. They started dueling below me with their pillows. She was quickly jumping and diving. He didn't land a hit. I couldn't tell if he was trying to or not, but I had to believe he was letting her win.

Lana swung hard, landing a good blow to Derek's chest. The pillow tore and duck feathers went everywhere. I was on my knees on the bed now. My chest hurt I was laughing so hard. Derek's face fell when he saw the feathers fly from the pillow.

My eyes met him. He looked at me in disbelief, like he couldn't believe I would let this happen. I burst out in laughter, watching as the feathers float to the ground. Derek spun in a circle taking in all the feathers before his stern eyes landed back on me. My eyes went wide.

"No." I screamed as Derek came barreling into me. We rolled on the bed, my pillow flying from me as I lost my grip. Derek and I rolled until he was on top.

"Lana, help me!" I pleaded. The girl did not disappoint me. She jumped onto the bed and then onto Derek's back, wrapping her legs and arms around him.

"Hey, not fair," Derek whined. The door creaked open, and we all turned our heads to see Derek's parents gaping at us.

"She did it!" Derek and Lana said in unison. Both pointing at me.

My mouth opened but no sound came out. I was shocked, in disbelief. Derek held his fist up to his sister and she fist bumped him. I laughed at them. They were so cute. He dismounted me with Lana still on his back. Holding his hand out to me I grabbed it, and he helped me off the bed. His mother was still watching us as we approached the door.

"We are going to go calm this one down by finishing our movie downstairs." Derek says using his thumb to point to Lana on his back.

Derek pulls me with his other hand as we gingerly walk past his mother. She doesn't say a word to us as we pass. Her arms crossed she shook her head at us. His father was already gone, probably kept walking to their room once he saw the mess we made.

We settled on the coach. The movie was already half over. Curling up, all three of us shared a blanket. We finished the movie and Derek took a sleeping Lana to her room. I followed as he laid her down and covered her, kissing her forehead before he left her side. A small smile on my lips at this sweet gesture. He turned her light off and shut her door.

"So, we are sleeping in your room tonight." He stated.

"We?" I questioned, grinning.

He pinched my side getting a laugh. Wrapping his arm around me, I sighed and leaned into him as we walked into my room. Completely content with us and this new life I was living with Derek. He turned his head and kissed my forehead. A smile playing on my lips.

We laid gazing at each other. Derek grabbed my hand and placed it on his chest. "What's it like when you are dreaming? Does it really feel like a week? Do you get hungry?"

I laughed, "No not hungry. It does feel like a week, honestly longer because I don't sleep either."

"So, you don't get tired. What kind of training is Mary giving you?"

"I don't get tired. Mary is teaching me to open all of my chakras." I paused, almost embarrassed, "She's also teaching me combat training." Although in the dark, I could still see his raised eyebrows.

"Mary is doing all that?"

"She is." I yawned.

"One more question. Is it hard, feeling like being gone for so long?"

"It wasn't as hard as I thought it would be, but somehow I feel like tonight will be harder than last night."

"Why is that?" He asked as he brushed a loose hair from my face.

"You said one more question." I laughed, but continued, pausing, unsure how to answer, "The hardest part was… not seeing you." I felt my face flush. "The more time I spend with you, the less I want to be apart."

He leaned in to kiss me. It was soft and gentle. "I don't think I could do it. Even thinking of you moving back home... What can I do to help?" He asked.

"I can feel you holding me, while I'm there. Feel your touch. It made me feel safe and protected last night." I smiled softly at him.

He gave me another quick peck on the lips. "Turn around then, I'll be big spoon." We repositioned ourselves. Derek holding me. One arm under my head the other draped across my stomach. I placed my hand over his and laced our fingers together. His head rested above mine.

"Where do you go when you sleep?" He yawned this time.

"To a garden... I don't know where it is... if it's just a figment of my... imagination." I paused to yawn. "But there's a waterfall... so many flowers... and fairies... it's... beautiful."

"Sleep beautiful. I'll keep you safe, protect you."

35

SEARCHING THE
SCHOOL

❧

Elissa POV

Getting ready for the day seemed to take a bit longer than usual. Thinking back to last night's incident and how Rebecca had behaved made me ashamed. How had I missed her feelings towards the Alpha's son? To also learn that my sweet child was the school bully had me feeling emotions I was not used to. Emeka was growing restless in my head.

'We have failed her and now use her as bait,' Emeka growled. She was pacing back and forth within me, now making me restless.

'We endanger many more by not keeping quiet, the Alpha is right. In a few days, those that wish to use her will realize she doesn't possess the gift of Leoht, and she will be safe.' I reminded her.

She was still not happy with this decision. For the most part she saw the reasons why we were here. To be a part of a pack helped ensure our safety and the safety of our children. Convincing my sigma wolf was difficult, but at the thought of losing her mate, whom was the Alpha's Beta, she was inclined to stay. Richard and his wolf, Artemis, were the only reason she agreed. She was like a lovesick pup in their presence. She tried to rebel at first. She hated following the rules. At times I am still given leniency when she misbehaves, like if she would have shifted during the Council meeting. It's not something I can prevent at times; she is stronger than I am.

"Rebecca," I called as I descended the stairs.

"I'm coming." She answered with a bit of annoyance.

I was giving her a ride to school today since I was meeting Dr. Warren there for our tour. Ethan had left earlier with Derek and Autum. It was apparent to most of us that Derek and Autum would be mates. After last night's display it was obvious how protective they were of each other. That only comes from our most animalistic instincts. It's like your mind and body know and you can't fight it.

We walked out to the car and Rebecca was sullen. As I pulled out of the driveway, I tried to make conversation.

"How are you feeling today?" I asked her.

"Like a child, who needs to get a ride from her mommy," she pouted.

"Well, you do sound like a child." I retorted. She rolled her eyes. "I don't understand what happened to you. Why are you being this way?" I questioned her.

"Everything was good until Autum came. That bitch ruined everything." Her anger was apparent.

"Rebecca, you can't blame others for your misbehaviors. Everything that has happened has been your own doing. You can't blame her and Derek for being mated, that wasn't decided by them." I reasoned with her.

"They don't even know if they are mated!" she screamed. I pulled the car over. My baby needed to vent, and I needed to be there for her. I couldn't do that and drive at the same time. I turned to look at her and grabbed her hands. She tried to pull away, but I held firm.

"Rebecca, you can tell their feelings are deep for each other. You will understand what I mean when you get your wolf." I spoke softly.

"When I get my wolf, I will finally be able to prove to you all that Derek is mine. My wolf will know, and my feelings will be validated."

"Honey, I think you are mistaken your feelings for him. We all feel the pull to our Alpha's. We love and adore them; they are our protectors. The mate bond is... different."

"How do you mean?" She asked.

"For instance, your father, right now he is doing border patrols with Alpha Darren. I haven't seen him for two hours. My skin is itchy, waiting for his touch. We have already mind-linked each other four times. Just to hear each other's voice. If I saw another female come close to him with the wrong intentions, I would cut her throat." I gripped her hands tightly, even thinking it made my wolf want to rage. He was ours. Rebecca looked at me with an eyebrow raised.

"Sorry," I muttered, loosening my grip, "But you see what I mean."

"When I kissed Derek last night, it didn't feel the way I thought it should feel." She admitted, "I was expecting sparks, like you all talk about, but I felt... nothing. The way he looked at me only fueled my rage at being rejected."

I nodded my head. Lifting one of my hands, I placed it on her cheek. "When you find your mate, he will only have eyes for you. You will feel sensations just from making eye contact. And when you do look into his eyes, you will feel like you are the only two in the room." A single tear fell from her eyes. I wiped it away, leaning forward I kissed her forehead. She let out a long sigh.

"I don't know how to move on. I had it in my head for so long, that I just feel hate towards Autum. I know the things I did were wrong, but I felt justified in doing what I did." She sighed again. "She is weak, she even allowed me to ride with them to school yesterday after everything I had done. She is not strong enough to be our next Luna."

"My love, do not confuse empathy for weakness. It is a Luna's job to protect the women and children. Autum was able to look past your wrongdoings to forgive you. Then you betrayed her again last night when you kissed him. Your brother is the only reason you are sitting here uninjured right now."

As if some understanding finally sunk in, she nodded her head. Anyone who was paying attention saw the way Derek and Autum were looking at each other all night. The fire in her eyes when Rebecca kissed him. Thankfully, Ethan was quick to respond the moment he realized what was happening. He will make an excellent Beta to Derek and Autum. And Autum, there is something about her that has me intrigued. Since the moment I met her on the day of my mother's death, Richard and I agreed, she seemed familiar.

Rebecca leaned forward and hugged me. I held her tight for a few moments, letting her know I was there for her. We separated and I pulled back out onto the road.

"Now I just need to figure out how to get my friends back." She moped. I looked at her briefly, not wanting to take my eyes off the road for too long.

"You could apologize." I suggested.

"Right, and that will just make everything better." She answered sarcastically.

"Well, it couldn't hurt. Being humble will go a long way." I didn't see her eyes roll, but I felt it. My daughter was so stubborn and strong willed. She needed her friends, hopefully they were willing to forgive her... again.

Pulling up to the school, I parked next to Dr. Warren. Rebecca jumped out and gave me a hug before walking in.

"I love you, thanks mom."

"I love you too honey."

She ran inside. Hearing a croaking noise of sorts, I looked around. A raven perched on the tree outside the entrance garnered my attention. He was a beautiful bird. I tried to talk to him but all he would say was that he was waiting for a friend. He was beautiful with blue eyes; I'd never seen a raven with blue eyes before.

Dr. Warren got out of her car. "Talking to the bird, I presume?" She asked.

"Trying to but he isn't very talkative." I laughed.

"Rebecca looked to be doing better." Dr. Warren stated.

"We talked and cleared some things up. Hopefully she will make better choices." I replied. We started walking towards the school.

"How are you feeling today, you look tired," I asked her.

"I didn't sleep well last night. But I'll be fine."

"I'm sorry, did you think of where we should start then, on our tour today?"

She laughed, "Yes, I did actually. I was thinking we should walk the perimeter first. Then the main hall. After that we should visit the nurse's office. If Amy had been injured the nurse would know. That could be where the witch or Heiress got her blood." Dr. Warren answered. It sounded like a good idea to me. We began by walking the perimeter. Nothing unusual stuck out to me.

"Are you sensing anything out here?" I questioned.

She gave a faint sigh. "No, let's move inside." Before we began walking the halls, we visited Principal Smith.

Walking into the main lobby, Rebecca was sitting behind the counter. She was the Office Assistant for first period. "Long time no see." I smiled at her.

She smiled back, "Principal Smith is waiting for you in his office, you can just walk in."

"Thanks honey." Principal Smith was behind his desk when we walked in. He stood to greet us.

"Dr. Warren, Elissa, welcome. Thank you for coming so soon to ensure the safety of our students." He shook both our hands.

"Of course." I responded.

"I'd like to jump right in," Dr. Warren started, "Can you tell us if you have noticed anything peculiar. Or if any of the teachers or other staff have acted out of character?" She questioned.

He seemed to ponder her question for quite some time. "Most the staff have worked here for years. There have been a few complaints made this year that you could follow up on." He stated.

Dr. Warren pulled a notebook out from her purse and a pen. "I'm ready."

He began. "Lunch lady betty was said to be harassing one of the students, it was said she even spit in her food once. I couldn't substantiate the claim and the student refused to write a statement. They said it was a misunderstanding."

"Who was the student?" Dr. Warren inquired.

"The student was Autum Moore."

Dr. Warren nodded and took some notes. "Anything else?" She asked.

"Yes, I have had multiple complaints about Counselor Robin. It isn't really a valid complaint in my opinion, but I'll let you decide. Some students feel neglected because she has had to miss so many days of work."

"Do you know why she's been absent?" I asked.

"Yes, her son has been ill, and she has needed to take extra days to care for him." He replied.

"I can confirm that, I have been treating her son." Dr. Warren waved her hand dismissively.

"There hasn't been much of anything else. Just student rivalry." He shrugged.

"Which students have you had problems with?" Dr. Warren asked.

"It's really not that big a deal, it's normal for students to act out at this age, they are just discovering who they are as wolves. Their minds and body's going through changes for the first time."

I sighed, "Its fine Principal Smith, I know you are just reluctant to name my daughter since I am here. But if we are going to help, we need to know." I reasoned with him.

He rubbed the back of his neck. "Yes, it is Rebecca, she really has been having a difficult time this year. She, Amy, and Autum had a confrontation on the first day of school in the girls' restroom next to Mrs. Landon's classroom. And several smaller things throughout the last eight weeks."

"Okay, anything else." She asked.

"Autum punched Derek a few weeks ago, but I'm sure you heard about that?" he said.

"Yes, yes, I did. Okay well if that's it. We are going to walk the hall and then head to the nurse's office. Probably see the counselor as well."

"She called in today. But you are welcome to look around her office." He informed us. We both nodded and headed out of the office. As we left the bell rang ending first period.

"Rebecca, would you mind showing us the girl's restroom next to Mrs. Landon's classroom?" I asked her.

"Sure." We followed her down the hall, it was very close to the office right past the library.

"Thanks honey, I hope you have a good day today." She smiled at me but didn't respond. She kept walking, entering Mrs. Landon's classroom for her second period class. I followed Dr. Warren into the restroom. She walked to every stall and looked up at the ceiling. Then she looked under all of the sinks.

"Are you seeing or feeling anything?" I asked her.

"No, not in here. Let's move on." We continued to walk around the main hall. We entered any other restrooms and any empty classrooms. We didn't see anything out of the ordinary.

As we made the final turn. The nurse's office was on our right. The counselor's office is also inside the same space. A bit further down was the entrance and the office lobby. We had made it all the way around and had found nothing so far. We opened the door and stepped into the shared space. There was a desk with another student aid, assisting with check ins. There were three additional doors. One led to the nurse's office, another the counselor's office and the third looked like a sick room.

"How can I help you?" asked the student aid.

"We are here to see nurse Danielle." I answered.

"She is in the sick room with a student. You can wait in her office if you'd like."

"Yes, thank you." We both responded and moved toward her office. Nurse Danielle's office was filled with plants. She had several jars with plant starters in them. As well as a hanging garden on the wall with all kinds of herbs. While we waited Dr. Warren started riffling through her things. Opening cupboards and drawers.

"What are you looking for?" I asked her as I kept watch.

"I'm looking for notes or symbols on loose paper or in a notebook. Sometimes when you are casting spells or practicing a skill, you absentmindedly start to scribble notes or draw pictures." She answered. She looked in the trash bin last and then took a seat in front of her desk. I joined her and a few minutes later Nurse Danielle came in.

"Hello, how can I help you ladies today?" She asked.

"We are wondering if you keep a log of injured students that seek treatment?" Inquired Dr. Warren.

"Yes, I do." She logged onto her computer and started typing rapidly.

"What are you looking for?" She asked. Dr. Warren and I had discussed keeping Amy's name out of it. So, the questioning would be non-descriptive.

"We want to know if any students have visited you since school started, with serious injuries.?" Dr. Warren requested. She started typing again. She moved the mouse around and clicked a few times.

"Ok, what would you consider a serious injury." She asked.

"Well, I think any large injuries or multiple small injuries." Dr. Warren answered.

"Also, we only need students in their senior year." I included. Dr. Warren nodded to me. Our thought was a large injury could produce the blood needed or multiple small injuries could produce it over time. We also only needed people that would be close to our kids. Underclass man was not in that group.

"Ok, let me change the search." She paused while she typed some more. "We have five students that have been seen for a large injury or multiple times."

"How about you give us their names first and then we'll discuss the injuries." I suggested.

"Alright, we have Samanth Rowe, Brian Tillis, James Brook, Derek Bell and Amy Dord." Perfect, she named Amy. We would let her tell us about the other students then focus on Amy.

"Please continue with their injuries," I asked her. Dr Warren was ready with pen in hand.

"Samantha has several injuries, she injuries herself quite a bit in P.E. Sprained arms. Multiple bruises. She was this way in elementary school too. She is a very clumsy girl. She even broke her arm and ribs when she was younger." I remembered that about Samantha. She would go to training but always hurt herself. We excluded her from sparing because she would always get injured. She was a bright girl, but she was no fighter.

Danielle continued, "Brian was injured during football practice, he sprained his ankle and had to use crutches for three weeks. James hurt himself during track and field, the pole snapped when he was mid leap and fell pretty hard. He broke his wrist. He is still recovering from that. Derek was punched and broke his nose... I'm sure you are familiar with that incident.

"We are. And what about Amy's injuries?" I asked.

"Yes, Amy has been here three times since school has started. It looks like the first time was on the first day of school. She was concerned after her confrontation with Rebecca and Autum in the girls' restroom. She came to me with a migraine. She thought she had been persuaded by Autum."

"You mean by Rebecca?" Dr Warren questioned.

"No, she said she thought it was Autum, Rebecca was mad at her for not helping her and she doesn't know why she just stood there and let Autum leave."

Dr. Warren scrunched up her eyebrows, I tried to act surprised as well. I was mad at the nurse for disclosing this information. Alpha Darren had been very clear he didn't want anyone to know about Autum. We never would have thought this nurse would be the one to spill the beans. It's not like she knew what she was saying, she obviously didn't believe it was a valid concern. If she did, Principal Smith would have known about it.

"But you didn't report it to Principal Smith?" I asked her.

"Well, no. It's absurd. Of course, it had to be Rebecca." She scoffed like we were idiots.

"What about the other two times you saw her?" I asked.

"The second trip she had a bloody nose from getting hit by a volleyball. And the third trip here she had a migraine again."

"When was she here for the bloody nose?" Dr Warren inquired.

"That was two weeks ago."

"And the migraine?"

"Let's see, that was a week ago. The day of the windstorm it looks like. Oh, I remember that one, Counselor Robin had actually brought her to me. She had been visiting with her when she developed her headache."

"Okay, I don't think I have any other questions at this time, would you like to ask her anything Elissa?"

"No questions, just to let us into Counselor Robin's office." Nurse Danielle called Principal Smith to get confirmation we could go into Counselor Robin's office while she was away. He confirmed and she unlocked her door for us.

36

MAGIC IN THE AIR

ℰ↝

Elissa POV

We entered the office and asked Nurse Danielle to excuse herself. She looked annoyed, but we didn't want her in the office with us. Our suspicions went on high alert at hearing Amy had been in this very office the day of the attack on Autum. Not to mention she had a bloody nose the week before that. Giving the counselor access to her blood.

When we walked in Dr. Warren visibly shuttered.

"What's wrong?" I asked.

"There is definitely residual magic lurking in this room."

She walked to the desk, and I started searching the bookshelf. Now that I knew what she was looking for, I could help. We started rummaging through everything. I flipped through every book and opened the cupboards at the bottom. In the cupboard I found a brass burning plate. There was a piece of paper half burned on it. I could barely make out the writing on it. It looked like some kind of binding spell.

Turning around. Dr Warren was still opening drawers at the desk.

"Elissa, look!" She exclaimed.

I walked over and peered down at the bits of loose papers she had scattered across the desk. They were very eerie. They had symbols all over them.

"I found something too," I told her.

She looked up to me as I brought over the burning plate. I held up the burnt piece of paper. It had not been completely burned.

"What do you think she was trying to do?" I asked Dr. Warren

"I'm not sure, from the looks of these scribblings she could have been trying to cast a Binding Spell. There are also incantations for the blood magic curse." She answered.

"From what is still left on this burnt paper. I can make out 'R.O.B.,' I think she was trying to bind herself. Why would she do that?"

My mind was trying to make sense of this. She must have been the one to curse Amy to hurt Autum. Blood magic was used. But then she tried to bind her own magic. I looked to Dr. Warren, she also looked confused.

"We should go see if we can find her. Her boy has been in the hospital for a while, maybe she is there. We can ask her some questions before we turn this all over to the Alpha." She asked.

"I'm not sure, she could be dangerous. I also don't want to jump to conclusions either."

"Well, I can go under the guise of doing a follow up with her boy. We can pretend we don't know about any of this stuff."

"Yes, let's do it. We can meet with the Alpha after to see what he wants to do next."

We left the school in our own vehicles; I followed closely behind Dr. Warren. When we arrived at the hospital everyone greeted us as we walked by. Dr. Warren led the way as we took the elevator to the second floor. We walked briskly to the children's ward and entered. We approached the room with caution. Dr. Warren peered in through the small window. She shook her head at me, and we walked in. Robin was not here. Her son lay unconscious on his bed. Dr. Warren walked in first but abruptly stopped me right inside the room. We both peered down at the floor. There on the floor was cast a white circle around the bed of the child. A candle next to the sink had been used but was not currently lit.

"Do you think she put a protection spell on him?" I looked to Dr. Warren. Her hand still on my chest, keeping me back.

"There's only one way to find out." She stepped forward allowing her hand to cross over the circle and immediately cried out in pain. Losing her footing, I grasped around her waist before she could fall to the floor.

"Thank you." She panted. Bringing her injured arm closer to her chest. "Why would she do that, stopping us from helping her own son?" She questioned.

"We need to find her. I'm going to talk to the Alpha. You need to go talk to the staff and find out when she was here last. No one has obviously been in here, or they would have informed us of the danger before we entered." She nodded. We left the room, and she went towards the nurse's station. While I stepped away to mind-link the Alpha.

'Alpha' I mind linked.

'Elissa?'

'Yes, Alpha. We finished our tour at the school. The only place we found anything was in Counselor Robin's office.'

'What did you find?' He inquired.

'We found spells in a notebook in her desk. One spell looked to be the one for the blood magic curse used on Amy. We confirmed Amy had been to the nurse's office for an injury the week before the incident and again the day of the incident that took place at Omega Julian's home.'

'Ok, you said spells? What else did you find?'

'Yes, the second one I'm still trying to make sense of. It was a binding spell. She also had a burning plate. It's weird because it looks like she was trying to bind her own magic.'

'What did she have to say to that?' He questioned.

'She was not here today. She called in. Her son has been sick and in the hospital. Principal Smith said she has missed many days of work. We came to the hospital next to see if she was here visiting her son. Now I have even more questions. Her son has a protection spell on him. Dr. Warren was injured when she tried to approach him.'

'I'm going to go to her home, see if she is there. Tell Dr. Warren she should stay at the hospital the rest of the day to see if Robin returns. Elissa, I want you to go back to the school. Inform Principal Smith of your findings and see if you can pull Amy aside and talk to her about Counselor Robin. See if she remembers anything from that day.'

'Yes, Alpha.'

He ended the mind-link and I found Dr. Warren to inform her of the plan.

"How long will the protection spell last, on the boy?" I asked her.

"Until she removes it, or she dies." Dr. Warren replied.

"I have a bad feeling about this whole thing. I'm heading back to the school. Alpha Darren wants you to stay here with the boy if Robin comes call us."

She nodded in agreement, and I set off for the school. When I arrived, I went straight to Principal Smith's office. I waved to my new bird friend who was still perched outside the school as I entered. Principal Smith had Amy already in the office. Ethan was also there. Ethan stood. I approached him and gave him a hug.

"Son, why are you in here?" I questioned him.

"This is Amy's first day back at school." He glanced at Amy and their eyes met. "I'm not leaving her to deal with any of this alone." He crossed his arms and walked back over to her. He didn't sit in the chair. He stayed behind her and put a hand on her shoulder.

My boy, he was going to be her protector. It made me happy as a mother to raise such a fine young man. But it also worried me to drag him into all of this. I sat in the available chair next to Amy.

"I'm so sorry to drudge this up dear and on the first day you felt comfortable coming back to school." I spoke to her. She nodded and Ethan gave her shoulder a small grip.

"Can you tell me what happened on the day of the windstorm. Everything you remember from the time you got to school until you left?" I questioned her.

She took a moment to answer. "I came to school like any other day. Went to my classes. Before last period I had a headache, and I went to the nurse's office. Nurse Danielle gave me some pain killers and then I went to PE. After school Derek gave us all a ride home. You know the rest."

"Do you remember talking to counselor Robin before seeing the nurse?" I probed.

"Counselor Robin?" She was lost in thought for a moment. "I do remember seeing her while I waited. But it's so foggy." She placed her hands on her head as if trying to pull the memory. The cry that left her lips next startled all of us. Ethan quickly moved in front of her and kneeled down to be eye level with her.

"Amy. Breathe. It's okay. You're okay. Look at me." Ethan pleaded with her.

"I'm sorry," She cried. "It hurts when I try to remember." She sobbed. I shared a worried glance with Principal Smith.

Ethan was holding her now, while she cried into his shoulder. He suddenly stood, picking Amy up bridal style.

I stood, "Ethan?" I reached out to put a hand on his shoulder.

He stopped walking, "I'm taking her home." He said sternly. He didn't turn to look at me. He was not asking for permission.

I dropped my hand, "Okay." I replied. I watched him walk out of the office. I sat back down and put my head into my hands.

"It will be alright." Principal Smith reassured me.

"I'm not too sure about that." I sighed.

"What has you worried?" he asked.

"Something Dr. Warren said to me earlier about Robin's son." Taking a moment to organize my thoughts. "She said the protection spell could only be lifted if Robin removed it or if Robin died."

"And?" he pushed.

"What if the blood curse is still on Amy, that's why she can't remember. What if Robin isn't done using her yet?" He seemed to contemplate what I was saying.

"Then we better have a plan for when Amy goes rogue again." Principal Smith gave me a box and I went back to counselor Robin's office and boxed up everything I thought had to do with her spells.

'Elissa?' Richard mind-linked me.

'Yes, mate of mine.' I smiled, mind linking back.

'We need you to come to Robin's house. I'm here with the Alpha.'

The smile left my face, now what, I thought to myself.

'I'm leaving the school now; I'll be right there.' I ended the mind-link.

Grabbing the box, I got the address for Robin's house from Principal Smith and told him I'd call later to fill him in.

Arriving at Robin's, Richard was waiting for me outside. He looked uneasy.

"What's wrong?" I asked worriedly.

He rubbed his hand down his face, "You need to see inside." He grabbed my hand, and we walked inside. I didn't know what to think at first. The house was destroyed inside. There had definitely been a struggle.

"What happened here?" I asked.

"We are not sure yet. Robin wasn't here. Her mate is Stephen. He didn't show up for border patrol last night either. I had Dr. Warren check already; he last visited his son yesterday. No one has seen him since that visit. Alpha and I tried to mind-link both of them too. Robin is blocking us, and Stephen must be sleeping or unconscious somewhere, we can't get through to him at all."

"So, we don't know if he did this or if someone else broke in?"

"Exactly, but this isn't why I asked you to come." He slowly pulled me through the living room to a bedroom at the end of the hall.

When I walked in, I gasped. Rebecca's picture was littered across the walls. Pictures of her at school with all of her friends. All of the kids were pictured sitting down for lunch. Pictures of her out walking in town and a few from outside our house. Passages across the walls about the Kingdom of Rune and the gift of Leoht, written right on the walls. I felt my legs become shaky and Richard guided me to a chair.

"What is this? Why is her picture all over the walls?" I panicked.

"Shh, Love, we will protect her. We'll protect them all." Richard looked into my eyes.

After a few minutes of thinking about what I had seen. I gathered my thoughts. Alpha Darren walked into the room at that time. I told them my thoughts about Amy still being cursed. I stood up and examined the wall. Then I started looking through the desk drawers. I found a black onyx mirror. Almost like the one my mother had, that I gave to Autum. Looking around the room I saw a white line in the doorway.

I scrunched my eyebrows. That white line looked just like the protection circle around Robin's son. I started checking the trash can. I didn't find anything. Next, I saw the burning plate on a little table in the corner.

I approached, there was another burned piece of paper. The letters I could make out were M. I. N. of the first name and R. E. looked to be the last two letters of the last name.

"I don't know what all this means. But it looks like she cast a protection spell against whoever this is." I held up the burnt paper.

"How do you know it was a protection spell?" Asked Alpha Darren.

"The notebook on the desk. It's what's open on the page right there. I just don't understand why we're allowed to walk past the barrier here but not at the hospital. Maybe this spell didn't work."

"Maybe it only works on who it was intended for," Richard added.

"Yes, I could see that being a possibility. So, she wanted us to find this. But why? She is obviously stalking all of the children, but more so Rebecca."

"She must think Rebecca will get the gift of Leoht." Alpha Darren added.

It made the most sense. "The birthday will clear all of this up. Two more days." I sighed.

"In the meantime," Alpha Darren interjected, "We will double the patrols on your home and on our street to ensure everyone's safety. I don't know if Robin is the real threat or if it is her Mate, Stephen, at this point. Or if they are both being used. We need to be extra cautious until we know more or find one of them to interrogate."

We packed up everything we could and made additional security plans for the twin's birthday on Saturday. Leaving that house, I felt exhausted, and the day was only half over. I needed a nap and an aspirin. Richard walked beside me and kissed the side of my temple. Lacing his fingers with mine, his touch calmed me. This entire day was stressful right from the beginning. Now to go and spend some time digging through all this stuff we collected until it makes sense.

37

HELPING AMY

❦

Derek POV

Driving home from school my eyes kept drifting to Autum. I took her in, letting my eyes roam over her body. The way her shirt holds her plump breasts. Her black mini skirt snatches that small waist. Her legs were bare. Her black flats I kept picturing as stilettos. My mind imagining her bent over the bed again while I spank that tight ass of hers and make her pussy throb. Imagining the first time her pussy will clench around me. Hearing Autum clear her throat, I look up and see her staring at me. Her cheeks blushed, as she pulled her skirt down to cover up more. I reach down and adjust my pants.

"I can feel you undressing me with your eyes." She smirks, almost bashful.

"Yes, I am. So, stop trying to cover up those beautiful legs of yours." I say playfully.

She shies away and I place my hand on her knee. She's so fucking cute. Even after everything we have already done, she's still embarrassed. She doesn't know how captivated I am by her. Or she still doesn't believe it. I slowly drag my hand up from her knee. The tingles leaving goosebumps on her skin as I push higher. Stopping right before I reach her core, I hear her breath hitch.

"I want to see these beautiful legs." I slowly drag my hand back down and up again. Squeezing a little when I get back to the top.

"But my scars." She tries to pull her skirt down where I have exposed her scars high on her leg. I grab her hand in mine. And smile devotedly at her. She raises an eyebrow at me in question.

"I told you; you are beautiful. I will tell you every day if I need to." I brought her hand to my lips and kissed it. Making her blush more. "You have been in a mood all day. Do you want to talk about what happened while you were dreaming last night?" Putting our hands down, I rest them on her leg. Lacing our fingers together, hers on top. I slowly drag my hand up again, feeling for any resistance from her. When I get none, I continue moving closer to her core. I let my pinky stray as we reach her core and brush against her silky panties. A gasp leaves her lips.

Smiling to myself, continuing to watch the road as I guide our hands back down and up again. Each time squeezing her thigh a little harder and letting my pinky stray to stroke her folds through her panties. I could feel and smell her arousal. My member strained against my pants, twitching with every small noise that left her lips.

Pulling into the driveway, I could see her disappointment when I removed my hand from hers to put the truck in park. I laughed.

"What's so funny?" She asked amusingly.

"You are. You are going to be the death of me." I laughed.

"Me? You started it!" She pouted.

"Come here." I patted my lap.

"What? Why?" she questioned, squinting her eyes at me.

I offered my hand to her. "Come here." I drawled out.

She took my hand and swung her leg around as I moved the seat back with my other hand. She straddled me. Her petite frame fit perfectly on my lap. Her breasts were right at eye level. I reached up and popped a few buttons from her shirt. My eyes devouring her. "Tell me what happened while you visited Mary last night, hmm, how'd the training go?"

"It didn't go, I couldn't get past the Sacral Chakra…" She huffed annoyed. "What are we doing? What if someone sees?" She asked as she looked nervously around to see if anyone was watching.

I made eye contact with her as I undid the rest of the buttons on her shirt. Pulling her tucked in shirt up and opened it, I stared at her beauty. If only she could see what I see. "No one is watching, what's the Sacral Chakra?" I asked as I caressed her skin, rubbing my thumbs over the fabric of her bra.

"Its fine, I'll figure it out." She deflected.

I leaned forward kissing the exposed part of her breasts while still keeping eye contact. "Tell me."

Her face was flushed as she enjoyed the slow pleasure I was giving her skin.

"I have to feel worthy. Allow my inner self to be seen and expressed, believe I'm a work of art." She looked away from me as she finished her sentence.

I pulled her bra down taking her nipple in my mouth. She covered her mouth with the back of her hand to stifle a moan. Her nipple instantly stiff as I tongue around it. Placing one hand on her lower back I pulled her in closer. My other hand reaching to role her other nipple between my fingers. Her breathing picks up with mine and I notice the windows start to fog. I cup her whole breast in my hand and squeeze, I want so much from her, she is a work of art. I pull away from her breast and blow a little air on them. Goosebumps cover her breasts and her already stiff peaks harden.

Autum moans again, "Mmmm Derek."

Her nipples are so sensitive to my touch, I feel my dick twitch against my pants. Letting my hand fall, I wander down to her hips. I could feel her scars under my fingers. I squeezed.

"I love every part of your skin; you are a work of art." I panted out as I moved my mouth to her other breast.

She moaned for me, and I felt her hips buck a little. She was so nervous about letting her body enjoy what it was feeling. I moved both hands to her hips and pushed her down. Letting her pussy rub against me. My hardened length straining to be let free. The bulge was obvious as it made contact with her wet core. Her panties hardly held her wetness from escaping.

"Derek" She let out a breathy moan.

"You do this to me." I told her as I thrust my hips into her as I drag her down on me. "You are worthy, you are beautiful, all of you."

I buried my face in her breasts as I continued pulling her hips into me. She started to pick up the rhythm on her own. Bracing her hands on my shoulders. I moved one hand to the small of her back. Pulling her closer. Her hands now around my neck pulling on my hair forcing me to look up at her. Her lips captured mine. I moved one hand to her neck, pulling her in closer, my thumb wiping away the solum tear that left her. Our kiss filled with passion as we devoured each other. It was sloppy and forceful, and filled with hunger.

I was going to come. The friction from her wet pussy and her aroma filling the small space had my head spinning.

Reaching down between her legs, I hooked two of my fingers around her panties letting her grind her clit on the back of them. Our lips parted as she threw her head back to moan. My lips moved down to pull on her nipple as she picked up her pace. I felt her body heat and saw her face flush.

"Are you going to come for me Autum?" I groaned as she continued rocking her hips on me.

"Yes, yes, yes." She cried out.

Looking up at her as her orgasm consumed her. She looked like a goddess. Her head thrown back exposing her neck. Her face glistening with a thin sheen of sweat as our body heat warmed the truck. The sounds coming from her making me cum like a pre-pubescent teen in my pants. As I let the sensation take over my body, I gripped her hip tighter pulling her into me over and over again, as I thrust up, until I finished.

As I rested my head on her chest, I pulled my fingers from her underwear and hugged her tight. Her breathing was still harsh as my head lay on her. Her arms around my head. We stayed that way for a moment, catching our breath.

"We need to go inside and get cleaned up quickly." I sighed.

She laughed, "Why quickly?"

Pulling away to look up at her. I pushed some of her hair behind her ear. "Ethan asked me if we'd go with him to talk to Amy. I was hoping you would say you would."

While she pondered my question, I started buttoning up her shirt still looking at her. Her eyes seemed lighter than usual. They were breathtaking. She smiled down at me. I grabbed her chin and pulled her closer to take her lips again. This time softer, more sensual. Our tongues were like silk against each other, tasting every bit of her and her me. I slid the back of my hand across her jaw and down her neck. We broke our kiss and held our gaze for a moment. Her eyes held so much emotion in them. I half smiled at her. I loved her… I loved everything about her.

"Derek…" She whispered.

"Hmm?" I saw her eyes become glossy and I knew what she wanted to say. Her brows pinched and I could read it all over her face.

"Derek, I L…"

I stole another kiss before she could answer. She tried to pull away, laughing as I tried to keep her tongue tied. I smiled through our kiss not letting her get her chance. There was no way I would let her say it first! I already planned on doing it at the twin's party. It would be a beautiful clear night at the beach under the stars. It would be perfect. And what can I say, I'm a romantic at heart. But who am I kidding, I would be whoever she wants me to be, just to see her smile.

Breaking our kiss, she tried to speak again, but I covered her mouth with my hand. She raises both of her eyebrows then both her hands in surrender. I removed my hand.

"Okay, okay, I get it. You're not ready. That's fine, I can wait." She sighs. I squeeze her sides getting her to laugh.

"Come on, we really need to get changed, and me especially." I look down, getting her attention. Her eyes go wide when she sees the mess on my pants.

"That was all you." I lean in and whisper into her ear before I pull on her ear lobe with my lips. She bites her bottom lip, her face stained with a pink blush. She was making me hard again already. I look around outside. My parents still aren't home, and it doesn't seem like any of the neighbors are outside.

"Let's make a run for it." She nods as I swing the door open. I give her my hand so she can step down. I reached across the seat grabbing her bag, intending to use it as a shield. Watching her run in front of me laughing like we were going to get caught doing something dirty had me laughing as well. Making it to her room we quickly shut the door behind us. Both of us up against her door laughing like we were some criminals who just got away with a bank robbery.

I drop her bag on the floor and give her a quick peck.

"I'm going to go shower and change. I'll meet you downstairs?" I asked her. She was biting her lip again. What was going through that mind of hers? I wish I knew. It couldn't be like the dirty thoughts going through mine.

"I thought, I told you, that drives me crazy." I say to her as I reach for her chin and rub my thumb down her bottom lip, pulling it from her teeth.

"You did." She looks down at the floor, then looks up at me through her eye lashes.

This dirty, dirty, girl. She was having just as many dirty thoughts as me. I smirk at her. Pulling her into an embrace. Lowering my voice, I leaned into her ear.

"We will play later as long as your good." I give her ass a little slap and squeeze it.

"What if I'm not good?" She whispers back.

"Then I'm going to bend your ass over that bed again and show you what happens to bad girls." I panted out. My dick already hard again. My little temptress giving my self-control a run for its money. How I hadn't taken her already should be a testament in itself. But she's not ready for that even though she's acting like she is. She's going to shift in the next couple of weeks and her libido and hormones are going crazy.

Coming back to reality, I hadn't realized I had her pushed up against the door. Our breathing elevated she put her hands on my chest. Feeling my muscles through my shirt as she slowly moved her hands down.

"The death of me." I rasped out as I grabbed her hands and held them above her head.

She captured my lips and rolled her hips into me. Fuck, this was painful, the restriction from my pants becoming unbearable. I pulled away.

"Our friends need our help." I try to get the words out as she takes my lips again. "We need to get ready." I managed to get out.

She was insatiable. Wanting more and I wanted to give it to her. Giving in, I released her hands. She instantly moved them to my neck. Putting both my hands on her legs I lifted them, and she wrapped them around me.

"We are taking a shower," I groan out as she rolls her hips on me.

I was losing myself in her scent. Hungrily leaving kisses up and down her neck. Fumbling with the water faucet to turn it on. My mind was a fog. She drops her legs and starts undressing me and I her. Our lips crash against each other, my willpower dwindling. Her need apparent and my body ready to sate her. She grabbed my dick and started stroking it, I groaned in approval as I cupped her pussy with one hand. The other on her back as I walked us towards the shower.

The warm water cascading down her breasts made me lose what control I still had. I pushed her into the tile, eliciting a gasp from her. I pinned her hands above her head with one hand and went to work on her plump breasts with their hardened peaks. My tongue was relentless as it swirled and licked every inch of them. My hand still cupping her pussy, I spread her legs wider with my knee and slapped it. Her cry was short but wanting, I did it again. Her legs were shaking as her pleasure overtook her body. I inserted two fingers, curling them as I dragged them in and out. Over and over, she cried out, wanting more. Her juices were spilling from her as she grew wetter with each pump of my fingers. My dick twitching as it stands erect, throbbing to be inside her.

"Let me touch you." She begged as she squirmed in my arms. Once I released her hands, she moved one to my neck and one to my dick. The sparks ignited a feeling of euphoria when her skin made contact. I groaned and her arousal flared further.

I would never get enough; I will spend hours making her mine when that time comes. Pleasuring her over and over again until she begs me to stop.

Autum pulled my hand from inside her and dropped to her knees. Taking me in her mouth and still stroking me with one hand. I put both my hands on the shower wall, not wanting to lose control. I wanted to grab her head and make her take me deeper, to the back of her throat. But I didn't want to hurt her. My need now matched hers and she wasn't even finished off yet. This shower was not going to work.

"Come here." I beckoned her. She stood; I picked her up swiftly as she wrapped her legs around me. Shutting off the shower I walked quickly to the bed.

I fell on it, and she straddled me. Deep in a kiss as she grinded her slick folds up and down my shaft. Coating me in her arousal. I let out a frustrated groan, I wanted to be in her, buried deep inside her. I rolled her off me and she got to her knees.

"Come up here and straddle my face."

"Do what?" She panted.

Instead, I moved and placed my head between her legs. I buried my face in her heat, delving my tongue in and out of her and she cried out. She was so close. I was going to make her scream.

Realization hit her, and she leaned forward. Taking all of me in her mouth. I thrust my hips softly making her gag. The sound only fueled me more. She rocked her hips on my face. Using my fingers to circle her clit and the other to hold one of her breasts. I pinched, rolled, and pulled her nipple as her moans vibrated me all the way to the base.

I groaned as I took her whole core in my mouth letting the vibration send her over the edge. Her sucking became faster as she let the orgasm roll over her in waves, heat after heat pulsing through her. I found my own release and she sucked harder, not letting any of it slip out. Her hips were still grinding as her orgasm subsided. My dick was still twitching with each stream of hot seed that coated her throat.

She rolled off of me. Both of us were panting. Goddess how would sex feel with her when this already felt so good. Our hands joined and we stayed this way for some time.

Autum eventually moved first. Not far though. She sat up and spun around and put her head on my chest. My heart was still beating out of my chest. She rested her hand on me sighing. Completely content at this moment.

We lay there for ten minutes before I felt Autum's breath even out. Now it was almost nonexistent. Looking down at my goddess, she lay sleeping on me. Lulled by my beating heart. I kissed her forehead, she felt cold. Giving her the shirt pillow in my place I got out of the bed. Pulling the blanket up over her, I watched her sleep for a minute. I needed to go call Ethan, let him know we'd be a bit before we could come over. Autum was out cold, and I wasn't going to wake her right away. Grabbing a towel, I wrapped it around my waist and headed to my room to get dressed.

My thoughts ran rampant as I dressed. Autum's calling was so strong, I was lost in the haze and could have really lost control. It was crazy the effect she was having on me. It didn't feel like she knew what was going on. Her grandmother home schooled her and I'm not sure how much she actually knows about all this. Sighing I go to talk to the only person that can help me.

"Hey, my son!" My mother embraces me. I lean down and she places a kiss on my forehead. "You're a little warm, are you feeling ok honey?"

"Yes, it's not me." I sheepishly respond. She raised an eyebrow at me as she walked away. Going back to her sandwich making I interrupted.

"It's Autum. Her calling has me all riled up." I ran my fingers through my hair, slicking it back. I can't believe I'm having this conversation with my mom, but then again, she did bring us condoms, so...

"It's a little soon for that, isn't it?" She questioned. As I eye bawled the sandwich she just finished, she rolled her eyes and handed it to me. She started to make another one as I took a big bite.

"Mmm, so good, thank you," I mumbled, my mouth full of food. Swallowing it down I spoke again. "Her birthday is in a couple of weeks. If the twins are phasing early, she probably will too."

"Yes, I know but for her to be calling to you, that's something that typically happens right before a shift, maybe one or two days before not two weeks before."

"Well, there is nothing typical about Autum. She is going to be strong; I can feel it. But she is definitely not acting like her usual timid self." I took another bite, finding the sound of the lettuce crunching satisfying.

"Hmm, yes, you're right. I think that's a good thing though." My mother smiled, amused with herself.

"What are you smiling for, what did you say to her?" I pried.

"Nothing much, just that it was time for everyone else to see what we all see. A strong, confident, and beautiful women. I told her stop being pushed around." She narrowed her eyes at me, "Are you two using protection?"

"Mom!" I said wide eyed, this conversation just moved into nope land.

"What? It's a perfectly valid question. Nothing to be embarrassed about. It would be unreasonable for me to assume you weren't having sex, especially if Autum is already using the calling." She smirked at me.

"Well, we aren't." I finished my sandwich in one last bite and stood from the island.

My mother now looking confused. "But you said she was using the calling? You can't fight the calling; it will demand more."

"Well, I did fight it, for now at least. I was so close to losing control. I don't think Autum even realizes what is happening. I can't lose control with her mom, I can't. She's not ready for that yet." I felt my face flush. This was embarrassing.

"Do you want me to talk to Autum? We can give her something for it." She suggested.

Running my hands through my hair again, "What do you mean give her something for it?" I probed.

"Elissa whipped something up for Rebecca after the funeral. A cocktail of sorts, it seems to be working."

"How do you know it's working?" I asked.

"Well, for starters she hasn't mauled anyone else." She smirked.

Completely taken by surprise at her statement. "Rebecca kissed me because of her calling?"

She gave a heavy sigh. "Autum has you and Ethan has Amy. Rebecca's mate isn't here so, she kissed you."

My mother's eyes went wide for a moment, but she recovered quickly. What was she hiding? "So, Ethan took the cocktail too?"

"Oh, no!" she laughed, "They've been going at it like rabbits!" I burst out laughing, I can't believe I'm having this conversation with my mom. It felt good though, to confide in her like this.

I gave her a hug and thanked her. "I'm going to go call Ethan. We were supposed to hang out today." She gave me a tight squeeze before letting go.

"You can always ask me anything." She smiled at me. As I walked out of the kitchen, I played her words over in my head. Stopping in my tracks, I slowly turned to face her again.

"What?" She asked.

"You... you said her mate isn't here."

Her eyes went wide again. As she started looking around us to make sure no one else was listening. Lana engrossed in the TV watching Shrek today and no maids here this late in the day. She pinched her lips together. She didn't want to give it up, whatever she was hiding.

"Dad told me before, that he knew Rebecca wasn't my mate. And you... You should have said she doesn't have a mate, but you didn't. Who is it and why aren't they here?" I stepped closer to her. How could they hide this from everyone?

She didn't speak. "Mom! You just said I could ask you anything." I pleaded with her.

"Your fathers going to kill me." she sighed. She sat at the island and messaged her temples.

"Mom...?"

"Ok, ok. We've known about Rebecca's mate for almost five years."

"What?" I whisper screamed.

"Calm down," She begged.

"Rebecca has been making my life hell, and you knew the last five years she wasn't my mate." I scowled at her.

"It wasn't that bad, stop."

I let out a frustrated grunt. But this was good news. "When is her mate coming back?"

"Soon." She replied.

"Mom...?!"

"Geeze, ok. He will be here for her birthday."

"Why did he leave?"

She rolled her eyes. "I told you the calling can't be ignored. He had to leave."

It was starting to make sense. "How old is her mate now?"

"He is twenty-three."

"So, she was only thirteen when he phased."

"She was twelve, soon to be thirteen. And much too young for any of that. His wolf knew instantly that she was his mate. They didn't want to hurt her. So, they left. They weren't supposed to return until next year when she phased. But-"

"She is phasing early." I finished her sentence.

"Yes," She paused, "And. Well, he felt it when she kissed you and his wolf went berserk thinking she was with another. It took your father hours to calm Kiel down and explain what happened."

We all grew up knowing about the mate bond but to actually experience it was another thing. We were taught that once your wolf found their mate, they could feel infidelity. Why anyone would cheat on their destined mate was beyond me. I didn't even have my wolf yet, but the bond between Autum and I was so strong. She consumed my every thought, even thinking of another was impossible. No one compared.

I shook my head, clearing my thoughts. Wait, did she say Kiel!

"Kiel! My cousin Kiel? Is that why he never visits? Does Emivy know?"

"No. No one knows. You can't tell anyone either!" My mother said sternly.

"How is it possible Emivy doesn't know?"

"He made us promise not to tell her, we decided not to tell anyone."

"He didn't want his own mother knowing, that's strange, isn't it? If you think I'm keeping this from Autum, you'd be mistaken. I won't lie to her." I argued.

"It's his business, he didn't want anyone to know. It's not lying, just don't tell her." She pleaded.

"That's a slippery slope, one I'm not willing to take." I said firm.

"Just wait until the party. Then there won't be a chance to let it slip to anyone else."

Sighing, "I'm not making any promises, she already has a hard time trusting men. I won't give her a reason not to trust me."

"Alright." She hugged me. "You're a good man my son. Don't ever doubt that." Pursing my lips, I nodded.

"So did you have Dorothy make him a suit too. For the party?"

"Shush," she swatted me with a tea towel. "That was supposed to be a surprise, how do you know about that."

I laughed at her, "I ran into Dorothy and saw her picking out fabric last week. She couldn't resist my charming personality." I wiggled my eyebrows at my mother. "I asked her to make a dress for Autum and helped pick out the fabric."

"That sneaky old lady, I asked her to make a dress for Autum the day she moved here. She didn't tell me you had already asked. I even offered to pay her extra for the last-minute addition. She wouldn't take it!" She laughed, "She lied to me."

I shook my head, "No, she didn't. She just didn't tell you." I raised my eyebrows and smirked. She smacked me with the towel again. Leaving the room still laughing, I walked to the study to use the phone. Calling Ethan's house, his mother answered saying he was already at Amys. I rang Amy's house next.

"Hello." Amy answered.

"Hey, Is Ethan still over there." I asked.

"Yep, he sure is. But he can't come to the phone right now." She giggled.

"Oh yea, and why is that?" I asked, amused.

"Well, you see he is passed out. Been sleeping for about thirty minutes."

My face reddened at the thought of why my future beta was sleeping. Glad I was on the phone and not face to face. My mother's early comment ringing in my ears. 'Going at it like rabbits' I shook the thought from my head.

"So, how long do you plan on watching him sleep?" I asked playfully.

"He said we had plans to go shopping, so probably not much longer."

"Yes, we were planning on taking you girls to Dorothy's boutique to pick out some accessories for the party." I spoke.

"Us girls? So, Autum will be coming?" She almost whispered. I could hear the strain in her voice. She still felt guilty over what happened. She needed to know we didn't blame her. This double date was meant to help them get close in a public place to ease the tension. And what girl doesn't like shopping?

"Yes, Autum is coming. Neither of us blame you for what happened Amy. We know it wasn't you." I spoke softly so she wouldn't feel threatened. I could hear her sniffle on the other side.

"Autum wants to go with you, Amy. She doesn't hate you. I promise, it will be ok." I pleaded with her.

"Ok." She sighed.

38

BLACK STILETTOS

❦

Autum POV

Waking to soft caresses on my arm, I slowly blinked my eyes open. Allowing them to adjust, I sat up. Realizing I was still naked from our earlier escapades, I gripped the blanket bringing it higher to cover my breasts. I felt the bed dip as Derek stood up.

"Let's get you dressed; I told Amy we would meet at her house at five."

"What time is it?" I asked.

"It's five." Derek laughed. He walked into my closet and grabbed some clothes. Bringing them back to the bed.

"Why'd you let me sleep so long?" I pouted. I still felt tired, and I was so cold. "Do you mind grabbing me a long sleeve shirt?" I handed the t-shirt back to him.

"Sure. How are you feeling?" A slight hesitation in his voice.

"Pretty good, still tired, a little cold honestly." I yawned and stretched my arms above my head. Derek tossed the new shirt to me. He was eyeing me suspiciously. I met his gaze, but he looked away a few seconds later. His hands in his pockets, he rocked on his heels.

"So," He began. "What do you know about the calling?"

"Well, I know my grandmother said I was doing it to you last night. Although I don't remember doing anything special. Also, I'm pretty sure she was wrong, because it's too soon for me to be able to do something like that."

"What if I told you, you were doing it last night and again today." He grinned.

Pinching my brows together I asked, "What do you mean today?"

"Well, love." He approached me. "I tried my hardest not to give in to you again in this room after our little adventure in the truck. But I couldn't. I couldn't resist you. It will only get stronger as we near your birthday."

"Is that a bad thing?" I questioned. Biting my bottom lip. I see Derek's shoulders tense. And he turned away from me. His fists balled in his pants pockets. Was he mad at me? I jumped off the bed.

I approached him and hugged him from behind. "Did I say something that upset you?" I asked. Why was he acting mad at me? I didn't understand how he could be calling me love one minute than acting angry the next. Laying my head on his back, I felt him flexing. His delicious scent calmed the anxiety I was having. Feeling his sculpted muscles under my fingers, I tightened my grip. Goddess he was consuming my thoughts.

"Autum!" His voice came out deep and strangled. "You haven't upset me, but please I need you to get dressed!"

Reluctantly I stepped away. Already missing the warmth his body gave me. I got dressed and looked at him, his back still to me. Sitting on the bed I put my head in my hands. Was he trying to tell me the calling was the only reason he wanted me? Were my feelings for him wrong? I was getting so confused. I let out a frustrated sigh.

"Hey what's wrong?" He asked, still not looking at me.

"For one, you won't even look at me. For two… Do you even have feelings for me or is it just because of the calling?" I asked reluctantly, my voice felt small.

Derek turned and walked to me quickly. Kneeling down next to me he grabbed my chin and forced me to look at him. My emotions were all over the place. I could feel the sparks, I knew he could feel them too. Why was he being so hot and cold?

"I do have feelings for you Autum. Before the calling." He said sternly.

Looking at his lips, I licked mine. He stood and backed away. I frowned instantly. Derek looked rigid. He drew his hands to the bulge I hadn't noticed. Biting my lip, I thought about taking him in my mouth again.

"Autum!" His loud voice startled me, and I met his eyes.

"Hmm?"

"I am having a very difficult time controlling myself around you." He closed his eyes, and I could see a bead of sweat forming on his brow. Watching him lose his self-control was kind of turning me on. I was doing that to him.

"Autum!" He called my name again, this time almost panting.

"Derek." It came out almost sultry.

He let out a long breath, "I want to bury myself so far in you, you won't be able to walk! If that's what you want, I'm ready. If not, then we both need to drink from that thermos on the nightstand. I will be happy either way." He tilted his head towards the small table.

I felt my body heat at his words. Earlier in the shower I felt like I was ready for sex, but now I knew I wasn't, not yet anyways. I looked at the thermos. "What is it?" I asked.

Derek's whole body was leaning towards me. But his feet were unwilling to move, grounded to their spot. I felt his uneasiness now. He really thought he wouldn't be able to hold himself back much longer.

"I'm not sure exactly what it is, Elissa gave it to my mom." He gritted out.

Watching as he closed his eyes again and took a deep breath in through his nose. I watched as the bead of sweat slowly rolled down the side of his face. My chest and cheeks heated as I watched, and I gripped the bed sheets at my sides. I felt my lips part and my breathing increase.

"Autum, please decide!" His voice was strained, and his eyes were still closed. He sounded like he was in pain. I felt it too, the need to touch him to be consumed by him. Quickly I grabbed the thermos, opening it, I poured a cup and drank it. It was some kind of tea. I poured a second cup and held it out to Derek.

"Here." I spoke softly.

He moved forward almost robotically and extended one hand. He drank it quickly, "Pour me another one." I did and he drank it just as quickly. I took the cup and drank another as well. Setting the thermos back down. I looked at him, watching his chest rise and fall with each breath.

"How much are we supposed to drink?" I asked.

"Elissa said a cup a day." He answered softly, his self-control slowly coming back to him.

"Until when, my birthday? Will the calling stop by then?" I asked.

Derek was shaking his head, but finally opened his eyes to look at me. A small smile playing on his lips. It instantly made me feel better seeing him start to smile.

"Can you explain the calling to me? Honestly, who knows how much I was paying attention when Gram was talking about it. I thought it had to do with a wolf when she was in heat?"

Derek slowly walked to the bed and sat next to me. A large gap still between us. I smiled to myself. He really didn't realize how much more I fell for him when he didn't take advantage of our situation. He could have. I would have let him. He readjusted himself as he sat down. I tried my hardest not to watch him, but it was damn hard. I could feel the tea working. I didn't want to jump on him anymore, so that was a good sign.

"You're partially correct. The calling is how a female finds her mate when she goes into heat after shifting. Her scent will spread out over miles. Unmated males can't resist it. The calling will be greater to the mate once in her presence."

"But I haven't shifted yet?"

"Right, before a shifter phase phases for the first time, our hormones go crazy. Both woman and men have a calling for their first phase. It's to help ensure you find your mate. The calling will have a pull to the mate, even if they don't have their wolf yet."

"So that's why Amy could feel Ethan. And why you... Could feel me?" He nodded and put his hand out for me to take. I did and he brought it to his lips and placed a soft kiss on the back of it.

"What happens if the mate doesn't come?" I asked curiously.

"If the mate doesn't come, then there is usually a duel. The males will fight until there is a victor that gets to claim her for the duration of her heat."

"That sounds barbaric!"

"Really, do you think she would resist?" he asked.

"I guess I hope she would. To just have sex with anyone doesn't seem like the best choice." I responded.

Derek scooted closer, the tea finally working. He leaned into my ear. "Did you want me to stop in the truck... Or in the shower...?"

Chills ran down my spine at his rough voice vibrating through me. I shook it off and he laughed. He was right though; I would have done anything for that release. In fact, it was all I could think of at the moment.

"Nowadays, we have roller shutters on most homes. When a female goes into heat. She can stay hidden if she desires to." He spoke, leaning in to give me a quick peck on the cheek. "Come on we need to go meet Ethan and Amy."

"What are we doing exactly?" I asked.

"It's a surprise, but Amy was hesitant to go when I mentioned you were coming. I may have told her you weren't mad at her and didn't blame her for what happened."

"That's fine, I don't blame her."

We walked downstairs hand in hand. Finally able to function without our desire going wild. His sister was finishing up a movie that looked to be Shrek. She didn't even see us leave. His mother waved us out the door asking Derek to pick up some packages while we were out.

After picking up Ethan and Amy the ride was a little awkward. I really didn't know what to say to her. Like 'hey I know you tried to kill me, but it wasn't your fault.'

"Are you girls excited?" Ethan asked.

"I mean I would be if I knew what we were doing?" I answered truthfully.

"Derek didn't tell you?" Amy asked.

"No, do you know?" I asked her, turning in my seat to look at her in the back seat.

"We are going shopping!" she said excitedly.

"For what?"

Derek laughed as we pulled up outside a place called Dorothy's Boutique. Everyone got out of the truck. They guys walked ahead, and I hung back with Amy.

"This place looks expensive, look at those gowns in the window." I said to Amy.

"Yes, Dorothy makes them all by hand, she is the best seamstress in town."

"Why would we be at place like this?" I asked her.

"Because the twins party theme is masquerade and Dorothy made all of our gowns." She replied.

I was a little shocked to learn about the party theme, and that everyone else would be dressed in a gown like this. I didn't know what I was going to wear that would even compare. Walking in, I found that the space was much bigger on the inside than it appeared. An older woman stood behind the counter.

"Hello. How are you all doing tonight?" She greeted us.

"We are good Dorothy, how have you been?" Derek asked her.

"Very busy with the party tomorrow. Business is good." She smiled warmly at us.

"My mother would like me to pick up all the packages while we are here." He told her.

"All right, I'll bring them out. You kids go ahead and pick out your other accessories while I fetch them." She replied.

We walked out of the room filled with the elegant dresses into one with all the accessories you could think of. Jewelry, gloves, masks, stockings, hair accessories, purses, shoes! OMG, I love shoes. There was even a small dressing room and a lingerie section.

"So, ladies." Derek rubbed his hands together, "you can buy whatever you want to accessorize your dresses for the party tomorrow. It is on us!" He smiled, fist pumping Ethan.

Amy squealed and ran off towards the lingerie section with Ethan close behind her.

"Where would you like to start?" Derek asked me, lacing his fingers with mine.

"I guess first, I should figure out what I'm wearing. I could wear that mint green dress your mother gave me?" I looked at him.

Derek was shaking his head. "You will be wearing a beautiful, off the shoulder, sapphire blue gown. It is short in the front and long in the back to show off these beautiful legs!" He finished smirking at me.

"I could never afford one of these dresses." I said shyly.

"Your dress is already made, it's one of the packages we are picking up tonight. I have a matching tux as well." He smiled warmly at me.

"I can't let you buy me a dress. You already took me in and pay for everything else." I protested.

"Firstly, my mother would never allow you to pay us back. Secondly, if you insist on compensating me," He leaned into my ear. "I can think of other ways you can pay me back." He pulled his head away, my face heated. He reached over and slapped my ass and guided me towards the shoes.

"I saw you eyeing these when we walked in." He smiled.

I cleared my throat, shaking off the dirty thoughts in my mind on the ways he may want me to pay him back. Avoiding eye contact, I look at the shoes. I can feel my face is heated and I hope it's not too noticeable. I grab a pair of white heels and admire them. They have a white flower on the toe with a blue tint to it and smaller flowers flowing up one side. The white gemstones give off a sparkle when the light hits it. They are gorgeous. I keep turning the shoe looking all around it.

"What are you looking for?" Derek asks.

"The price."

"You won't find it on the shoe." He laughed, "Besides I already told you it's on me." I huffed; I didn't like feeling like a free loader. "Let me spoil you a little, please! I just want you to have fun and not worry about it."

I rolled my eyes but nodded at him. "Do you like these white heals?"

"Try them on, let me see you walk in them." He suggested.

I did and took a stroll around the area we were in. I hadn't walked in heals a lot, but you couldn't tell. Derek was watching me as I paraded around him. He smiled and nodded in approval. I bit my lip and looked down at them. Pointing my toe out to look at them, they were so beautiful.

"Derek, dear. The boxes are ready on the counter when you are." Dorothy rang out from the other room. Stepping out of the shoes, I put my flats back on.

"I'm going to go put those boxes in the truck with Ethan, will you try talking to Amy more." He asked. I nodded and leaned forward giving him a peck on the cheek.

"Thank you." I said softly. "For the shoes." I smiled at him.

He kissed my forehead and smiled down at me. "I'll match you as much as possible too." He said before grabbing Ethan and heading into the other room. Grabbing the heels I walked over to the mask wall where Amy was currently comparing two masks.

"What do you think?" She asked, holding each one to her face.

"What color is your dress?" I asked her.

"It's a deep green."

"Well, the white mask gives more contrast, but if you are getting those black heals, I think the black mask would match better." I offered.

She nodded her head back and forth then selected the black mask. Looking at the masks, I selected a white mask off the wall. It had white flowers up one side, with the same blue tint as the shoes. It would match perfectly. There was also a white male mask, which would look good on Derek. Both only covered above the nose.

Thinking of how our outfits would match was oddly satisfying. Everyone would know we were together and had planned how we would dress.

"What are you thinking about?" Amy asked. One brow raised suspiciously at me.

It was then I realized I was smiling. "Nothing." I lied.

Amy laughed. "You two are cute together by the way."

"Thanks."

"But for real how are you two able to keep your hands off each other?"

Scrunching my brows together, "What do you mean?" I asked.

"Well, Ethan and I snuck away during several classes and again when we got home!"

I looked at her and our eyes met. We busted up laughing. "While you were at school?" I asked incredulously.

"Oh yeah! It was hot too!" She winked at me. I felt my face heat, embarrassed for her. I couldn't imagine doing that at school of all places. Hearing the door ring, I saw the guys come back in and carry a few more boxes out.

"Derek and I haven't done that yet." I told her.

"What? How are you fighting the calling like that?!" It was her turn to be surprised.

"I don't know what you're talking about." She didn't know I was a white wolf, why was she asking me that.

"I saw you Autum… That night as Samantha's. My body wasn't in my control, but my mind was. I saw your eyes glow. You called to that lightning, asked it for help. You are some kind of super conductor or something."

"Amy…"

"I haven't told anyone, not even Ethan… So how are you not having sex?" She asked again.

Okay, so she knew I was a white wolf. She hadn't told Ethan. More impressive, Ethan hadn't told her what my actual gifts were, and I wasn't going to correct her. Also, this girl was shameless. Looking at her I realized we had walked to the lingerie section. She was looking at a very seductive red lace piece, which left nothing to the imagination.

Looking around to ensure the guys weren't back, I walked over to a white bra and pantie set.

"We are taking some kind of cocktail Elissa made. It helps with the incessant desires."

"Oh, that makes sense. Rebecca is taking that too." I looked at her questionably. Noticing me, she kept talking.

"Ethan has me and Derek has you. Rebecca doesn't have anyone. They didn't want her mauling anyone else. Not after what she did to Derek." She smirked at me. I never thought about that being the reason Rebecca acted the way she did. Now I felt bad for being mad at her. Goddess I was hopeless.

"If you're not going to get actual lingerie, you should get that black lace bra and panty set. They're hot!" She pointed behind me.

Rolling my eyes, I looked behind me. I didn't want to give Derek the wrong idea. But maybe I could be ready to do more by my birthday. Biting my lip, I grabbed the black set. I looked at Amy and she smirked.

"Shut it!" I laughed at her. She put her hands up in surrender and we walked to the counter where Dorothy was waiting. I placed my items on the desk.

"Oh, I need a pair of gloves." I remembered.

"I'll bag what you have so far. The gloves are on the far wall." She pointed. I went to look before returning with a pair of thick, white lace gloves that would go all the way past my elbow. She added them to the bag.

"No jewelry?" She questioned.

"No, thank you." I answered quickly. As I saw Derek and Ethan enter. I didn't want Derek to spend so much.

"Hey, did you girls get everything you needed." I nodded.

"And some!" Amy teased winking at Ethan.

Derek approached trying to peak in my bag. I pulled it away quicky not wanting him to see the undergarments.

"I just want to know what color you settled on, so I can match." He smiled at me.

"Right." I laughed. "White, everything." I told him.

"Everything?" He slanted his eyes at me in question.

Did he see me pick out that bra? I was about to ask when Amy grabbed my hand. "Let's go wait in the truck while they get their things." Amy said, pulling me to the truck.

Derek walked away laughing as Amy pulled me outside. Getting in the back seat with her, we settled in. I glanced through the window and could see Derek and Ethan walking around. You could see around the mannequins in the windows.

"Do you think they were watching us?" I asked her.

Amy leaned over to look through my window. "Definitely." She stated.

"Oh goddess." My face flushed and I put my hand to my head.

"Hey, what's wrong?" She asked worried.

"I don't want Derek to think I'm ready for sex. I don't want him to think I'm teasing him either. If he saw me buying those black undergarments. Geeze, I'm an idiot!" I blubbered out.

"Stop worrying. If he knows you guys are waiting, he won't push you, Autum. I've known him my whole life. He's a good guy." She reasoned with me.

"What if he gets tired of waiting? And goes back to an ex-girlfriend or finds someone else?

"What!" She laughed. "Don't be ridiculous."

"I don't understand how any of this is funny." I glared at her.

"Autum, Derek hasn't dated anyone before you." She said seriously.

"But he's surely been with others." I questioned.

She was shaking her head no. "Derek's never been with anyone that I know. I mean if you two aren't having sex, then he's probably still a virgin. He's never shown any interest in any girls at school. Why do think Rebecca was so mad when she thought you guys were sleeping together? She's been trying for so long. Here you came in a matter of weeks and have him wrapped around your little finger."

I opened my mouth to say something, but nothing came out. Is Derek a virgin? Could I ask him... No, I shouldn't. Should I? Amy reached over and shut my mouth. I hadn't realized it was still open. I looked over to the boutique and saw the guys at the jewelry counter. Damn old lady probably told him I didn't buy any.

Amy started snapping her fingers in front of my face. "Earth to Autum." She laughed.

I turned to look at her. "Did you hear anything I just said." She asked.

"Um, I heard virgin. That's the last thing I remember." I answered honestly.

"OMG, you two are perfect for each other. So, innocent. You should see your face right now. It's as red as an apple." She continued laughing. She was crying from her laughter. The guys opened the doors at that time. Looking at us, wondering what was so funny.

"You two doing okay?" Ethan asked.

"Sooo good!" Amy answered.

I could feel my face now. No way I could hide it. Derek looked at me and I quickly looked away. Oh goddess. Thinking back on how he had been with me. How he hadn't been with another. It was making me want him more. I needed some more of that damn tea, like, right now. I looked at Amy. Damn her for telling me this now.

"Autum, you good?" Derek questioned.

Lowering my head, I took a deep breath. Looking up slightly through my eyelashes I responded. "Yes, I just feel a little warm."

"Is that what you call it?" Amy teased.

I slapped her playfully and avoided eye contact with Derek. Thankfully, he didn't ask anything further, but he kept glancing at me through the rear-view mirror. Amy and Ethan kept eyeing each other the entire drive as well.

Only I could see her fidgeting with the hem of her skirt. Her face became as heated as mine had been. Good, glad they are suffering, I smirked to myself.

When we pulled up to the pack house Amy jumped out swiftly. Running around the truck she jumped into Ethan's arms, wrapping her legs around him. "I got you something in this bag," she said seductively between kisses. He slapped her ass and started walking towards her house. Leaving all of his bags in the truck.

I looked at Derek and he was rolling his eyes.

"What should we do with his stuff?" I asked.

"We can just bring it in our house. Pretty sure they plan on coming over here tomorrow to get ready anyways." He shrugged his shoulders.

"Why is my grandma's car here?" I questioned noticing it for the first time.

"Oh, um the movers brought your stuff while we were gone. Remember?" He said, turning to me and moving some loose hair behind my ear. "She is staying for dinner too." He finished.

Thinking back on his words I repeated, "Our house?"

He smiled deeply, "Don't tell me you've changed your mind?"

I shook my head. Looking down, I remembered mine and Amy's conversation. The slight breeze helped keep me from overheating. Derek pulled my chin up making me look at him. "What's going on with you?"

I cleared my throat. "Nothing, just… Nothing." I chickened out. Looking at the back of the truck I started talking again before he could ask more questions. "Where did all these bags come from?"

"Well, these four are mine. Those two are Ethan's. And all these boxes are the gowns and tuxes for Amy, Ethan, Rebecca, Samantha, you, and I."

"You have more bags than I do." I laughed.

"Well, these two," he lifted two bags, "Are for you." He answered.

"Me? But I already got-"

"One of them is for that compensation we talked about." He cut me off. Winking, he patted my ass with one of the bags, ushering me forward.

At a loss for words, I started walking. Amy's words once again played on my mind. We walked into the house and laughter could be heard from the kitchen.

Derek leaned into my ear from behind me. "Go see your grandma, I'll get the rest from the truck."

I looked over my shoulder at him and pinched my lips together. "You should bring that tea down from my room too." I smiled at him. Smacking my ass, he nodded.

After visiting Gram and eating dinner, we said goodbye. She was going to come over tomorrow to help me get ready. We needed to get to bed. Tomorrow was going to be a long day. We also had to stay up past midnight for the twins to phase as well. Yawning again, Derek grabbed my hand and pulled me up the stairs.

"Let's go, sleeping beauty." He taunted as he opened the door to my room. We both got changed and climbed into bed. I felt exhausted. After braiding my hair to one side, I finally let my head rest.

"Why are you shaking?" Derek questioned.

"I'm a bit cold." I shrugged.

"Come closer, let me warm you up."

Wanting his warmth, I complied. Turning so my back was towards him, he wrapped his arms and legs around me.

"You're like an ice cube. Why didn't you say something sooner?"

"I wasn't cold then." I teased.

"That's right, in the truck earlier you looked like you were overheating." He mused.

I stiffened slightly. Derek noticed. He lifted himself slightly off the bed to look at me. "Is everything okay, I mean with us? You have been off since earlier. I don't want to pry, but…"

"Everything is good, better than good." I smiled up at him, placing a hand on his cheek. "Kiss me."

He complied. His lips spreading warmth through me. I deepened the kiss and parted my lips, our tongues mingling against each other in a seductive dance. He pulled away, biting my lip. Then gave me one last quick peck. The tea doing its job for the night, didn't leave me feeling crazed for his touch. Resting our heads back down. Derek tightened his hold on me.

"Will you see Mary tonight?"

"Yes, I need to."

"To open your Sacral Chakra?" he asked.

I smiled to myself that he remembered. "Yes." I held his arms around me tighter.

He kissed the side of my face. "You are worthy, you are beautiful, you are my everything."

I smiled to myself, feeling that Derek's words were true. I let sleep take me.

39

BREAKING
THE FEVER

❧

Derek POV

I woke up sweating. But it wasn't because of me. Autum was burning up. Her fever still hadn't broken. I could feel her still shivering in my embrace. The clock read 2:12 a.m. I rolled out of bed and heard Autum whimper at the loss of contact when I let her go. I furrowed my brow. Maybe she was sick. I went down to the kitchen to grab some fever medicine. I grabbed the thermometer and another blanket as well. Walking back up the steps, my mother was waiting at the top for me.

"What are you doing up son?"

"It's Autum, she has a fever. I'm worried."

"Do you want help?" She asked.

I nodded and she followed me into the room. I could hear her teeth chattering from the doorway. I looked at my mother, now she understood why I was concerned. We both approached the bed. I threw the other blanket over her. I ran the thermometer across her forehead. It came back at 104 degrees.

"We need her to take that fever reducer." My mother whispered. Sitting next to Autum. I tried to shake her shoulder to wake her.

"Autum. Can you hear me? I need you to wake up."

"Derek... I'm so... cold..."

"I know, can you take this medicine for me, love?"

She squinted her eyes to try and look at me. Seeing the cup of medicine I was holding, she opened her mouth. She took it but gave an awful look when she swallowed. I know that stuff tasted like crap, but now I had a new concern.

"Mom did you see that?" I whispered. I turned to look up at her. She was covering her mouth with her hand nodding.

"Autum?"

She didn't answer, already falling back to sleep. I pulled her lip up to look at her teeth again. To make sure I wasn't hallucinating. Looking back up to my mother. She waved her hand towards the door. I left the medicine on the nightstand in case I needed it again and followed her out.

Fisting my hair outside the room my mother just stared off into nothing.

"Am I crazy or are her canines elongated?" I asked her, hoping I was wrong.

"They were! When did you say her birthday was?" She asked.

"Not until November 5th, that's still two weeks away." I replied slightly panicked.

"That can't be right. There is no way she would be having these symptoms right now."

"We had to drink that entire thermos of tea today! Elissa said one cup a day should be good until next week. I don't understand what's going on." I sighed frustrated.

"What's going on out here?" My dad asked walking over to us in his bath robe.

"It's Autum, she is running a fever, and her canines are elongated." My mother answered him. The shock on my father's face was how we were all feeling.

"I have a bad feeling about all of this. If she is already getting this sick. How bad is it going to get over the next two weeks? She must have been having toothaches before now and not said anything. We need to go talk to Elissa and ask her for the remedy she is giving the twins. I know Ethan started feeling pretty shitty about four days ago, his mom made him and Rebecca something to help with the pain and fever." I paced in the hall.

My mom wrapped her arms around me. "We can call and talk to Elissa tomorrow. For now, you need to go monitor her for a bit and make sure her fever goes down. You can give her more medicine in two hours. If that doesn't work, you need to make her take a cold shower."

"Okay." I started to walk back to the room.

"Derek. If you need help come get me." My mother added before I walked in and shut the door behind me.

Grabbing one of the notebooks off the nightstand, I sat next to Autum. I couldn't lie next to her without sweating. I also didn't want to fall asleep yet until I knew her fever was coming down. She turned and lay on my lap, a small smile making its way to my face. The mate bond was strong, it excited me to think that we had found each other. Opening the book, I began to read the notes Autum had made. These notes were from the book on the Kingdom of Rune that were written in old English. She had translated about half of it so far.

An hour went by before I felt sweat under my hand. I ran my fingers through Autum's hair for the thousandth time, relief flooding me as her fever finally broke.

I kept reading, wanting to finish the section I was on. I wonder if Autum realized that she was decoding her own history. The parts she had finished translating were about The Gift of Leoht and the original families.

"The three families were the Boern, Gewitt, and Haelan."

"Boern, the warriors and protectors."

"Gewitt, the intellectuals and problem solvers."

"Haelan, the naturals, forgivers, and white wolves."

"A daughter born from a Haelan mother and a father who was both Boern and Gewitt."

"This child received a gift like none before it."

"Elders later named this the Gift of Leoht, meaning the gift of Light."

"A conflict grew, those who thought this new gift gave that family more superiority and those who did not."

"To keep peace a fourth blood line was created and named Leoht."

"Time passed and the young girl was found to be truly special; kind, honest, forgiving, extremely rational."

"Though she was not a fighter, she was unmatched at problem solving and verbal comprehension."

"The young girl soon became a woman and was loved by all, having characteristics of all three families."

"The Leoht name became a Royal one, the women becoming the first Queen."

"Since the queen's passing only two others had been born with the same gift. Both daughters and both first born."

"Born during a time of need to protect the kingdom from peril."

"The last Queen was Patrina. Saving the world from the Heiress of Darkness."

That was the last thing she translated. My mind slowly wondered as I traced my hand up and down Autum's back. What peril was she born for? What would she be facing and what was she expected to do? It was becoming more apparent that the Heiress of Darkness had returned, but why now? Would she be protecting us from her? I knew one thing was absolute, I would be here to help her. I put the book down and the pages turned on their own. Autum had scribbled notes in the middle of the notebook. Reading them, I realized these were notes from when Mary died. They were jumbled ramblings of odd things Mary had said to Autum.

"The Heiress is watching."

"Someone I know and was using my energy to shield herself."

"She doesn't know what I am… what am I?"

"I must go back and watch… must find her?"

"Mary put the blocks in my head, they will fall as I'm ready…?"

"Something happened at the hospital, Mary saw something when I was six."

"Watch it again…watch it again… eerht fo eno era uoy… What did she mean?"

"Mary's Onyx mirror… could have been used for scrying. Did she locate the Heiress?"

Autum POV

I woke up drenched in sweat. So gross. It was made worse when I realized I was lying on Derek's lap. Why was he sleeping sitting up like that? Getting up from bed, I realized all of my clothes were completely soaked. My hair was stuck to the side of my face and where my head had been resting on Derek looked wet as well. So embarrassing. I got up as quietly as possible from the bed to take a shower. I felt lightheaded and still tired. Grabbing onto the nightstand to balance myself I saw a bottle of medicine I didn't remember being there before. After a few minutes I had regained my balance and walked to the bathroom. Getting into the shower felt amazing. The fresh water rinsing my skin of the sticky sweat feeling. While I washed my hair, I remembered Derek waking me to give me medicine. I must have had a bad fever to have warranted medicine and to wake up sweating like that. Turning the dial of the shower colder, I braced my hands on the tile walls and let the water run over me. I still felt dizzy and lightheaded, the cool water felt good on my skin.

What was wrong with me? Getting sick today was not an option. I wanted to go with Derek to the twins' party and wear our matching outfits and feel pretty. A wave of nausea hit me, and I gripped my stomach. Turning the water off, I grabbed a towel and wrapped it around myself. My mouth filled with saliva, and I knew I was going to be sick. After failing to talk myself out of throwing up, I emptied what little amount I had in my stomach. After flushing the toilet, I put the seat down and sat there for a moment. My hands were shaking, and I really needed to eat some crackers or something. My teeth and head were aching, and I felt like I was coming down with the flu. A knock on the bathroom door pulled me from my thoughts.

"Autum, can I come in?" Derek asked.

"Sure." I answered reluctantly.

"How are you feeling?"

"I've been better." I answered honestly.

Derek walked to the linen closet and grabbed another towel.

"Do want help drying your hair?" He asked. I smiled up at him and shaking my head yes, he approached. "Lean forward if you can." He put his hand softly on my back.

I placed my hands on his hips to balance myself as he dried my hair. When he was done, he kneeled down in front of me. Putting the back of his hand to my forehead he nodded in approval.

"Your fever is down. You're still a bit warm, but much better than last night." He smiled up at me.

"I hate to say, but I may be coming down with something. I feel awful."

"I heard you getting sick, do you want some toast or something light to eat?" He got up and went to the sink to get me some water.

I nodded my head. After drinking the water, I stood and walked to the sink. I rinsed my mouth with mouth wash and walked out of the bathroom. Getting dizzy again, I swayed on my feet. Derek grabbed my arm and helped balance me. Without warning he picked me up bridal style.

"Derek, I can walk." I argued.

"Just let me help you. I don't think you're sick. You're just having symptoms of the phase." Seeing that arguing was pointless, I let him carry me. He didn't stop at the bed though. He carried me towards the door.

"What are you doing?" I asked puzzled.

"Taking you to my room, your bed sheets need to be changed." He laughed.

"But my clothes?" I protested.

"I'll come back for some clothes, or you can just where some of mine. You need to rest a bit longer."

I sighed, giving in, and laying my head on his chest. Derek put me down softly in his bed. He walked to his closet and grabbed a pair of shorts and a t-shirt and handed them to me. I put them on and climbed under his blankets to get comfortable.

"Elissa has been giving Ethan and Rebecca herbs the past few days to help with the phasing symptoms. It's in addition to the tea we've been taking. I'm going to go there and see if we can have some for you. Then I'll bring you something to eat." He pushed my hair to the side and placed a kiss on my forehead. "You just get more rest."

I nodded and closed my eyes. I still felt tired, like I hadn't slept. I heard the door open and close and knew he was gone. I wasn't going to argue with him, although there was no way I was having phasing symptoms this early. But I would try anything if it helped me feel better so I could go to the party. Maybe my mind wasn't resting because of my activity in my dream state. I wouldn't go tonight, or right now. Just sleep, I had finally opened my Sacral Chakra and was actually quite happy with myself.

Rebecca POV

Hearing a knock on the front door, I went to it. I was surprised to see Derek outside my door.

"What do you want?" I asked. Derek rolled his eyes at me and crossed his arms. I guess that did come off kind of rude.

"I need to talk to your mom." He asked.

"She's out running errands for the party."

"What about Ethan?"

"He's over at Amy's. He stayed there last night and hasn't been home yet." He just looked at me for a second. I crossed my arms and started tapping my foot impatiently.

"Never mind, I'll just come back later." He said turning to leave.

"Wait, what do you need? I can try and help." I bargained with him. I needed to make amends for what happened the other night. I just didn't know how to apologize. Derek rubbed the back of his neck.

"I need to know if your mom has any more of the herbs she's been giving you two for your phasing symptoms?" He asked reluctantly.

"Um, yeah. In the kitchen." I turned and walked towards the kitchen. Leaving the door open so he could come in. He waited a few seconds then followed after me.

"Why do you need it?" I asked.

"Its... for Autum."

I looked at him questionably, it was too soon for her to need it. But I would give him whatever I needed to, to get back in their good graces.

"Which one do you want?" I asked him.

"What do you mean?" He questioned.

"The one Ethan takes is just for phasing symptoms. The one I take has more herbs to help with... other cravings too." I said hesitantly, feeling my cheeks flush. Remembering how I kissed him and how he looked at me. I felt ashamed and looked at the floor. Hearing Derek sigh I looked up at him.

"I need the one you take." He said sternly. I nodded and grabbed one of my water bottles from the fridge.

"Here, you can have this whole thing. I have two more." I handed the water bottle to him.

"Thank you," Derek turned to walk out of the house.

"Derek, wait." I pleaded.

"What?" He asked his back to me.

"I, umm... I'm sorry... sorry for kissing you." I stuttered out.

"Just forget about it." He replied.

"I can't. I can't forget about the way you looked at me. You hated me." I felt tears brimming in my eyes. I reached and grabbed his arm. Derek turned abruptly and grabbed my wrist. I tried to step back. "I just want us to be friends again, please." I pleaded.

"That's not up to just me anymore." He let go of my wrist and walked out of the house. This was going to be harder than I thought.

Samantha POV

Running around with Elissa today to finish up the twin's party décor was exhausting. But Elissa was paying me. What can I say, I have superb party planning skills. I might open my own business someday when I leave this place. Rebecca was going to love this. The fairy lights hanging from the pavilion. The white linen chair covers and black accent bows around them. White table linens and black napkins on the tables. Center pieces were either black and silver LED balloons or white feathers in a black vase.

There was a picture area with a silver tassel curtain. It was surrounded with black and silver balloons. Some balloons had LEDs and others didn't. There was also a table with extra masks if someone didn't bring one. A table for gifts and an area for the food. Down from the pavilion, towards the shore where changing tents for those who wanted to go for a swim. There were five tents in total. One belonging solely to the Fawn Family and another for the Alphas family. The remaining three were for anyone's use, complete with towels and a hanging area for gowns and tuxes in each one. Each also had an assortment of flip flops for walking on the beach.

Out at the beach were several sitting areas with white loungers or chairs. More balloons with LEDs and fake candles would help keep those areas lit. Blankets were also available for those who wanted to sit on the sand. They had a crew go through and comb the beach to ensure it was picture perfect. The photographer was already taking pictures of the entire area.

It was just after 3 p.m. when we finished. The caterers were planned to be there at 6 p.m., an hour after the party started. The baker would be there at 4:30 to place the cake. She already had directions on where to put it, so we didn't need to stay for that. Elissa waved me over and we walked to her car.

"Thanks for your help, Samantha." Elissa said.

"No problem, I enjoy party planning. It's also more fun when it's not your money!" I laughed.

"True." She laughed with me. "But honestly, you're so meticulous. You really thought of everything and the timeline you created helped so much with ensuring everything was received on time." She continued praising me.

She handed me a check next. It was for $500.

"This is way too much! I can't accept this, Elissa." I said astonished.

"You can and you will. You did so much. I won't take it back." She winked at me. Completely at a loss for words, I took the check.

"What else can I help with? I need more to do to accept this." I begged her.

She laughed at me, "Well, I actually do have something else you might be able to help with."

"Anything," I replied.

"It doesn't have to do with the party. Without going into too much detail now. I need help going through all the evidence we found at counselor Robin's office and home."

"Why do you need help with that?" I questioned, a bit confused.

"We are missing something. You have an eye for detail. I think you might be able to shed new light on it. I will have to get Alpha Darren's permission first. But I have been staring at it for the last two days and I just can't put the pieces together."

"Well, I have been reading everything I can get my hands on about white wolves and the Kingdom of Rune. I might be able to connect the dots between what happened then and what is happening now with the stuff you found, but I have to speak to my father first." I answered.

"Perfect, I'll talk to the Alpha too, in the meantime we both have a party to get dressed for." She smiled at me.

She dropped me at my house. I went inside to get all my makeup and everything I would need. We were all to go to the pack house for our gowns and to get ready there. I was so excited to see everyone dolled up!

40

WHAT'S IN THE BOX

❦

Derek POV

Everyone was here now, hanging out in the living room and chatting with each other. It was 3:30, giving everyone about an hour and half to get ready. We set the girls up in the conference room. Mom had planned to have Jenna over; she was a local makeup artist. The best in her field, the girls had no idea. She had arrived right before everyone else. I needed to go wake Autum. I had given her the herbal tea a few hours ago, hopefully she was feeling better now. Excusing myself, I went up to my room. She was still sleeping so peacefully. Placing my lips on her forehead. I gave her a soft kiss. Her fever was gone. That was a good sign. Half the toast I had brought her was gone. Sitting on the bed next to her I rubbed my hand up and down her arm.

"Hey." She stirred quietly.

"Time to wake up sleeping beauty." I whispered into her ear.

"What time is it?" She asked.

"3:30, just the right time to get up and get ready… if you're feeling better?"

She sat up. "So much better. Whatever you gave me worked." She smiled. Stretching her arms above her head.

"So… all the girls are here. We have the conference room set up for you all to get ready."

"All the girls?" She asked.

"Samantha, Amy, and Rebecca. Ethan and I will get ready in here." I answered her.

"Rebecca's here?" She pinched her eyebrows together.

"Yea, about that. She was at her house when I went there to get that herbal tea. She apologized for everything and asked if we could be friends again?"

"What did you tell her?" She asked.

"I told her that it wasn't up to only me. And then I left without responding further." I grabbed Autum's hand in mine. "She doesn't deserve to be forgiven again. But it also isn't entirely her fault for what she did."

Autum seemed to think about what I was saying. "I agree… she is phasing tonight. We all had our hormones on high alert that night." She gave me a quick peck. "Plus, she knows she can't have you." Her cheeks blushed.

"No, she can't!" I pulled Autum onto my lap, grabbing her head between my hands, I pulled her in for a kiss. She leaned in deepening our kiss, placing her hands around my waist, she pulled herself in.

"I could do this all night, but then I wouldn't get to see you in your dress." I said pulling away. She blushed again and I stood up. Autum lowered her feet to the ground as I kissed her one more time.

"Come on." I led her out of the room. We walked down the stairs together and I called the other girls to follow behind us. I showed them to the conference room. Allowing Samantha and Amy to walk past and held Rebecca and Autum back.

"Rebecca, we aren't going to have any problems, right? I know it's your birthday but that doesn't mean you can cause issues."

"No problems, I am sorry for what I did. I am trying to be better." She turned to look at Autum, "Autum, please accept my apology for the way I have behaved since you've arrived. It is still hard to see you two together, but I understand that my feelings for Derek and your feelings for him are different. I hope that, with time, we can become friends."

She bowed slightly and I allowed her into the room. Keeping Autum behind this time, we both looked completely bewildered. Had Rebecca grown a conscience in the last two days? She seemed to have grown emotionally in the last few days as well, it was like talking to a different person.

"Well, that was unexpected," Autum broke the silence.

"Agreed. So, what do we do now?" I asked her.

"We move on and let her actions speak for themselves." She answered.

"You have no idea how special you are! Have fun getting all dressed up." I kissed her forehead, slapped her ass, and pushed her through the door. Noticing the tinge of pink on her cheeks from the compliment.

Walking back out to the living room I called out to Ethan, and we walked up to my room.

"Dude, you look sharp." Ethan called out to me.

"Thanks bro, you too."

I took one last look in the mirror. The sapphire blue tux looked good. I bought white shoes and a white mask to match Autum's. Ethan was wearing green with black shoes and a black mask, to match Amy.

"We only took thirty minutes to get ready." Ethan laughed.

"We can go get a drink in the study while we wait." I suggested.

Ethan nodded and we headed down to the study. My mother and father were both in the study as well. I laughed. I walked over to the liquor cabinet and poured four bourbons. My father rolled his eyes at me but accepted the drink. It was difficult to get drunk being a werewolf. Our metabolisms processed the alcohol so quickly. It wasn't uncommon for teens to drink either because of this. It really just took the edge off.

"You got ready fast mom; I expected you to be in with the girls still." I smirked as I handed her a drink. She was wearing black and so was my father. They both had white masks. Same as Autum and me.

"I've had many years to perfect this." She laughed as she jested to herself. We all had a little laugh. But I noticed her smile didn't reach her eyes. Something was bothering her.

"So, when is Kiel picking up his tux?" I directed the question at my mother.

My father spit his drink all over the place and my mother's eyes just about bulged out of her head. Ethan was completely indifferent, having no idea why I was asking. I took another sip of my drink, taking time to look at each of them. My mother turned to my father and lipped 'sorry.'

"He is coming by after we all leave." My father finally answered.

"Does Emivy know he is here?" I asked. My father does not like me calling her by her first name.

"Dr. Warren does not know; it's a surprise." He answered back.

"I bet." I responded sarcastically.

I was still mad they hid this from me. Everyone would find out tonight anyways. So, I saw no point in hiding that I knew. Ethan was eyeing me suspiciously now. My father lifted my mother's hand and placed a kiss on the back of it. Telling her, he wasn't mad. She got up and walked towards me.

"You couldn't wait another hour?" she rolled her eyes at me. "I'm going to go check on the girls. The corsages are in the fridge. Ethan, be a dear and go fetch them please." He nodded and walked out with her.

"That was pretty immature." My father started the conversation.

"Was it? Why would you hide that from everyone? Don't you think Rebecca would have been easier to manage if she knew who her mate was?" I asked frustrated.

"It was Kiel's decision. He didn't want anyone to know. You can ask him later why he decided that. But it wasn't my place to disclose it." He took another sip of his drink.

I shrugged my shoulders. That decision caused the last five years of my life to be hell, but I guess it led me to Autum. Not having been with anyone because Rebecca scared them away. In a way I could be happy it happened the way it did.

"Next time I'll use more tact." I winked at my father. He wasn't amused.

"You know, running a pack takes a lot out of you. It would be wise for you to remember that. We have so many more responsibilities than making sure your feelings aren't hurt. Things will happen the way they are meant to. We can't change what has happened... Your mother is struggling right now... She is trying to be strong for you... for the pack... for me. You need to stop being an ass." I thought about his words, I had noticed she was not completely herself.

"What's going on with her?" My tone more serious now.

He ran his hand through his hair, "Your mother had a rough childhood. She can't help but draw lines from her experiences to those of Autum's... " He paused and glanced at the door, "She helped Autum into her dress earlier... Your sister saw too..."

My mother and Ethan entered back in the study at that moment. Both were grinning ear to ear.

"Here." Ethan said handing me Autum's corsage, "They are all ready and thirty minutes early too!" he laughed.

"Autum is still in the conference room, waiting for you, son." My mother smiled.

She looked too happy. "Why are you so smiley?" I questioned.

"You'll see... you are lucky my son." She hugged me.

I leaned in and whispered in her ear, "I'm sorry for being a jerk."

She smiled and nodded then pushed me out the door. The other girls were standing around the living room. They looked really nice. Rebecca was in a form fitting silver dress. It was long and went to the floor. It had a large slit that went up to her thigh. You could see her matching silver heels with white and black accents. Her mask was black and white with silver accents. Amy and Samantha both looked radiant as well. Amy in green and Samantha in white. Corsage in hand I walked to the conference room.

Autum's back was to me when I walked in. The dress already looked amazing from the back though. Her long legs were stunning, and her brown curls cascaded down her back. Her hair was partially up and was shining from the lights reflecting from above. She was wearing the white heals and white lace gloves. They covered her entire arm, up past the elbow. I cleared my throat. I saw Autum stiffen and slowly turn around.

Autum's POV

Derek had just pushed me into the room with the other girls after slapping my ass. My eyes wide I stared directly into Luna Synthia's eyes, mortified that she just witnessed that. Samantha and Amy started giggling while Lana approached me.

"Derek spanked you again, what did you do this time?" Lana asked innocently.

I grabbed her to me, quickly covering her mouth. Horrified to even glance at Luna Synthia now. I chanced a look at Amy and Samantha first, both were holding their mouths trying not to laugh. Looking at Luna Synthia she was smiling. I frowned, why was she smiling? I could feel the heat coming off my face, my chest, my whole body. Looking towards Rebecca, she was trying to remain indifferent, but honestly not hiding it well. I'd hoped her words were true earlier, only time will tell. Then I turned to an unfamiliar face. A woman, tall and beautiful. She had short, dirty blond hair. Her hair was straight, longer in the front then in the back. The length ending mid neck. She pulled the style off well.

Synthia followed my gaze, "Ladies, this is Jenna. She is a beautician; she will be assisting with hair and makeup if you so wish. Lana, come over here, let's get your dress."

Lana ran to her mother, and they walked to the table to get their dress boxes. Her comment about my spanking was already forgotten in her excitement.

I gazed around the room. Jenna had a station set up with two chairs. It appeared she had an abundance of makeup and beauty supplies. Her station had several books as well, with the newest hair trends and styles. In addition to her station there were six more for each of us. A mirror was stationed at each one. The other girls seemed to have brought all their own supplies. I had not, I left everything upstairs. I shrugged it off, I would let Jenna do my hair and makeup. Next to each of our stations was a partition to dress behind. Looking inside the closest one, there were full length mirrors concealed as well. I walked towards the dress boxes. They were lined up on the center conference table with little tent cards atop them, our names elegantly written on each one to identify our dresses. Rebecca was already standing in front of a box. As I approached the table, I walked over and stood in front of mine.

Sam and Amy approached. As Amy passed by, she couldn't help herself.

"You like getting spanked?" Amy teased.

"Shut it!" I slapped her arm. Each of us stood in front of our boxes now.

"Rebecca, would you like to go first, being as it is your birthday?" Luna Synthia asked her.

"Yes!" She answered happily.

She ripped the lid off quickly and pulled the dress out. She flung the dress open and then held it against her chest. It was gorgeous. Silver with black embellishments. It was floor length with a deep v neckline and a slit that went all the way up to her thigh. She swirled in a large circle.

"It's perfect... exactly how I asked for it!" She laughed. I had never seen Rebecca this happy; it was almost unnerving. I was glad for it though; it was helping ease some of the tension between us. Rebecca took her dress and walked to one of the six partitions.

"Rebecca, after you change, Jenna will start with you. Alright ladies let's open these boxes!" Each of us lifted the box lid.

I stood momentarily stunned as I looked upon the dress I would be wearing tonight. The fabric shimmered as the light cast its warm glow upon it. I dropped the lid to the floor and slowly pulled the dress from the box. It was how Derek described it. The color, sapphire blue. It was sleeveless, it would cover most of my back and front. The gloves would cover my arms. I would need to wear my hair down to cover the rest of my back. As I held the dress in my hand, I hadn't noticed the other girls had moved on. Already putting their dresses on.

"Autum, can you zip me up?" Samantha called.

"Yeah, hold on. Let me put my dress down." I walked to the empty station and placed my dress over the chair. I crossed the room over to Samantha's station and walked behind the partition. Her dress was mostly white, and she looked angelic. The dress was floor length with long sleeves. The front and back were not too revealing. The back only dipped down to her mid back. The front scooped just enough to show some of her cleavage. The end of her sleeves and hem of her dress were a dark grey almost silver color that transitioned to white. The dress had intricate designs in silver that flowed from the grey sections and then turned lighter as they disappeared into white.

As I zipped Samantha's dress, I couldn't help but notice the deep bruising on her back. She sucked in a harsh breath as I zipped her up.

"Are you going to be okay? That bruise looks pretty bad."

"Um, yeah, it's fine. It happened during training. Should have taken it a little easier knowing we had this coming up." She tried to laugh it off, but I could tell it pained her to breathe too deeply.

"Well, let me know if you need any help, even later, okay?"

"Sure, of course." She smiled.

I left her area to walk back to my dress. Amy was sitting at her station doing her own hair and makeup. Her dress was the dark green she spoke of while we were at Dorothy's Boutique. Her dress was short, ending right above her knees. It was form-fitting with a deep open back, nearly to her butt. The front was low as well, showing ample cleavage. Her black stilettoes looked amazing and made her calves flex, showing off her firm form.

Luna Synthia was doing Lana's hair. Synthia was in a black gown. She looked elegant in everything she wore. The dress was simple. Floor length with one strap over her shoulder. She finished putting half of Lana's hair up and then allowed her to put on a tinted lip gloss. She was very excited about this it seems as she squealed with excitement. All the girls let out a small chuckle as she drew everyone's attention.

Samantha was leaving her partition as I reached mine. Headed towards Jenna's station for hair and makeup. I grabbed the dress and examined it once more. I had never worn something so nice. I undressed and pulled the dress up. I couldn't quite reach the zipper. I peeked my head out of my concealed area to look around the room. Rebecca, it seemed was done already. Jenna was truly good at her job, a passion it seems that she greatly enjoys. Rebecca's hair was in an up dew, with a few, small, curled strands loose around her neck.

Jenna was starting on Samantha's hair while I saw Luna Synthia and Lana headed towards me.

"Do you need help?" Luna Synthia asked as they approached.

"Please." I smiled softly at her.

"I'll help!" Lana volunteered cheerfully.

I stiffened unintentionally; I didn't want Lana to see the scars on my back. Luna Synthia hadn't seen them either, but I felt more comfortable with her helping me. Lana was just a child. I instinctively took a step back, forgetting the mirror was behind me.

Lana's eyes shifted and her eyes grew concerned.

"What happened to your back Autum?" She asked innocently.

I couldn't think of a response. Luna Synthia quickly walked behind me and started to zip up my dress. Our eyes met in the mirror, a quiet understanding passing between us. I extended my hand for Lana, and she took it coming to stand in front of me. She gazed up at me inquisitively. Her purple dress made subtle sounds as she shifted uncomfortably on her feet. Synthia had finished zipping me, so I kneeled down to be at eye level with Lana. Synthia moved to my side, placing her hand on my shoulder.

"When I was little, I got hurt very badly... but my grandma came and rescued me." I tried to explain to her, "I'm all better now."

"Did it hurt? Does it still hurt?" She asked.

"I hardly remember the pain anymore." I lied to her. I felt a light squeeze on my shoulder, Synthia offering her support. Lana moved to sit on the floor and pulled her dress up over her knee.

"I have a scar too," She smiled up at me, exposing the long scar above her knee. "It hurt really bad, I was foraging with my dad and fell down a ravine. I used to hate how it looked. I thought it was ugly and made me look ugly too. He told me scars show the story of our lives and how strong we are. That they shouldn't be hidden. That they should be worn proudly."

She stood back up and I embraced her in a tight hug.

"Thank you, Lana." I whispered into the side of her neck.

She pulled away to look at me, "The story of your scars means you must be very strong."

Her statement was followed by a moment of silence, where I looked upon her with wonderment. She was truly a smart child, her wisdom not from years of knowledge but an innocent statement of truth. The unfiltered ramblings of a ten-year-old.

"I'm going to go check on the boys." Synthia patted my shoulder and walked towards the exit.

"Can I stay with you?" Lana asked.

"Yes, but Lana… could you please keep my scars a secret for now."

"Why?"

"I'm still trying to be strong." I answered her as simply as I could.

Standing up I smoothed out my dress. An audible gasp left my lips as I looked at the dress in the mirror. It was gorgeous. Short in the front, right above my knees and long in the back. The skirt was made of tulle layered over silk. The silk extending in the back creating a small train that ended right above the back of my ankles. The chest was tight, it reminded me of a heart the way it was shaped. It clung to me in all the right places, the silk hugging me like a cocoon.

"You look very pretty Autum." Lana smiled up at me.

"Thank you, Lana."

"Are you going to let Jenna do your hair and makeup?"

"I think I'll do my hair. I'll have her do my makeup."

I decided to wear my hair half up and half down. Derek liked my long hair, the way it flowed down my back. It would also cover the remainder of my scares that could be seen. Pulling half my hair up, I put it in a bun. Pulling a few hairs out to frame my face, I curled them with an iron. Satisfied I stood and grabbed my gloves, I removed my elbow sleeve and pulled the gloves on. Next, I headed towards Jenna's station. She was finishing up Samantha's makeup. Samantha decided to wear her hair down. She had Jenna straighten her hair and give her bangs. It was different for sure, but she looked good with bangs. Her makeup looked great, her steely grey shadow matching the silver in her dress.

She and Amy were having a casual conversation when I approached.

"Looks like your next Autum, last but not least." She smiled up at me as she stood from the chair.

I was feeling nervous. I had never had someone do my makeup before. She would have to touch me. I worried my hands in my lap as Jenna put together the pallet she would use for my complexion.

Samantha and Amy moved towards the conference table and joined Rebecca while Lana stayed next to me in the other chair. Jenna asked me a few questions about my preferences of which I told her I really didn't have any.

"Can you turn me away from the mirror, while you do my makeup?" I inquired.

"Sure, that's not a problem," Jenna smiled down at me. "That will make the reveal more dramatic."

I finally started to relax as Jenna's touch was delicate to my face. Lana started spinning in her chair, to occupy herself. I noticed Rebecca's gaze on me several times. Although bothered by it, I didn't let it show. Jenna had finished my foundation and was now starting on my eyes. The pallet she had was filled with blues, silvers, and browns.

Lana jumped from the chair and walked over to the table. She picked up a blue velvet box. The box was medium in size, slightly larger than my hand. Walking back over to us she held it out for me.

"What's that?"

She shrugged her shoulders, "Not sure, it was by your box. Looks like a necklace box to me."

I took the velvet box but didn't open it. The exterior of the box felt soft against my fingers. I couldn't bring myself to open it. I knew Derek was going to get me jewelry. This looked to be expensive, I already felt overwhelmed with the dress and its exquisiteness.

The conference room door opened, grabbing everyone's attention. Luna Synthia and Ethan walked in. Ethan walked to Amy and presented her corsage. White roses and what appeared to be green hydrangeas. The hydrangeas were lighter than her dress, it made a nice contrast. Luna Synthia gave Rebecca her corsage, a mixture of white and black roses with baby's breath. Then she gave Samantha hers. White roses with grey poppies. She approached us next and placed a corsage on Lana. It was a purple iris surrounded by white daisies.

Jenna finished my makeup and took a step back, ensuring everything looked alright.

"Ready?" Jenna asked before she swiveled my chair towards the mirror.

I nodded but didn't verbally reply. Holding my breath, she spun the chair around. Luna Synthia approached and placed her hand on my back, and I released the breath I was holding.

"Absolutely radiant." Luna Synthia spoke as she leaned in and gave me a side hug, our eyes meeting in the mirror.

The girl looking back at me in the mirror, took my breath away. I had never worn much makeup before, and Jenna seemed to bring out all my best attributes. Blue and brown eyeshadow pulled my eyes into more focus, making them pop. Blue eyeliner made them even more defined. Blush highlighted my high cheek bones and made my face appear slimmer. The black mascara coated each lash, they fanned out and appeared to be longer. Jenna spritzed my hair and face with glitter. As I turned my face in the mirror, I could see the small crystals shining as the light hit them.

"Alright ladies, let's move out into the great room." Luna Synthia announced.

"Could I have a minute alone? Please," I asked quietly. Luna Synthia nodded and pulled Lana along with her. The girls all exited. Jenna started packing up her belongings, but then stepped out to use the restroom.

I couldn't bring myself to open the jewelry box. I started pacing trying to syce myself up. I could do this. It's just a necklace. I didn't own much jewelry, but the more I thought about it the more my emotions pulled at me. Derek cared about me, he really cared about me. Having someone who understood me and who helped me find myself and supported all of me... I needed to clear my head and stop overthinking right now. I was going to start crying and I didn't want to ruin my makeup.

The door squeaked as it was pushed open. I knew immediately who it was without looking. His scent hit me, sage and sunflowers. I slowly turned around but didn't lift my head. I hadn't reeled my emotions in yet, I needed a few more minutes. Tea, I also needed that damned tea.

Derek stopped abruptly right inside the doorway. I couldn't help but finally raise my eyes to meet him. He looked at me like I was the only one in this world. His mouth was slightly ajar as he gazed at me. I approached him and smiled deeply, lifting my hand, I closed his mouth. I took a step back, but Derek closed the distance immediately, moving forward and taking my hand with the jewelry box in it.

"Why haven't you opened the box?"

"What's in it?" I asked, lowering my head again. I really didn't want to cry; I was so emotional. Derek lifted my chin, and we made eye contact. I could see my eyes reflecting in his, the sapphire looked like flames in his eyes.

"Absolutely stunning!" He spoke as he leaned in to kiss me. No matter how hard I tried, I couldn't stop the single tear that fell. He wiped it away with his thumb.

"Why are you crying, why are your eyes glowing?"

"I've never worn something so nice or felt like... this before." I whispered.

"Felt like what?"

"So… cared for… so… loved." I gulped and looked down again, trying to think of something else that would stop me from crying and ruining this beautiful masterpiece Jenna had created.

"Autum, look at me please."

Derek's POV

She looked up through her eye lashes and I felt like my heart stopped right there. She was gorgeous. She had no idea how beautiful she was, how kind and forgiving she was. I couldn't wait until we were at the beach to tell her. Tell her how I felt about her. I took the box from her hand and opened it. She gasped. Inside was a diamond and sapphire necklace with matching earrings. It went with everything she was wearing. I took the necklace from the box, and she held her hair away for me. I reached around and clasped it. Her hand instantly went to her neck to touch it.

Next, I took her hand and pulled her to the mirror. She put the earrings on, and I enjoyed watching the smile creep to her face. I took the corsage from the box and placed it on her wrist. Blue periwinkle and white jasmine flowers to match her dress. Bringing her hand to my lips I placed a soft kiss on the back. I could see her holding back the tears.

"We are going to walk out of this room, and you are going to be the most beautiful woman at this party. Because you are beautiful in here too," I pointed to her heart, "You are just wearing it on the outside now too!" I leaned forward and kissed her forehead.

"What about my eyes?"

"Let the nervous energy go. And if you can't, who cares." I placed my hand on her cheek, "You will phase in a couple of weeks, and they will all know anyways. Let them see." She took a couple of deep breaths trying to relax.

I bent my elbow out for her to take it in her arm and she obliged. Her eyes started to fade to normal and we joined everyone in the living room.

41

WHITE MASKS

❦

Autum POV

Arriving at the beach I was breathless. It was so beautiful. Derek and Ethan got out of the truck first and opened Amy's and my doors. Standing outside the truck I took in the site, a huge smile on my face.

"Why do you look like you're seeing this for the first time?" Amy asked.

"Cause I am." I said breathlessly.

It was so gorgeous; the sea went on for miles. Huge rock formations were peeking out of the sea as waves crashed against them. Maybe I'd find a seashell today.

"What do you mean?" Derek asked.

"I've never seen the ocean." I looked up to Derek. His face contorted. Looking at the other two they shared the same look.

"You are a bad boyfriend." Ethan said, patting Derek on the back as they walked past us. It caught me off guard for a moment. Derek being called my boyfriend, but I guess that's what he was. I felt my face heat slightly and I tried to ignore it. My mask would cover most of it, fortunately. Derek extended his elbow again and I took it.

"I am a bad boyfriend; how did I not know you haven't been to the beach before?" He asked as we descended the wood steps from the parking lot down to the pavilion next to the shore.

"You never asked, and it really never came up in conversation."

"Of course, it did. When I said the twin's party is at the beach. You could have said 'oh, the beach I've never been there before.' Hmm." Derek had changed his voice to a girly one.

"I don't sound like that." I playfully slapped him. "Oh, the beach. I've never been there before." I said sarcastically.

Derek rolled his eyes, "See, it was that easy. I do feel like a bad... boyfriend though. But for real, how have you never been here?" he asked.

I smiled to myself when he paused at the word boyfriend. "Well, I lived in White Mountain Pack for my whole life. We never traveled, my grandmother and me. When we moved here, it was right before school started. So much was going on with me and my meetings with Dr. Warren and school. We just never found the time, I guess."

I heard more cars pulling up behind us. We stopped our descent and turned to see Samantha arriving with her parents and Rebecca arriving with hers.

"Mom, it looks just like how I imagined it!" I heard Rebecca squeal.

"Well, you need to thank Samantha. She's the one that made your vision come true." Elissa hugged her daughter.

Smiling to myself again. I saw Rebecca leave her mother's embrace and run over to Samantha and hug her. Samantha's face was comical. She was not expecting that at all! As Rebecca squeezed her, Samantha's face changed, she looked like she was in pain. Her mother looked away awkwardly and her father almost looked angry. Her parents were so strange.

"Thank you, thank you, thank you!" Rebecca said as she squeezed the life from Samantha.

"You're welcome, it was no trouble at all, honestly." She tried to speak between trying to gasp for air. Turning around we continued to walk down the steps.

"I didn't know Samantha helped with the party planning." Derek spoke.

"Yeah, it's why we haven't been hanging out so much. She has been so busy with ensuring everything was ordered on time and planning how it would all be set up. She spent most of the day here organizing the team for setup too. We've only been able to hangout and talk at school the last few weeks." I answered.

"She did a great job, maybe my mom should get her help for your party." He winked at me.

"I don't need anything fancy like this; I'd be happy with something simple... very simple." I half pleaded.

My birthdays consisted of my grandmother and me. I'd never had a party before. I'd never had friends before, let alone a boyfriend. The entire concept was foreign to me.

"You have to let me plan a party, let me spoil you." Derek continued.

"You've spoiled me enough." We had reached the bottom of the steps. I stepped out and let go of his arm. I twirled around, to show just how much he had already spoiled me.

He grabbed my hand pulling me towards him and leaned into my ear. "I've only just begun." Blushing slightly, I turned around when I heard a familiar croaking noise. Lifting my arm, the raven landed gracefully.

"Where did he come from!" Derek asked startled.

"He's been following me around." I shrugged, "Hey Blue, my pretty bird." I petted his head.

"You named your black raven Blue?" Derek laughed.

"His eyes are blue; I think he likes the name. Don't you Blue?" I baby talked to him.

"He does like it!" Elissa laughed as she passed us by.

Derek rolled his eyes and I laughed. "You stay out of trouble Blue, but I need to go inside now." I lifted my arm in a quick motion, and he took flight. He didn't go far, landing nearby on a tree.

Shaking my head, we continued towards the pavilion. Ethan and Amy were waiting off to the side to enter. We walked past them. Samantha rushed ahead to the DJ, to announce the twin's arrival.

The pavilion was fabulous. The decorations made the whole area seem very high end. It matched the masquerade theme perfectly. Rebecca's dress matched as well. Her silver dress with the black, white, and silver theme of all the decorations was definitely intentional. The fairy lights hanging around the entire perimeter made it feel like we were in another world entirely. Paper lanterns hung from the high ceilings. Samantha really did a fantastic job.

"Would you like something to drink?" Derek asked, breaking my focus on the room.

"Yes, that would be nice."

The sun was slowly setting, we still had a good two or three hours of light left. The food smelled amazing and everyone in town was there. Derek walked us to a table that had our names on little cards. He sat me down and left to get us something to drink. Samantha came and sat next to me as the DJ announced Rebecca and Ethan's arrival. Everyone turned to see them enter and started clapping. Reaching over I grabbed Samantha and pulled her in for a hug. She hissed silently, but I heard it.

"Sorry, I forgot about the bruises." I cringed.

"I'm fine."

"You really out did yourself, you know, this is stunning. Everyone is going to want you to help plan their parties when they find out you did all this." I complimented her.

"Stop." She laughed.

"I'm serious. This is breathtaking."

"Okay, okay. Thank you. Now stop complimenting me, it's going to go straight to my head." She said, as we laughed together. She seemed better now.

"We all need to go take pictures while we look fresh!" She added.

"That's a good idea, I'll talk to Derek when he gets back with the drinks." She nodded at me and walked away to go tell everyone else. Lana came and sat next to me at that moment, she looked adorable.

"Autum, will you come take a picture with me, just me and you?" She tried to do puppy dog eyes through her mask.

"How could I say no to that?" I joked. She smiled brightly. "I just need to wait for your brother for a minute, why don't you go save us a spot in line and I'll be right over."

She jumped up and hugged me. "Deal!" she stated as she skipped away. So, freaking adorable. I'm in love with that kid. We took multiple group photos. All of the girls, then all of the guys, then the whole group. I was surprised when Luna Synthia asked me to join their family photo.

"Autum, honey, come take a picture with us." Luna Synthia requested. I stood there for a moment, Amy nudged me, and I turned and glared at her. Not that she could really see it though the mask. She laughed at me, not scared of my scowl at all. As I approached Derek held his hand out to me.

"Are you sure?" I asked hesitantly.

"You are a part of our family now," She smiled at me as Alpha Darren and Lana nodded in my direction.

Lana stood in front of me and Luna Synthia, holding both our hands. Derek was at my other side with his arm around my waist. Looking at everyone now, I noticed we all had white masks on. They were all designed differently but the main color was white. It looked planned; it couldn't be a coincidence. After a few pictures were taken Luna Synthia wanted pictures with no masks on. We all obliged.

As we walked away from the picture area, I couldn't help but inquire. "Was it planned that your whole family would wear white masks?"

"My mother made the decision." He answered.

"So, I just happened to get a white mask... but didn't you get a white mask after I did, to match me?" I didn't notice but Derek had led us to the dance floor. He placed my hand on his shoulder, and he placed his on my waist as he took the lead.

"Yes, that's correct." He answered, as his eyes looked into mine. His features were soft, he seemed relaxed and happy. Suddenly he extended his arm and spun me and then brought me back to him. My hand landed on his chest as our eyes met again. He smiled down at me at my surprise and I let out a little laugh.

"Your ridiculous." I playfully slapped his chest.

"You enjoyed it, don't lie." He smirked.

"I did." I smiled even brighter, "Now about the masks." I raised one eyebrow at him.

Derek pulled me away from him again, I spun out from his arms. When he pulled me back in, he spun me under his arm then dipped me. My breath caught. He was making my body do things I didn't know I could do. He was a very good dancer. We stayed that way for a moment, Derek's hand on my thigh, as one of my legs was lifted.

"My mother picked the mask color, after we had ours. She wanted us all to match. She sees you as family, Autum." He didn't give me time for a response, he leaned in and kissed me. Not a quick kiss, but one filled with passion. He broke the kiss and moved us to stand. I held his cheek in my hand for a moment. I really couldn't picture this being any other man other than Derek. He was completely and irrevocably mine and I was his.

"Derek!" I loud male voice broke our trance. He glanced behind me. Grabbing my hand, we headed in the man's direction.

42

BIRTHDAY WISH

❧

Rebecca POV

I was trying so hard not to feel sorry for myself. Ethan and Amy looked great together. Even Derek and Autum looked like they were meant to be. I got super jealous when we were taking pictures. We took a couple of group photos then the couples wanted some alone. I can't blame them. That's what I would have wanted too. I was more jealous of Autum than Amy. But it was so hard to stay mad at her. She was just so damn nice… all the time. Now I was watching them dance. They were gliding across the dance floor. Meant for each other's arms, their moves were graceful and pulled the attention of party goers. Letting a sigh leave my lips it garnered the attention of the crowd of girls around me.

"Rebecca, you look amazing. Why are you so sad?" One girl said.

"I just wanted to have a date for tonight, my only birthday wish." I replied.

"Well, then take your pick." Another wiggled her eyebrows at me.

She was right, there were so many boys here to choose from. All were ogling me from afar. Most were too scared to come any closer. I really did make a reputation for myself for being a bitch. None of these boys would do. None strong enough to handle me and I'm a handful, I know it!

"Who is that?" A girl purred behind me.

Turning around I saw him walk in. Tall, dark, and handsome. Too bad his mask was hiding most of his features. I swear he was staring right at me. Who was he? I didn't recognize him, though he seemed familiar.

"Girl, he's looking over here."

"No, he is looking at her." Another said pointing at me.

"And he's matching you Rebecca, it was meant to be. Go over there!"

I felt heat creep to my cheeks, I was lost in his eyes momentarily. Was he looking at me? I saw Derek and Autum make their way over to him. His head turned from my direction to theirs. I felt overwhelming jealousy at that moment. What was wrong with me? Derek extended his hand, and they shook before embracing for a moment, patting each other's backs. They were laughing and smiling. Next, he took Autum's hand and kissed the back of it.

Before I knew it my feet were taking me closer to them. I didn't want him touching her. Wow, now I sounded crazy. One thing was for sure, he could be my prince for the night. We were coincidently matching; I couldn't have planned it better myself. His tux fit snug. Every inch of him seemed ripped, but hidden well, under all that clothing. I pulled my fan open and started fanning my face as I approached. The heat outside was finally getting to me. Or was it this man's presence?

"Derek, introduce me to your friend?" I asked. I could smell something like pumpkin spice, and it was making my mouth water.

"Rebecca, this is Kiel, you may remember him." Derek smiled.

Kiel extended his hand, and I took it. Wishing I wasn't wearing gloves right now, so I could feel his skin when he slightly bowed and brought my hand to his lips. His eyes never left mine, I felt my breath hitch. He straightened back up but didn't let go of my hand. The smell was him; it was subtle, but I could smell it. I saw his nose flaring too. Was he smelling me?

"You're Dr. Warrens son, I remember you. You've been away for school, right?"

"Yes, I actually finished school early. So, it was time to come home. Have you seen my mother by the way?"

"She is at the hospital. She is watching over one of the children whose parents are missing. There's a lot going on around here right now actually."

"Well, then I will just have to go surprise her there. She doesn't know I'm home."

"Oh, will you be leaving then?" I asked, hoping he'd stay a bit longer.

"No, I plan on spending my evening here." Pulling my hand, he was still holding, he leaned into my ear, "Happy Birthday Rebecca." His tone was deep, and it vibrated all the way to my core. Feeling more flustered than I cared to admit, I continued to fan my face.

"Accompany me to the dance floor." I said sternly. It wasn't a question. A slight smile taking form on his lips.

"I heard you could be a bit… demanding." He smiled as he led the way to the center of the pavilion.

"What can I say, I know what I want."

"So, I've heard." He glanced at Derek and Autum. For a brief second, I felt disdain in his voice.

Blushing now, I cleared my throat. He must have already heard what happened. Bloody hell, I wish people could just keep their mouths shut.

"That was a mistake, a result of the phase. I blame my hormones and the death of my grandmother. It had been a difficult day." I reasoned, assuring myself more than anything.

Kiel spun me out from him and then spun me back in. "That's good, because after tonight, Derek will be the last thing on your mind." He rasped out.

Then I felt it. His hand grazed my jaw. In that moment, the smallest amount of tingles spread across where he touched. My lips parted and a small gasp left my lips. Was this what everyone talked about, the tingles you feel when you find your mate? Was Kiel my mate? I had no time to process when the beat of the music picked up and Kiel started leading us into a dance. I felt like a puppet to the puppeteer, as he continued turning and spinning me around in all directions. Glancing around I noticed everyone had backed off the floor. It was just the two of us now, everyone else in a circle watching. His eyes never left mine as he spun me around. He guided us as we glided across the floor, and I felt like no one else mattered.

Time slowed as we danced, and I moved with him. Flourishing my arms or legs when I could. I felt seductive, beautiful, and alluring trapped in his gaze. He had eyes for no other. The song came to an end, and he dipped me. Grabbing my bare leg through the slit in my dress. He held me there, my arms around his neck our noses practically touching. The rise and fall of my chest were unmistakable. I hadn't exerted that much energy in Goddess knows how long.

His gaze felt hot on me. It made my heart beat faster. I stared back into his deep grey eyes and for the first time ever I forgot about everything else. It all fell away. I could feel the intensity of his emotions through those eyes. I bit my lip, enticing him. I know he wants to kiss me. Goddess knows I do. He licked his lips, and I felt my entire body heat. I saw my eyes in his reflection. They started to glow. Goddess not now, I didn't want to make him kiss me, I wanted him to do it on his own. Is he a pack member? I wasn't sure. But one thing was for sure, I wanted to know he wanted to. Closing my eyes, I turned my head. Ending our stare off.

Kiel stood us up. And we were applauded as we left the dance floor. I could make out a slight frown from under his mask. Was he already regretting this, was he going to reject me? He didn't kiss me, so he must not be feeling the same way. This was like Derek and Autum all over again. Pulling my hand from his I walked off, out pacing him and cutting through the crowd of people. Nodding and thanking people as I walked by as they said Happy Birthday. Getting outside the pavilion I took a deep breath in. His pumpkin spice was still lingering. I took in the view. The sun would be setting soon. This beach had the most beautiful sunsets. My teeth started to tingle, and I smiled to myself. I would phase tonight and meet my wolf. She would never reject me or abandon me. It was exciting to think I would have a friend for life soon.

"Did I do something to upset you?" I heard Kiel's voice come up behind me.

"It's… nothing. Not anything I'm not used to anyways." I half pouted. I kept my eyes on the horizon and hugged myself.

"I don't ever want you to feel that way."

"What way?" I asked, intrigued.

"Like your feelings don't matter." He said softly, coming closer. I could feel his chest on my back. His hands reached for mine and I let him take them.

"Are you a pack member?" I asked.

"No, does that matter for some reason?"

I felt defeated at that moment. My own gift was making me feel helpless. I had used it so many times on people growing up, that I didn't even realize when I was doing it. I wanted someone to want me for me. Not because I persuaded them to like me. I wanted what Derek and Autum had, I wanted to be loved by someone.

"You didn't answer me." He probed.

"Why aren't you a pack member? I remember you from when I was a kid."

He walked next to me. "From what I remember, my mother brought us here when I was about ten years old. Alpha Darren wanted me to understand what it meant to be a part of the pack. So, we waited. I had never really understood that we were werewolves. My mother is human, and she raised me in Ilwaco while she attended medical school. She probably didn't want me running around telling people I was a werewolf."

"I could imagine, that would be a problem." I interjected.

"Yes, it would have. After Alpha Darren gave us permission to move here, I learned about who I was and what it meant to be a part of the pack. It was planned that I would officially join the pack on my thirteenth birthday."

"Why your thirteenth birthday?" I asked.

"No special reason, really. We had decided to do it sooner than that, but when Luna Synthia realized it was my golden birthday, she talked us into waiting. It would be more special in her opinion." He rolled his eyes.

"When's your birthday, if you don't mind me asking?"

"It's August thirteenth."

"So, you never became a member, what happened?" I probed. Leaning down I removed my heals. We were at the end of the path and my heals wouldn't do in the sand. We kept walking towards the beach.

"It's hard to say exactly. When we had moved here not everyone in the pack was here yet. The town was still being rebuilt and many pack members were still living amongst other packs. That summer before my birthday, many people were moving back in, the hospital was reopening, and many shops had started business back up. I remember my mother coming home one night, days before my party. She was furious. She wouldn't tell me why exactly. She only said that there were people here she didn't know were a part of this pack and that she wouldn't allow me to join. When I argued with her, she said I wasn't an adult, and she wouldn't allow it."

"But you are an adult now, why didn't you do it after you turned eighteen."

"A couple of reasons. As I got older, I could tell there was bad blood between my uncle and my mom. He never really believed I was his nephew, until I phased that is. Also, when I turned eighteen, I planned on going to medical school. I really didn't see the need to be a pack member."

"What do you mean Alpha Darren didn't believe you were his nephew until you phased?" I asked curiously.

"When I got my wolf, his wolf recognized the familiar bond. He apologized to my mother for not believing her. I never realized until then that he never saw me as family, and I was honestly hurt. I was glad that I was leaving for college at that time and decided to wait to become part of the pack."

We were now at the beach. Kiel guided me to sit down on one of the loungers and he sat next to me. How could I ensure I don't persuade him? I felt my eyebrows pinch together. This is probably the only time I ever wished I didn't have powers.

"What's wrong? Why so many questions about being a pack member?"

"I guess it really doesn't matter if I tell you, you'll know in a few hours anyways. I'm a white wolf. I have the gift of persuasion." I blurted out quickly.

"I still don't see why being a pack member matters," He questioned.

"Aren't you surprised? You're not acting surprised."

"I told you; I moved here when I was ten. You moved back right before I turned thirteen. You were all everyone talked about. You and how you persuaded students and teachers to get what you wanted, you were only six years old, almost seven and already so talented."

"Really, that's embarrassing, that was your first impression of me."

"Truthfully I thought you were brilliant." He grinned.

"I think I do remember you; you and Derek were always ganging up on me and picking on me! He thought you were so cool, how you didn't spell your name K.Y.L.E like normal." I laughed.

"I wasn't picking on you, just trying to get your eyes to glow." He laughed back.

"My eyes to glow? But then I was trying to persuade you?" I asked confused.

"Yes, and you were so angry when it didn't work! But it was worth it to see them glowing. Like they were tonight, your emotions bring your power forward." He leaned closer. "They looked radiant tonight!"

I gulped; his close proximity was making me flustered. I could feel the warmth coming off my cheeks. If I wasn't wearing a mask, this might be embarrassing. "Wait, I'm confused… what do you mean they didn't work on you? I mean the Alpha has commanded me not to be able to use them on pack members recently, but you're not one… so?"

"He commanded you?" He raised his voice angrily.

"Calm down, it was… necessary at the time. Now answer my question."

"I think I'll wait a bit longer." He teased. I really didn't have the patience for this. Maybe he thought it was cute or something to toy with me, but I was phasing tonight, and I hadn't drunk any tea recently. I was way past patience at this point.

"Listen, I don't know everything that you have been told, but let me fill you in on one thing. I don't like games. So, if you have something to say then say it. I'm not going to wait around and be toyed w-"

"So, demanding!" He cut me off.

I stood from the chair. I really just couldn't do this, not on my birthday. Now my patience was zero. I could just feel the irritation growing, goddess damn hormones. Turning to walk away, Kiel reached out and grabbed my hand. Pulling me back towards him.

"Wait, I do have something else to say." He said as I pulled my hand from his.

"Out with it then." I crossed my arms.

Kiel reached up and removed his mask and dropped it on the chair. "There is one more reason why I left after I turned eighteen." He reached up and pulled my mask off. I was captivated by him. I couldn't help the smile on my face. His face was perfect. Shaped by gods. His smile was just as sincere when he removed my mask. His words were like silk as they left his soft lips. He reached up and caressed my cheek, "When I turned eighteen, I found my mate."

Well, that was like being doused in cold water! Why do I keep having feelings for these boys who feel nothing for me? I could feel the heat on my face, and I knew my eyes were glowing. I turned to leave again.

"Just wait a minute." He tried to pull me back.

"Why, why would I stay here? Did you not just hear me? I have no patience for this, especially today. I want someone to want me for me. I don't want to accidentally persuade you; you have a mate. Why are you here?!" I yelled,

"Rebecca, you can't persuade me, I told you already."

"Stop talking in circles! You know what I'm going through today, with the phase! These kinds of conversations are driving me to the edge of madness." I needed to calm down, I knew this, but he was making me so angry.

"Ok, I'm sorry, you're right! I'm here because my mate is here. I left because my mate was too young. The calling wanted me to have her, and my wolf couldn't control himself. I had to get far away. I didn't join the pack because I didn't want to feel any connections to the pack while I was gone. I needed the space from her, to wait for her. Until she phased herself and could recognize me as her mate."

"Why are you telling me all th-"

His lips captured mine. The sparks coming alive as our skin made the connection. I felt the anger leave me. It melted away like it never existed. My hands found his neck and I pulled him in. His hands around my waist started roaming my back. Anger turned to arousal and in an instant, I became very aware of the bulge in his pants rubbing against me. This was madness, how long he had waited for... me? I would phase tonight, and my wolf would claim him, I could feel it in my heart, it felt right. He broke our kiss and gazed at me. The sun was setting, the most beautiful sunset from the perfect spot and neither of us cared. I could see my eyes aflame in his eye's reflection.

Reaching up he wiped away a tear I didn't know was there. "Stubborn woman couldn't wait a mere three more hours to phase and have your wolf claim me. Made me give it all up now." He smiled sweetly at me. I didn't have words for this moment. It would only be surpassed by the moment we have when I shift. I was ready for it too.

"What's your wolfs name?" I asked him.

"Avery," He answered, pulling me in to whisper in my ear. "And he can't wait to taste you."

My arousal perfumed the air, and I saw Kiel's nose flare. His eyes were flickering from light brown to black. His wolf was coming forward. "Mate." His wolf growled!

"Calm down boy," I purred back, "It's only three more hours."

43

BEST PART OF
THE PHASE

❧

Ethan POV

I needed to cool down, it wasn't even that warm out today.

"Amy! Cool me down with your fan!" I panted.

"My poor baby, are you feeling hot?" She asked sarcastically. Beads of sweat were forming on my brow. I unbuttoned my tux jacket and removed it. Amy moved closer.

"Babe, you don't look to good." She said concerned, putting her hands on my face.

"I know, I'll be fine. I didn't drink enough of that damn tea today. Didn't think it would get this bad."

"You wanna go for a swim? We can go change and watch the sun setting from the water?" she beamed.

"That's a little too romantic for me." I teased her. Amy playfully slapped my arm.

"Help me up?" I asked her.

She rolled her eyes then extended her hand. I threw my jacket over my shoulder, and we made our way to the changing tents. After cutting across the dance floor, we ran into Derek and Autum. They were both staring out at the beach.

"What are you two up to?" I asked curiously.

"We were just watching Rebecca and Kiel. They hit it off good, but then your sister stormed off and he followed her." Derek said, pointing to the two walking across the beach.

"Yeah, I saw them dancing. They looked amazing together." Amy piped in.

"Where are you two off to?" Autum asked us.

"We are going for a swim and then to watch the sunset from the water." Amy answered before I could.

I rolled my eyes, "First, I'm going to get you out of that dress!" I smacked her ass and watched her face flush.

"You brought swimsuits?" Autum asked.

"We have changing tents down by the beach. There are suites for all of us in the tents, even you." I pointed below us. Autum obviously didn't know. She looked uncomfortable all of a sudden. "But you don't have to swim." I added.

"It's not that." She turned and whispered something in Derek's ear.

"I made sure there was a cover up for you." He smiled at her. That seemed to put her more at ease.

I knew she had scars; Derek had mentioned it to me. I didn't know how extensive they were, apparently bad enough to make her uncomfortable in a swimsuit. I had noticed she always wore a sleeve over her elbow too. Even the gloves she picked for her dress tonight went up past her elbows. Derek never told me how she got them, just that they were inflicted by her mother at a young age. It made me angry to think someone had hurt our future Luna like that and as a child. I really needed to burn off some of this tension.

"Hey, are you ok?" Derek asked me.

I hadn't realized I was growling. "Shit, sorry. No, it's the phase. Everything is getting to me. I feel like I'm in a damn sauna." I apologized. Amy started fanning me again and we excused ourselves. Making our way to our family's tent.

Amy sauntered in first, I hung the sign outside saying 'Occupied.' She was shaking her ass on purpose, and she knew it. I watched as she bent over slowly to take off her shoes.

"Leave those on!" I growled softly.

She smirked as I walked over and undid the zipper on the back of her dress. Slowly I pulled it down as I kissed her shoulders. This was the best part of the phase… the sexual desire. The others were crazy for suppressing it. I couldn't get enough of her. The dress hit the floor and Amy stepped out of it. She turned around to face me. She was so confident in her appearance, and she should be. She was a living goddess. Her muscles just toned enough to be fucking irresistible. I would expect nothing less from the best trained female in our pack, and she was mine.

She put her hands on my chest as I slowly unbuttoned my shirt. Leaning forward, I kissed her forcefully, and she moaned into my mouth. She reached down and undid my pants and they fell to the floor. Looking around the room, I didn't have much to work with. No hard walls to throw her up against, no bed. A couple of bench seats, those would have to do. Dropping my boxers to the floor my dick sprung free.

Amy dropped to her knees and took me in her mouth.

"Fuck, that feels good." I cursed out. I went to reach for the back of her head, but she stopped me.

"Don't mess up my hair." She said sternly.

"Fine." I said, slamming my dick back in her mouth making her choke.

She grabbed my ass with both hands pulling me in deeper. Fuck, joke was on me, she could deep throat! As she squeezed my ass, her throat squeezed my cock. I could smell her arousal and I wanted to be in her. Slamming my cock so deep in her that she screamed, the vibration pushing me close to the edge. Looking down watching her take me in and out was fucking hot! I don't want to finish this way.

"Get up here!" I groaned.

Amy stood and I pinched her nipple between my fingers. I took her other breast in my mouth. Her moans filled the tent. I didn't give two fucks who could hear us. I just wanted her, wanted to hear her scream.

"Bend over, put your hands on that bench!" I said as I turned her around. Her heals were making her the perfect height for me.

Her plump ass in the air. I spread her legs further and slapped her pussy. She moaned for me again. The wet sound from her juices spilling out sending me into a frenzy. I slammed into her; her back slightly arching at the feeling. I pulled my dick out, drenched from her and ran it across her ass. Her nails scrapping against the bench fueled me further. I slapped her ass hard, and she yelled out. Pushing back inside her, I felt her pussy clenching. My dick twitching within her. I placed my thumb over her ass and applied pressure. Pumping in and out of her with a steady rhythm as she moaned. Her knees started to wobble, and I knew she was close.

Pulling out of her I grabbed a towel quickly, folding it, I placed it on the bench.

"Put your knees on the bench."

Amy did, looking over her shoulder at me and biting her lip, she knew that turned me on. I placed one hand on her stomach and pulled her into me as I thrust back into her. My other hand grabbed her throat. Pulling her head to my chest.

"Touch yourself," I demanded. Both of her hands slowly slid up her body as she grabbed hold of her breasts and started massaging them. I loved watching her touch herself. "More." I said dropping my voice an octave.

One had slid down; she reached all the way back soaking her hand as I pulled out and back in. Her fingers brushing my cock made it twitch again. It was so hard, painfully hard.

"You feel so fucking good." I rasped into her ear.

Her fingers now rubbed her clit, and she matched the rhythm of my pounding. Her moans vibrated my hand as I tightened my hold around her throat slightly. Increasing my thrusts, I watched as her hand circled her clit faster. Her legs were shaking and my hand on her stomach tightened. She pushed her ass into me harder with each thrust and she lost her voice. Her mouth opened in a silent scream.

"Breath baby. Make it loud for me, I want them to hear you come."

Her hand holding her breast moved to the back of my neck and her pussy clenched. She let out the most seductive sound I'd ever heard her make. I felt like the whole room was echoing our sounds. My teeth began to ache, and I ran them along her neck. I bit down on her neck where my mark would soon rest, and she came hard. My teeth were not long enough yet to fully mark her, but it felt so damn good. My cock swelled in her, and my hot seed began to coat her. Her moans drove me on with each thrust as her orgasm rolled over her wave after wave. Her hands fell to her side. My grip on her was the only reason she was still upright. I moved my hand from her throat to her breast. Our chests both rising and falling as we caught our breath.

Pulling myself from her, I moved her to a sitting position and grabbed two bottles of water for us. Dampening a towel with one of them a tossed it to her. I watched as she cleaned herself. Fuck even that was hot. She stood up and dumped the rest of the bottle down her body. The water droplets dripping off her hard peaks. I felt my dick twitch again. Looking down I realized

I was jerking off. Amy lifted an eyebrow as she watched me. She stood up and took a towel laying it on the sandy ground.

"Lay down!" She purred.

Fuck yes, round two!

44

PERFECT SUNSET

❦

Autum POV

Changing into my swimsuit became quite a hassle. The noises coming from the tent next to us made me giggle. Those two were always so horny. I heard the DJ turn the music up and it made me laugh. I don't know who picked out this swimsuit, but it is sexy as hell. It was all white, making my white ass skin seem tanned. The bottoms looked like a mini skirt, showing off my legs and covering the scars on my hips. The only scars that could be seen were on my torso and arms.

"Can I come in yet?" Derek called from the door.

"Yes!" I replied. "You could have just stayed from the start," I winked at him.

He cleared his throat, "No, I really couldn't." He loosened his collar while he took in my appearance.

"That looks better on you than I imagined it would." He proclaimed.

"Is that so? Are you the one that bought me this? It's a little revealing don't you think?" I said as I spun around. Bending over to pick up my shoes on the ground, I locked my knees, keeping my ass in the air.

"Here, put this on." He handed me a swimsuit cover. He was being no fun.

"Fine." I pouted, pulling the cover over my head. It was super cute too. White lace, just thick enough to hide my skin but still show off my curves.

Derek laughed at me. "Come on, I want to go sit on the beach with you."

I rolled my eyes and took his hand that was extended towards me. He walked us to the door. "Wait out here while I get changed really quick."

"Mm hmm." I crossed my arms while I waited. I could hear Ethan and Amy. They were having a really good time. It made me laugh when I noticed people looking towards me. Even Blue was tilting his head from his perch at me. Goddess how embarrassing. I laughed to myself when Derek finally walked out. Grabbing his hand quickly, I pulled us towards the beach.

"Those two are shameless!"

Derek slowed us down, smiling and shaking his head at my remark. "Let's take a wide path around those two." I followed his gaze to Rebecca and Kiel and nodded in agreement. Derek took my hand, lacing our fingers together. I turned, walking almost backwards and jumping excitedly.

"This is so beautiful, Thank you!" I smiled. Derek pulled me in, bringing my hands to his neck. He put his around my waist.

"Yes, it is!" His lips crashed into mine.

He was so perfect, taking every opportunity to compliment me. Always making sure I was the priority. His hands lowered to my thighs and pulled me up. Wrapping my legs around him, I let him carry me. He broke our kiss, our foreheads touching, he walked us in silence the rest of the way.

The beach was stunning, white sand, huge boulders throughout and a few obelisks. Peculiar. "Who built these?" I questioned as we walked closer to the shore, stopping next to one of the obelisks.

"Not sure." He responded shrugging his shoulders.

"This one has similar symbols from the book your mother gave us."

"It does?" Derek finally looked at the thing.

"Look at the top too. It looks like the pyramid at the top is made from glass or something." I pondered why these huge obelisks were here and who put them here.

"You should see them during a thunderstorm, if they get struck by lightning, they light up and sometimes it's so strong they arc to each other."

My eyes bulged. "Then it's not glass at the top, its most likely quartz crystal."

"Your sexy when you talk smart like that, now you just need some black framed glasses to complete the look!" he joked, but he wasn't really joking. The look in his eyes said otherwise, he looked like a predator, stalking his prey. Me, I was his prey. He leaned in to kiss me. It seemed like he was holding back. His hands shook a little as he gripped me tighter. I became breathless as we continued and had to pull away.

"You're intoxicating to me right now. I feel like I could lose control at any minute." He finally admitted. Heat crept over me. I had been thinking of him in the dirtiest of ways. I wanted his hands on me, all of me, his skin closer to me. "Is that why you left the tent while I was changing?"

He nodded, "You feel like you're getting warm again."

"Hmm." Was all I replied. I wanted this man. He continued past the obelisk and stopped near a lounge chair. He'd been being standoffish because he wanted me too. He was leaning forward getting ready to sit us down, but then changed his mind. There was a mischievous glimmer in his eye. He started to walk towards the shore. My eyes went wide.

"Don't you dare." I squealed.

"What, you are getting hot again. Only one way to cool off out here!" He laughed.

"Derek, no. Oh, my goddess it's cold! Stop, stop!" I laughed and screamed at the same time.

Derek held me firm in his grip as I wiggled, it was no use. Pulling him closer to me for the warmth, he put his face between my breasts.

"See, this was the best idea ever!" he mumbled as he walked us into the water up to his chest. I laughed, but stopped abruptly when I felt his bulge between my legs.

"See, you weren't the only one who needed to cool off." He grinned.

Blushing, I bit my lip. Derek, shaking his head, dipped below the water. Fully submerging himself but lifting me slightly, leaving my head above water. When he emerged, the water glistened off him. He walked us closer to the shore. His pecks were visible, and I hadn't taken the time earlier to admire them properly. He was a gorgeous man. Moving one of my hands down to his chest, I scratched softly while I ran my hand up and down him. Derek leaned his head back and smiled.

"That feels good." He spun us in the water so that I was facing the sunset, him facing the shore.

I giggled at him. "Should we get out so you can see it too?" I asked.

"I've seen it a dozen or more times, I like this view better." He smiled at me warmly.

Pulling him in closer and pretending to smother him in my breasts did not have the desired result. He just laughed and pulled me in tighter. I loosened my hold when I saw the sky fill with vibrant colors, as the sun made its final descent behind the horizon. The mixed colors of magenta and violet were dominant, with streaks of orange and yellow. The water shimmered in the sun's final moments with all the same colors. The smallest breath of wind exciting the sea to ripple. I could feel my smile widen; the view was breathtaking. I wanted to see it again, to come here again. Darkness was immediate as the sun disappeared. The water felt warmer now, the air cooling around us. I looked down at Derek and his gaze was piercing mine.

I responded to him with a kiss, one filled with passion. Both my hands on each side of his face. His hands on my thighs, squeezed. I parted my lips giving him access. Our tongues danced back and forth with each other. We pulled away, each taking a deep breath. The silence was broken by Derek.

"I love you, Autum Moore!"

One of his hands reached up and cupped my face. And I leaned into it closing my eyes. I could feel the tears wanting to break through. Those words I'd waited to hear, knew in my heart that I loved him too. Opening my eyes, they were aflame, I could feel it. Not only by the way Derek gazed into them, but by the emotions I had coursing through me. The throbbing between my legs grew the longer we held our gaze. Goosebumps covered my skin at the thought of letting Derek take me right here and now.

"Derek-" I started.

"You don't have to say it back." He cut me off.

"Derek James Michael Francis Bell." I laughed.

"Remind me to scold my mother for telling you my full name," he joked as he spun us around in the water. Our foreheads touching.

"It was your sister." I laughed. He stole my laughter with another kiss, slow and passionate. I pulled my lips from his. The tingling lingered as I licked them. I ran one of my hands through his hair and down to the base of his neck.

"I love you, Derek." I spoke softly.

Derek squeezed my legs a little tighter as he held me in the water.

Hearing singing, we both turned towards the sound. Everyone was in the pavilion singing happy birthday to the twins. Which meant we were all alone out here. Biting my lip, I turned back to him. When he turned to face me, I met his lips again. I wanted him more than I had ever wanted anyone before. Grabbing a fist full of his hair I pulled him in deepening our kiss.

Derek pulled on my swim cover, and I lifted my arms. He threw it to the shore. I undid my top and Derek's eyes went wide.

He looked over my shoulder to make sure no one was nearby.

"They are all busy in the pavilion. Plus, the music will be back on in a minute." I reasoned.

"What does the music have to do with anything?" he shook his head at me.

"So, no one will hear me scream," I whispered into his ear.

45

UNDER THE STARS

❦

Autum POV

I threw my top to the shore. Derek smirked at me and immediately took one of my breasts in his mouth. Snapping my mouth shut, I moaned, throwing my head back looking up at the brilliant night sky. Derek moved from my chest to my neck. Sucking and kissing up to my jaw.

He walked further toward shore, and I unwrapped my legs from around him. Standing about thigh deep in the sea, Derek pushed my swimsuit bottoms down. Getting on his knees, I lifted my feet so he could remove them. I looked over my shoulder to the pavilion. The music was playing now, and everyone was dancing. No one was on the beach with us.

Derek caught me off guard when he took my pussy in his mouth. I was already so wet. I threw my hand over my mouth as I moaned. What we were doing was exhilarating and felt so naughty. The fear of being caught actually excited me. His hand caressing my ass as the other one spread my lips open. I felt my legs shaking as the knot in my stomach tightened. We'd been denying the calling and it showed. I already felt my climax coming. Derek moved his hand to my opening and pushed in two fingers. I could hear my juices as he slid his fingers in and out.

"Fuck, you're so wet!"

I grabbed onto his head to balance myself with one hand. The other I lowered to my pussy and helped him spread my wet lips. His tongue shot out circling my clit. His hand on my ass started pushing me towards him, in a pulsing motion, making my pussy grind on his tongue. He started moving his head side to side while I moved back and forth. The motion creating a feeling of euphoria as my climax ripped through me. My mouth sealed tight as I fought the urge to scream out in pleasure. His fingers moved faster inside me as he curled them, creating more friction. But it wasn't enough, I wanted more. My climax felt like a wave of heat, rolling over my body. Goosebumps followed as I came down off my high. He stood and I crashed my lips into his, tasting myself on him.

He may not know it yet, but I was far from done with him. Lowering my hands, I pushed his swim trucks down. Freeing his cock, it sprung forward. He was so thick. I wonder if it would hurt. Grabbing him in my hands I started stroking him. He moaned into my mouth. I moved closer to him, positioning him right between my slick thighs. I rubbed myself on him, teasing him the best that I could.

"Autum." He panted, "We should stop."

"Why?" I asked between kisses. I rolled my hips hard on him. Feeling his dick twitch below me, only aroused me more.

We walked closer to shore, and I guided Derek down to the lounge chair. He looked up at me and I saw it… Desire… Hunger… Craving… Lust. I wanted him to feel how he just made me feel. How I still felt. The need coursing through me was unsatiated. My body warmed, there was a fire in me, a flame that could not be extinguished. I dropped to my knees. The soft sand embracing me. I licked my lips.

"Autum." Derek grunted low.

He started stroking himself, I watched for a moment. My mouth filled with saliva as I imagined tasting him. I felt starved, the phase was affecting me, but I didn't care to try and control it. I let it consume me as I pulled his hands from his member. I placed both his hands on my head, and I leaned in. Precum dripped from him, I licked from his base to his tip. Derek's hands tightened in my hair. I licked again, swirling my tongue around his head before taking him in fully.

Derek was so still; I knew he was trying to stay in control. So, I slowed my movement to drive him crazy. I hummed as a slowly pulled him out and then applied pressure with my tongue as I glided back down. My movements slowed more.

"Autum," He rasped, hardly able to speak.

I smirked to myself; he was still stiff. I wanted him to lose control, it's the only way he'd agree to take me here on this beach. I continued my slow assault on his pulsing member. He strained slightly, then I felt his hips start to move. I hummed louder, the vibration making his cock twitch and it excited me even more. His hands tightened on my head, and he pulled me down on him.

Yes, finally, I quickened my pace. I was wet too; I could feel slickness between my thighs. I clenched my thighs together to stop the ache that was forming there. Derek inhaled sharply and his eyes locked on mine, he moved his hips harder. My arousal mixing with his. His new awareness of just how much I was enjoying this. I felt his legs move between my knees. He forced my legs apart as he panted.

"Touch yourself." His voice was low, demanding. I hesitated for a moment. I hadn't touched myself before.

His chest rumbled as he strained to keep himself from coming. "Do it now." His voice was soft. Yet I felt compelled to obey. My hand slid down, and I moaned as my fingers brushed my sensitive clit. I moved my hands to the same rhythm Derek was moving my head on him. I felt him grow in my mouth as he hit the back of my throat over and over again. My swirling finger created the friction I needed to go over the edge. I was so close. So was he. As I gagged repeatedly from how full my mouth and throat were. He grunted, enjoying it.

"Come with me Autum…come with me."

And I did. My moans around his bulging cock had him losing his rhythm as he came hard. His seed hitting the back of my throat. I swallowed, panting hard as I licked one last time up his shaft. I looked up at Derek. His chest was rising and falling with such force. He pulled me up to him. I sat on his lap. Wiggling my hips until his cock was resting between my thighs. Grabbing one of the towels, I threw it over my shoulders. I small chill making its way through my body.

"Kiss me?" I asked.

Derek reached up and cupped my cheek. His gaze was intense. He slowed his breathing, steading himself. Slowly he pulled me into a kiss. The kiss was gentler now. Slow and passionate. My hands playing with his hair as my body took control again and slowly started grinding on him. His hands started roaming every inch of me, tingles following every path he took, goosebumps never leaving.

"Are you cold?" He asked softly.

I shook my head and continued kissing him. His hands moved to my hips, and he helped me grind on him. My nipples had hardened and were rubbing on his chest. Water dripping from the ends of my hair, left my body glistening.

"If we… keep going… like this." He panted out between kisses.

"I know…" I cut him off.

He pulled away to look at me. I met his gaze, I wasn't scared. I just wanted him.

"Autum?"

"Derek, this has been the most perfect day." I leaned forward and pecked his lips, "I want you; I want all of you."

He looked back towards the pavilion. Then scanned the beach. We were already so far from people. He pointed farther down the beach to a rock formation. "You see that down there?"

"Yes."

"Come on." He stood us up and grabbed the other towel from the lounger. He wrapped it around himself. Grabbing my hand, we ran down the beach towards the rocks.

Walking around the giant rock was another small beach. We were completely out of sight now. I couldn't even hear the music from the pavilion. One look in his eyes and I knew... He wanted me too. We crashed together, in a frenzy. Towels forgotten as they fell to the sand below. He grabbed the back of my neck and pulled me to him demandingly. I felt his need through the kiss. His tongue was slow but rough, and it sent shivers to my core. Reaching one hand to his neck, I pulled him in. My other hand slid down his abs to his v-line. Hesitating only for a moment, I grabbed onto his member. It pulsed and twitched in my hand already fully erect. His breath caught in his throat as I started stroking him. I craved him, wanted every part of him. His touch was like fire that fed my hunger.

He pulled my hand from him and lifted me. My legs clung to him as I rocked my wet pussy on him. His hands held my waist firm, not allowing himself to enter me. My hands tangled in his hair. I pulled away to breathe, but he did not need air. He latched onto my breast. I whimpered as I felt heat pool between my legs. My thighs were wet from my need. I needed him, my mind could not form words. I stuttered what I could.

"Derek... p- please." I moaned as his lips pulled tightly on my nipple. The pain mixed with a pleasure I had not known. I pulled his head back, taking his lips with mine. The kisses become harsher, wetter. It was not enough; it would never be enough.

"More... I need... more." I moaned. All rational thought was gone from my head.

Derek stilled; our eyes lost in each other's gaze. I panted, my chest rising and falling harshly as neither of us broke the stare. I nodded as if knowing his silent question. He moved his hand from my hip to his cock. I could smell his arousal, could taste it, it was so thick in the air. He lined himself up to me, I could feel him at my entrance. I gripped his neck tightly as I slowly slid down his rock... hard... cock. He groaned as he forced himself to be still. His grip on my hips was bruising as he restrained himself from thrusting.

I did this to him, I made him feel this need. It matched my own. Tears pricked at the corner of my eyes as I lowered myself. I could feel his member pulsing, twitching as a drew lower and lower. Derek moved his hand to my thigh, his thumb reaching around, rubbed circles on my sensitive bud. I moaned in ecstasy as the pleasure over road the pain.

"Autum... "he purred in panted breaths.

He filled me, stretched me to the brim. I started to grind on him. Tears fell from my eyes as the pain disappeared, replaced with fire once again. It was just us, there was nothing else that could tear me from this moment. In a sudden movement Derek dropped to his knees, driving even further into me. I cried out, the pleasure radiating through me. I felt my back touch the cool sand. I was burning up, burning with desire. My legs began to shake and fell from his sides, as his pounding became harder and faster. I felt the pressure building, it was stronger than ever before. Derek groaned into my ear. Startling me into unfathomed pleasure. All I could hear were my cries, they were sending Derek into a frenzy of emotion. I felt my hands tighten in his hair as the pressure raised, my release was coming. He moved relentlessly,

his lips on my neck now had me arching off the ground. My marking spot…
It felt so… Fucking… Good…

His dick twitched within me eliciting another moan. My peaks hardened and I felt my whole body heat up. I cried out again. His lips captured
mine, his groaning matching my cries. He grew inside me, with each thrust.
I moved my hips faster and harder meeting his thrusts. Moving one hand
down his back and up his arm. His biceps were huge as he held his weight
above me. Running my fingers down, it fueled me more. He was so strong,
so masculine, he was mine.

He pulled my leg up and around his back. I lifted the other, locking
my ankles around him. He held onto one of my thighs, holding himself up
with one arm. The muscles rippling with each thrust as he went deeper than
before. My teeth were aching, and I wanted nothing more than to mark him
here and now. I pulled him closer to claim his lips once again. The kisses
were sloppy, wet, and aggressive. I yanked his head to the side, my hands
in his hair and kissed his neck hungrily. Stopping at his collar bone, where
his neck meets his shoulder. I savagely bit him, his cock twitching with each
aggressive move I made.

He fisted his hand in my hair and pulled me in tighter. He bit me back,
neither of us actually marking each other, but the pleasure from the pressure
made my stomach tighten. I threw my head back as I felt my orgasm coming.
Releasing my grip on him as I dragged my nails across his back. My hands
now gripping the sand below me and my back arching up off the ground. My
body felt like it was on fire. I could feel my hands heating.

"Autum?!"

"Oh goddess, don't stop!" I cried.

Digging my nails into the ground, my orgasm hit me with a force I
hadn't felt before. My moan was long and breathy, and I didn't care who
heard. Heat was pushing through my body; my hands were heating the sand
below them. I felt Derek jerk out of rhythm then pull himself from me. The
absence of him, left me feeling empty. He circled my clit with one hand as I

rode my orgasm out. His other finishing himself off. Watching him beat his dick, glistening with my juices made me moan louder. Ropes of his seed shot out all over my stomach as we both filled the air with our sounds of pleasure. Looking up at him as he came made me hot all over again. His head craned towards the nights sky as he groaned. His muscles were bulging. Damn, I wanted to do it again. Our haggard breaths only second to the sound of the rolling waves crashing into the shore. Slowly catching my breath, I realized I was holding something warm.

Lifting my hands from the sand they were glowing. Pushing myself up onto my elbows, Derek and I both looked down at the sand. A shiny surface with my hand imprinted in it was on either side of me.

"What is that?" I asked. Derek tried to touch it, but immediately pulled his hand away.

"It's still hot!" he said astonished, "I think... you made glass!"

My eyes widened. "What!"

"I didn't think our first time would be that good, even I'm impressed." He smirked.

Derek got up and extended his hand. "Time to go skinny dipping."

"Huh?" I was still confused that I somehow made glass. "Aren't you even a little freaked out?" I asked.

"Nothing about you surprises me anymore."

I reluctantly took his hand, and he helped me to stand. We walked into the water; it was warm against my skin. I pulled my hair pins out and fully submerged under the water. There was no point in trying to keep it up, it was a mess after all of the fooling around we had done. My body ached all over, but it was a delicious kind of ache. I broke through the surface of the water as I felt hands wrap around my waist.

"You're so warm" Derek mussed.

"Am I?" I asked, but all I could think about was his hands on me.

My desire still unsated, I wanted him again. Our eyes locked and he smirked, knowing exactly what I was thinking. Our lips met, still bruised from moments before. Already breathing hard his hands traveled to my ass and lifted me up. I felt weightless in the water, wrapping my legs around him he penetrated me with one quick thrust. My head shot back, my back arching. I would never tire of this. Holding me with one hand, his other traveled to my core. His thumb was moving against my already swollen bud. I yelled out his name. The moans coming from me didn't sound like my own. His lips captured my breast, stealing my breath away as he furiously pumped in and out of me at a rapid pace.

I felt the heat coming again. But this time I controlled it. Taking two fists full of his hair, I pulled him in tighter to my breast. His thumb still moving against my sensitive bud and his cock filling me. I still wanted more. He moved his lips to my neck and pleasure radiated through me. I rolled my hips into him relentlessly. I knew my desire would not end. I was completely and utterly consumed by Derek Bell. I was putty in this man's hands… His voice was like a thrumming to my heart.

"Scream my name when you come Autum."

"Ohhhhh… Dereeeekkkkk." Heat coursed through my body as I gave into the feeling of euphoria as I reached my climax. I felt his cock twitch inside me. My grip on him forced him to stay close. I rode out my orgasm as his rapid movements came to a climax. His words and groans in my ear as he came undone only fueled me further.

"Fuck, this feels… so fucking good." He rasped into my ear. As both his hands grabbed my ass pulling me in harder and faster as I felt his warm seed shoot into me. Deep, deep inside me. The feeling was earth shattering. I pulled his head back and stole his lips. His tongue fighting mine for dominance as we consumed each other. Wave after hot wave my body rolled through its climax. His cock twitching with in me, still hard even after two rounds.

I dropped my legs. My body lowered further into the water. My hands still around his neck he dropped his forehead to mine. We sat there in silence for a moment trying to catch our breath. My chest moved with his, our breaths still labored but in sync with each other's.

"You looked like a fucking goddess, bouncing on me like that!" Derek groaned.

My eyes piercing his, forbid him from looking away...

"Autum your calling is so strong..."

"Hmm..." I murmur as I lean forward pressing a delicate kiss on his lips. He strains himself to pull away. Resting our foreheads together again, eyes still locked.

"I can't resist you." He panted. His hard cock pushing into my stomach, makes me smile at him, mercilessly.

"Then don't." I purr.

46

NO TIME LEFT

ᏋᏒᎩ

Derek POV

Walking back from the beach we tried to be discreet. Neither of us were dressed, just covered by our towels. I had to drag us from the water. I took her four times, and I still had a semi. I needed to get her back to the house. We needed to drink some tea... or not. But either way we couldn't stay here.

We made it to the changing tent and tried our best to get back into our clothes. Autum was grunting away, her body still wet making it difficult to get back into her gown. Watching her was difficult. Her naked body was driving me mad. She really had no idea what she was doing to me.

"Here," I tossed a bag her way.

"What is it?"

"A change of clothes for you. I brought it in case it got cold." I answered her.

She looked at me with a soft smile. The gratitude in her 'Thank you' that followed was genuine. Yeah, I loved her, I didn't even bring myself extra clothes. She braided her wet hair, and I watched as she applied light makeup to her face.

"How do I look?" She asked as she finished up.

"Beautiful, as always." I smiled at her.

Her cheeks were still flushed, and she beamed up at me for the compliment. I closed the gap between us, placing one hand around her waist and the other on her cheek. Autum stiffened suddenly and a small gasp left her lips. I followed her gaze down. She was staring at my neck.

"What's wrong?" I asked confused.

She reached for my neck and her touch stung a little. Pulling her hand away, there was a small amount of blood on it. She dashed to the mirror and opened her mouth. She swayed on her feet, and I quickly walked to her and steadied her.

"What's happening to me, this isn't right?" she asked scared.

Confused by her words I looked in the mirror. I had two small puncture wounds on my neck, where her canines bit into me. But she shouldn't have been able to leave a mark like this. It wasn't deep enough to actually mark me, but I could see why she was concerned. I pulled her over to the bench and had her sit down.

"Let me see." I asked her.

Autum opened her mouth, and I pulled up her lip. Her canines were extended. I was startled but I didn't show it. I needed to get her out of here. There was no way her birthday was still a week away. I didn't want her phasing in front of everyone. My gut was telling me we needed to keep this a secret. Every fiber of my being told me she would have the gift of Leoht. Her hands were fidgeting in her lap, so I grabbed them.

"Everything is fine." I tried to calm her. "Do you want to go home?"

She nodded slowly. "I'm scared."

"We can wait in here for a while. Whatever happens we will face it together, okay?" She gave a soft sigh but nodded in agreement.

"My body feels like it is burning inside," She said.

"What can I do to help?"

"Just, don't stop touching me… it burns when you're not touching me." She looked at me longingly.

I picked her up and sat down on the bench. Sitting her on my lap I held her close to my chest. She wrapped her arms around me and took a few deep breaths.

Ten minutes went by before her heart rate started to decrease. I held her the whole time. She pushed off of me after a few more minutes and went back to the mirror.

"I don't understand why they are still glowing." She said as she gazed at her eyes in the mirror.

I wrapped my hands around her stomach, my chest against her back. I rested my head on top of hers and met her eyes through the reflection of the mirror. I would never get bored of those stunning eyes that pierced right through me. I dipped my head and kissed her cheek softly.

Watching crimson color her chest and neck as it worked its way to her face. I was happy to see her so reactive to me. On the other hand, her fever was back. Furrowing my brows and lost in thought. She is definitely phasing tonight.

"What's wrong?" She asked, breaking the silence that had formed.

"Your fever is back…" I spoke while turning her towards me. I place my lips on her forehead and Autum closes her eyes briefly. I feel her sway in my arms slightly and pull her in closer.

"How are you feeling?" I asked worriedly.

"I am a bit dizzy, I just assumed it was from us… from earlier." She half stuttered, turning her gaze to the floor.

She was so adorable. She was shy now, embarrassed from what we had done. Just wait until she sees what I have in store for her. I planned on molding her little body into every position my mind could conjure. It may have been my first-time having sex, but I was no stranger to porn. My mind was already picturing her plump ass in the air, her hands bound behind her back and her pink juicy peach getting wet for me.

"Derek?" Autum spoke breaking my train of thought. "I don't feel good." Her knees gave out and I carried her to the bench. Shit, I need to tell my parents what's happening. We need to leave.

"Autum, sit here. I'm going to go get you a bottle of water. Okay?" She nodded faintly. I rushed out of the tent to see my parents and everyone else that was left walking towards me.

"What's going on?" I asked Ethan as he passed by, his eyes also glowing.

"It's almost midnight, were heading down to the water for the show!" Amy was holding him up as they walked. He looked haggard.

Kiel walked by carrying Rebecca, she was drenched in sweat. She was wearing loose clothes now. She must have changed in anticipation for tonight. Her eyes were closed, but I would guess they were also glowing.

My parents walked by last, and I pulled them into our tent. My mother was about to scold me until she saw Autum looking worse for wear on the bench.

"What's wrong with her?" She asked concerned as she walked to Autum and put her hand to her forehead.

My father also noticed my neck at the same moment. He tilted my head to the side and eyed me. Taking large strides, he stopped in front of Autum; he moved her lip up to see her teeth. My mother gasped at the site.

"I need to take her home, now. We can't let her shift in front of everyone." I explained.

My mother looked at my father in panic, then to me. "But I thought you said her birthday was next week?" she said alarmed.

"We don't have time for that right now. All I know at this moment is that she looks just as bad as the twins right now and I'm not taking any chances."

My father nodded, "Take her home, we'll have to do this without you two."

"If you can't make it home, make sure you are somewhere secluded when you pull over." My mother urged.

I picked Autum up and my father held the door open for me as I strode through. There was some yelling coming from the beach. I turned to look at my parents.

"Go, we'll take care of whatever that is." My father assured me. With that I carried Autum through the pavilion and up the stairs to the car. We didn't make it very far when she awoke in pain.

"What's happening? Why do I feel this way?" She asked groggily.

"Shh, just hold on a little bit longer." I pulled her hand into mine and lifted it to my lips placing a small kiss on it. Only a few more minutes had passed before she sat up, fueled with adrenaline.

"Derek, pull over, pull over now." She half panicked.

We were too exposed on the road, but I still pulled over. I didn't know what to do. Autum rolled out of the car and a scream left her lips as I heard some of her bones start cracking. Her scream was agonizing to me. I wanted to hold her and tell her it would be all right, but it was dangerous to be too close to her right now. My thoughts were broken from the annoying croaking coming from a nearby tree.

"Blue, get out of here, you are distracting me." I called out to the annoying raven, who seemed to follow Autum everywhere. But he wouldn't shut up. Finally lifting my head to look at him, he jumped down off the tree and kept croaking. Then, as if he was pointing, he turned his beak, and I followed the movement. Right behind the tree line was an abandoned house.

"You crazy ass bird!" I said astounded. "Autum, we need to get to that house over there, come on." I grabbed the back of her arm but then I heard her ankle crack.

"I can't, I can't," She cried. "I shouldn't be shifting, what is happening?"

"Fuck it," I picked her up carrying her bridal style as I ran towards the house. Her skin was scolding. I could feel my skin blistering as I ran through the brush. Her hand cracked and a claw scrapped a crossed my arm. I kicked the door open of the house and laid her on the only furniture in the whole room, an old sofa. My arm was bleeding, and I was blistered. The couch started steaming as she laid there. If this took much longer, she'd catch the damn thing on fire.

I sat by her head and brushed her fallen hair from her face, "You're doing so good, not much longer now love."

"It hurts" She cried. A few more bones cracked, and her skin started turning to fur. Tears were streaming down her face. Her cries were like daggers to my chest. Her body started to glow, her whole body.

"Derek, get away from me!" She yelled, sitting up.

"I won't leave."

"I don't want to hurt you." With that she stood up, her eyes turning white as light and just as bright. "Derek, step away now." Her aura hit me hard, like an alpha command. I strained against the command as it brought me to my knees. I refused to leave her. Forcing myself to look at her, I refused to turn my neck in submission. She was so strong. Her body looked like it was suspended in the air, her feet not touching the ground.

Our eyes met and she had a look of shock on her face. "I'm sorry!" She cried as she pulled her aura back. "Please!" She begged. I did as she asked, this time, but only because I heard the thunder approaching. I remembered one of the pictures in the book. It was a person in a bubble of light with a lightning bolt through it. It suddenly dawned on me that being in a house might be a bad idea.

The thunder cracked and I felt the entire house rumble. The next moments happened in slow motion. But actual slow motion. Time literally slowed down. The lightning was shooting down through the ceiling, debris looked as if it was suspended in the air, moving incredible slow.

"Don't be scared, I'll protect you." Autum's voice rang in my ears, she sounded calm and angelic. But her lips weren't moving. She raised her arm at normal speed although everything else was slow around us. Light flew from her hands at me. I was blinded by the light.

47

A KNIFES EDGE

❧

Amy POV

It was 11:30 and almost time for Ethan and Rebecca to phase. We were slow dancing when I became hyper aware of Ethan's labored breathing on my neck. I pulled away to look at him. He shook his head rapidly as if he was trying to focus.

"Shit, I feel dizzy." He spoke. But his words sounded slurred. He lifted his hand to his mouth. It slightly startled me to see his canines extended.

"It's almost time babe!" I said excitedly. He slowly nodded his head. And I realized I was somewhat supporting him.

"Do you need to sit down?" I asked him. He shook his head no.

"We should head to the beach." He replied.

Our conversation was interrupted by a few gasps as Rebecca ripped a tablecloth from its place to stop her fall. I'd never seen anyone move as fast as Kiel did then. Reaching her before she hit the ground, his water bottle still in hand. It was impressive to say the least. He opened the bottle of water and made her drink some.

"I'm fine, I'm fine." she tried to stand, but he picked her up bridal style and followed us out of the pavilion towards the beach.

It was crazy to think how time had flown by. I remember being five years old and playing with Ethan and Rebecca at the pack house with Derek. I liked him then too. He always acted so tuff around me and I remember thinking he was my knight in shining armor. I quickly became an equal to him as my father is the pack trainer. I was no match compared to his strength, but I was unmatched in agility. I was lightning striking fast, which was pretty remarkable if you think of his goddess gifted powers. We were a match, and it couldn't be denied. But tonight, his wolf would come, and he would claim me as his. I knew it with every fiber in me. I loved him.

We walked past Derek standing out of his tent. Ethan let him know we were heading down to the beach. The beach was beautiful, the moon was shining on the surface of the water, the reflection lighting the entire area. Huge boulders scattered across the area and three obelisks ran the shoreline, it was one of my favorite places.

Reaching one of the many lounge chairs we took a seat. Kiel sat with Rebecca on his lap. My parents were still taking a leisurely stroll with Ethan's parents.

My hand reached down grabbing the knife I kept in my thigh holster. What was I doing? Panic started to fill me. No one was paying attention. Kiel stood, placing Rebecca at his side, they walked towards the beach stopping near a boulder that Rebecca rested on.

Dread filled me as I stood. It was happening again. I couldn't speak, I had no control of my body. I stood silent in front of Ethan.

"Babe what are you doing?" Ethan asked. I couldn't respond. He stood, cupping my cheeks.

"Why are you crying, babe." My body spun behind him, placing the knife to his neck. Right at his carotid artery. 'Stop this!' I screamed to myself, 'Fight this!' I cursed and screamed. But no one could hear me.

"Amy! Wake up! What are you doing!" Ethan bellowed.

This got Kiel's attention. He moved towards us, and I took a step back. My parents and Ethan's parents were now moving towards us. 'This can't be happening again.' I cried to myself. If I killed him, I'd take my own life next. The knife pressed harder, drawing blood as everyone moved closer. The blood trickled down his neck. Everyone froze.

"Everyone, calm down." Elissa said in a stressed voice. "Amy is under the blood curse; she can't control herself." She paused; her breath labored as she saw the blood trickling from Ethan's neck. Richard pulled his wife towards him to comfort her.

"Robin, come out. Show yourself!" Richard yelled.

I saw Robin sneak out from the boulder where Rebecca sat. 'Turn around, someone, anyone turn around!' I screamed to no avail.

"Mom!" Rebecca screamed, as she was pulled to the ground. Robin now holding a dagger to her neck as well. A furious growl echoed through the air; Kiel's gaze was murderous. He started shaking and we all watched as fur sprouted on his arms and in one quick motion he phased. His wolf was snarling, he looked crazed. Saliva dripping from his fangs as he started stalking back and forth. Trying to find a way to save his mate.

Ethan's POV

There was too much going on. I couldn't focus. All I could hear was my own pulse. The dagger was already in my neck, another few centimeters and I'd lay dead in a pool of my own blood. I didn't even want to speak, for fear of moving too much.

I could smell Amy's tears. Her right hand on my throat, her other hand holding me firmly against her body. I rested my hand on hers, making circles on the back of her hand with my thumb.

"Amy, I love you. I know this isn't you. It will be ok; we will be ok." I whispered, trying to soothe her. I remember her saying she could hear everything that was going on the last time. I remember her saying she was screaming trying to get out of the bonds that held her. "I know you're in there, everything will be okay." I continued to talk softly to her.

A loud growl broke me from my thoughts as I watched Kiel phase. His clothes in shreds, his wolf snarling, hair on end. As he stalked closer to Rebecca.

Fuck Rebecca! Robin had her kneeling on the ground with a dagger to her throat.

"What do you want?" My mother pleaded. "Let her go. She has done nothing to you!" A crazed laugh rang through the air. Robin was crazed. Only one thing drove a wolf to be and look that deranged. The loss of a mate.

"Your foolish games have cost me everything!" Robin proclaimed. "She killed him, she killed my mate!"

"Rebecca hasn't done that!" My mother countered.

"The Heiress of Darkness did it!" Robin spat. "She did it to get to you and your family. My family got stuck in the cross hairs." She laughed again. Completely deranged.

"What do you want?" My father asked, the hair on his arms was growing. He was fighting off the shift. Beads of sweat glistened off his brow.

Amy's hand stiffened under mine. She was trying to fight the blood curse. If she just loosened a little bit, I would be able to pull her away from me and bind her. "You can do this babe. Just loosen a little bit. You will need to trust me... I know you trust me." I whispered to her.

My body started shaking and I could feel the shift coming upon me. Dark clouds started rolling in. Lighting over the water was getting closer.

"You!" Robin pointed to me. "Stop the lightning!"

"I can't stop it; I can only create it. And I didn't do this." I panted as I felt sweat beading on my skin. Fur appearing on my arms and legs.

"Liar! Do you know what will happen if she gets the gift of Leoht! The Heiress will kill us all!" She looked at my sister, a look of regret passed through her eyes, but she quickly replaced it with hate. "She must die, one death to save many more!"

"No!" My parents screamed; Kiel growled furiously. Rebecca was trying to keep herself sitting upright, but the shift was upon her.

'Crack' The sound of one of Rebecca's ankles shifting, followed by her scream that will be burned into my mind forever. My mind went blank for a moment as my mother's final plea filled the air.

"She is not the first born. Her sister died shortly after being born, I had triplets that day. Please let her go." My mother bagged.

"Liar! Do you take me for a fool? Do you see the lightning approaching, it comes for her!" Robin ranted.

My sister started shaking as the phase had started. Kiel was pacing, waiting for his chance to rip Robins throat out. I did not summon this lighting, but I would use it. If I was able to channel it at the right time, I could strike her down. I had never directed lightning before, but I had to try. I really haven't meddled with my gift that much. Always too scared that I would do something that couldn't be reversed, like when I was born and caused the tsunami.

"Amy, you need to loosen your hold, I believe in you. I'm only going to have one chance at this. I'm about to shift and I don't want to hurt you." I whispered to her.

Lightning started all around us. Mostly behind us. This whole thing felt so surreal. But I could feel that it was going to be ok. I don't know why, but I had a feeling of warmth. I saw Amy's parents out my peripheral, they were edging closer. My parents were still arguing with the mad women. The

Alpha and Luna had been slowly approaching on my other side as well. Robin was about to meet her end. And my mother had a lot of explaining to do, but I couldn't think of that now.

48

TRIAL OF SELF AWARENESS

❦

Autum POV

I was suspended above my body. It was like when I was meditating.
I had a bubble of energy around me, and I had created one around Derek
as well. The house looked like it was about to explode. My body was in the
middle of the shift. Fur covered most of me, white fur. The skin that I could
see was luminescent. It looked like a lightning strike was coming through
the ceiling, but it was moving so slowly. I reached for it.

"Child." A voice came from behind me. "I wouldn't do that if I were
you." Turning, I saw the most beautiful women. She looked regal and had
poise. Images started flashing through my mind, images of this women. I
gasped and bowed.

"Queen Patrina!" I started to bow.

"Do not bow to me, Autum." She approached, placing her hand under my chin. She lifted my chin till our gazes met. "A Queen does not bow."

"Is this real?" I asked her.

"Yes, you will take your rightful place on the throne. But your journey will not be easy. I have come for the transfer of power, as you will do for the next Queen. The last of my energy will be gifted to you and it will now be your burden to bear. Please take my hand." I gingerly placed my hands in hers. "Before we begin, there is a choice that must be made." She said, my hands were still in hers.

I felt my body tense, "What choice?"

She didn't answer in words, imagines started playing in my mind. It was of Ethan and Rebecca at the beach with their parents. But my goddess, I watched as Amy drew her knife and took Ethan by the neck!

"What! No! Not again!" I gasped. I then saw as Counselor Robin came from behind the boulder and grabbed Rebecca. "I won't allow them to die because of me. Robin is only after Rebecca because of me...Can I save them?"

She nodded. "Yes, but you must be back before that lighting strikes your body."

"And if I'm not?"

"You may not wake up…"

I hung my head, hot tears pricking at the edges, threatening to escape. I looked longingly at Derek. "Can he hear us?" I whispered.

She followed my gaze. "If you want him to," She answered.

I nodded, his eyes found mine, but he was still suspended in time. "Derek… Robin has Ethan and Rebecca at the beach… she is going to kill them." The tears broke through. "I can't let her kill Rebecca thinking she has the gift of Leoht." I approached him. My translucent hand resting on his cheek. I touched my forehead to his and shared every happy memory I had ever had with him. "I love you." I spoke only to him.

Stepping away from him, I looked to Queen Patrina, "I choose them."

She took my hands once more, "I'm going to show you how to do the transfer of power," she pulled me closer and pressed her forehead to mine. Images flashed in my mind again, this time of the ritual for the transfer of power. It really looked like more Reiki. I knew these movements.

"That's all I have to do?" I questioned.

"The hand movements, and you have to will it. You are the only one on this earth strong enough to will it." She spoke softly, "Chanting helps, if you can create an incantation."

I nodded my head, this felt so surreal. I knew this was my purpose now. Placing one hand on her solar plexus and the other on her Third eye I began. The words flowed out of me like I had known them all of my life.

"I summon the power here and call forth all energy that now belongs to me. May the goddess bless me as her heir, as I carry on her gift of Leoht. I bind myself as protector of her children." Light engulfed my physical body as I watched on. The light faded from Queen Patrina as the transfer of power flowed. My wolf started to take form and the lightning bolt was now a few feet closer.

A searing pain formed at the base of my neck and at the front of my forehead. All I could see was white light for a brief moment.

"Breathe child, your wolf has taken most of the pain for you. That is why you are outside your body. This will make her stronger, making you stronger as well." She informed me.

I took a deep breath, I could feel the energy running through my veins, every inch of my skin covered in goosebumps. My hair raised over my whole body. I wiped my eyes. And swallowed back my fear.

"You have passed the test of Selflessness." She said solemnly.

"Test...?

"Choosing others over yourself, your heart is pure."

She nodded and sent me more images. It was of a much younger Queen Patrina. And another child. Something felt familiar about her. They were ice skating on frozen lake.

"That is my sister Nervia. She is my twin sister. My test was different than yours. One of my gifts is foresight. I would have dreams of my death at my sisters' hands. I refused to believe it. I tried for years to change the outcome. Sometimes the way I would die would change, but I always died in the end. Then this happened..."

The images moved faster, until it was like watching a movie. Nervia skated farther away as Patrina was warning her about the thin ice. The ice gave way and Nervia fell in and disappeared. Patrina was screaming for her sister, frantically searching for her. She peered down and saw a glimpse of a face below the solid ice.

"In this moment I paused, she would die if I didn't save her. Then I would live. I could see it. But I couldn't live with myself if I let her die."

The images continued. Removing her ice skate she struck the ice, over and over and over again frantic to free Nervia. The ice chipped away and then finally cracked, removing a large piece, she pulled her sister from the icy water and sprinted home with every breath she had.

"You saved her, knowing you would die in the end?" I questioned.

"I made a decision, just as you did. If I didn't make that decision, I would not have become the Queen. I would not have been pure of heart. But in that moment, I found clarity. Two things changed after that. First, I forgave her for what she would become. I knew it didn't matter what I did in this life I would die. So, I did what I could to change what would happen after my death."

She didn't give me time to ask another question, she continued explaining.

"To weaken her, I took her wolf. Freed her spirit to return to the goddess and not be tainted by my sister. You see she drove her wolf crazy, and it fueled her hatred for others. Seeing that outcome as a certainty I removed it as a possibility. I saw the future change for the better. It was not fixed completely, but it was the first step. Secondly, I could see how hatred and jealousy would fill her heart, so I gave her a reason to love, I gave her a mate. Someone to desire her for everything that she was and could be."

"But she still killed you!"

"Yes, like I said, that was always the outcome. She was blinded by her hatred, but without her wolf she was not as strong. With the last of my strength, I bound her magic to the tree of good and evil and to myself. I begged the goddess, my dying wish, she created mates. Without a wolf and with no magic, she had the strength of an ordinary human. Using my powers was the only way to stop her and what she would become. Using all of my strength left me vulnerable. She stabbed me through the heart to try and stop me. I had nothing left to save myself."

"The goddess created mates because of you?" I questioned.

She smiled, "Yes."

"How is that possible, mates have been around for centuries?"

"My reign was over 200 years ago."

"I'm lost, how is your sister still alive?"

"The goddess granted my wish for mates but cursed my sister in my stead. Cursed her to wander the earth in search of him. I would never have wanted that for her. But the goddess was angry at my death. And wanted my sister to see the errors of her ways, for her to feel powerless. Made her immortal until she found her mate, she could not even kill herself."

"So why is she here now?" I asked.

"I was not here to stop the unforeseen." She stated.

As I watched the images, I saw the back of a women with her child in her arms. They were seeking higher ground. Then the image of a man appeared. He was far away, He appeared to be looking for the women and the child. A loud thunderous noise was approaching. My view zoomed out and I was now above the trees. I could see a tsunami approaching the area where the man was. In mere seconds the entire area was underwater. The imagine zoomed back to the women and child. They had been picked up on a road and were safely in another town. But the women dropped to her knees suddenly, grabbing her head, her child still in her arms. The scream of pain that left her will stay with me forever. That was the break of a Mate bond.

"She found her mate and then he died, now she seeks revenge?" I asked.

She only nodded.

"Will I die today?" I asked her.

"No." She responded.

I looked at her confused, "But you said I may not wake up?"

"Yes, look at the lightning coming towards your body." She asked.

It was about a foot away now. It was moving so slowly.

"Your mind must be connected to your body by the time the lightning strikes. If it's not, your body will be but a hallow vessel." She answered.

"I should have left at the beginning, but I got caught up in your story." I closed my eyes to leave and send myself to the beach. She abruptly grabbed my arm.

"You could not go then, just as you cannot go yet now. I have seen this play through already. We must wait or you will choose the wrong course and all will be for naught."

Completely frustrated I asked, "Is there any chance that I will be able to wake up?"

"Yes, you will be able to become one with yourself after some time. But it will be… difficult." She paused and took in a very dramatic breath of air. I found this funny considering we did not need to breathe. "Have you noticed the time difference when your meditating?" She inquired.

"I have, I know that roughly one hour in my meditation state is equal to only five minutes to my physical self."

"That is almost exactly correct. When I had my Trial of Self Awareness, my physical body was in meditation for twenty-seven days." She stated.

If I had legs right now, I would have fallen to the floor. "That means you were in your meditation state for nearly ten months! Locked in your head for ten months, how am I …"

She cut me off, "I was able to choose when I would undergo this trial, you however will be forced into it. This will be a test of sheer willpower and it is all completely mental and up to you. You will have to move through each one of your chakras to reopen them to connect your mind and body again. This will be one of the hardest obstacles for you to overcome."

"How will I know what to do?"

"You already know what to do and are better prepared than I. Mary and Ellen made sure of that. Your body will need to be protected…" She didn't finish her whole thought. "You need to go now!"

49

WHISPER IN THE WIND

❧

Autum POV

Lightning struck all around me. The sea was angry. Taking in my surroundings, the situation was dire. Time slowed like before. Amy had Ethan by the throat. I placed my hand on Ethan. Giving him my calm. What could I do in this situation? I looked around and saw that Patrina was not here. What did she mean if I had too much time, I would make the wrong choice?

I could see they didn't have much time left already. Elissa was on her knees, begging Robin to let Rebecca go. Richard was mid shift behind her, no longer able to contain his beast. Rebecca and Ethan were both half-phased. Both covered in hair. Rebecca was on her knees, and Ethan was barely able to stand.

There was too much going on, I didn't know what power I still held in this form. I caught Robins gaze; her eyes were wide. Turning, I saw the largest lightning strike I'd ever seen. It was behind everyone else; only Robin was facing it. It was the lightning strike for me. It was glorious. Obvious to me that it was no ordinary natural phenomenon. It was massive and lit up the sky. I could read her mind at that moment. She knew she was wrong, but she was angry. She wasn't going to let Rebecca go. She was hurting, her mate was gone, and her child was hospitalized. She blamed them still.

Looking at Ethan, I saw him gripping Amys arm across his chest. Fur and claws were taking over. His eyes on the sky. His focus was on a lightning strike about to hit the obelisk. Robin's hand raised about to plunge the knife into Rebecca. Kiel was about to pounce no matter what happened. He would kill Robin, even if it meant his death.

I looked at Amy. I felt for her. She was in there. I tried to speak to her. Not knowing if she could hear me. The answer came to me in a split second and there was no time to waste.

"Amy I'm going to put you to sleep. Everything will be ok."

My mind was racing, and time started before I could stop it. In a split-second Amy started to fall to the ground, knife falling from her grip. I grabbed Ethan's hand in mine and together we directed it. As the lightning struck the obelisk it arched off and connected with the knife in Robins hand. That gave Kiel his moment. He pounced on Robin, his teeth savagely ripping her throat out as they slammed into the ground.

Robins last words were not that of sorrow.

"My Queen, forgive me. Save them all." Her gurgled words were heard only by Richard, Kiel, and me.

Could she see me? The thought was fleeting for the lightning cracked in the distance. The bright light drew everyone's attention. Ethan and Rebecca both shifted as the boom echoed through the sky. The blast caused air to rush out in all directions. Everyone dropped to their knees and bowed in the direction where my body laid, no one fully understanding why.

Howls filled the air. Looking around me, everyone shifted except the unconscious Amy and her parents at her side. Howls could be heard all around us. Elissa and Richards howls filled me with an emotion I could not name. It was filled with… pain. But their children still lived. Sorrow pulled at my heart, and I grabbed my chest feeling pain I did not recognize.

I felt a strange pull in my mind and my body felt numb. My vision started to blur, and I knew my trial was about to begin. Darkness took me.

Derek POV

I held Autum's body to mine. Everything happened so quickly, my mind was having trouble working through it all. It was like I could only make out bits and pieces of it. I felt exhausted but I knew I couldn't stay here. I couldn't rest. The words played over and over again in my head.

"You'll need to protect your body." The Queen had started to say to Autum before they disappeared. The dead Queen who said it had been 200 years since she lived. The dead Queen that I had seen with my own eyes. I had seen them both, their glowing bodies. They looked like holograms. I would never fully believe what I had seen or heard.

I was completely unharmed as was Autum, well her body anyways. The house, on the other hand, was completely blown apart. Walls were now scattered amongst the trees. It quite literally looked like a bomb had gone off in the middle of the forest.

I brushed her hair away from her face. She looked so peaceful right now. Remembering how she had transformed and that I had gotten to witness it. The light had been radiating off of her as she was surrounded in a bubble of light. She phased into the most beautiful white wolf I had ever seen. Her fur reflected specs of gold in the light as she was lifted further off the ground.

The lightning that struck was blinding. Her eyes had opened at that one moment. The white consumed them as the lightning passed through her.

The house exploded as a shock wave left her body. I closed my eyes as the light engulfed us completely. I dropped to my hands and knees and bowed. I didn't feel forced but compelled to do so. When I opened my eyes, she lay on the floor. She was beautiful, her skin still had a glow about it, but she was still, unmoving, lifeless, back in her human form. Completely naked.

I removed my shirt pulling it over her. Lifting her, I started walking towards the car.

The car was completely destroyed. The windows were all broken, and it wouldn't start. My gaze went to Autum where I had laid her in the back seat. I punched the steering wheel. "Fuck!" Getting back out of the car I paced for a minute thinking of what to do next. The annoying sound of croaking wouldn't stop, and that damn bird was about to get a rock to its face!

"Blue, stop!" The bird quieted and as if pointing looked down the road in the direction of the pack house.

Bits and pieces of what had happened were slowly coming back to me. I felt a calm wash over me as my memories returned, flashing in my mind. I remembered Autum telling me about what was happening at the beach. I knew that everything was going to be ok. I remembered her voice; she was talking to me. Her voice was but a whisper in the wind, but I remembered it. She said she loved me and then she touched my cheek and I remember her warmth. I saw memories of all the times I had made her smile, or blush or feel loved.

I picked Autum up out of the car. Looking down at her I whisper, "I heard you; I hear you now my love." Kissing her forehead I vowed, "Sleep beautiful, I'll keep you safe, protect you, until you return to me. Let's go Blue." And the journey begins.

To Be Continued…